T H E
O L D
M A N

Yuri Trifonov

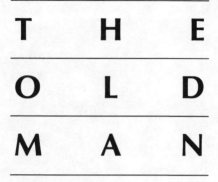

Translated from the Russian
by Jacqueline Edwards
and Mitchell Schneider

SIMON AND SCHUSTER
New York

Library of Congress Cataloging in Publication Data

Trifonov, IUrii Valentinovich, 1925-1981
The old man.

Translation of: Starik.
I. Title.
PG3489.R5S713   1984   891.73'44   84-14067
ISBN: 0-671-25283-6

The letter came in July:

DEAR PAVEL,

I am writing to you on an off chance, in care of the magazine in which I read your piece about S.K. Unfortunately, by the time I stumbled on it it was already five years old. I was recently visiting a friend of mine in Berdyansk and there, among the old magazines we were going to give the kids for scrap paper, I came across that issue, number 3 of 1968, which contained your piece and the little picture of S.K. You can't imagine, dear Pavel, what I felt at that moment. You see, I knew absolutely nothing at all—I didn't know that you were alive or that S.K. is considered almost a Civil War hero.

You may have forgotten me, but I remember you extremely well and will always think of you with fondness: there is so much that links us together. I am Asya Igumnova, your neighbor from Vasilevsky Island, Liniya 15; you, Pavlik, were a great friend of my first cousin Vladimir who lived with our family; he was killed by Krasnov's men in the winter of '19 in the Mikhailinskaya *stanitsa*.* I barely survived. You probably remember. It was Sergei Kirillovich who saved me. You were a clerk or an orderly in the Revkom commanded by one of your relatives and I was a typist at the headquarters of Sergei Kirillovich's Corps. I was eighteen at the time and you were the same age or a bit younger. I remember that the three of us—you, Vladimir and myself—all attended Prigoda's school and that we were in the same class. I also had an elder brother, Alexei, a student. He fought on Kornilov's side and I was so very worried that I didn't know what to do with myself. Vladimir was my first husband. Mama cursed him and me after Alexei was killed. Then I became the wife of Sergei Kirillovich Migulin. I loved him very much; he brought me back to life. But it lasted only a few months and in May came the tragedy you know about.

* See Glossary for Russian words.

5

Dear Pavel, there has been a great deal of suffering in my life, but I'm not going to tell you all about it now because I don't know whether you will get this letter, or if you're alive and well and will want to correspond with me. I would very much like to see you now as I approach the end of my life; there is nobody left from that time. My brothers have perished and my father died of typhus in Rostov. Mama and my sister Varya and her husband left for Bulgaria in '21 and then went to France. I know nothing of them.

I am glad the stigma—which I never believed in—has been lifted from that marvelous person S.K. They told me nothing about it, because nobody knows that I was his wife and that I had a son by him. Even my family didn't know. I don't know why I am writing to you so frankly. The piece you wrote upset me. I've been like a stone all these years. I don't understand why it was *you* who wrote the piece. Can it really be true that there's no one left? My name hasn't been Igumnova or Migulina for a long time; it's been Nesterenko since 1924, when I married Georgy Fyodorovich Nesterenko. Georgy Fyodorovich was an army engineer; we used to travel around the country the whole time; we visited the Far East and Mongolia. He died in Leningrad during the blockade. He loved my son like his own child. My son died of a blood disease three years ago. I live not far from Moscow in a township called Klyukvino. There's a big institute here where my grandson works. His mother also works here. It is not difficult to get to Klyukvino from Moscow: railway to Serpukhov and from there it's about forty minutes by bus. I would love to see you, dear Pavel! There was a time when it wouldn't have been possible for me to see you, but that didn't last long. I hope to God you're alive and well.

Sometimes at night—especially recently, since I became an old woman—I dream of our street on Vasilevsky Island, our three-story house with the bay window and that sort of attic where sometimes we used to hide from the grown-ups. I have no complaints about life, though there have been a lot of hard times. Do write back, Pavel—even two lines. I send my love.

> Your old friend
> ASYA
> ANNA KONSTANTINOVNA NESTERENKO

P.S. I am seventy-three years old, my hair is completely gray, I am scrawny and, of course, sick. I have trouble walking but I do all the housework, because it's very difficult to find help. For no particular reason I am sending a photograph of my grandson and his wife Svetlana; it makes her look much more youthful and naïve than she is in real life. They have been married for a year and a half. Pavel, I'll always remember that you were the first one to come to me that time in Mikhailinskaya. I remember your words, your face—everyone thought I was unconscious, but I could see and hear; I just couldn't feel anything, of course. Pavel, do forgive an old woman and write back.

Pavel Evgrafovich turned the photograph over and looked at the lobster-eyed bearded young man, aware only that something very like a heart attack had seized him—anxiety, shivering, a stifling memory from far, far back which constricted his chest, causing a sensation of fear. He used to try to tell himself at night, Calm down; you're feeling better; the pain is going, going. . . . And it went. Right now was the same: It's nothing special. It's just an ordinary letter; you shouldn't get excited. Big deal, so you haven't seen each other for fifty-five years!

He had remembered Asya Igumnova immediately. And the street, Liniya 15, and the house with the bay window and the gates of wrought iron. Suddenly he felt happy—he would go and tell the children! It would be interesting for them—after fifty-five years. But at once he realized that he could not tell them, because they had had a falling out. Yesterday there had been a serious and painful quarrel and yet again he had run up against a lack of understanding. No, that was the wrong word: they all understood, but went on regardless. It was worse than that: it was a lack of thought. A lack of feeling. As if they did not share the same blood. He was reluctant to tell Ruska or Vera or his sister-in-law or anyone. If only Galya were alive.

He took the letter and read it through once more. Again his heart began to pound, and he quickly thrust the letter deep into the desk drawer under some papers. Yesterday a vile conversation on workaday matters had started up. It was strange how his son and his daughter, who were so different, always quarreling about everything, instantly joined forces. And they went for him with such spite, arguing relentlessly. Vera said, "I'm fed up with our eternal blissful indigence. Why do we have to live worse than everyone else, more cramped and wretched than everyone else?"

Ruska spoke threateningly and shook his finger. "Just remember that the sin will be on your conscience. You think only about your own peace of mind, not about your grandchildren. But it's their future, not ours."

Something was said about senile egoism, something unfair and disgusting. He was such a fool, so heartless. No, that was unforgivable. Yesterday he gave up on them and walked away, because there was no point in talking. Wrong, wrong! It was not yesterday, but the day before. Yesterday was an empty day. He did not talk to anyone; he sat upstairs in the small room over the veranda, free for the moment because his sister-in-law had gone to Moscow to collect her pension and see the doctors. And he had drafted a reply to P. F. Grozdov, from Maikop, who had sent a long illiterate letter making an utterly nonsensical allegation: that the Kashkinskaya *stanitsa* had been taken in January 1920, although everyone knew that that Cossack village had been captured in February—on February the third, to be precise. The letter had been forwarded to him from the Veterans' Board. It was difficult to answer; he agonized over it, choosing his words, but his head was troubled and his heart was aching because of those fools, and even the simplest words eluded him.

Vera came upstairs, knocked crossly and said defiantly, "What's the matter? Why don't you answer? Are you irritating us on purpose? Come and drink some tea."

More nonsense. Irritating them on purpose. As if they didn't know that he was hard of hearing.

And all because he refused to do their bidding, to have a word with the chairman of the board about Agrafena Lukinichna's wretched little house. But he couldn't, he couldn't, once and for all he *could not*. How could he? Go against Polina Karlovna? Against Galya's memory? As far as they were concerned, since their mother was dead her conscience was dead, too, and everything could start from scratch. But no, Galya's conscience was alive; it had not disappeared and would not disappear as long as he was still of this world. Of course, it would disappear, and soon. Then you can do what you like.

Seething at the memory of the insult and suddenly forgetting Asya's letter, Pavel Evgrafovich descended the dilapidated staircase with the intention of fetching the covered dishes from the kitchen to take with him to the sanitorium. It was a bit early. Lunch was available from noon. But he liked to take his time walking there, have a rest on the benches by the riverbank and be the first one into the kitchen so as not to have to grow weary waiting on line. The line there was nothing like the one in town at the Dietetic or the provisions store. Everyone was either boasting about something or complaining about something. Pavel Evgrafovich took the newly washed dishes that were lying spread out on the windowsill drying in the heat of the sun—quarrels apart, Valentina was still terrific, an expert at her job—gathered them up, took the milk can and went out onto the veranda, where he found a crowd of people.

As it was Sunday, everyone had gathered together: Ruska; Vera with her Nikolai Erastovich; some friend of theirs, a dumpy woman in a sarafan who had appeared yesterday evening; and his grandson Garik with his friend Petka too. Viktor, his other grandson, was there also, and Valentina was darting in and out— from the veranda to the kitchen, from the kitchen to the veranda. Some had already eaten; some had finished their tea; and at the end of the table Garik and Petka had moved the dishes to one side and were playing chess. Pavel Evgrafovich had grown used to people not waiting for him at mealtimes; in fact, nobody waited for anybody; everything was catch as catch can. Valentina fed her own family—that is, Ruslan and Garik; Verochka seemed to eat on her own with Nikolai Erastovich whenever he was around, and if he was not she seemed to eat with her Auntie Lyuba, Galya's sister. Myuda and Viktor, who used to turn up quite frequently although no one invited them, seemed to eat with Verochka and would always bring her candy. As for Pavel Evgrafovich, he would sometimes eat with one group, sometimes with another, and sometimes alone, on what he would bring back from the sanitorium. At times, however, they all sat down together at the big table, causing total confusion. But in former times that was how it used to be: together. When Galya was alive.

But Galya died. It was like the linchpin falling out; the wheels were dangling loosely and any minute now the axle would fly off. Let it! Pavel Evgrafovich had neither the strength nor the desire to put the cart to rights again; anyway, it would be impossible now. As if through a depth of water, the muffled voices and cries of his children and his grandchildren reached his conscious mind: things were happening in their lives, but Pavel Evgrafovich was not paying attention. Some things he knew nothing at all about, some things he guessed at: for example, the fact that Ruslan had a woman again, that Valentina was upset, that perhaps they would separate; also that Verochka had some illness and ought to quit her job and start treatment. But what illness Pavel Evgrafovich did not know. He was afraid to try to find out, and if he did find out he did not know what he would do, because Galya was the one who used to deal with all that.

And so, right now they had assembled on the veranda, jostling, causing a din, quarreling—but about what? Probably about some nonsense they'd seen on television. One actor is good, another one is bad, and that makes a quarrel. They could drivel on for half a day like that, even though it was Sunday. No, he listened and was able to make something out: they seemed to be talking about something else. About Ivan the Terrible, was that it? Some historical subject. It was all the same to them, so long as there was a din, an argument; just so that each could have his say.

Naturally, Ruslan was an especially nasty wrangler, and he

was forever crossing swords with his sister or with the tiresome Nikolai Erastovich, whom one couldn't figure out: was he really a pious man and, despite his years, ingenuous, or was he pretending, dissembling for some reason? Pavel Evgrafovich was not all that keen on old Erastovich—not even because Verochka was not happy with him and probably never would be; the thing had been dragging on for seven years and it was still at square one because the fellow was sort of deluded, incomprehensible. He seemed to be an educated person—he was with Verochka at the Institute—but when it came to the Bible, icons, church holidays and such nonsense, he would argue like a devout graybeard.

"Papa, aren't you hungry? Haven't you eaten yet?" asked Vera, throwing her father an irritated but totally blank, unseeing glance.

Pavel Evgrafovich indicated his answer merely with a gesture of his hand—"Don't bother, and don't interrupt the conversation!"—sat down at the table and drew a cup and saucer toward him. It was true, he did fancy a little tea.

Meanwhile a battle royal was raging around the table. Nikolai Erastovich was rattling on in his rapid nasal twang, and Vera, of course, was echoing him in great excitement—and all on the subject of Ivan the Terrible; how they took it to heart!—and Ruslan was upbraiding them terribly for something, pointing his finger at them and thundering away in his deafening, tub-thumping voice, just as in the old days. He always did bawl in an argument. What people used to call "ramming yourself down their throats." Pavel Evgrafovich had long since vowed never to argue with him. Well, to hell with him. If only the pressure would ease.

"Those were diabolical, brutal times; take a look at Europe, the world. What about the Religious Wars in France? The Saint Bartholomew's Day Massacre? What about what the Spaniards did in America?"

"You're trying to make excuses for a crazy fanatic! A sadist— a devil! A sex maniac!" yelled Ruslan, leaping up from the table and brandishing his huge hand in Nikolai Erastovich's face; he had clearly been at the bottle that morning. "The times? The times? What are you talking about, for God's sake? What about the Renaissance, Michelangelo, Luther...?"

"Listen, we've gotten off the subject. We were talking about Dostoevsky," piped up the dumpy woman in the sarafan.

"You can't just remember the bad—the executions, the barbarity. Your Belinsky called him an extraordinary person—"

"He's *your* Belinsky! You can have him!"

"What about the extension of our boundaries? Kazan? Astrakhan?"

"They're no good to me! What do I care about the extension of the boundaries? They were extended by bloodshed and drowning!"

"No one calls Charles IX a villain even though Saint Bartholomew's Night and Novgorod were almost at the same time; but the Russian Tsar is automatically a big monster."

"Listen, we approached Tsar Ivan from the standpoint of 'everything is permitted.' But everything is permitted only if there is no God."

"Tsar Ivan did an enormous amount for Russia!" Nikolai Erastovich shouted out in his thin voice. His face turned dark and stony from a rush of blood.

Why had they gotten so heated up over a tsar? Take Ruslan over there: flared up, flushing bright red and looking as if he were just about to anathematize someone.

"Be quiet. You get one out of five for history, Comrade Candidate of Sciences! Tsar Ivan tore Russia in two and corrupted everybody: some he made the butchers and others the victims. Oh, but what's the point of talking? When Khan Davlet-Geray attacked, it was necessary. It was...." Ruslan suddenly flagged, sank into a chair and concluded in a weak, stifled voice, "The *oprichniki*, the bastards, couldn't even fight. How could they be expected to? He ran away himself, the so-called Tsar. He profaned us; those heathens burned Moscow...." He muttered something unintelligible as he wiped his palm over his cheeks and beard.

Then, of course, tears. Whenever he drank he became shockingly maudlin.

Pavel Evgrafovich looked at his son with sadness and secret disgust. The one good thing was that Galya could not see. Five years ago when Galya was still with them he never used to carry on like this.

All of a sudden, Ruslan jumped up and rushed inside as if responding to some urgent summons. In the house there was a crash. That was he slamming a door. Vera shuddered. Garik, who was playing chess, said, "Gosh, Papa's at it!" Valentina calmly went on clearing away the dishes as if she had heard nothing. And Pavel Evgrafovich thought of her with bitterness and anger. It was not his own bitterness that he suddenly felt, but Galya's: no, he thought, she doesn't care about him or love him. She's no good. The main thing for her is to hang on to him; it doesn't matter whether he's a drunkard, an invalid or any sort of wreck you like, so long as he stays with her. That's why she tolerates such swinish behavior. In fact, she even encourages it, because once he's deprived of his will he won't run away. She's a cunning woman; she realizes that. What is there to do? Galya could have helped, but not he, Pavel Evgrafovich. He's not able. He never was. By now everything was done with. Even the children's lives were done with. But behind the customary sadness which had been the underlying tone of his thoughts in recent years an unexpected something from afar was producing a vague flicker of warmth. He did not guess immediately that it was Asya's letter. He felt like leaving quietly to be by himself, to recall everything in great detail, and he made a movement. He tilted his body forward to get up from his chair, but Vera stopped him.

"Papa, I forgot to introduce you to my friend Inna Alexandrovna. She's a lawyer and works in a legal-advice office. By the way, you can get some useful advice from her without waiting on line, and free of charge."

"I shall take my fee in the form of your wonderful air!" The

dumpy woman in the sarafan smiled and took a deep breath, her
eyes shut in a display of exceptional enjoyment. "The air here
is absolutely divine!"

Not spitefully, but just because he liked to see the funny side,
Pavel Evgrafovich thought: The air may be divine, but that doesn't
stop her from helping herself to a third piece of cake. She's right,
of course. You do need air. Pleased to have you. Legal science
has marched forward, but *he* was one of its fathers; he was involved
in a trial fifty years ago. He was about to embark on the story of
Migulin's trial—very dramatic and tempestuous, instructive for
the young ones—but after the first sentence, "In the autumn of
1919, when Mamontov had broken through the southern
front...," he sensed that no one was particularly interested.
Valentina left, Vera and Nikolai Erastovich started whispering
about something, and Ruslan, who had just reappeared on the
threshold, gave a blank stare, and so he fell suddenly silent.
What's the point? Pearls before swine. They'll manage without
Migulin's story. But what a fascinating figure he was! Really,
what fools, not wanting to know anything about him. And again
he fell to thinking about the letter and Asya, and imagined with
what rapt attention—in his mind's eye he could even see the
expression on her face—Galya would have listened to him.

The dumpy woman in the sarafan was explaining something
about Agrafena Lukinichna's house to Vera. How could it fail
to get on a man's nerves? A bore to listen to. Once again Pavel
Evgrafovich braced himself to get up and leave, but Ruslan stopped
him and even pressed his hand down on his shoulder, forcing
him to sit.

"Listen to this, now, it's helpful for you." And, turning to the
lawyer, Ruslan said, "Do you realize what they're insisting on?
The fact that for eight years they rented it from Agrafena and put
work into it—and that they submitted their application before
everyone else."

"But you have advantages on your side too. First, you're the
cooperative's oldest residents. Secondly, the family has grown...."

Now everyone was talking at once. Knitting her brows im-
portantly, the lawyer was enunciating very loudly and authori-
tatively. She turned out to have a voice like a foghorn. Pavel
Evgrafovich noticed that now that he was an old man—a lot of
nonsense, of course!—he had become fearful of people with loud
voices. At the beginning he felt like joining the conversation and
explaining the crux of the matter to the lawyer. Why was he
against this house venture? Because Polina Karlovna was Galya's
friend and Galya had enticed them all out here eight years ago.
If Galya were alive the whole argument would have been unimaginable. But as the children saw it, the fact that their mother
had gone meant that they could go ahead. Anyway, Polina herself
would be joining Mama soon. The whole matter had been talked
over at shouting pitch.

So to hell with them all.

"I told you, I'm not going to discuss it with anyone!" Pavel
Evgrafovich, frowning morosely, started to crawl up from the
table, leaning on his stick and inclining his torso forward.

"For heaven's sake, Papa! Whatever you want. We'll manage."

Nikolai Erastovich's voice could be heard as he left. "By the
way, about Tsar Ivan Vasilevich: you, Ruslan Palych, you cast
aspersions on the Tsar, but what about yourself? You're also
trying to extend your territory and you have no compunction
about. . . ."

Noise, laughter and a clatter of dishes; no one noticed Pavel
Evgrafovich's departure, and the never-ending morning-to-night
tea party continued. Erastovich's nasal chatter, Vera's thin little
voice and Ruslan's booming bass continued in his wake. The
minute Pavel Evgrafovich had descended the porch steps—always a problem for him because of their height—he immediately
started thinking about Asya's letter. He had decided to reread it
later after his walk to the sanitorium. Then he would get down
to the business at hand. After dinner. He had quite a distance
to cover, about one and a half kilometers through the whole
township to the asphalt road; he could go by the river way—it

was longer, but there were benches, so he could make short stops and have a rest. The day was turning out just like the preceding ones with this terrific heat. The black dog Arapka who generally accompanied Pavel Egrafovich on his travels refused to move today: overcome by the heat, he lay in the shadow of the veranda and did not budge, even though he heard the familiar jangling of his leash.

"Aren't you coming?" asked Pavel Evgrafovich. The animal scarcely managed a shake of his tail and did not even raise his head, which was resting heavily on his paws.

Thousands of young people with their music and beach balls, and dressed in bathing suits, were flocking toward him from the trolleybus terminus to the riverbank beaches. Pavel Evgrafovich saw nothing and no one. He was thinking about the letter when suddenly some incomplete thought, something he had not fully absorbed, began to gnaw at him. Some trivial matter or other. A mere trifle: that brief sentence, "I don't understand why it was *you* who wrote the piece." How is it she doesn't understand? In fact, the whole letter was sort of, God forgive me, a bit, well, old-womanish and rather silly.

More and more, my days flow over into memory. And life turns into something strange, a duality: there is one life that is reality and a second one that is an illusion, memory-made, and they exist side by side, like a double image on a broken-down television set. So I wonder: What is memory? Boon or bane? Why is it given to us? After Galya's death, there seemed to be no crueler suffering than the suffering of memory; I wanted to follow after her or else turn into an animal—anything to stop remembering. I wanted to go away to another town, to see some friend or other, another old man just like me, so as not to get in the way of the children's lives and so that they would no longer torment me with their constant reminding. But none of my friends are left; there's no place, no one to go to, and I decided that memory was given to us as an inextinguishable flame of self-judgment, to singe us—or rather as a self-torture. But after a while, after maybe four or five years, I began to feel that there was joy in the sufferings of memory, that Galya had remained with me, that her absent presence continued to cause pain but that I rejoiced in that pain. Then I thought that memory is repayment for the most precious thing that can be taken away from a human being. Memory is nature's way of making up to us for death; therein lies our meager immortality. I did not know whether Asya—my classmate from Prigoda's school, my friend from the southern-front days—was alive; she was not near, not far, not anywhere. Time had caved in and buried her like a mine shaft caving in and burying a miner—and now how am I to rescue her? She is still alive, still breathing fifty-five years later, somewhere under the shale, under the lumps of unyielding ore, in the pitch-dark, airless catacombs. . . .

She was still breathing. But I thought she was dead. I ran into the house and the first thing I saw was a motionless whiteness on the floor, a heap of something white and rounded. Early dawn; half-light: I did not realize that it was a naked person on the ground. An absolutely naked woman. I did not see immediately that the snowy object, a strange, frozen mound, was not white at all. It was dirty, covered in bruises and scratches. But in the darkness I could make out only whiteness and, when I touched it with my hand, cold. I lifted the woman up, cried out, shouted: no response. I carried her in my arms and still I did not guess *whom I was carrying*. Because the face was lolling back, dead. The woman's body smelled of raw vodka. For a second it seemed that she was totally drunk. And very heavy. But then, suddenly—I was still holding her in my arms but did not know where to take her or for what—it came to me in a terrible flash and suddenly I realized *whom I was carrying*. In that instant I realized everything. Everything. The full horror of what had happened during the night, and what now, fifty-five years later, seems far more horrible than it seemed then.

Those were days of numbed senses. Too many deaths, acts of violence; crushing tension day after day. Intellectually I understood then that it was horrible, but that understanding did not make my blood run cold, did not make my knees give way. Some sober thought in my head said, Get alcohol. First warm her up if she's alive. They've killed the child. And at the same time astonishment—again intellectual. I was holding a naked woman for the first time in my life. But whom? A terrible thought— even more horrible than the first one, but everything was topsy-turvy and distorted. I was only eighteen and I had seen so much, experienced so much. I had seen nothing, experienced nothing. It was all the delirium of the moment, suppressed by intellectual horror, but now my knees really were giving way under the excessive weight, and above it all there were the malicious, blinding words "Shoot the whole pack of them like wolves!"

Then some people rushed in, Migulin's staff officers. Migulin himself, wearing a reddish-brown felt coat and breathless from running, pushed through a group which had run on ahead of him. Shura was among them. Migulin snatched my burden from me; tore it from me roughly, with authority, tossed his coat onto the ground and wrapped it round her. Then I realized for the first time—from his face, from his wild movements. . . . Poor Volodya! But Volodya was no more. That same night.

The lights came on. I'll always remember how life returns: not with the eyes or with a groan, but with the hiccups.

It was February 1919, Mikhailinskaya *stanitsa*. The north Don. Migulin and two cavalry divisions were driving Krasnov's men southward. The front was two hundred versts farther south. But Migulin rushed into Mikhailinskaya with four hundred men, having found out about Filippov's gang. Several hours too late. And Shura and I, had we not spent the night in Solyonoye, would now be lying on the snow in a pool of dark blood. Volodya and eighteen Revkom—or Revolutionary Committee—mem-

bers, including four Latvians from the Fourth Latvian Regiment
and three workers from Petersburg (the rest were locals) were
lying outside one on top of the other, thrown down any old way,
already stiff, arms and legs in every direction. All of them barefoot. The dead faces were covered in hoarfrost, the legs petrified,
bare, frosted over, and the blood in dark stains on the snow. The
nauseating smell of blood on the frost. The raid had been at
midnight. Everyone in the Revkom building had been slain. And
that was precisely where they had been sitting until late, arguing
furiously. Even though Shura and I weren't present, we knew
that the arguments about what to do with the hostages had been
going on all week. About seventy people were being held. Filippov released them all, but the Revkom members were bound by
the wrists, dragged outside and, according to all the rules of
Cossack butchery. . . .

A woman related: it lasted about ten minutes. You could hear
the inhuman wailing. In their haste they hacked down an old
Cossack called Mokeich, seventy-eight years old, for no reason
at all, merely because he had been sitting in the Revkom hut
dozing. And a lad of thirteen, the son of a Petersburg man who
used to drag the boy along everywhere with him. There he was.
I can see him lying beside his father, clutching his father's bare
foot. Everyone's boots had been wrenched off. There was Volodya, clutching his torn throat. The mouth was open and monstrously distorted, so he was not recognizable as Volodya. But in
his eyes was this fierce look of desperation, this amazement,
frozen there forever. "How can they execute innocent people
without a trial, without an investigation?" They say the hostages
that Filippov released volunteered to butcher the Revkom members. They didn't know that Volodya had fought for them tooth
and nail, what a beating he had taken; that Shigontsev, Bychin
and other Revkom members had skinned him alive and stig-
matized him as a Menshevik, a "putrid intellectual," or that
Shigontsev had declared that if Volodya hadn't been so "wet
behind the ears" he would have put him on trial just as he had

done in Rostov in 1918 with Egor, a former prisoner and an old friend, because he had whimpered Menshevik drivel. Now he had his throat slashed and there was that look of amazement in his dead eyes. I had always sensed that there was drama, blood and turmoil in his future.

"I can't for the life of me understand: how could they? Without a trial, wantonly, simply because he was a Cossack."

"It's because of people like you that the Revolution is dying!"

"Because of people like *you!*"

"No, because of people like you!"

Volodya had two innate qualities: amazement and stubbornness. That was why he joined up with the Bolsheviks: he was suddenly amazed at the idea. I loved them both, him and Asya. I spent my childhood with them. Now there he was lying with his throat slashed, but Asya they took to a warm house. She will live, Migulin will take her in and she will become his wife.

And then this: a year later, Rostov, the house on Sadovaya Street, some sort of ridiculous cold, dimly lit room seemingly uninhabited, its paneless windows carelessly boarded up with plywood, and outside, the intense cold, unprecedented for these parts. I am standing at the door to the next room, the room out of which Asya should be emerging. Something is being heated up in there: there is a smell of smoke. Instead of Asya, Elena Fyodorovna comes out. I used to visit their home in Piter so often, used to drink tea in the living room where a cast-iron knight held a lamp on a bronze chain, used to eat homemade ice cream smelling of milk. Elena Fyodorovna would call me Pavlik. She's wearing a coat; her head is wrapped up in something white like a turban. She is almost unrecognizable. The look on her face is full of such coldness that I recoil. She does not invite me in, does not say, "Hello, Pavlik!" She looks at me with hostile eyes in inflamed eyelids. Either she is ill or she has been crying, and she states firmly, "Leave my daughter in peace. Do not torment her." For ages she called me *ty*, but these commands are addressed to me as *vy*. She tries to shut the double door, but I manage to insert my foot into the opening and cry out, "Asya!"

I don't give a damn. I am oblivious to everything. Who is Elena Fyodorovna anyway?! I am impervious to it all: the tears, the hatred, the fact that she doesn't call me Pavlik anymore and addresses me as *vy*. I must see Asya, and, peering above the turban, I cry out louder, "Asya! Are you there?"

An unfamiliar voice answers from within the house, "Yes!" It seems to me to be a man's voice.

I have to tell her that last night in Bogaevka Migulin was arrested together with his whole staff. Asya raises herself up somewhat on her pillow and stretches her neck. Her head has been shaven because of her typhus and it is covered with a kind of down, like a newly hatched chick's. There is bewilderment in her eyes.

"What about Bogaevka? Nothing happened, did it?"

My face tells it all, but my tongue can't form the words, so I lie. "No, nothing; they send greetings. They're worried about your health. Look here!" I take eggs and a scrap of pork fat out of my bag.

"Isn't there any letter? How is that possible? I can't believe he didn't write anything."

I had not expected that. I continue to fib. "He didn't have a moment to spare. And anyway, there was nothing around: no paper or pencil."

"What do you mean?" She gave me a look of terror and pity. "Pavlik, what happened? I *know* that he always carries with him a field notebook made by the Warrior firm. A yellow, glossy thing."

What am I to do? I mumble and mumble. She must not be told anything. She's in a very bad state and her mother is standing in the doorway, aiming for me through the slits of her swollen little eyes as if she is about to pull the trigger at any moment. But that doesn't bother me at all. I am afraid that her mother has already guessed what has happened and may even be glad about it; this seals my lips even tighter. I continue my fibbing. She won't forgive me for this afterward, just as I was never forgiven for having been *appointed* court secretary in Balashov.

She did not understand that I always did what I could. I did my best. I did the very best within my power. And, practically speaking, I was the first to start agitating for his rehabilitation when it became possible to do so. And even at that time, fifty-five years ago, I did everything that a court secretary could do. I arranged his meetings with the attorney. And what about her last meeting with him? And after all that, she's surprised: "I don't understand why it was *you* who wrote the piece."

How strange that I loved her for so long. She did not understand me. And, realizing that, and anguished by it, I was still unable to rid myself of the thought for so long. Even when Galya had appeared on the scene, during the first few years when we lived in Novorossisk, I could not entirely forget her. I could never be the one to leave her. Even that time in Rostov, that bitterly cold February, when everything had been said, when all the fibs had been told and there was absolutely nothing to do in that home where they were missing someone else and where her mother hated me—even then I still could not make myself get up and leave.

A burning pity fills me with heaviness and chains me to the spot: pity for an unsightly, thin woman with chick's down on her head and with deathly fear—not for me, but for someone else—in her eyes which fix me with a vacant stare, just as they might stare at the postman or a telegraph pole. Like a chessman with lead-weighted feet, I cannot tear myself away. I feel that something else will be said, that something will happen. But they are too well brought up to chase me away. Elena Fyodorovna brings in the teapot and we drink a hot brew of indeterminate flavor. The scrap of pork fat has somewhat mollified Elena Fyodorovna.

But then an argument flares up. There had to be an argument. First a tearful story about how Asya's father Konstantin Ivanovich had died in that very apartment in November; how Asya's elder brother Alexei had died during the volunteers' retreat; how they lived in poverty; how there was nothing to live on; how everything had been sold; how Asya's elder sister Varya was earning money by doing duty with typhus patients and how her husband, a literary man, had been working on *The Don Wave* which now had no funds at all and how he was absolutely unable to get any work because he belonged to the gentry class of parasites. As someone had in fact declared to him in one office, "As a parasite on the working masses you will be given the hardest of physical labor. And you'll thank us." He would have thanked them, but there was no physical labor either. What were they pushing him to? What was he to do? How was he to live? Why did they call him a parasite when he had lived by his own toil from his early years and had had no estates or capital? He'd been a positive credit to the gentry.

As I recall, Elena Fyodorovna could quite justifiably be counted as a parasite: she did hold stocks and shares. But when I think of it, they had probably all been lost by that time. Hence the animosity. Mama, seeing my attachment to the Igumnovs' home, had often said, "Now, don't you forget that the Igumnovs are typical bourgeois. She's a very rich lady and he's a servant."

The rich lady sips her brew out of a tin mug and sits at home wrapped in a fur coat. I feel sorry for her, but not because she has lost everything and is starving, but because she is Asya's mother. I try talking to her calmly and seriously. No social revolution takes place without upheavals. It is naïve to imagine that the well-off classes will surrender their position without a fight. Think what happened in Robespierre's day! Read the Vicomte de Brok, an author Shigontsev and I used to love reading. Shigontsev had taught me, "Never miss a chance to look back into history."

"But the Revolution was three years ago!"

I have to explain the simplest things: the Revolution continues. So long as enemies remain, the Revolution will continue.

"But you'll always have enemies!"

The woman is blinded by her hatred. She has suffered. I understand. But talking to an uncompromising person is difficult. I should leave immediately; it's time. I simply must. But like a silly dog I am rooted to the spot. I am not in control of myself. There is nothing more long-lived and deceptive than a childish love. What was it about her? What still remained of that little girl who had once bowled me over? After everything that had befallen her and me: after Volodya; after Migulin, who was old enough to be her father. . . . But when she was living on Sadovaya Street I remember clearly that she looked a real fright. And I can feel her incredible love for another man. She is thinking about him and does not see me or hear me arguing with her mother. She even finds it difficult to speak; she is silent and smiles weakly. Sometimes she waves her hand at her mother in protest. But her thoughts are far away and she senses misfortune.

By now, Elena Fyodorovna and I are having a full-scale shouting match; harsh words have been uttered, words like "criminals," "murderers," "crimes." Elena Fyodorovna smiles at me maliciously. "I've talked too much. Now you can arrest me. Hand me over to the tribunal court: that's what it's called, isn't it? You are a commissar, aren't you, Pavel? You are authorized to arrest me on the spot, aren't you?"

"I am not a commissar, Elena Fyodorovna."

"Of course you are. You're a commissar through and through. I can tell by your face and your double-breasted jacket. You're wearing a commissar's jacket."

"Mama!" cries Asya. "He's not a commissar!"

Then Varya suddenly appears with her husband, whom I have not seen before. They say there is shooting in town. Some volunteer units have forced their way through to the suburbs and a real battle is under way.

True enough, for about two hours now there has been the sound of shots and the thunder of guns, but no one has been paying attention. Everyone is used to that music. With a look of cheerful resignation, Elena Fyodorovna makes a gesture with her hand and, turning to me and Asya, says, "Oh, you'll get the upper hand! You'll beat them off."

But Varya agitatedly protests. "But, Mama, this is serious. They're erecting a barricade on Sadovaya Street. God preserve us." She crosses herself wearily, looking like a nun in her long gray dress closed to the throat. Varya is an insincere, unpleasant person; I have never liked her.

Elena Fyodorovna introduces me to Varya's husband. "Vikenty Vasilevich, man of letters, at present out of work owing to his unfortunate pedigree—Pavel, our Petersburg friend, now a commissar. By the way, he might be able to help you. He has big connections in the committees. Isn't that true, Pavel?"

Again, caustic remarks. Pathetic, impotent. Varya's husband is a bit older than I am; he is pale and thin, as I am, but everything about him bespeaks another world, another age; everything is different. The little beard, the mustache, the quiet voice, the passive, unmasculine look in his eyes: some sort of flyaway fluff, not a look at all.

"Please don't trouble yourself," he says in his quiet voice. "I am quite content with my situation."

"What do you mean content?" Elena Fyodorovna exclaims. "You have nothing to buy bread with! You don't have any shoes!"

"It's sufficient for Varya and myself. I don't ask for anything. A person who can hear the inner voice does not need..." Then followed some strange prattling—like the gibberish spouted by a religious sermonizer or a Tolstoyan ranting about some society

of True Freedom, about doing good, about the classes on free-
religious knowledge where he had just delivered a lecture and,
gracious me, about some newly established "Bureau for the Pro-
tection of the Opponents of Violence."

"But you've haunted the threshold of the Soviet institutions,
haven't you? And you were turned down, weren't you?" yells
Elena Fyodorovna, looking wrathfully at her son-in-law. "Or are
you going to deny that too?"

"No, I did haunt their thresholds. But I did it for your sake."

"Ah, so you were doing *me a good turn*? What did you eat
today, you wretched man?"

The strange fellow explains that as a lecture fee he had been
given a plate of pearl-barley pudding and a cup of coffee.

Meanwhile the shooting had intensified. Nearby, a shell crashed
thunderously, and from the adjacent room came the sound of
shattering glass. By now it is high time for me to make tracks,
but I dawdle. I cannot conceive of such a preposterous situation—
that Denikin's men are in town. The front was far away. And
Denikin's position was not of the best. How could be indulge in
such escapades? Yet he had: he had taken the risk and General
Gnilorybov had broken through the front, reached the outskirts
of Rostov and joined battle in town. I know nothing, therefore
I am calm. Shooting. Some gang or other is being wiped out. It
happens every day. Artillery fire makes me sit up a bit, but not
enough to make me rush immediately out onto the street.

"Good Lord, good Lord..." whispers Varya, standing by the
window, making a rapid small sign of the cross. "If only, if only,
if only...."

"Varvara, come away from there!" orders Elena Fyodorovna.
Everyone is on edge now that it is quite obvious that a very real
battle is under way. The battle of Rostov. Outside, people are
shouting. Suddenly the sky is illuminated and a yellow-pink light
fills the room: the building next door is on fire. We cannot see
the building, but the glow of the blaze is nearby. We can hear

a tree cracking; the dull thud of something hitting the ground; people crying out. A smell of burning seeps into the room.

All of a sudden, Varya shrieks, "I can see the Russian standard! They're holding the Russian standard!"

Everyone rushes to the window, but I go over to Asya to say goodbye. She grabs my fingers in her hot hand and asks me in a whisper, "Pavlik, tell me the truth: has something terrible happened to Sergei Kirillovich? Is he dead? Have they broken through the front?"

I do not know what happened yesterday or the day before. Three days ago in the morning everything was absolutely quiet on the lines held by the Corps. But Denikin could break through the front farther south.

"He is in trouble! I feel it. I see it. It's because of Shigontsev's murder, isn't it?"

For a moment I hesitate. Perhaps after all I should tell her? Her mother, who can think quickly, says, "The volunteers will arrive and find out that Migulin's wife is here. What do you think they're going to do with us all?"

"God, let them do what they like!" cries out Varya. Suddenly she starts to sob.

I do not manage to say anything or make any decision—or to leave. Completely unexpectedly—as if this were the theatre and they were leaping out from the wings—three men appear in the room, an officer and two soldiers. The officer rushes over to Elena Fyodorovna. Embraces, tears. Some old acquaintance. At once he starts telling—it seems that this is why he came— about how Alexei died. The soldiers move over to the window and one of them gives it a cool, powerful blow with the butt of his gun and knocks out the frame, which hurtles down to the street and reverberates below. The soldiers position themselves on the windowsill and open fire. But the shooting does not last long. I have no idea what they can see there: the street is full of smoke. I have my Smith and Wesson in my coat and feel calm.

I keep my hand in my pocket. I remember with remarkable clarity that I felt calm. I do not know why. Perhaps because Asya was there. We were together—she and I.

The officer first gives me a cursory glance and then looks me over more carefully. He is unshaven, with a sallow complexion, and the whites of his eyes are yellowish. His look changes in the space of two seconds. My double-breasted leather "commissar's" jacket has set him on his guard. Probably something else as well: perhaps the fact that my face shows neither joy nor anxiety. Elena Fyodorovna and Varya are crying in each other's arms.

"Whom do I have the honor?" asks the officer without rising from his chair, yet leaning toward me with his whole body, with his eyes and with his hand, which is gripping the hilt of his saber.

I see that the eyes of the champion of True Freedom have suddenly lit up. Vikenty Vasilevich cannot conceal a suggestive smile.

But Asya's mother says tearfully, "That's Pavlik, our friend. . . ."

Two days later, Denikin's men were driven out of town. When was that? February. It was bitterly cold. I crossed the Temernik in the morning and saw corpses, hoary with the night frost. The end of February 1920.

Shigontsev was murdered in January. They found him dead, shot through the head, in a gully not far from the *stanitsa* where the Corps headquarters was housed. After Novocherkassk, the failures had begun. Marking time on the Manych River, making fruitless attempts to entrench ourselves on the left bank: lost time. During which everything hostile and harmful to Migulin began to stir, and then suddenly—Shigontsev murdered. He had turned up quite recently. It was Shigontsev's third appearance. The first was in January 1918 in Piter [Petrograd] after long ordeals: after Siberia, Australia and the Far East. The second was on the Don in 1919, and the third meeting was now. And each time he was different. Now he was nervous, peevish, sick, coughing all the time. "You should get treatment," Migulin told him peaceably. "You're rotting away. Diseased through to the core. Why on earth do you want to go to the front?"

But Migulin is rarely peaceable. More often than not, he is tense, suspicious and rude. The first instant when he saw Shigontsev with the orderly in the yard of the headquarters building he recognized him and was somewhat taken aback: the telegram from the Revolutionary Military Council of the Southern Front about the appointment of a commissar had arrived the day before, but Migulin had not connected Shigontsev's name with the man he had had such a cruel run-in with in 1919 at the time of the ferocious onslaught of the Steel Detachment. In addition, enraged by the gauchely pompous Shigontsev—who did not look like a Cossack at all, sitting like a sack on his horse, slouched over to one side—Migulin wheezed out sarcastically, "Ah, my respects to you! We are old friends!"

Because of Shigontsev's black beard and his eyes like coals looking out from under bushy eyebrows, he had taken him for a non-Russian. And during the whole first day, Migulin was full of the kind of insinuating sarcasm and malicious innuendo of which he was capable. I could also hear rabid angry swearing— not in Shigontsev's presence, but among our own men in the headquarters building: "What are they doing this for? Are they doing it on purpose? Are they trying to exasperate me?"

The point is that these are old scores. From 1919. Perhaps even earlier. And naturally Migulin feels insulted: they have sent him a man who was at one time an unyielding and malicious adversary. I was unable to find out whether it had been done intentionally or whether it was mere clumsiness, haste. Later, once the acerbic telegraphic swearing match flared up between Migulin and the Revolutionary Military Council, retreat was even more futile. And so they dug in their heels. "THE RMC SEES NO REASON TO REPLACE THE COMMISSAR. THE MATTER NOT OPEN TO

FURTHER DISCUSSION." Something along those lines, something extremely annoying, was the message our telegraphist Petya Gailit received. By that time the air was dry and crackling; saturated with electricity.

I remember the Cossacks' alarm cry at dawn: "The commissar's been killed!" In an instant I guess it; the thought flashes, "They've killed Migulin." I bump into Asya on the street running somewhere bareheaded, heaven knows where—the madness of the moment, there is nowhere to run. At the time Migulin was spending the night about six versts away at Durnaya Polyana, a farmstead—I remember thoroughly all the details of that night: fateful memories. I remember Asya running into me in the darkness, falling straight into my arms as if on purpose. "Do you understand what this means?" I do understand. I hold her tight. She is shivering although she is wearing a warm fur coat over her shoulders. Is she trembling from the cold or from terror? I remember distinctly that I began to shake. . . .

After all, he was an old man! Forty-seven. And she was nineteen. Forty-seven. My God, how that age of splendid and happy maturity seemed Methusaleh-like, because I myself was not quite nineteen. That "not quite" was torture. It always was. Especially as a child. That time when I embraced her in the dim light of that January dawn, a trembling creature with darkened face, charred by a lightning bolt, I felt such an acute sensation, so strong that it has remained with me to this day. A chill of the soul: pity for her, fear for her. It did happen, what they call love. But I never talked about it. Everything became confused. And I do not remember what I felt during that instant when the thought came to me: They have killed Migulin.

The first autumn of the war. Fog, Petersburg, the whole class of us walking after school to a military hospital on Liniya 22. She is fourteen years old, I am not quite fourteen, though I soon will be. But not soon enough. I am in agony; it seems to me that all my troubles stem from that "not quite." She is offhand with me, pays little mind to what I say, runs out of the classroom whenever I go up to Volodya, and all because of those damned missing months: she cannot pay attention to a thirteen-year-old boy when she is being pestered by fifteen-year-olds. No. What I have to do is catch up with her as soon as I can, even just for a little while, six months or so. At least those six months would be mine.

We are walking along our unprepossessing Liniya 15, past the shops and the gray houses, and I am suffering from her indifference. She talks to everyone, looks at absolutely anyone, dogs, young high-school boys walking toward us, but not at me. Although I am walking alongside her, her gloved hand only once in a while brushes absently against my hand. It would not be difficult for me to walk closer to her, because everyone knows that I am Volodya's friend and that he and she are brother and sister. Well, first cousins actually. But they live in the same house, in the same apartment, Volodya living with the Igumnov family like a son. His mother is in Kamyshino and his father is abroad, exactly where no one knows. They don't talk about him— perhaps he left Volodya's mother, Elena Fyodorovna's sister, or perhaps he's some kind of anarchist, a fugitive. I remember someone mentioning in passing, "The man's a nincompoop." My attraction to Volodya is not merely friendship, but also that common link which we never discuss: fatherlessness. For I too have a father "somewhere." And "something" has happened to his mother. Sometimes I conjure up a crystal-clear picture of Volodya's life in the Igumnov home, that dear home that I loved to visit: that hurly-burly, that crumpled, noisy, cozy, benevolent

household where they chaffed one another, where they invented
all kinds of jolly amusements for their own enjoyment: coin games
or word games. Or else, just like that, young and old alike would
get carried away with sculpture. They would walk around with
grimy hands, the floors would get caked in filth, there would be
a smell of wet plaster, everyone would madly vie with everyone
else, and a domestic contest would be organized. Konstantin
Ivanovich once invited a famous sculptor to be the judge and he
found the best work to be a piece of nonsense by the hand of the
servant Milda. That home where everything was almost one's
own, but not quite. It was so close, that home where Volodya's
not-quite father and not-quite mother were so kind to him. Both
he and I suffered from "not quite."

Volodya and Asya were extraordinarily close. While Asya would
quite often quarrel with Varya about the slightest trifle, as happens
between sisters—even going so far as minor scuffles, with very
spiteful expressions on their faces (in fact, I once saw them beat
each other with their fans, not hard, but with spirit)—and while
she was totally distant from her elder brother Alexei, she was
bound to Volodya by an unfathomably deep friendship. To me
there seemed nothing extraordinary about it, just the friendship
of two very good people. Such a rare thing in life! I believed in
this for a long time and that friendship did not worry me. I was
much more alarmed by Gubanov the soldier. It all starts pouring
out of your memory once you get down to excavating, and it
turns out that nothing has been lost. Memory is a storeroom for
unneeded things, an attic where dusty baskets crammed full of
old shoes are kept until they are eventually thrown out, along
with suitcases with broken handles, odd rags, umbrellas, bits of
glassware, albums, pieces of wire, a solitary glove and dust, dust,
the thick, limp dust of time. There is the name of a soldier who
flickered on the threshold of existence. A soldier named Gubanov, slightly wounded at Suvalki. He lies there like a diamond
in the unimaginable dust.

It is not the first time that we are on our way to the hospital on Liniya 22. We have our own ward on the fifth floor. We carry gifts in bags: apples, candy, cigarettes, half a pound of tea, and paper and pencils. As soon as we appear in the fifth-floor corridor, Private Gubanov cries out joyously, "The inquisitors have arrived!" He can never get it straight that we are not inquisitors but visitors.

"Hi, blondie! Anyuta! My darling!" bellows Gubanov. "Come over here, honey!" And he scoops Asya up with his long arms, rakes her toward him and sets her on his lap as though he were her father. What's so surprising about that? She is the most radiant, and the most beautiful. She is so nice and plump, so superb, so ripe, so towheaded, so unlike the pale Piter ladies— she is like a farm lass from the Baltic, a Finnish wench, a dairymaid's daughter. With her white-blond eyelashes. To me, Asya's beauty is an indisputable fact, just like the value of those earliest British postage stamps with Queen Victoria on them. And, of course, people see that beauty and make advances to her. I cannot defend her, since I have no right to. Why should I? Besides, private Gubanov isn't doing anything wrong. It's just that I feel— in fact, everyone feels—that there is something vile about his manner.

Private Gubanov reads aloud a composition that for several days he has been writing with Asya's help, "The Battle of Suvalki." We have hit upon the idea of publishing a magazine, and each of us has to help a wounded soldier to write down something he remembers. I have someone in my care, too, but he is curt, uncommunicative and reluctant to remember anything, mumbling morosely, "What's the point of describing how they shoot the hell out of you?" Gubanov, on the other hand, is quick and efficient and has written several pages practically by himself. One hand is turning the pages as he reads, and the other is holding Asya on his lap. I can see that she is embarrassed and ashamed; she is not a little girl anymore, but a young lady, and has, as they say, "filled out nicely." Now she is making delicate efforts to free herself from Private Gubanov's grasp, but to no avail.

Gubanov has caught her and holds her fast. The first pages describe the battle, his injury, how he ran back to the trench and saw the staff captain who asked him pathetically, "Wounded, brother?" and "Where's your bandage?" and other points of detail.

I look at Asya anxiously, wondering how I can help her. What can I think of to say to Private Gubanov? He is a hero and Asya doesn't want to offend him. He may be a hero, but he's a swine all the same. I hate him. He goes on to describe how the wounded were brought back to Petrograd and how much he liked everything in Petrograd—the trolley, the hospital, the nurses, the soft mattresses, the white sheets and the fine towels. "They treated us very well indeed. In the morning the nurses came and said hello. I also remember that we were given a good wash in the bathhouse. When you're out of the bath, they immediately dress you in clean shirts, drawers and socks." All this seems stupid to me and not at all suitable for our magazine. Everyone is listening, however, including the wounded. Gubanov goes on reading, and with his right hand, which is clasping Asya, he gives her little strokes and pats as if she were his property. "On October 9 we had a visit from someone from the governing body of the book department of the *Supreme Authority*," reads Gubanov, placing particular emphasis on the last two words, "who gave us psalters and Gospels. . . ."

Suddenly, Volodya walks up to Gubanov, who is sitting on his bed with Asya on his knee and, without a word, pries back the arm which is holding her. Asya, now freed, jumps up and runs away from her tormenter. Private Gubanov, however, goes on reading just as if he has not noticed a thing. Volodya has done something amazing: there are times when words are not needed, when one simply has to go forward and act.

Volodya often amazes me. It is impossible to predict what he will do. Take the story about the rat which caused such a furor at the school. It was a marvelous coeducational school—I was lucky, it was the best one on Vasilevsky Island, probably even in the whole of Piter. It was called the Prigoda School, after Nikolai

Apollonovich Prigoda, the founder and principal and a great enthusiast; he was an admirer of Thomas More and Campanella and he taught history, while his wife, Olga Vitalevna, taught biology. Strange people! They needed nothing more out of life, required no occupation other than their school and their pupils. School councils, which were introduced after February 1917, had existed much earlier at Prigoda. All decisions were taken by a vote. Olga Vitalevna asked if someone could bring in a rat to dissect in the anatomy lesson. Somebody promised to catch one, did not succeed for a long time and then finally produced one. The whole school knew that on that day our class was going to cut up a live rat. A boy had brought it in a cage and for some reason had said that its name was Fenya. He actually volunteered himself to do the cutting. Out of the blue a deputation from a senior class led by Volodya appears at the lesson.

"We don't want a living creature to be killed in our school. We feel sorry for Fenya." Some cry "Shame!" Others "Cut it up!" A terrible argument begins. As I recall, Olga Vitalevna stirs up the argument even more. The fact that someone has said the rat is called Fenya proves to be fatal, for it stops being merely a rat: it becomes an individual. People take a closer look at it. It behaves like a Fenya. Impassioned speeches are made at the meeting, and, forgetting about the rat, which is humbly waiting for its fate to be decided, people debate science, history, the guillotine and the Paris Commune. "Great ends require victims!" "But the victims disagree! You ask the rat! You're exploiting the fact that it's dumb; if it could talk, it would answer!"

In the end we decide to vote on it. Our class is not the only one voting, for the rat question has aroused the entire school. The rat is pardoned. Volodya triumphantly carries the cage out into the yard and, in the presence of everyone, frees Fenya, all but a victim to science. A thrilling moment! Olga Vasilevna is especially excited and we too realize that the issue was not the rat but something more important. The finale casts a slight pall over our mood: finding itself freed, our Fenya is disoriented and stands gaping, upon which it is immediately caught by a cat which was running across the yard.

Winter in Siverskaya. A cloud of dry snow blows down from the pine trees, the Finnish sleigh is being drawn at a gallop up the slope, so fast that the runners tilt upward so that you have to hold on tight to the bar; on the veranda of Matisen the forester's dacha a multicolored garland of ice kegs has been hung. This is the third winter we have spent in the Matisens' house. Not far from us live the Igumnovs. They have their own house. On the turn, Asya slides off the seat of the sleigh—I think it was called a *pottkuri*—and lands head first in a snowdrift while I flounder about in the snow on the other side. Covered with ice, the road gleams with a porcelain sparkle. Asya's red hat has flown a long way off and her wonderfully thick black-and-white-striped pullover—bought in a Swedish sporting-goods shop, where they called it a "sweater"—is covered with snow and Asya is guffawing like a lunatic. Her laughter sometimes frightens me. I feel that she is laughing because of someone, because of something.

This is how the little ice kegs are made: you pour colored water into cups and put a piece of string into each. Asya's father, Konstantin Ivanovich, has bought a car, but driving it to Siverskaya in winter is dangerous; he once got stuck and had to be hauled out by horses. There is a story going around that roaming the area around Siverskaya is the gang of one Gribov, a deserter they have been trying unsuccessfully to catch for several months. Which winter is this? Christmas holidays. Mama is no longer working in the statistics office, but in the publishing house as a proofreader; she has to travel to work into Piter. I go to the station to meet her, since she is bringing back heavy packages—and also because "Gribov is up to his tricks." Nobody has seen this Gribov fellow in the flesh, although people tell all kinds of horrible cock-and-bull stories about him. In particular, they say that Gribov hates the cops, financial bureaucrats and Livonian landowners. Those three categories of people had done him dirty in his lifetime and he had sworn to have revenge on them. They say that he robs the rich dachas but doesn't touch the poor ones. That winter I was ecstatically reading thin little volumes about Nick Carter and John Wilson and imagining myself as one of them—in a fight with Gribov.

And then I bumped into him face to face.

It is evening on the wooded hill where the four of us—myself, Volodya, Asya and Mama's brother Shura, recently returned from Siberia—have gone to ski. Shura! At that time I am still sizing him up. He intrigues me. Alexander Pimenovich—or Shura, as Mama calls him—is quite young, about thirty, but is all sort of grimy-looking, charred, his face marked with blotches and scars, his head shaven and gray, and there are steel-framed spectacles on his nose. Mama says he has changed. They have not seen each other for many years. Shura is a revolutionary, but exactly what kind or how he made a name for himself one does not know. Nor can one ask—that rule I know better than to break; sometimes mysterious individuals appear at our house and I have been instructed how to behave with them. Even so, something makes me impatient to get Mama to tell me about him. What is Shura's profession? A revolutionary. I know that, but does he have some kind of profession? He's a professional revolutionary. But before he became a revolutionary? He always was one. As far back as I can remember him. He went to the parish school as a small boy and already at that time... Gradually I find out: a *druzhinnik* in the first revolution, exiles, escapes, the murder of a guard, then exile again and penal servitude. It was not as Alexander Pimenovich or as Danilov that Shura had arrived in Piter, but as Ivan Spiridonovich Samoilenko, and this does not surprise me. Mama too uses a false name. Everyone thinks she is Anastasia Fyodorovna Merks, a petit-bourgeois woman from Revel, while in fact she is Irina Pimenovna Letunova, nee Danilova, a peasant from Novgorod province.

We are standing atop the hill about to ski down, but Asya is afraid. She is guffawing and says she won't ski down, that she'll take her skis off and go down on foot. We are egging her on, when suddenly three men in sheepskin coats appear from behind the pine trees.

"Greetings, my gentle skiers. Don't be afraid," one of them says. "I am Gribov." They too are on skis. They have sneaked up on us undetectably. We are dumbfounded. I take a look at Gribov: nothing terrifying about his appearance—a young man with a dark beard and a very ruddy complexion, wearing a peaked fur hat with the earflaps down, like the ones the Finns wear. Gribov's expression is quite good-natured—he even seems to be smiling.

"Ah, Gribov!" says Shura.

"Hello, brother."

I hear the creak of ski poles, the whoosh of skis—I look round and Volodya is tearing down the hill. With a thump of his skis as he flies down the jump, he is off, darting through the pine trees. He turns right, fleetingly appears in the thicket and disappears. "Spunky!" says Gribov, and one of his companions gives a brigand's whistle.

Shura goes up to Gribov and they exchange words in a low voice. Then the three of them say farewell and move off, and we go homeward. In a clearing we set up a small board as a target and Shura fires his Browning. He allows Asya and me to have a try as well. Shura has poor eyesight—it suffered because of the beatings he was given in prison—and he takes aim slowly and carefully.

The spent cartridges sink into the snow with a hiss. For some reason I pick them up; they are warm. Dusk is approaching, making it impossible to shoot anymore. On our way home, we try not to talk or think about Volodya. What happened is catastrophic. "Did he really get frightened off?" asks Asya in a whisper.

It's a complete mystery to me. There is astonishment in her voice, but we are even more astonished by what had happened before our very eyes: Shura and Gribov talking together like two good friends. I am dying to find out from Shura about Gribov, but I keep quiet, remembering my mother's injunction: *Don't ask questions.* Three years later, when Shura and I are wearing ourselves out traveling across Russia by train, spending whole nights together, I find out that it was through Gribov that they obtained their weapons. Not long afterward, Gribov died, killed by border guards.

It is quite dark when we reach the Igumnovs' dacha. Shura and I are left to have supper. What delicious, hot, life-giving tea! How warm and cozy it is in the dacha! It smells of Konstantin Ivanovich's cigar and burning candles. The stoves buzz, the wood crackles. Volodya sits at the table, his head hanging. I can understand him. In fact, as I see it, you have to have a fair amount of self-possession to sit there after what *he* just pulled and drink tea, even with such a stonelike expression on your face. The tea-drinking continues peacefully. Konstantin Ivanovich asks Shura about Siberia, but cautiously, without letting on that he knows what Shura was doing there. They talk about the Siberian people's hunting and fishing and their customs, and they talk of the war, the Mad Monk, the fact that Germany is exhausted, epidemics, spies, bribery and the increasing acts of plunder and violence— of which, as a lawyer, Konstantin Ivanovich has firsthand knowledge.

Suddenly, Asya blithely and insouciantly—and, I am sure, unintentionally, just thoughtlessly, as a foolish well-meant act— says to Volodya, "It's a pity you ran away, Volodya. The outlaw turned out to be very sweet!"

What outlaw? Who ran away? The questions begin, and somehow it comes out about Gribov. But we keep quiet about the most important part. Suddenly Volodya jumps to his feet, his face aglow—for some reason it is the top part of his face, around the forehead and eyes, that has blushed especially red—and rushes out of the room.

"What happened?" asks Elena Fyodorovna in a whisper.

"That's exactly how he shot off... when Gribov appeared."

"Oh, so he got scared?" Alexei's eyes show a gleam of surprise and malicious enjoyment. Asya looks frightened. She is distraught and does not know what to do—should she go after Volodya or stay and defend him? I put forward a theory: that he was standing on a slope, on a very slick ski track, and a single movement was enough to make him slide right down it unable to stop. But why didn't he come back? We were talking with Gribov for at least a quarter of an hour. Well, what *is* cowardice, in actual fact? A momentary blackout of the conscious mind. It can, if you like, be grounds for nonliability. I start to go after Volodya, but Elena Fyodorovna says don't bother.

"From the legal point of view," says Konstantin Ivanovich, "cowardice is esteemed so characteristic of man... as Tagantsev wrote, a man cannot be punished for—"

"What about a display of cowardice in wartime?"

"Ah, well. Evading danger is deemed punishable by law." But Shura says that everyone has moments of a searing fear which clouds the reason. A moment and Volodya was skiing down the hill, unable to stop, unable to return, unable to look us in the face—unable to live. You can't define everything in the world in terms of laws and paragraphs. Yes you can. Moreover, you have to. That is the guarantee of the world's viability. Do you call a rotten society a viable world? It is rotten precisely because its laws define so little. They are too weak. Hell, but everything is collapsing before our very eyes! The temple is crumbling and you talk about laws! Laws are the only thing that can save it. In that case, the world is divided into two categories: what falls within the purview of law and what does not. Where do you put all the rest? There isn't any rest. Come on, what about the judgment of one's own conscience? A moment of cowardice might mean a lifetime of torture. Let me illustrate the great power of laws by giving you an example, says Konstantin Ivanovich. Let us say that Volodya got scared. At that critical moment when you happened upon the criminals in the forest, he ran away. Thank God, it turned out happily, and the criminals did you no harm. But if some misfortune had occurred...

At these words Volodya appears wearing his hat and coat. Perhaps he has heard everything. I shall never forget his face: sort of gray papier-mâché with a frozen expression. Without looking at anyone he utters into space, "I'm going into town; please, no one follow me. If anyone comes after me I shall shoot." And he shows his pistol.

A few minutes afterward, when the stupefaction has passed, we rush after him. But in the garden and on the road there is a thick fog. He has disappeared. Nor is he at the station. Four days later a telegram arrived from Kamyshino, from his mother. But those four days...

Everyone had it. Including me. A moment of fear—not physical, not a fear of death, but precisely a moment of mental blackout, a crack-up of the spirit. A moment of compromise. Or perhaps a moment of self-knowledge? But afterward a person says, *I was weak* that once, but I shall never give in to you again. In 1928. No, in 1935. Galya said, "I feel extremely sorry for you. *You* didn't say it. *I* said it, our children said it." She thought everything was for their sake. Mental blackout—for their sake. Now Galya is no longer. And the children—are they or are they not? Peter, who denied Christ in the Garden of Gethsemane, did not have children, yet later he did earn his name Petros, meaning rock: that is, hard.

Many times after that half-childish fear or, let us say, that moment of weakness, Volodya was staggering in his exceptional presence of mind at critical moments. What about the summer of 1917 on Ligovsky Prospekt? By some crazy chance, he and I landed smack in the middle of an assemblage of monarchists. We had gone into a pharmacy. I ask for some ricinine oil, and, without saying a word, the pharmacist pulls us into the back room, flings open the door to the corridor and, giving us a prod in the back, whispers, "Down the steps! Hurry up, it's already started!" In the basement there are about forty people, listening attentively to a portly gentleman who is pouring forth names and figures, speaking excitedly and with constant spite in his voice. "Those traitors," "Judases of the Russian people," "the so-called government." If we had asked simply for castor oil we would have been given a bottle and would have gone calmly on our way. "Ricinine oil" turned out to be their password. Only in those days could that gory nonsense have taken place. Kornilov had not yet advanced, but some people knew and were waiting for him. We were nearly shot dead in that basement, but Volodya smashed a lamp and we made a getaway in the darkness.

Those early days—March, heady spring, the crowds of thousands on the streets of Petrograd, streets wet with slushy snow, and the three of us, Volodya, Asya and myself, wandering about from dawn to dusk. The complete freedom from everything and everyone! No need to go to school, where there is nothing but meetings, elections, discussions of the "school constitution"; instead of giving a lecture on the great reforms, Nikolai Apollonovich tells us all about the French Revolution. At the end of the class we learn "La Marseillaise" in French and there are tears in Nikolai Apollonovich's eyes. Mama spends her days who knows where. In the publishing house, where all sorts of lists, programs and manifestos are being printed, in the Tavrichesky Palace, or else she visits the sailors. I do not see her at all and often do not spend the night at home because Mama does not come home, but rather with the Igumnovs, on the trestle bed in Volodya's room. It is very comfortable there. Volodya and I talk through the whole night or play chess. And Asya is close by, just the other side of the wall! But at the same time, what torture!

Suddenly one morning she runs along the corridor in her dressing gown and cries out in confusion, "Oh! Pavlik! I'd forgotten." She always forgets that I am here. But never for a minute do I forget about her. Strange relationships in that house. They are all friendly, but a little indifferent to one another. All of a sudden in the evenings they will disperse in different directions. Or it can happen that they all assemble and have a jolly old time joking and horsing around. Konstantin Ivanovich will tease Elena Fyodorovna a little, Alexei will pull Volodya's leg, and Asya... Asya has shut herself in the bathroom and Volodya is cooling his heels in the corridor waiting for the bathroom to be free, when suddenly Alexei brazenly knocks on the door and even opens it slightly, saying, "A brother is permitted, but you, cousin, kindly wait outside." I can see Volodya's face darken. He is the only one in the house who is not very much inclined to joking. He takes everything too painfully seriously. Konstantin Ivanovich and Elena Fyodorovna, as well as Asya, Varya and Alexei, regard everything taking place in town not exactly flippantly, but sort of half jokingly, half fearfully: on the whole like a big game. Oh yes! Kindly but not very bright. But I live as if in a dream. Everything around me is a noisy, enveloping dream, coaxing me somewhere. Asya is now sixteen years old, and I am still only fifteen; she is more and more hopelessly breaking further and further away. A pal of Alexei's, a student, invites her out for a poetry-dance soirée at the Lancelot Club on Znamenskaya Street, a place to which Volodya and I are not admitted. Then some cadet takes her for a spin in his father's car—but that, I think, was in the summer.

In March, however, there is nothing but endless running, crowds, shooting, news, terror and rapture. All the eagles on the Palace railings are swathed in red cloth. There are red flags everywhere. There is a red flag on the Fortress too. Documents burn in the police department, and the street is strewn with ash. In the Igumnovs' building a housing committee is organized to search all the apartments and attics to make sure there are no policemen in hiding. Konstantin Ivanovich is elected chairman. He wears a large red rosette. A game, a game! And our Shura is now a great man—Commissar of Workers' Deputies for Vasilevsky Island; he is Ivan Spiridonovich Samoilenko, a martyr of tsarist penal servitude. The funeral of the Victims of the Revolution takes place at the end of March. Unbelievable slush and filth, the streets not swept. Every day, enormous crowds of people wade through the mud, splashing the wet snow around and turning it into puddles. We are walking in a long procession toward Mars Field. On Nizhegorodskaya Street we are joined by a factory contingent, then a medical school, Mensheviks, Ukrainians, firemen, a reserve regiment; coffins draped in red emerge from the Army Medical Academy. We proceed along Liteiny Bridge, past the burned-out lockup; red and black flags are hanging out on the buildings. We stand for about two hours on Nevsky, and from everywhere we hear people singing "Eternal Remembrance" and "You fell a victim..." A man in a black coat leaps up onto the granite base of an entrance staircase and, grabbing onto the lamp with one hand and snatching his hat from his head and waving it about with the other, he cries out, "Friends! We have to let the Petrogradsky district through! Keep calm and be patient, friends! Today is a day of great sorrow and great freedom. No country in the world, friends, is freer than Russia is today...." He utters something disjointed and desperately loud, and as he slowly turns his black bent body around I see the coaly face, the grizzled crewcut, the gleaming steel-rimmed spectacles of—Shura.

Migulin wrenched Asya's body from my arms so peremptorily, with such rude haste, it was as if he was grabbing *what was his*, as I realized later. And that whole sudden raid to save the Revkom, albeit unsuccessful... Why not just dispatch four squadrons under the command of anyone at all? I galloped over myself. I saw an old man's face distorted by excruciating torment—dark deep bags under his eyes, cheeks covered with black-gray stubble, the furrows on his brow tightened in martyrlike horror. When Shigontsev came up and asked with a malicious, almost mad smile, "So what do you think now, defender of the Cossacks? Who was right?," Migulin recoiled and gave him a long, hard look—although you cannot scare a former prisoner with a look—and answered, "I was right. There are brutes among our people as well." But Volodya—in the snow with his throat slit.

    Then in April—after the Finland Station, Lenin's reception, Kshesinskaya's palace where Shura had dragged me— when it was warmer, in the spring, Volodya, Asya and I are prowling around town, busy collecting money for the Soviet of Workers' Deputies. In about three hours we collect six rubles. We walk as long as our feet will carry us. On the streets there is still the same chaos, the same confusion, the rather terrifying churning of the crowd; meetings, fights, shooting. I see armed workers from the Parviainen factory coming along Nevsky holding a banner: DOWN WITH THE PROVISIONAL GOVERNMENT! Moving toward them, making their way down Liteiny Prospekt, is a demonstration of students, officers and some well-dressed ladies, carrying a banner: LONG LIVE MILYUKOV AND THE PROVISIONAL GOVERNMENT! People are throwing stones from a rooftop. Impossible to say at whom. The two demonstrations merge into each other, the women shriek, there is a scuffle; some fall, some run, a banner is noisily ripped and the flagstaff is broken. Some gentleman is standing up in an open car by the Moika Canal haranguing the crowd, thrusting out his right hand with its white cuff as if tossing money to the throng. "America!... Has declared!... On the Huns!..." Shouts of Hooray! A rather fierce-looking man in a *papakha*, pushing his way toward the car with arms outstretched, fighting everyone off, wheezes out, "Just let me at that flea. I'll squash him against the wire with my ass."

    Then I hear two people who are standing in conversation by the wall of a building. One of them says in an undertone, "You know what these street crowds remind you of? They're just like guts pouring out of a ripped open belly. Russia won't live through this stabbing." "Good Lord!" "You'll see. It'll be fatal. But the nice part is," he chuckles softly, "I am dying. And Russia is finished, too, in one fell swoop. So I don't even feel sorry about dying."

I look at him, an old man with a bushy white beard and a hat pulled down low over his eyes. And it is so that he remains with me, and always will remain.

We drag ourselves along to the Igumnovs' house in the darkness. I am with them, Volodya and Asya, from morning to night; I cannot tear myself away. What an idiot! I sometimes notice that when they are hemmed in by the crowd Volodya and Asya cuddle up to each other. Volodya puts his arms around her to try to shield her from jostling—and the only thing that occurs to me is, Lucky Volodya; he can embrace her like a brother! That evening as well, I should have gone home. We had walked our feet off and had had plenty of talk. I should have given them a break from me, but Asya—probably automatically—asks me in for a drink of tea. "Pavlik, let's go in, shall we?" Her voice sounds absentminded; she is tired, Volodya is yawning and I myself am unbelievably weary, yet I manage to trail after her through the front door. I haven't got the strength to refuse. I must really have outstayed my welcome!

Soon Alexei arrives. There is dried blood on his face, and his jacket is torn. Excitedly and unintelligibly he tells of some clashes, of how Kirik Nasonov was beaten up and pursued. Suddenly he catches sight of the mug we ran around town with, collecting for the soviet. "And what kind of rubbish is that?" Then, to Volodya, "Are you involved in *that?* You nothing! You bungler!" And he even raises his hand to strike him. Why is he a bungler? Because it was out of place and stupid. For the first time I see a quarrel brewing between the near-brothers, brewing swiftly and nastily. All of a sudden, Alexei comes down on his uncle, Volodya's father, and for some reason calls him a chatterbox. The connection is unfathomable; all I see is that things that were kept inside are bursting out into the open. How dare you talk about my father like that? You are living in someone's house, so kindly abide by the rules of that house! What rules? Ours! Both Varya and Elena Fyodorovna are present—and no one is in a joking mood, because there is a crowd outside on the street and Alexei's face is covered in blood. Asya rushes to Volodya's defense. Apologize immediately! What do you mean, *our* rules? I mean it's come to that: people are being killed. Half an hour ago, before my very eyes...Kirik Nasonov....

Everyone knows Kirik Nasonov well. He is the nephew of Nikolai Apollonovich Prigoda and a student at the Land Surveyors Institute. But Kirik is beside the point. Everyone starts arguing with everyone else, but I am out of it. It's as if I am not there in the room. Even though the whole ruckus is my fault. Mama had asked me to lend a hand collecting funds; I want to join the Party: I long to join, but my age is an obstacle. I am almost old enough—but again, *not quite!*—and, because Volodya and Asya had nothing better to do, they decided to help me, out of friendship. But neither Volodya nor Asya actually held the collecting mug: they simply walked along with me.

Once again, Volodya suddenly rushes headlong out of the room in the middle of the conversation, actually interrupting himself in midsentence, and Elena Fyodorovna tries in his absence to mollify Alexei and reconcile everyone. Konstantin Ivanovich discourses on the duality of Order Number One: on the one hand, on the other hand, but ultimately history will decide—come back and see in four hundred years—all the while devouring a piece of *vesiga pirog*, the acquisition of which was a miracle, attainable only by the genius of Elena Fyodorovna, and I am thinking that perhaps it is also time for me to take my leave. The only reason they are not scolding me is that they are too well-mannered. But their silence, as well as the fact that they leave me out of the argument, is in itself a rebuke. We have stood together on an ice floe for so long, and it has cracked; now the two halves were drifting slowly apart. Mama has already guessed this is happening. "Don't they dig at you at the Igumnovs' house because your uncle is the district commissar? They're good people, but only up to a point. But never forget they're bourgeois."

No, they don't dig at me. I don't feel that they do. But then there is a lot I don't feel.

Once again, just as in that winter in Siverskaya, Volodya is itching to leave, but this time they grab him and hold him back; Varya and Asya take his suitcase from him, and Elena Fyodorovna, practically in tears, implores, "Children, I beg you, whatever happens in town, in the world, you must remain friends. You, Volodya, and you, Pavlik, all of you, children, shake hands at once."

Alexei cannot offer his hand at once, that very second, as he is tending his wound. Asya has washed it and poured iodine over it and he has to hold absorbent cotton on it with his fingers; his expression is one of suffering but also of determination—no, he cannot forget Kirik Nasonov in an instant. People were walking along, quite peaceably and unarmed, when those others appeared out of the blue with a banner. Insults and threats began. And just because he had cried, "Traitors! With German money!"— At this point I can no longer contain myself: One cannot shout out abominations. Yes one can, dear Pavel; one can shout anything one likes. That was why they made the Revolution: they have abolished censorship. But kicking someone in the head— that one cannot do. They were all trying to get at him, those animals. Once they'd knocked him off his feet and toppled him over, they kicked him in the head—when he was lying there.

Kirik Nasonov died in the hospital a few days later. But we do not know that yet. Konstantin Ivanovich unexpectedly takes my side. What a pliant lawyer's mind! I can see him now: plump, slightly pockmarked, fair-haired, always vaguely smiling at something, and, framed by a pale-red mustache and a short little beard, his full, moist lips, which are always twitching, on the verge either of laughing or of saying something amusing. His lips are the liveliest feature of his face, livelier than his eyes, and this imparts a somewhat ladylike expression to his whole visage. That is he exactly, smiling and moving his large white fingers about in the air before him and saying, "But don't let's incur the wrath of God. One feels frightfully sorry for Kirik; he suffered through his imprudence, but, that notwithstanding, Russia is a very fortunate country. A very great revolution has occurred virtually without bloodshed and with an insignificantly small number of victims. Read Aulard to see what went on during the French Revolution."

Elena Fyodorovna fervently supports him. "Yes, yes, boys, do read Aulard!" She kisses Volodya, embraces her son and gives me a soft, happy smile. That woman is always happy. She radiates health, and her rosy complexion glows with kindness and an appetite for life; her diamond brooch glitters like a terrifying false eye on her magnificent bosom.

I am selling *Pravda* in the Duma with a Baltic soldier called Ganyushkin. We collect five hundred copies at a time from the editorial office and return in the evening with the money. Then there's the bread to get hold of—about an hour and a half in line. And then off to the municipal office to register the bicycle or else to someplace on Golodai Island for firewood, which is issued by coupon through the soviet. Everyplace you go there are lines. Hungry, strange, inconceivable time! Everything is possible, yet you can't understand a thing. Shura will sometimes disappear and go around with a stuck-on mustache and an assumed name—not even Samoilenko but something else—or else will take command again on Vasilevsky Island, organizing the police or buying up weapons. Konstantin Ivanovich alternately extols the government and abuses it in the foulest language. He is on the commission to expose secret collaborators with the Okhranka. He is ecstatic, on edge; never-ending phone calls and visits. His smile has vanished; he no longer moves his white fingers about in the air and now merely pounds away with the flat of his hand. In the evenings he announces mysteriously, "If you only knew the pike that has turned up in our net!" Well, who? Papa, do tell us! No, no. Don't badger me, my friends. We have freedom of information, but not to that extent. You'll find out from the newspapers. He did tell us about one, a bank employee who lived on the second floor and was well known in Petrograd as a punter. One evening Volodya lay in wait for his schoolboy son and gave him a good beating up.

Shura says, "They haven't got much longer to fool around with this game. They won't last the summer. They'll drive them out."

True enough, by midsummer Konstantin Ivanovich had grown despondent and was cursing the government for all he was worth. "Fools! Scoundrels! They want to win the Great War, but they can't even score a victory in a petty domestic squabble!" The commission is disbanded. None of the informers is properly punished. Konstantin Ivanovich's car, in which he proudly rode in the mornings, is commandeered for military purposes. Someone set fire to the old dacha in Siverskaya and it burned to the ground with all the furniture and books. Konstantin Ivanovich makes an attempt at legal action to obtain the insurance—some hope! No one is in the mood for anything. It is August; there are terrible rumors about imminent carnage, the revenge of the Cossacks. Some are glad, others are in a panic, but all are excited. Many people are leaving Piter. There is a rumor afoot that Kerensky has ordered Kornilov's arrest and that Kornilov has ordered Kerensky's arrest—all by telegraph. Krymov's corps is headed for Piter. At this stage I stay side by side with Ganyushkin. I don't drop even a single step behind him. With him I have nothing to fear—either General Krymov or the "Wild Division," which they also say is on its way to pacify the capital.

Oh, Savva Ganyushkin, always dumbfounding! How did he just fall out of life? What became of him later? Savva Ganyushkin: ex-sailor; hoarse, coarse bawler; reader of newspapers, and fierce street fighter! He shoves himself with ease into any argument, gets mixed up in a fight with anyone at all, even with soldiers or cadets. Surprisingly enough, he always gets the better of them. He lays out one or two at the first blow, and the rest of them take to their heels. Because they sense that Savva has inordinate strength. We went with him to the Naval College back in the spring to hear Lenin. Shura had gotten hold of some tickets; there was an immense crowd of people, about five thousand; they were even hanging by the gym's wall bars. Some smart alecks start breaking down the door from the corridor. There is confusion. Savva does not like confusion and I can see him tossing them out: turning his bear's back to them and straining his hands at the doorposts, he squeezes them all out like a piston. Come on, Savva! Oh, Savva. How can I ever forget him?

The winter when Mama died. Savva says, "I used to dream we'd start a life together, lad, in the same house." His words to me.

I say nothing. That seems to be right, as though I knew about everything. In fact I hadn't the slightest inkling. It came to me like a bombshell, albeit a distant, belated and noiseless one. They have rushed by, flown somewhere; Mama knew nothing of my life, or I of hers.

Late summer. The Kornilov panic was at its height. Someone brought a Military League leaflet entitled "On Guard." An appeal to do everything to assist the rebels. Many copies were scattered about on Bolshoi Prospekt. The printing office stood there brazenly—Number 5, Liniya 16. I run over to Shura at the District Council, which assigns us some Red Guards, with Savva as their commanding officer, and we go off to the address. When the door is flung open, the first person we see is Alyoshka: Alexei Igumnov! He looks at me, struck dumb, then suddenly guffaws. "It's you? How delightful! What a quirk of fate!" With the lightest of movements, Savva shoves him to one side as if he were a curtain and dives into the room. In the inner recesses of the apartment are some people who welcome us coldly and talk to us with arrogance. "You're being hasty, young men. General Krymov will be here in two days, and we'll remember you all, every single one of you." Two days later came the news that General Krymov had shot himself.

He asks me, "Pavel Evgrafovich, why are you so doggedly concerned about Migulin's fate? You aren't a relative of his, are you? A distant relative? On his wife's side perhaps?" No, I say, I am not a relative. "What's the point, then?" There isn't one really. I'm just reaching for something, that's all. For you there *always* has to be a point. But for me there isn't any point except that my heart aches. "That's what we're concerned about, Pavel Evgrafovich. Your bad heart. You aren't a youngster and this is the third time you've come to Rostov. You're wasting your strength and your time. We're surprised at your persistence. How old are you, Pavel Evgrafovich?" I answer. Now I, I say, am surprised that there are some who are not the slightest bit interested in the history of their own people. To them, it's neither here nor there; it's all the same. A little old man, sickly and hysterical, jumps up from his chair. "In that case explain why you are defending a lie. Okay, he may have been a successful military leader; he fought with Krasnov and Denikin; he was awarded the Weapon of Honor. That's all true, but why make him into a revolutionary? Why tell such a lie?" The old man's eyes are gleaming, his blotchy fists are clenched, but I answer him calmly: I have never defended a lie and do not intend to. If I speak it means I have the facts. "There are no facts!" says the old man, shaking. "He was a Trudovik! A People's Socialist! I was graduated from the ataman college with his brother and know his crowd well. They were all obscurantists and served the Bolsheviks only under the lash." That's what I don't understand: black and white, obscurantists and angels. And no one in between. Yet everyone is in between. There's something of the angel and something of the fallen angel in everyone. Who was I in August 1917? When I look back now, I can't understand or get a clear idea of it. Of course there was my mother, there was Uncle Shura and some new friends. General intoxication. Yet in fact it would have been enough when Mama died in January

to veer off slightly either in the direction my father was asking
me to take or in some other direction, in which the old Prigodas
were beckoning me. Or perhaps if Asya had asked me to go with
her. I don't know who I would have been today. The merest trifle
like a slight turn of the switching points will hurl the locomotive
from one track onto another and instead of Rostov you land up
in Warsaw. I was a small boy, made drunk by a powerful time.
No, I must not tell fibs like other old people. My track was
determined by the flow of the stream—it is such joy to flow with
the stream—and by chance and instinct; but not in the least by
any vigorous mathematical volition. People shouldn't tell lies. It
can be different for everyone. My God, why am I getting into
an argument? It was probably different for other old people. One
should not offend anyone. I was a little boy, solitary, given to
daydreaming, who was living a street life and was, besides, head
over heels in love.... The one who took Asya away from me
nearly died on August 30, 1917, in the Ust-Medveditskaya *stanitsa*. He narrowly escaped being killed by *Sotnik* Stepan Gerasimov.

Is it really possible that the only revolutionaries are those who
are able to talk about themselves and to prove their points in
scarcely audible but lively voices? What of those who were bursting to go; who raged, choked on foaming blood, disappeared
without a trace and perished in smoke, fumes and obscurity? I
see before my eyes a *stanitsa* assembly: a lava flow of many
thousands of peaked caps and *papakhas*, windows flung wide
open, young lads on the roofs and swarthy Kaledin, haggard from
the intense heat, wearing his pale general's tunic. Thick dust and
heat. I am not there, but I can see and hear. A high-pitched
croaking voice of doom says, "Our program is well known to
everyone—as Cossacks we are not traveling the same road as the
socialists; we will go with the Party of People's Freedom...."
Two months previously, Kaledin had been selected ataman of
the Don Cossacks at their assembly. At the time of the mutiny,
Kaledin sends the provisionals an ultimatum: if they turn down

the agreement with Kornilov, then he, Kaledin, with the assistance of the Cossacks, will cut Moscow off from southern Russia. The provisionals have given orders to arrest the ataman. But Kaledin does not know this and has galloped off into Ust-Medveditskaya to "raise the Don."

Nor does he know what is happening around Piter: the regiments are straining not toward the capital, but toward the houses. What strength will be needed to "raise the Don" anew after so many years of strife? The swarthy old general, who is craning his neck and shouting things that everyone knows, hollow words heard long ago, does not have that kind of strength. The old men who have been elected pound their hands and yell Hear, hear! while the front-line veterans cuss and whistle. Migulin tries to force his way through to the rostrum, but they hold him back. Migulin is the lieutenant general, assistant commander of the Thirty-third Don Cossack Regiment. And still the Cossacks keep pushing him through, using their shoulders to open up a path for him. He makes a speech. He likes to take the floor; I have heard him several times. Two years ago, in the summer of 1919, when he was organizing the Special Don Cossack Corps and we were dashing about in our special train from station to station, at every little stop he poked his head out the window, called the people over and held a meeting. He has a knack, quickly and without hemming and hawing, to latch onto some vein that sets the crowd aquiver and starts them buzzing.

"Citizens of the *stanitsa!* The most important thing for the Cossacks was, is and will be..." Then, after a pause, to relish the split second of general silence, he sings out thunderously and with a flourish of the hand as if hurling a grenade into the crowd, "Freedom, Cossacks! It's been a long time, about two hundred years, since the Cossacks have enjoyed that sweet pleasure, although they like to chatter about it and wag their tongues about it. Freedom, freedom... What freedom is there when the Cossacks are the bung of every barrel? Wherever there's commotion or rioting, that's where they get chased to, like firemen sent to put out a fire. They don't ask for freedom. The Revolution put an end to that false 'freedom.' Enough of making the Cossacks the scourge of all Russia! We want to live in peace and work quietly on our land. Down with the counterrevolutionary generals!"

Those are the words Migulin hurls at the audience seated in the room. One after another they jump up from their seats, yelling and shaking their fists. The windows of the jampacked hall are open and the throng in the market square, upon hearing the din and the shouting, begins to seethe menacingly. Any minute now and they will smash down the doors and burst into the room. Migulin tries to go on with his speech, but the infuriated old men and Kaledin's followers drag him down from the rostrum, and a fistfight ensues. Suddenly, up jumps Captain Stepan Gerasimov from the crowd (an indelible name; although it was not till later that I read about Stepan Gerasimov when I was rummaging through the archives of the Ust-Medveditskaya Gazette for 1917, at which time I remembered that one Matvei Gerasimov had served with the commandant's platoon of the Eighth Army staff; he was another northern Cossack and so possibly a relative of the other, hotheaded one) and shouts to Migulin, "Apologize to the ataman or I'll whack your head off!" And he brandishes his saber threateningly. Migulin whips his revolver out of his holster and strikes him over the forehead with the barrel. "Drop your saber!" For a moment they stand there rooted to the spot, piercing each other with hate-filled looks. Then a Cossack snatches Gerasimov's saber from him, breaks it and throws it out the window. Kaledin meanwhile disappears out the back door.

Then Migulin goes out onto the square. In the midst of his speech to the buzzing crowd, clerks have been elbowing their way through to the steps with a telegram from the Minister of War, Verkhovsky: Arrest Kaledin as an accomplice in the rebellion. Migulin calls over a group of front-line Cossacks who are loyal to him and they rush off to search for the ataman, but he has vanished without a trace. He has skipped off to Novocherkassk. The Cossacks have been dispersed—not by bloodshed so far but by bloody words. What is to be done? Whom can one turn to?

I have almost forgotten my father. I had forgotten him even when he was still alive. The last time, in 1912, he arrived in Piter from Baku, then he moved to Helsinki. I recall his dark curly beard, his spectacles, his long soft hands, his constant fiddling around with his pipe and his never-ending joking at Mama's expense. He was an engineer. Mama felt sorry for him; she spoke of him as a kindhearted outsider. "The trouble is, he's timid. I don't mean a coward—physically he's brave—but timid in his thinking." They separated many years later. I don't know exactly why. I think the reasons were ideological. During his student years he too rebelled, protested and was exiled to the North somewhere for a year, but then he went back to his engineering.

And so, he is sitting in an enormous cold room, drinking tea and warming his fingers on the glass and speaking under his breath with Shura. What about? Mama is seriously ill. She has pneumonia following on influenza. She may die. Someone let my father know and he has arrived from Helsinki.

January 1918. They have just announced that the bread ration has been reduced from six ounces to a quarter of a pound. I have spent three hours on the street, first queuing for kerosene, then for bread. There is no water. The trolleys aren't running. What are my father and Shura talking about? They are whispering; Mama has been unconscious since morning, so she won't hear. They are whispering so that I won't hear, but certain phrases reach me. "Now, since the decree... An independent country..." "Let *him* decide..." "I think she would be in favor of such a decision...."

I sense that they are talking about me. Father is a distant, successful person. He has become corpulent and has shaved off his beard, except for a scarcely noticeable little wedge under his lip—like Lunacharsky's. He has brought with him a basket of food, a medicine—urotropine—difficult to get hold of in Piter and a large bottle of milk. Mama does not eat or drink anything. She lies there with her eyes closed and sometimes babbles incoherently.

Shura gives me a somewhat strange, cold look, screwing up his eyes the way he looks at new people, weighing up what they might be good for, and says, "Father suggests that you go back with him to Helsinki. What do you think?" Impossible. How could I possibly leave now? "Not now; not today, or tomorrow," Father whispers. "I'm talking about soon; in principle." Father is wearing a beautiful warm suit of gray checked cloth, woolen socks and thick-soled boots; he is sitting cross-legged, swinging one foot. He has a kindly look. So penetrating and sympathetic through his spectacles—the sort of look strangers overflowing with goodwill give you. He and Shura talk as if Mama were no longer. Suddenly Mama's eyes come unglued; yet she is unable to look at either me, my uncle or my father. Her eyes fix on our museumlike stucco ceiling, grimy with smoke from the stove, and she declares distinctly, "Stick with Shura."

I know that already.

We bend down toward her, try to give her something, then something else, but once again she cannot see or hear anything. Then Savva arrives carrying a rifle and wearing cartridge belts and two holsters around his waist; with him is a bearded old man, a doctor, uncommonly small of stature like a gnome. Savva has brought him in the car: the same car that is to take Shura to the Tavrichesky Palace where the Congress of Soviets is to open. The gnome examines Mama, asking no questions; he merely hems, grunts and clears his throat as if he were sick, too, or had just had a good, hearty meal. The four of us stand around and stare at him; he ceases to be a gnome and grows before our eyes. His face becomes coarse and heavy, we see his thick pearlike nose and his cheekbones like rocks.

"It may happen within the hour. Maybe during the night," says the doctor. He stands by the bedside holding his satchel in both hands, his leg slightly to one side, scrutinizing us patronizingly and very piercingly as if to work out how much longer each of us has to live.

A car horn below the window. A call for Shura. Time to go to the Congress. He hesitates. Savva sends him off: "Go ahead, Alexander Pimenovich. I'll stay with Irina." But who is Savva? An ordinary sailor. A stranger. Shura is sullen, taciturn, unhearing. He despises other people's advice. Shura is accustomed to deciding everything himself—quickly, firmly and finally.

The gnome vanishes. Again, the car horn sounds below.

Shura casts a long look at his sister, lying there completely motionless with her eyes closed, when all of a sudden she amazes us once more: slowly she raises her hand somewhat and lets it drop. Mama whispers, "Shura, go." Shura leaves. The car gives a rattle and a snort and is off. Whereupon a vicious conversation breaks out between Savva and Father. It is as if they are shouting at each other, only in a whisper. It began when Father, with a sinister smirk, mumbled something as if to himself: "Yes, it's obvious now... there's no defeating such people." "What people?" "People like Irina's brother. It's become perfectly clear to me now. There's nothing to hope for, either." "What is it that you desire to say about Alexander Pimenovich?" I ask them to lower their voices and to go into the next room. Again Mama raises her hand and whispers, "Let them stay here." They talk, whispering to each other, arguing till they are hoarse; Savva might conceivably shoot or arrest Father because of his insulting words— I am amazed how fearless he is of everything; and yet Mama said he was a coward. He calls the sailors bandits: not Savva, but the ones who killed Shingaryov and Kokoshkin. The sailors killed them in the Mariinskaya Hospital. "I can't answer for the anarchists," whispers Savva; "I would have strangled them myself."

"Yes you can; you're answerable for everything. Everyone and everything. Including the fact that Irina is dying." Father buries his face in his hands and hunches over. He stands there, stooped, tall; I can see his bald patch surrounded by a halo of dark hair. The bald patch sways and a loud, cavernous sound booms out from under the hands covering Father's face. He strides quickly out of the room into the hall, then moves even farther away into the kitchen. Savva follows him, but I stay with Mama. There is nothing to be done. You can kill a million people, overthrow a tsar, make a great revolution, blow up half the world with dynamite, yet *it is impossible to save one particular life.*

That is what I am thinking about. That the person who is dying cannot be saved. There is a lot of this later on in my life. It sort of becomes enmeshed with life, mingling with it and forming a kind of strange, nameless mixture like a supernatural whole, a life-death. All those years, the accumulation of deaths, absorbed into the blood, into the very fabric. I am not talking about the soul; I never did know what that was and still don't. It is not cholesterol that causes hardening of the arteries: it is death seeping into you in constant, small doses. Mama's departure was the first. Galya's departure will probably have been the last. Then as now I am abandoned by that *one* person. But between those two deaths, between the time when I had not yet become myself and the time when I stopped being myself (at least in the eyes of others, because nobody knows that you have stayed the same; you have to play your role to the end, pretending that you really have changed, which is glaringly obvious from your appearance, proclaimed by the way you walk and borne out by your failing strength—although it's a lie), between the two deaths lay a long life in the course of which it was not you that changed, but your attitude to that whole nameless thing: to that life-death. In your youth you felt a certain way, now you feel completely differently. How ardent, impetuous, frivolous I was in January 1918, in spite of all my grief! Terror and pity, that is what oppressed me then. Terror at the mystery that has revealed itself and which I find myself facing alone; pity for Mama, that she will not be able to see what is going to happen in the beautiful world, the completely devastated and rebuilt world, or *what is going to happen to me.* She loved me so much, in addition to her ferocious desire to live, to learn, to understand, to participate!

What is to happen later—when each death has made its home inside you—has not yet happened. The longer you live, the more fearsome that burden becomes. When Galya died, the weight became so heavy that it was almost the end of me.

Father holds himself stiffly, as if the cemetery frost has numbed him; not a twitch, not a blink. He sees no one, he answers no one, until suddenly his legs give way. He crashes down to his knees, his fur hat flies off and he lands with his head in the snow.... Later we see him off at the Finland Station. Savva has forgiven Father everything and has come along to say farewell to him, too. Savva says to Father, trying to convince him, "Now, don't you just disappear in Helsinki—stir up a bit of commotion, now! You're one of us, the intellectual proletariat, and you'll get it but good from the bourgeois."

Father sighs, "It's not as simple as that."

"Well, make a start; join up with us!"

Father says that he will come again in February and then we'll decide what will happen—whether I will go to him or he will come to us. But there's nothing to decide. He is a nice stranger. He does not come in February, because by late January, and without any help from him, a "bit of commotion" does get stirred up out there—first the Red Guards, then the Germans; everything starts spinning, everything is cut off. I got some sort of postcard when I returned from the Urals, then nothing forever. So many people disappeared. The great wheel of life has taken us up; people, ordeals, hopes, killing in the name of truth. Yet we can't guess what lies ahead. To us all that has to be done is to smash the Kaledinists and scatter Dutov's gangs in the east, and the Revolution will triumph throughout the whole country. Victory is at hand! In January we have already taken Orenburg! A matter of two or three months.

Not only I but Shura and many others also think this way. Shura is working on the board for the organization of the Red Army. I am assisting, typing out the newspaper on large glossy sheets. The paper is called *Information Sheet: The Movement of the Red Army Organization Across Russia.* What, where, how many, what difficulties. I recall that almost everywhere they need money, agitators, literature. They need two, three million rubles. At first, it's like some sort of paper game. And there aren't many of us playing that game in the board building. Later on an invincible strength emerges from there.

Old people don't remember a damned thing; they mix things up, fib; you can't believe them. Don't I do it, too? Can I be believed? But I remember perfectly well that Migulin was thickset, broad-shouldered and of medium height. Uncommonly strong hands. The hands not of a cavalryman but of a blacksmith. The suppliers had brought along a consignment of new boots. Migulin became absolutely furious with the suppliers about something or other. He grabbed hold of a boot and ripped it apart at the seams with his bare hands. "Is this the kind of rotten stuff you bring us, damn you?" Others tried with might and main, but no one was able to tear up a single boot. The boots were the regular kind. About four years ago I was chatting with some old men in the museum in Rostov and looking at photographs. They all remembered Migulin well. One old man said, "I was a kid. I saw him in Rostov. He was thin, well-proportioned, like a youth. About thirty." Another old man objected: "No. He was forty-five when he died." A third one, a shortish chap, said, "He wasn't tall—about my height." You see, everyone imagines that only he knows the truth. Another one, again in Rostov, put me through a trial by ordeal: "You tell me, then, if you saw him. What was his most distinguishing feature? In his appearance." I was at a loss. He said triumphantly, "His most distinguishing feature was his left eye, which squinted when he became excited!" I remember absolutely nothing at all about the eye. It's quite possible he was lying.

Kaledin shot himself early in 1918, I think. If not actually in January. That meant the end, utter despair. The Don Cossack *stanitsas* announced their recognition of the Soviet regime. The conflagration on the Don need never have occurred.

Saying goodbye to Volodya, the first fall of snow. A few days after the October uprising. I had gone to the 1886 Electric Company to pay for the whole summer—for some reason Mama didn't want to, so Shura gave me the money and told me to go and pay—and on the way back I bumped into Volodya near the house. He showed me a telegram: "SICK COME IMMEDIATELY." It later turned out that his mother had simply summoned him out of fright at what was happening. Getting train tickets was out of the question. Everyone was rushing to leave Piter. Volodya waited for me a whole hour; he wanted me to have a word with Shura to ask him to get hold of some tickets. Waiting for Shura, Volodya and I sat in a large room—the owners had turned tail and fled and the whole apartment now belonged to us—and rummaged about in the enormous library by candlelight. The apartment owner had been the manager of a metal-pipe factory. I had seen him several times. An unpleasant type. He addressed Mama as "madame." And always with some caustic remark: "Madame, pray do not take offense if I offer a piece of advice—not at all political in nature—to your sailor friend. For goodness' sake do not be offended. Give him delicately to understand that one should not sit perched like an eagle on the toilet. The toilet is a fragile thing and the sailor weighs about seven poods." Mama's face would turn white after speaking with him. But she restrained herself. All of a sudden the manager assembled his whole family and departed without saying where to. They did not leave so much as a note. We had arrived back home very late, at about midnight, and were surprised to see that the door onto the landing was wide open. In the apartment too everything was inside out; papers on the floor, scraps of newspaper and pieces of string, like the aftermath of a burglary. Now we are sitting, leafing through someone else's books, many valuable and marvelous ones among them.

Volodya says he needs two tickets to Kamyshino; a fellow countryman, a student, will be traveling with him. But Volodya is incapable of telling a fib. I can tell quite clearly that he is fibbing. He doesn't look me in the eyes, he's on edge, he keeps on running to the window, thinking that a car has pulled up. The electricity is off. Outside is darkness. If you lean out the window you can see in the distance a bonfire on Bolshoi Prospekt.

I ask him, "What's the matter with you? You're lying."

"Yes, I am."

"But why?" He shrugs his shoulders. "God knows. . . . I'm going with Asya."

And that was that. Forgotten pain.

Agitatedly, hurriedly, Volodya starts to describe his misgivings, vacillations, the agonizing details. I ask him, "Did you read the article about Freemasons in the latest issue of *The Past?*" I don't want to listen to him. I don't want to know anything. Suddenly there is a knock at the door. When Shura arrives by car, the driver always signals with the horn at the doorway, and Mama rings a special bell.

"Who is it?"

After a pause, a man's voice answers. "Does Alexander Pimenovich Danilov live here?"

In walks someone in a sheepskin coat, a fur cap with earflaps, and hunting boots, but also dark glasses; he has a wizened, sharp-nosed face and carries in his hands a foreign-looking trunk which seems incongruous with his sheepskin coat.

"Shigontsev, Leonty Viktorovich," he introduces himself, removing his fur cap to reveal a peculiarly narrow, elongated skull. That skull hits you at once. It has sort of dents above the temples which make it look even more tapered. The man with the strange

skull like a badly baked loaf played a significant part in my life—
both at that time and in 1919—and cast his shadow over the
years ahead. That is why I well recall his first appearance on the
scene. I guessed at once that someone who referred to Shura as
Alexander Pimenovich Danilov must have known him for a long
time, perhaps through penal servitude or exile. Such people turned
up often. In springtime they descended on us in especially large
numbers, living with us for weeks on end, but this one's arrival
was somewhat belated. Where was he from?

"Australia," said Shigontsev. And quite right, he had known
Shura from penal servitude in Tobolsk. After that he had been
transferred to Gorny Zerentui and then was sent into exile, from
which he escaped and landed up in Australia; two months ago
he arrived back in Vladivostok. Right now was only his second
day in Piter. "I haven't seen anyone yet; I don't know a thing,
so my first move is to get hold of Alexander. How we used to
dream in the wastes of Tobolsk that when the Revolution came
we would be together in Piter. To make them pay off their debts
to us." What debts? "All sorts! Everything! The whole world is
in our debt!" Shigontsev made a sweeping gesture with his arms
as if to embrace the imaginary world—or perhaps a very large
woman—and clasp it to his bosom, waved his hands about,
smiled, winked; all with a sort of unnatural energy and frankness.
Then I saw glittering behind his spectacles the small dark-slate
eyes with their look of crafty defiance. When he talked he liked
to show his teeth as if from fervor and impatience, baring those
clenched teeth as he breathed heavily. I had never seen such a
spirited, slightly comical revolutionary. All the revolutionaries
who had previously visited our house had been staid, taciturn
people. Yet this one didn't shut his mouth all night.

Now Shura and Mama arrive and we sit down to drink tea.
Volodya asks Shura about the tickets; Shura makes a phone call
to someone and gives an order. Mama tells us the latest news:
Dukhonin has been dismissed; Ensign Krylenko has been appointed supreme commander in chief; there will be elections to

the Constituent Assembly on the twelfth. And all this is inter-
woven with, or rather accompanied by, Shigontsev's incessant
chatter.

He even speaks when no one is listening. As if he had been
simply dying for an opportunity to wag his tongue. My God,
what doesn't he talk about! His escape from Siberia, the Dukhobors, secret opium dens, the perfidious craftiness of the Mensheviks, sailing over the sea, Australia, living on a commune,
his girlfriends who did not want to go back to Russia, the fact
that mankind will perish unless it changes its mental attitude and
renounces feelings and emotions... As a joke, Shura calls his
friend the Count of Monte-Cristo.

Later, however, things take a turn that is no joking matter.
True, this does not happen immediately, but about a year and
a half later. At that time, in November 1917, there was talk and
jollification, people were remembering their friends: which ones
had disappeared, which had changed color. Many turned up in
Piter and joined the struggle. Egor Samsonov, for example, had
been the chief of the Putilovo police and was now a big boss in
the Red Guard.

"Egorka's alive?" Shigontsev cried. "He's here? Aha, that means
our Cell Eight's at the helm of Russia. Just as it should be!" In
hard-labor camp Egor was famous for poetry and beating up
informers. I knew him. A squat, rather gloomy person with a
pince-nez. They all seemed to have trouble with their eyes. Shigontsev became excited, as if he had been drinking wine—although nothing but tea had passed his lips—and immediately
was bursting to rush off and look for Egor. This was not possible,
however. Then the pair of them began to recall out loud Egor's
poems about camp life, constantly interrupting each other.

"The bell aroused us early
Those murky November dawns;
The glow of smoking lamps..."

Shigontsev bellows out, forgetting what follows. Shura prompts:

"... Dispels the shreds of sleep."

"The frenzied shrieks,
The hail of gutter cursing,"

Shigontsev continued, then, both together,

"Time to get up.
Get off your butt, you dog!"

Drops of moisture were trickling down Shigontsev's face from underneath his glasses. With shaking fingers he wiped his cheeks. Mankind's doom is inevitable: there is no escaping feelings.

"You mules:
You were able to stand it all, without begging or cursing.
In silence you laid your bare, branded shoulders on the block.
You go from here as heralds and harbingers of the brotherhood
Which spurned it all and stopped at naught."

If they had known what would happen three months later in Rostov, into which Egor burst with his Petrograd detachment, when Shigontsev would accuse him of softheartedness and demand that he be tried by the tribunal! But right now he is weeping because he cannot go to see Egor immediately, this very minute. That same evening he relates some stories about their student days: the political circles, talking to the privatdocent, the bastard of an administrator on whom their fate depended, the humiliation, being called on the carpet, the beetlelike non-Russian behind the enormous desk, the lackey standing disgustingly in the doorway, Shigontsev's muttering, his entreaties to take pity on his mother. If only for her sake: she will not survive another expulsion. The reply in icy tones: "Why put these worries about your mother on our shoulders now? You should have thought

about that before." She did not survive it. He awaited the sweet
moment for a long time, cherishing in his Australian dreams
thoughts of the time when he would enter that same office with
the same carpet—please God they hadn't requisitioned it—with
the same man sitting behind the same desk, scribbling away at
something with his beetle claw; when Shigontsev would grab him
by the chin and say, "Remember me, you brute?..."

And I believe that he did it: that he did catch up with him.
True enough, not in his office, not in that mansion on the
embankment with the doorkeeper and the lackeys, but at the
Finland Station. He plucked him out of his compartment from
among his suitcases and, in an hour—poof! he had vanished
into thin air. In December Shigontsev started to cut down the
hoarders and made a lot of headway there.

There was shooting in the streets. The rooms were very cold.
The hazy night of shooting dragged on; in its belly there lurked
enemies, dangers, plots, uncertainty. Candles gutter, two ex-
convicts are droning away, smoking, sipping tea; Volodya goes
out, Mama dozes and I am listening, yawning, dreaming, trying
to work it out. Everything in Russia has been churned up, everything swept away, gone.

In the middle of the night, when everyone is packing—it was
an enormous apartment, everyone had his own room—Mama
goes into Shura's room and asks him softly, "What do you think:
is Leonty clever?" I can hear everything because the door is open.

After a short pause, Shura says, "Not so much clever as passionate. I'd call him ebullient."

"And I'd call him very frothy," says Mama. They both laugh.
They understand each other and love each other so very much.

At breakfast Mama tells how Shigontsev tried to force his way
into her room at dawn, demanding that she open up. With an
absolutely transparent aim in mind.

"Typical of him," says Shura. "What did you tell the fool?"

"He's not a fool; that's just the way he is. I don't really know
whom he is like. Maybe Chernyshevsky's heroes? Or perhaps

Nechaev, as Zasulich described him? I know those sorts of people. I said to him, 'Leonty Viktorovich, you're the one telling mankind to overcome their emotions.' To which he replied, 'Irina, this isn't a question of emotions.' Well, what then?"

I think it's disgraceful, but Shura and Mama laugh it off. Shura says, "He never could tell a lie; it's his great virtue." Then he adds seriously, "Actually, you sometimes do have to tell a lie... *for the cause.*"

An ear-splitting noise of snoring resounds from the next room.

Shura remembers, wrinkles his swarthy brow and smiles: Shigontsev was the scourge of Cell Eight in Tobolsk Central Prison. Unreproduceable people! Their like does not exist on this earth; time has burned them all to ashes.

Asya nestles up to Volodya's shoulder, tears streaming down her pathetic, bewildered face. I have never seen her like this. Elena Fyodorovna is sitting opposite, so absorbed by the moment that she does not even answer my hello and says scarcely audibly, "Our insistent request when the Most Holy Synod gives its permission for the marriage..."

Konstantin Ivanovich looms up at the door, reluctant to enter the compartment; in any case there is no room. Such a crush: there are about six other passengers apart from Volodya and Asya, sitting huddled up together as in a trolley. Konstantin Ivanovich is forever bowing and apologizing, letting the crowd of sweaty people pass along the corridor with their luggage. Where are they headed? Where will they all sit? "Lenochka, don't worry! Lenochka, I have a contact in the Synod; I have an in with Vasily Karpovich...." He talks to Elena Fyodorovna as if she were an invalid. He does not argue with anything she says; he agrees with it all and goes along with all her nonsense. Perhaps she really is a bit touched. Good God, what synod? What's all this about, asking permission to marry? Nobody's asking any permission. Nine people crammed into what should be a compartment for

four. The synod has probably been abolished by decree. It is of
no importance.

I am bitter—stunned: they have hidden it from me. So this
goodbye is forever. It's of no importance at all. Volodya's face
meanwhile: a smile he cannot suppress and his eyes full of a
greedy, all-consuming happiness.

For more than a year I hear nothing and know
nothing about them. Dragged off down a crater, disappeared. I
did it all without them—the journey south with Shura, the
expedition of the Narkomvoen, then the Czechs; the Urals; the
Third Army; the retreat; Perm. I became a different person, I saw
death and buried my friends. It was not until February 1919,
when Shura was wounded and sent to the southern front—or
rather to the rear of the southern front, to the liberated areas—
when we found ourselves in the north-Don region, that I had
news of Volodya from someone, that he and his wife Asya were
attached to Migulin's staff in the Ninth Army. I couldn't believe
it. Can it be the same Volodya? The very same: the one from
Kamyshino, from Piter; Volodya Sekachev. Tall man, curly hair,
ruddy complexion, not more than twenty, perhaps even less, same
age as she. He's in the machine-gun detachment at headquarters
and she's a typist. She types out orders and various appeals,
leaflets, even poems which are composed by Migulin and scattered about by the thousand. We find Migulin's works everywhere
in his wake. "Brother Cossacks of Kargin's regiment! It's time to
come to your senses! It's time to put down arms and talk—not
the language of guns, but the language of men. . . ."

But how did Volodya and Asya come to be attached to the
staff of the Red Army? And not just on the staff, either, but at
the very core of the most victorious, the most famous army of
the day? Migulin's breaking through to the south. A fantastic
success. Almost the whole of the Don is liberated and Krasnov's
army has collapsed. He's tearing down to Novocherkassk; the fall

of the Don capital is a matter of days. And I had been thinking that Volodya and Asya were languishing somewhere in Ekaterinodar or that they had perhaps gone off to Bulgaria or Turkey.... But I can't see them. They're in the South and Shura and I are in the Mikhailinskaya *stanitsa*, on the district revolutionary tribunal staff. There are hundreds of versts between us.

We know about Migulin from what people say. Anyplace you go everyone is talking about him—and saying different things. Apart from the fact that he is the most distinguished of the Red Cossacks—after the deaths of Podtyolkov and Krivoshlykov and the recent death of Kovalyov there is no one more distinguished— apart from the fact that he is a lieutenant colonel, an expert commander, immensely respected by the Cossacks of the northern districts, fiercely hated by the atamans and branded by Krasnov as "the Judas of the Don," apart from these facts which all agree on, we are assailed, since we have landed in *his* territory, by a plethora of rumors, inventions, cock-and-bull stories and the smallest details about his life. Migulin's home village is ten versts away. What sort of man is he, then? The devil only knows; a strange, flickering figure. Sometimes you imagine you see one thing, at other times you think you see something quite different. Calls himself—not without pride—an old revolutionary. In his impassioned appeals, which are written in a provincial high-school style, very sincere and bombastic, and which he squeezes onto anything that comes to hand—wallpaper, a candy wrapper—he constantly repeats, "I, as an experienced revolutionary..." or "I, as an old fighter against the tsarist regime..." And apparently these are not just words, either. On the other hand, other people, like Bychin, the chairman of the Mikhailinskaya Revkom, say that he's spinning yarns; that he never was a revolutionary, and that all he ever did was bawl his head off at the assemblies. He did once go to Piter, all expenses paid, and delivered a few of his screeds before the Duma, but that was a matter of no importance.

I am intrigued by this man. And not only because Volodya

and Asya are somewhere near him or because the papers are trumpeting him: hero, triumphant over the Don counterrevolution, invincible, invulnerable. Whole regiments of Krasnov's men are going over to him. Then, all of a sudden they are abandoning him just as quickly. One wounded Cossack relates that Migulin had been releasing Cossack prisoners and sending them home—to "spread the propaganda." The information from the Revkom was different: he was releasing the prisoners because he could not overcome his sympathy for his brother Cossacks. He was first and foremost a Cossack, and *then* a revolutionary. *Migulin was playing a double game!* That was the word in the Revkoms, on the military staffs and in the tribunals. Based on what? There again: flickering, fog, indistinctness. What sort of game do you mean when he's in the Don?

A young man who publishes the political department's newspaper—a dropout with shaggy graying hair, called Naum Orlik—says the reason he's dangerous is that he's a secret separatist. He wants to turn the Don into something like Finland. He is very careful to conceal this, but people who knew him in former times say he's a separatist for sure. Although he now swears loyalty to the Bolsheviks, everyone remembers his former sympathies: he was a Trudovik, a People's Socialist. In Piter he was close to the Don Cossack deputies. "To put it more bluntly, he's a true Don nationalist! With all the endearing qualities that implies. And what's more—" Orlik shook his fist as if rubber-stamping something in the air—"with a Socialist Revolutionary stuffing!"

Orlik is difficult to argue with. He knows everything before you even start and has no doubts about anything. To him people are like chemical compounds whose basic elements he, like an experienced chemist, can instantly analyze. So and so is one-half Marxist, one-quarter neo-Kantian and one-quarter Machian. So and so is only ten percent Bolshevik, the outside ten percent, while his inside is Menshevik. "As for you," he says to me, "you're an elemental, unstable Bolshevik. You've got a strong liberal streak in you. You're two-thirds one of us and one-third putrid intellectual." The devil only knows where he gets it all from! Perhaps from the fact that I have been arguing with him and other members of the Revkom about the executions and the requisitions.

I have the impression, however, that the main subject of argument with Orlik—of all of everyone's arguments—is Migulin. If you could understand him or at least decide for yourself what he is, then a lot of things would become clear.

Despite our quarreling and even our cursing, I am friends with Orlik. I respect him. I look on him as a comrade even though he is ten years older, was a *druzhinnik* in the 1905 Revolution, was exiled, harassed and lived in poverty, and his left hand was slashed by a saber and is now useless.

During his exile to the Enisei region he read masses of books, and he knows a hundred times more than I do. And twenty times more than Shura. After all, Shura hasn't read very much. Nevertheless I trust Shura more. "First gather the facts," says Shura, "then draw your conclusions. Naum is always in a hurry."

Shura is a painstaking, thorough person. Fond of statistics.

The facts are as follows: Migulin is now forty-six. If he is a revolutionary he's really one of the old ones. But they say he's still a stalwart; strong on the march, and adept at horseracing and hewing and all the Cossack skills. Everyone claims he has other qualities besides: that he is educated, that a better read, more literate man you won't find. First he went to the parish school, then to the high school and the Novocherkassk Cadet College, and all by the sweat of his own brow, by his own strenuous efforts. For there was no one to help, since he came from a poor peasant family. When they were wondering whom to send to the Duma in Petersburg with the *stanitsa* assembly's verdict on conscription, they chose him. Because he had made an inflammatory speech in the assembly. Nineteen hundred and six. He was just back from Manchuria with his regiment, having won four decorations and promotion to the rank of sub-*esaul*. But at the assembly in his home *stanitsa* he immediately clashed with the authorities.

It had to do with a sore point festering on the Cossack soul—
something called the provision of "troop assistance to the civil
authorities." It was precisely at that time that the government
decided to build up the "internal" troops and call up the second-
and third-priority Cossacks in addition to the ones who had come
back from the Japanese War. It was not enough for them to have
Cossack units in their garrisons! It was stupid to imagine that this
service under the lash would be to everyone's liking. Everywhere
they began protesting at the assemblies. My boss in Mikhailinskaya recalled how the young ones hollered fearlessly while the
old men attempted to make them understand, but without any
particular ardor. Migulin journeyed to Piter with the demand of
the *stanichniki* that the second- and third-priority Cossacks not
be taken, but on the way back there was the sudden arrest, the
Novocherkassk guardhouse, his officer's rank stripped from him,
and dismissal from the Cossack ranks. Well, then, can that event
be considered to be a revolutionary act? In my view, definitely
yes. For a Cossack officer, such an attack against the authorities
was unheard of. And as far as his personal future went it was a
truly revolutionary deviation—everything was smashed, his career ruined and his life in military service thrown away.

Then a job in the land department in Rostov, the start of war,
conscription into the Thirty-third Cossack Regiment. Battles,
decorations—even the Saint George's Cross, I think. February. . . . While Volodya, Asya and I are rushing about the streets
of Piter collecting for the Soviet, Migulin is hollering away at
political meetings either in the regiment or else in his home
stanitsa. Rounded up some Trudoviks, took command of them.
He is made a candidate to the Constituent Assembly. Oh, yes!
No cause for astonishment: people nowadays are rushing back
and forth like mad; unpredictably, as if drunk. Only recently
some *voyenspets* was cursing the soldiers and calling on them to
fight "until victory," and now he is shouting Bolshevik slogans.
Another one was sitting in our headquarters yesterday drawing
up maps and giving orders, and today he's smoking French cig-

arettes with the volunteers. Just like Vsevolodov and Nosovich, former *voyenspetsy*, now turned Cain.

Colonels! Terrible nightmare of the commissars. How can you peek into someone else's soul? How can you divine whether it was from an honest and sincere desire and after deep soul-searching that they decided to rip off their epaulets and put on the helmets with the star, or whether it was a devilish, long-caclulated settlement of accounts? Yet there is no time to study the question, to scrutinize it.

Migulin too is a lieutenant colonel.

No one says directly that Migulin could turn his cloak—strange even to mention it when the Ninth Army, with Migulin in the vanguard, is ramming the Whites good and hard! Yet one thing runs as a constant through conversations among Revkom members, official representatives and local tribunal members: *distrust.* Or perhaps, to be absolutely accurate, *incomplete trust.* As far as ramming them goes, he's one hundred percent; he has practically cleaned out the whole of the Don, but what drives him to do it? That's the rub. I can sense something of his nature—something unutterable and muted, but incredibly tenacious and quite invincible—in all conversations about Migulin. "Just be aware," says Bychin. "Migulin doesn't care whether it's Bolsheviks or Whites, he loves them all just the same: as a horse loves the whip!"

I might even have believed Bychin—he was a local from Mikhailinskaya; though he was not a Cossack, but an *inogorodny,* his father had served as a workman for a rich Cossack, and Kolka himself had fished on the Sea of Azov; he came back a Bolshevik and pushed on right away to become a Red ataman and Revkom chairman. Bychin has a head like a haystack, broader at the bottom, with a brown face, slit eyes, pale blue with lead-gray whites, and flaxen baby's hair. He has pood-sized fists and carries them about like dumbbells. I would have believed him if it hadn't been for Slaboserdov. Slaboserdov the teacher. A middle-aged

man getting on for fifty (no age at all when I think of it now!),
his wife the same age, with two sons a bit older than I, ex-students
who don't work—hard to understand what they do. How were
Shura and I to know? The battle was raging, fierce and merciless.
Anyone who slipped up got a bullet through the head. Just as it
should be during a period of class struggle. We immediately
arrested all the moneybags, the monarchists, the ones connected
with Krasnov's people—about forty according to Bychin's list—
but we had no pretext for taking the Slaboserdovs. They were
not wealthy at all, nor were they counterrevolutionaries; on the
contrary, they had had clashes with the former regime.

Yet Bychin insisted. How were Shura and I to know? The only
thing we knew was: if you slip up you get a bullet through the
head.

"The old man we wouldn't have as a gift," explained Bychin.
"You can leave him alone, the bald coot, but as for the young
men, we need them as security. They could harm the Revolution." Shura hesitated, but Bychin said, "Just do as I say!" Difficult
guy, pays no attention to anyone, won't brook any argument;
Shura says he met thickheads like that during his time in hard-
labor camp. First they're a bit wary, he says, but then they'll
thrash the living daylights out of the whole bunch of you. On
the other hand, times are fierce, one is surrounded by enemies,
and these "difficult guys" are needed. Every day a Revkom member is killed, someone is wounded or else a unit dispatched to
carry out a requisition encounters machine-gun fire and you're
forced to engage in real fighting. Everything is in flux, everything
is restless and confused. There are joys too: the exultation of the
newspapers, the victorious cries at the mass meetings and a sort
of secret feverishness, an anticipation of turmoil. Because we are
walking along the brink. Shura does not care for a lot of what is
happening on the Don. His quarrels sometimes reach the point
of shouting and hurling the most outrageous insults at the local
Revkom members, at Bychin, Gailit, his comrades on the tri-

bunal and the people from the Don Revkom on whose behalf our friend Leonty Shigontsev suddenly landed on us in Mikhailinskaya.

Funny when I think back, the silly things they did: stripes down the trouser legs were forbidden; you couldn't call yourself a Cossack; they even abolished the word *stanitsa*—you had to call it a *volost*. As if names and trouser stripes were what it was all about! They got it into their heads to plane the people down in the space of three months. My God, the amount of timber they felled that spring! And all because of a sort of haste, fear, a mad internal fever: get entrenched! Rebuild at once, for all time, for ever and ever!—because the regiments have gone, the divisions have galloped off, but the soil is alive and throbbing. Of course, there were real enemies among them, full of ferocious hatred. And there were the rich, indestructible in their malice— they could not be altered or reconciled except by fire. But you can't place them all in the same basket.

Bychin says, "I don't trust the whole rotten tribe of them. They've always kept us down. We weren't people to them. A muzhik for them was just a cowpat. They never had a good word to say about us."

"Don't you trust anyone?"

"No one!"

"Surely they aren't all like that?"

"They're all wolves, only some show their teeth and others keep their muzzles low to the ground so you can't see them."

Shura patiently points out that not all Cossacks are the same; that in the South, for example, the average Cossack allotment is twenty to twenty-five dessiatines. How can you equate them? The same thing applies to Cossack rights and privileges: in the lower reaches of the Don they mean something, whereas in the North they are practically useless. Just take the fishing rights, the rights to the mineral resources: The South has always lived at the expense of the North. Marxism teaches that existence determines consciousness, yet existence there is by no means equal.

Bychin knows all about Marxism; he nods his haystack head in agreement, but his white, incorruptible eyes are leaden. "It's true that there are poor people and riffraff. But you know, Alexander Pimenovich, when my brother was nearly killed—they horsewhipped him and he's an invalid to this day—it wasn't just the rich who did it, there was riffraff too, who were every bit as brutal." It turned out that they had thrashed his brother because of a "juvenile matter: he had got the teacher's daughter slightly crumpled in the garden."

"So there was a reason for it?"

"A reason, Alexander Pimenovich? What does that mean? He was in love, he wanted to marry her, but their attitude was, 'You're a boor, don't even think of it.' How offensive! We're Cossacks, bluebloods, and you're damned coachmen, you swine; your place is digging manure. They may be teachers, but they're still bourgeois of the first water. They have two full-time workmen. An American mower, a herd of horses and a stableman, a Kalmyk. A superb house: stone foundations, two stories high. They have another house in Elets—his, and he's just a teacher. That one was given as the dowry, since she was the daughter of Tvorogov the ataman of the *stanitsa*. So it's a well-known family. They could do the Revolution a lot of harm."

That was a long time ago, about five years; the teacher's sons were still in high school at the time and now they're locked up in a cell. Bychin got them. He knows best; he knows the locals. Well, when they had taken the sons away and kept them in the basement for a couple of days, Slaboserdov calls on us: bearded man with a large forehead, dressed city style in a long black overcoat with a fur collar, a hat and muddy boots—the thaw had struck and you could hardly get through the mud.

We are sitting in a room—Shura, Bychin, his assistant Yashka Gailit, Petka's brother plus another three or so—discussing the news, the order sent over the wire from the Don Revkom. About requisitioning the carts and the harnesses. Orlik is there, too. The order hit like a bomb. We do not know what to do. We received the order yesterday and are keeping it a secret, but inexplicably rumors have leaked out and are spreading around the *stanitsa* like wildfire through dry grass.

And that is the most terrifying thing. If you're going to strike, then strike at once. A Revkom member informs us that during the night some Cossacks drove their horses with empty carts out into the steppe; he saw it himself. He tried to stop them. He shouted, but they answered by shooting and galloped away. So he didn't find out who it was. Of course the surest way would have been to overwhelm them as soon as the telegram arrived, that is to say the day before yesterday, before they got wind of anything; surprise in such matters is paramount. But there had been an obstacle: Shura was hemming and one of the local Cossack Revkom members was hawing, while Bychin and Gailit were goading them on to obey the order forthwith. We argue and shout. The reason it cannot be obeyed immediately is that the Red Army detachment is not around, having been sent to the Staroselskaya *stanitsa* at the request of their Revkom. The Cossacks were becoming agitated because of the Austrian commissar who had exasperated them with his ridiculous instructions. To start without the detachment was inconceivable. Shura sent a telegram to the Don Revkom: "REQUEST REVOKE ORDER TO REQUISITION HARNESSES CARTS SITUATION UNFAVORABLE," which was quickly followed by the reply: "NOT DISCUSS ORDERS CARRY OUT."

We have nine bayonets: the prison guard and the tribunal convoy. If everything goes smoothly we can get by with nine, but what if it doesn't? In the morning a courier arrives from Staroselskaya with the news that the detachment is delayed: the Austrian commissar has been killed, the detachment was attacked by bandits and the bandits were routed; things were quiet in the *stanitsa*, but retaliatory measures were required. Hence the delay.

February 1919. Dark nights, wind, pitch blackness, frost.

Enter Slaboserdov the teacher.

Bychin jumps up. "Who let him in?"

"Your sentry is asleep." The sentry, an old Cossack fellow called Mokeich—soon afterward killed by the Filippovists—was dozing on the steps. Why shouldn't he? Everyone was worn out, broken down by sleepless nights.

Bychin's haystack face grew thin and fell, and rings like bruises circled his eyes. He waves his hands at the teacher, shooing him like a fly towards the door. "No, no, no. I don't have time to talk with you! Come back later!"

But Slaboserdov walks over to the bench and sits himself down. "I can't come back later. It will be too late."

Yashka Gailit walks over to him and addresses him sternly. "Get out at once!"

The teacher removes his hat, screws up his eyes and shakes his head. I can see that his face is covered in sweat and his lips are trembling.

I tell them, "You can't throw the man out!"

Orlik too says, "Let him tell us why he's come!"

In meetings, Bychin and Shura are always sort of jostling each other with their shoulders as if surreptitiously vying with each other and each measuring his power against the other's: Bychin as chairman of the Revkom and a member of the *okrug* tribunal, and Shura as chairman of the tribunal and member of the Revkom. But although Bychin does puff himself up like a peacock, he nevertheless does understand reason. Shura is no match for him—Bychin has been in the Party only a year and a half as opposed to Shura's fifteen years. Makes a difference. That's why he's loud, bullying, and stupidly wants to squash you and force you to do things his way, but then all of a sudden understanding will dawn and he will be deferential, even ingratiating. Now too he asks respectfully, "What do you think, Alexander Pimenovich? Shall we allow this citizen to speak? Or should he come back tomorrow? It is Slaboserdov the teacher, who is married to the daughter of Ataman Tvorogov. His sons are being detained as hostile elements."

"Speak," says Shura, turning to the teacher. "Only be brief. There's very little time indeed."

Bychin makes a warning gesture with his finger. "And no requests about your sons! There's nothing to discuss."

Slaboserdov, seemingly calm, although his fingers are trembling as they knead his old hat, starts off on a long rigmarole about the Cossacks, their history, origins, customs, traditions... Shura stares at the teacher; Bychin's face turns a brown color— it seems to him that he's being made a fool of. Suddenly he bursts out, "What's this rubbish for?" And Naum Orlik adds, "We don't have time to listen to history lectures. Later, perhaps, when we have time to kill after the victory of the World Revolution." But Slaboserdov suddenly becomes firm: "But it is historical questions that you people are deciding. So it wouldn't be a bad thing for you to take a look at the history."

"What are you driving at?" Shura frowns.

"I'm driving at what they're buzzing about in the *stanitsa*: that there's an order out to requisition carts, saddles, harnesses—the entire wealth of the Cossack, without which his life cannot go on. Do you have any idea what would happen? A Cossack would rather give up his wife than his saddles and harnesses."

"He'll give us anything the Revolution requires," says Orlik. "And if he doesn't, he'll get it!" And Bychin raises his dumbbell-like fist up to Slaboserdov's face.

The teacher does not notice the fist, nor does he hear what Orlik has said. "I have come, gentlemen, to warn you. You do not know the Cossacks sufficiently well if you think you can keep putting pressure on them forever. First you imposed an indemnity on rich homesteads, which was collected by some unnamed detachment which landed on us from goodness knows where. Then the requisition of grain and fodder—"

"The detachment which collected those indemnities was a

group of anarchists," said Shura. "The Soviet regime had nothing to do with it."

"Why waste your breath gabbing with him?!" shouts Usmar, Bychin's Revkom deputy, a dark man with a flat Kalmyk-type face. "He's shown his true colors, the swine! Get rid of him!"

But Shura says no, let him have his say. The teacher says if it's true that such an order does exist and if they start implementing it, there will be mutiny in the *stanitsa*. And that's no idle threat, it's for real. Slaboserdov says he didn't come to scare or threaten us; he wasn't sent by any committee, but came of his own accord. His whole life he has been collecting material on the history of the Cossacks; he is writing a book; he is well acquainted with the Cossacks and ventures to believe that he is not mistaken about the present situation. Things have gone as far as they will go. Tragic events will occur: especially if everyone gets carried away by mutual animosity and feelings of vengeance— if the hostages are made victims.

"Are you aware of what is happening in Russia?" asks Shura. "Either we make the world bourgeoisie knuckle under or they'll do it to us. Yet you're still living on antediluvian ideas—'tragic events,' 'vengeance,' 'animosity.' This is a class struggle to the death, do you understand?"

"I do not deny Marx's theory, Citizen Danilov. I am familiar with it; I have even been somewhat carried away by it. But you must concede that theory is one thing and practice another. Regrettable as it may be, feelings of vengeance can intrude."

A strange impression of a meaningless, absurd excess of delicacy mixed in with a ridiculous, hard, unbending stone wall. I can tell immediately he's a goner. Doesn't understand a thing. And no one understands him.

"Don't listen to him! Get out, you crow! You've spread enough doom and destruction!" says Usmar. He is more bitter toward the teacher than the rest, even more than Bychin. Fedya Usmar, from an average Cossack family, neither rich nor poor; swarthy, rough. I distinctly remember his face, as flat as a pancake, and his eyes always screwed up so you couldn't tell which way they were looking. Soon after, it turned out he was an agent of the Whites. It was at his bidding, when the Denikinists seized Mikhailinskaya, that they hacked down everyone who had helped the Revkom. Bychin was a stupid oaf. That's why he died.

Usmar points his revolver at the teacher. "You know what you get for being an *agent provocateur?* That's what you are, you know!"

"I'm not afraid of you." Suddenly all the teacher's strength leaves him, his hat slips from his hands and he says in a feeble voice, "But why do you touch innocent people? What have my children done to deserve such a punishment? I implore you, Citizen Danilov, don't act hastily." There are tears trickling down Slaboserdov's face. They are spontaneous tears, yet his features are coarse, and frozen as if dead.

"Oh, so that's it! He's afraid of an uprising because we're executing his sons as hostages, is it?"

Slaboserdov says nothing. He doesn't need to. It's obvious that he has come for their sake. However, he cannot change a thing: the order has to be carried out.

In through the broken windows blows the wind, smelling of sweetness and damp—of earth, the far yonder and warmth. February 1919. The Ninth Army is beating its head against the north Don, though it would seem that its strength and thrust are spent. We can sense a fever. The Cossacks feel it in the air—something has cracked and has started to float down like an ice floe in a stream of meltwater. Before daybreak a courier is dispatched to Staroselskaya. By evening of the next day he returns with this jumble of information: things are quiet, muffled, in the *stanitsa;* six people charged with murdering the commissar have been executed; about twenty people have been taken hostage, but the commander of the detachment, a sailor called Chevgun, is in no hurry to leave the *stanitsa.* His message to Shura sent with the courier consisted of only five words: "A small spark is enough."

And suddenly in this prestorm atmosphere the deceptive quiet burst: first Volodya and Asya and a day later Shigontsev.

We had not seen one another for a year and three months; we had grown coarse and hard beyond recognition, but inside we were the same—the same uniqueness, the same aching warmth. You would think it would have vanished, faded away and been forever forgotten, swept off by the whirlwind. But no: nothing, nowhere. Even the first second, the first hour, it was as if it didn't matter at all; it was irrelevant that she was with him, and not just as a friend, but as his wife; that they even spoke the same sentences, one starting, the other finishing; that they gave each other too frequent glances, fleeting and unnecessary, but filled with the usual attentiveness and a mechanical touching as if to ask, Is it real? Are we here? Even that was not at all wounding but, as it were, reinforced the remembered warmth that suddenly welled up because the two of them were a single indissoluble whole. It was later—soon—that the torment began.

How had they ended up with Migulin? Once again, chance. The flow which caught hold of them and dragged them along with it. Because of Volodya's father who suddenly turned up. He had been friendly with someone on Migulin's staff and had latched onto him back in the spring of 1918 when Migulin was scratching together his first detachments in the Donetsk steppes. Volodya's father met his death in an armored train which was blown up by *haydamaks*. So this is how it happened: somehow or other his father reached Migulin, then Volodya joined his father, and Asya with him. The family cracked apart like a ripe sunflower seed. What had become of the parents? God knows. They were either in Rostov or in Novocherkassk, or perhaps they had headed off farther south. A prisoner had told them that Privatdocent Igumnov was apparently pursuing his career in Osvaga among Denikin's agitators in Rostov. Soon Rostov would be taken, and then... What would happen then? Asya was not thinking about that; she was concerned about something else: the baby she was expecting. But Volodya could speak of nothing but Migulin: with passion, with impatience. Confidentially he informed us, "The Revolutionary Military Council of the Front can't stand him. Even though he's winning, he's still a stranger. Even Trotsky winces when he hears his name. How does someone prove he's one of us?"

How do we know Volodya himself is one of us?

Only recently he was talking—and just as passionately as he is talking about Migulin now—about the peasant commune, dreaming about the Volga region, living the simple life with his friends. Back in November when he and Asya were fleeing a starving Piter neither of them had any thoughts about fighting for the Revolution. Time had changed them, raked them into the rushing torrent, carried them with it.

Volodya looked bizarre in his long-skirted cavalry greatcoat, his peaked cap with a star, his Mauser box dangling about carelessly and rakishly on his stomach anarchist style. His whole aspect was different, yet his eyes showed the same old youthful animation and an abiding amazement about life.

"Just think what a brilliant tactician he is, how wonderfully he knows people—both his own Cossacks and the Whites—and what a lucky devil he is! And that is the most essential quality: it is part of being talented. The traps he's managed to escape from! The scrapes he's wriggled out of alive!"

Asya too is completely different. When we are alone together I ask her stupidly, "How are you?"

"Same as everyone—if you've survived another day it means you're okay."

"What is it like with Volodya? Are you okay?"

Stupid again, pathetic; but I can't stop myself. Asya thinks awhile, then answers, "I don't know a kinder person than Volodya. Or braver or more honest...." She thought a bit more and added, "He couldn't live without me."

She does not even mention Migulin, about whom Volodya is jabbering so enthusiastically. As if she doesn't hear. And that catches my attention slightly. I still do not know whether there had been anything between them at that stage or whether it was still in the offing. Anyway, the times were such that there were no minutes to spare for dropping hints. Perhaps even the child she was expecting was Migulin's? There was no time for anything. Only for getting on with it: fighting, making split-second decisions. Indeed, almost immediately, not even two days after Volodya and Asya arrived, the Steel Detachment of the Don Revkom descended on Mikhailinskaya, about forty Red Army men including sailors, Latvians and Chinese from heaven knows where— a formidable and relentless force led by a pair of men: Shigontsev and Braslavsky.

Shigontsev represents the Don Revkom and Braslavsky the Civilian Administration of the Southern Front. These organizations are the power in the Don, in the liberated regions. And they let it be understood immediately that they are the power. As indeed they are. Genuine, steely power. In the name of the Revolution. They pronounce everything done by us, by the *okrug* tribunal and the Mikhailinskaya Revkom, headed by haystack-headed Bychin, a pathetic, rotten, bungling job. On the verge of being criminal! The main quarrel is centered around the directive recently sent by courier in a sealed package. Shigontsev and Shura meet not as two ex-prisoner friends with plenty of memories to share, but as opponents who at some point broke off in the middle of a fierce argument and now take up where they left off. Oh yes! It began a year ago. In February 1918. Shigontsev had come back after the taking of Rostov and angrily told how Egor Samsonov—the third friend, the convict poet— had unexpectedly spoken out in the Sovdep against executing and persecuting the bourgeoisie. At the time, this persecution was causing an outcry among the Rostov Mensheviks and the local citizenry. Then Egor arrived in Piter, dismissed from all his posts and having narrowly escaped execution himself. Yet

Leonty had made no attempt to save him. He had been saved by Putilovo workers, by Red Guards.

"I told you!"

"How did you lose Rostov? Why couldn't you manage to organize any defense?"

"Rostov was lost because of the damned Huns. Stop being a demagogue." Shigontsev pointed a threatening finger at Shura and shook his absurdly elongated head with its dented temples.

I remember how that head had once amazed me in Piter. Now it was shaven and yellowish gray from typhus. In the space of a year Shigontsev had grown darker and thinner as well as tougher and less garrulous—he had lost his voice and spoke hoarsely. In a barely audible but passionate huskiness he laid into the German proletariat for always being late: they procrastinated a year over their revolution and now they were dithering in Bavaria even though Eisner had been killed and they should be taking advantage of the situation.

"When it comes down to it," he says to Shura, prodding him with his finger, "what we're talking about is how to hang on to our gains. Surely history teaches us something, doesn't it?" And as usual he is bursting with quotations and examples from the French Revolution. "The decree of the Convention stated that a column should be erected on the ruins of Lyon with the inscription 'Lyon protested against freedom. Lyon no longer exists.' If the Cossacks adopt an enemy stance they will be destroyed like Lyon, and on the ruins of the Don Oblast we shall write: 'The Cossacks protested against the Revolution. The Cossacks no longer exist!' By the way, that's a first-rate idea: to populate the oblast with peasants from the Voronezh, Tula and other provinces."

"Why are you so afraid of the bullet?" Braslavsky asks Shura.

Shura is not afraid of anything. Penal servitude taught him that. There is nothing in the world that merits fear. He is sick. He is critically ill, although no one knows it yet. By evening he has collapsed and even now is running a fever: his face is burning.

He says that it isn't a question of being afraid of the bullet but of being afraid of a rear-guard uprising by the Reds.

Braslavsky asks, "How many people has the tribunal executed in the past three weeks?" Braslavsky is a small, red-faced man with the puffed-out cheeks of a sulky little boy. He is of indeterminate age: he could be my age or he might be forty or so. He is wearing a wide, ungainly leather smock, too long for his height, on top of leather motoring trousers. He has a strange expression, sort of sleepy, inert. What does he see from under his pendulous eyelids? What is he thinking about? At the same time there is something tenacious, clinging and importunately all-seeing in that look.

Shura answers, "Eleven."

Braslavsky's eyes are like two snails in the puffy red shells of his eyelids. When the shells contract the snails draw back inside. "Are you familiar with the directive?"

Shura says he is. The thrust of the directive is "dispossession of the Cossacks," going after everyone who had anything whatsoever to do with fighting Soviet power, and execution of everyone caught with a weapon. When he first read it, Shura had said, "It's a mistake, to say the least! We'll regret it. But it'll be too late." Saddles and carts indeed! It's a terrible act of defiance to the Cossacks.

Now when Shura says that, yes, he is familiar with it, his voice is calm.

"You know," says Braslavsky, "that I can hand you over to the court as saboteurs, don't you?"

Bychin mutters nervously, "Comrade, everything is ready. There are people serving as hostages; how many times have I raised the matter with Comrade Danilov?"

Incredible to see a huge, strapping, powerful man with his knobbly fists, practically squashed by that little sleepy-eyed fellow—pushed to the very brink of renunciation and betrayal!

Everyone sets on Shura. If the counterrevolutionaries had been promptly exterminated in Staroselskaya, Comrade Franz, the Austrian Communist, would not have died there and this kind of situation would not have arisen. Shura tries to protest: it's not always easy to decide who's a counterrevolutionary and who isn't, to determine that someone supports the Revolution forty percent, has forty-five percent misgivings and is fifteen percent terrified. Here he is lampooning Orlik. Each case has to be carefully checked; people's lives are at stake. But Shigontsev and Braslavsky chime in together: It's the Revolution that's at stake! Don't you know why the revolutionary court was set up? To punish enemies of the people—not to air misgivings and investigate cases. During the trial of Louis XVI Danton said, 'We're not going to try him, we're going to kill him!' And what about the Law of Suspects enacted by the Convention? Any former nobleman who did not show unceasing devotion to the French Revolution was considered suspicious. Don't be afraid of blood! Milk is good nourishment for children, but blood is the food for the children of freedom, as Deputy Julien said. . . .

To Bychin, Shigontsev's string of quotations is like the crackling of so many twigs in the forest.

"These are the ones for the ax!" he said, shaking a piece of paper. "The Antonovs, the Semibratovs, the Kukharnovs, the Dudakovs—related to *the* Dudakov. Slaboserdov the teacher: he's at the top of the list. Son-in-law of an ataman, but he's still at liberty, and yet how many times have I told Comrade Danilov..."

Slaboserdov is a sticking point. Shura is reluctant to give his consent. Hard to understand why. He had seen the teacher only once and had quarreled with him; they had talked angrily, and yet he really digs in his heels and won't budge. His face is blotchy and highly flushed; his eyes are aglow deep in the recesses of their sockets. He motions with his hand—water, water! I take him some water in an earthenware mug.

Naum Orlik shouts, "You're ill! You must have a temperature of nearly a hundred and four!"

"No, no; I'm fine. I want to say this: I consider the directive to be the fruit of overhasty reflection. I am going to write to the Central Committee, to Lenin."

Braslavsky looks at Shura and says nothing. A minute's silence. Braslavsky is thinking, working out what to do. After all, as representative of the Revolutionary Military Council of the Front, he was the highest-ranking person there. Slowly raising his hand with its gnarled little fingers, in a gesture of assent or a salute to the troops on parade, Braslavsky remarks wearily, "Write all you like! It's your right to spin theories: you're a former student, aren't you? Well, I'm a worker, a tanner, not versed in theories, and it is my duty to carry out directives." And he clenches his little fist and with surprising force bangs it down on the table so that the earthenware mug leaps up and starts rolling. "I'll march through this village like Carthage!"

That remark was so astounding that, unable to restrain myself, I say, "You can't march like Carthage. You can destroy something in the way Carthage was destroyed."

His fixed gaze freezes onto me from under his heavy lids. Clearly and firmly he repeats, "I'll march through this village like Carthage!" Then, after pausing for an instant to survey everyone, he suddenly yells, "Do you understand me?!"

Later, Shigontsev told us in confidence that Braslavsky had suffered greatly at the hands of the Cossacks; that his family had been slaughtered in the Ekaterinoslav pogrom of 1905. His mother was murdered and his sisters raped. But surely it wasn't the Cossacks, but the locals, who did the murdering and raping? The Cossacks helped, he said. Shigontsev announced almost gleefully that "you couldn't imagine a better fellow for that job!"

If Shura had not fallen ill, if he had not collapsed unconscious that same evening, perhaps that internecine battle... Since it was he who had summoned Chevgun and had given orders to station the tribunal detachment to defend the prison and not to hand over the hostages. Executions have begun in Staroselskaya, from where Chevgun has just returned. Shooting counterrevolutionaries. Revenge for killing Communists. For Comrade Franz.

So far things are quiet in our Mikhailinskaya; the hostages are
not being touched and Chevgun's guard is sitting on the front
steps of the prison, calmly cracking sunflower seeds, but only
because the Steel Detachment is marching "like Carthage" through
Staroselskaya. I have the impression that even Bychin is flab-
bergasted by such savage zeal. My God, is the tanner with sleepy
little eyes really a savage? Or was that Cossack really a savage,
the one we caught on the flats and shot on the spot because we
suspected him of having murdered Naum Orlik? Naum was found
in the neighboring village of Solyonoye, bound, riddled with
bayonet wounds, eyeless, and—most horrible of all—alive. Were
the Cossacks really savages who captured Boguchar and ten Red
Army soldiers and buried them in the earth with the words,
"There's your land and freedom for you!" And were the *stanichniki* of Kazanskaya and Meshkovskaya really savages, who lured
the Zaamursko-Tiraspol detachment into a trap, the detachment
which in the spring of 1918 had retreated from the Ukraine and
which, dead with exhaustion and not suspecting anything un-
toward, set up camp for the night in some Cossack huts. Some
of the detachment, consisting of Chinese, were shot in their sleep
and the rest were stripped naked and locked up in sheds. The
stanitsa holy man in Meshkovskaya held a service of thanksgiving
for the occasion and called for all the anti-Christs locked up in
the sheds to be burned alive. And were the Veshenskaya Cossacks
such savages, who that same spring, in an access of revolutionary
derring-do, killed off all their officers in one fell swoop and
declared themselves supporters of the new regime? And were the
four worn-out factory hands from Piter really savages—a Hun-
garian who scarcely understood Russian and three Latvians who
had all but forgotten their homeland—who, for years, had been
killing, first Germans, then *haydamaks* and then, in the name
of a great idea, enemies of the Revolution? Those are the enemies,
bearded enemies with brutal hatred in their eyes, barefooted, in
their undershirts: someone is shouting and shaking his fists, and
another has crashed to his knees, and the women are wailing

behind the slatted fence. And an ex-convict, beaten and flogged, an old man at thirty, croaks, his hopeless lungs bursting, "Take aim at the enemies of the Revolution—fire!"

Savage is the year, savage the hour over Russia. Like lava it flows, that savage time, submerging and burying in its fire. And in that fiery womb new and fantastic things are born.

When you're flowing in the lava you don't notice the heat. How can you "see the times" if you're in them? The years go by, life goes by and you begin to sort it all out; why this or that happened. Rarely did anyone see and understand it all as from a distance, with the mind and eyes of another time. Like Shura. It's clear to me now. At that time I doubted, as did many. He alone was genuinely horrified by the directive, which I was not allowed to read, which was kept secret and revoked two months later, though the harm it caused was tremendous. I read it fifty years afterward. By then it could evoke terror or pain in practically no one. It read something like this:

1. Mass terror against Cossack leaders.
2. Confiscate grain; force destruction of any surplus.
3. Organize resettlement of peasants from northern provinces to the Don oblast.
4. Newly arrived non-Cossacks to be equal in status to Cossacks.
5. Conduct complete disarmament.
6. Issue weapons only to reliable, non-Cossack elements.
7. Keep armed detachments in Cossack *stanitsas* until order established.
8. Exercise maximum firmness in respect of all commissars appointed to Cossack settlements. . . .

My God, and so few people were horrified; so few cried out! Because the lava blinds your eyes. There is nothing to breathe in the crimson fog. The land is aflame—not only our land, but all over the place: revolutionary strikes in France and England;

Soviet power almost consolidated in Germany; Romania and Bessarabia in the throes of peasant revolts. How can it be otherwise, how else can the couuterrevolutionaries be wiped out if not with bayonets and bullets? Almost all of them have been wiped out. But *that* was precisely the mistake, the fatal miscalculation that Shura saw and that he muttered about in his delirium—that victory was already in our hands. That Krasnov and Denikin would never recover after the winter offensive.

Nor was I horrified, nor did I cry out. My eyes too were dimmed by the red foam. I can see Orlik spattered with blood, his eyes put out and his lips whispering something incoherent. *Why did they kill Naum Orlik, who never did anyone any harm?* He was a reflective person who wanted to get to the bottom of everything with his mind. We used to talk about how, after the victory, university education would have to be reformed. He left alone, without a guard, carrying a bundle of the political department's newspapers—to propagandize and inspire. They jeered at his half-dead body. All the peasants from that village fled to the steppe during the night.

The following day, by order of the RMC of the Front, Braslavsky broke up the Revkom and appointed new people and a new chairman; he broke all the newcomers and Bychin to the ranks—for their leniency. And since Shura has typhus and is lying unconscious and on the verge of death, *I* am appointed chairman of the tribunal. I didn't want it. I did my best to refuse. The interview was stern; he used threats to bring it home to me that I did not have the right to refuse. No, I didn't want it. Not for anything. Not my sort of thing at all, sentences, executions.

I told him, "That job requires special people. People like Shura. Toughened by hard-labor camp."

He replied, "Not at all! It requires people who can write up records. There aren't any people. You're the only one. It's your duty."

Chevgun the sailor said, "Stick with the job, brother. Otherwise they'll give it to a scoundrel."

Chevgun too was hacked down by Filippov's men. But he was the only one of them all who was not hacked to death. They brought him round and he survived. He disappeared somewhere that same spring. Then, what, in about '32? Oh, yes. The Urals, the Turgayash State District Power Station. On Krzhizhanovsky's orders I had just been appointed chief operational engineer for Turgayash. Masses of work. Galya came with the kids and we lived in a wooden house surrounded by taiga. What went wrong there? What was the matter? The first of the three stages in the Turgayash project, two 3,000-kilowatt turbogenerators, had been completed in 1923. The second stage, two 10,000-kilowatt turbogenerators from the Leningrad Engineering Works, had been completed just prior to my arrival. The boilers were already in operation, but the turbogenerators—this was the devil of a job: while they had an exceptionally good steam-flow rate, they suffered from enormous problems in regulation. Always on the brink of blowing up. What a terrible headache! The third phase was still in the preparatory stages. The boilers were built over chain-grate stokers. However, the stokers are beside the point: there weren't any, as the factory had not yet built them. The point was that it was difficult to poke fuel into ten-meter-wide furnace openings; downright impossible, in fact. But those Turgayash coals had to be stoked. So, send off a report to Moscow! To have the chain-grate stokers replaced by dust-burning equipment. Moscow takes umbrage. They send a commission. The commission agrees with me. We're authorized to get new equipment, and we order a stoker from the English firm Combustion, Ltd. Suddenly, a month later, I am urgently summoned to Moscow. Why? What the devil for? "They'll explain in Moscow. Get moving!" The official in charge knows something; the others shrug their shoulders. Galya is terribly nervous. That was her weak point—at crucial moments she was not reassuring: her whole appearance, her terror, her anxiety just added fuel to the fire. She was all ready to take the children and go with me to Moscow, even though Ruska was sick at the time; it was all I could do to dissuade her.

But the mysterious summons—after I had been proven absolutely right about replacing the chain-grate stokers—really had alarmed me. It all suddenly became clear on the train. I bought a newspaper and there it was in black and white: "SABOTAGE BY COMBUSTION." I and an engineer named Sulimovsky were indicted. Nothing to do with the Turgayash power station, but with an earlier one in Zlatoust. All of us had apparently "confessed" our "crimes." The authorities had seen fit to punish the principal culprits and not the technical executive officers—myself and Sulimovsky. The article on the Combustion affair took up an entire newspaper column. Naturally I did not sleep on the train that night. Utter nonsense. If I am a saboteur, then why haven't I been arrested? If I am not guilty, then what right do they have to write about me as if I were a criminal? They say that some trial is going on, yet I, the accused, find out about it only from the newspapers.

The train arrives the next morning. Who is the first person I ought to run to see? Shura? Well, Shura, of course, is the closest, the very closest one, but he is no longer in his job; he has been set aside, pensioned off. He would be the only one to advise me. I phone him from the hotel. He gets the picture, no explanations needed: he has read the papers. "Go at once to see Alyoshka Chevgun!" He gave me his address, but at that hour Chevgun was at work, in the public prosecutor's office. That I knew. But I hadn't seen him for thirteen years. For myself, I had decided to make a strong protest, to draft a statement to OGPU, the Unified State Political Administration, and take it that very day to the Lubyanka. If I'm an enemy, then take me and put me on trial!

Chevgun lived in a huge apartment building near the Kamenny Bridge. About seven o'clock the next morning he received me in his office, I wouldn't say ecstatically, but somehow quietly;

cordially, but at the same time suspiciously. I showed him my statement and he read it and suddenly jerked upright in his chair. "What, are you off your rocker?! You're putting your head in a noose! And neither I nor Shura can get you out of it. Don't go anywhere and don't submit any statements!" Wise counsel.

Shura's delirium was monotonous—he kept harping on Slaboserdov. He would shout out in a horrible voice, "I won't give up Slaboserdov to you! Be quiet! Leave Slaboserdov alone!" Or he would start imploring, "Friends, I beg of you in the name of God Almighty—you can't, you just can't kill. I entreat you, do not kill Slaboserdov...." Or else he would just babble incoherently. His was a bizarre illness; he became a different person. To keep repeating the same name when tens, hundreds, are perishing is a mental quirk which is almost comic. But then he came to and, looking soberly at Leonty and myself— we two were at his bedside—asked, scarcely audibly but insistently, "What about the teacher, Slaboserdov?"

Leonty answered, "Nothing in particular. What should be, is."

"Well, what then?"

He replied that the question was redundant; that the question no longer existed.

Shura picked up his steel-rimmed glasses, shoved them onto his nose, looked at Leonty, looked at me and closed his eyes.

Leonty whispered, "Delirious again."

"No," said Shura. "It's you who are delirious. I understand everything perfectly." And to be honest, his voice did sound clear. Well, then, where was the delirium? Delirium is confusion, darkness, a gurgling down in the inner depths. A crimson fog clouding the reason. "You are delirious, not I." From under his glasses, tears trickled down his cheeks. I had never seen Shura crying. He never cried. Shura whispered, "Why can't you see, you wretched fools, what will be in the future? You've buried your heads in today. But all our sufferings are for the sake of something else, something in the future. Ah, fools, fools."

We were happy. Thank God, the crisis was over! Shura was getting better. He was not delirious; *he understood everything perfectly*.

In the ill-starred March at the height of Shura's illness, or rather in my memory of it, everything has become tangled and stuck together like old bloodstained bandages on a wound. I am powerless to disentangle and separate the strands. One should leave old wounds alone. When did Migulin appear? What were Volodya and Asya doing there? When was Braslavsky shot? And why did Leonty survive? Leave them alone, leave them alone. Impossible to bandage up all that pain again. Nothing will come of it. Don't do it. It's forgotten. The bloodstained bandages have stiffened, turned into stone, turned into coal. They are seams which will take a pickax to chop out. Impenetrable, complete and utter blackness, and somewhere inside it—Asya. She is alive.

This all happened in March, during the thaw; the ice had started floating down the north Don; the Whites were blowing up bridges as they retreated; and Migulin's brigade was marking time on the right bank. The offensive had petered out. But not just because of the thaw—no, no! The thaw was not the reason. It started in one *stanitsa* on the night of the eleventh to the twelfth and spread like a fire. What Shura had warned about. And before him Slaboserdov the teacher. In fact, we had all had a premonition of it, we were expecting it any day. There was something hanging in the chilly air. A kind of muffled feeling. We waited: even before these petty local troubles came to pass, the world would explode. All the revolutionaries, all the workers of the world, would rise up united. How could it be otherwise? What else could be befogging our eyes? That is our pain, our justification.

I am eighteen, and in my hands are held the lives of hundreds of men who frighten me, women I do not know and old people

I do not understand. But Shura was too late dispatching his wrath to the Central Committee; he delivered it later when he had gotten over his typhus, when everything was raging and the North was aflame. When it was too late. My God, why was it too late? After all, it was only 1919! Too late. The *stanitsas* were rising, the whole of the rear was ablaze and troops had to be withdrawn from the front. Braslavsky gave orders to "dig a mass grave for the hostages." That night the Cossacks scattered and there was no one to do the digging. The women and the old men couldn't. I am ashamed to say I wonder whether he is in his right mind. Am *I* in *my* right mind? Doing that kind of work every day you'd go batty in no time flat. No, it's not a case of going batty, it's a kind of numbness. You become insensitive, like a sack of sand. Someone could prick you with a needle and you wouldn't feel a thing—the needle is passing through sand. Shigontsev's dream— zero emotion. The supreme state you had to strive for.

February 1919. Early March. A raw spring wind disperses the shouts, swells, smoke, shooting, wailing. In my hands I have a list: number one for having been for Krasnov; number two because his family was; number three because he refused to surrender his horse. A fourth had been found with a rifle; a fifth had been a speculator; a sixth had abused the regime; a seventh was a former tsarist cadet; an eighth was related to a priest... Shigontsev says, "Vendée! Vendée! The French Republic triumphed only because it knew no mercy." I am supposed to sign it instantly. What difference does it make, Bychin's eighteen people or Braslavsky's hundred and fifty? People are horrified by numbers. As if arithmetic is important. Shigontsev would argue, "A person has to decide in principle whether or not he is capable of devoting himself entirely, of giving his whole visceral being, to a great result." My question would be, Is he capable of undergoing mortification—that is, of killing something of himself? It then turns out that, yes indeed, arithmetic is important. It has all become so irreparably stuck together and so mixed up: the things I read, the things people told me, the scraps I retained, the bits I imagined—and the things that actually happened. What really happened, then?

Volodya and Asya are in the next village, where a reserve regiment is being mustered. Migulin sends enraged telegrams demanding that the Revkom be dismissed and another district commissar be appointed. He threatens to come himself, to break up the Revkom at machine-gun point, condemn the lot of them to death and shoot them. He calls Braslavsky, Shigontsev and the new Revkom chairman false Communists. But how can he come? A war of telegrams. Braslavsky's response is rude: "He didn't appoint me! I'm not subordinate to him!" They are not afraid of Migulin, because they can sense that he is not trusted.

Volodya hates Braslavsky. He is even hostile to me: "If I were you I'd put a bullet through my head." He told me this in Asya's presence, in my own house. I was merely seeking his advice as a friend about what I should do. I was confiding in him, but he answered me truculently. He was always inclined to histrionics— sort of undigested Schiller. Asya was much cleverer. She looked at me dolefully, sympathetically and without getting into arguments. I remember she whispered to me softly, "You're done for." But I don't want to be done for! I see Orlik—dead, riddled with holes and alive. I can feel the hardening of the Cossacks, their intractability, their animosity and their desperation. *Now*, today, it is clear: the enemies of the Revolution exploited our mistakes with diabolical energy and strength. But at that time I was aware of one thing only: that fateful days were upon us that beginning of March. Volodya and Asya knew nothing about that night when I ran to Braslavsky. It was useless to run to Shigontsev. He had ersatz brains. I ran to Braslavsky. I was in such a state that I was capable of doing anything—shooting him or shooting myself.

The whole point was that on that night in March headquarters had already revoked the directive, but we did not know it! Actually, the Don Revkom knew, but was in no hurry to notify us.

How could I forget that night? Raw, dank, with the red flashes of a distant storm. I was a kid—silly, daring, and shaking as if from a fever. The one thing I knew was that *it had to be decided that night*. He would "march like Carthage" on and on and on. Figures were not important; it was a road without an end. At the gate some Chinese were squatting, their rifles between their knees. A machine gunner was sleeping on the front steps. A light was on in the end window. That means he's not asleep. He is in agony before the dawn. How can he fail to be in agony? A glimmer of hope stirs: what if I persuade him? In these pàst days his face has turned deep red, a black-cherry color, his cheeks have become even puffier; to look at him, you'd think he either has drunk too much wine or else is mortally ill. *Everything must be decided before dawn.*

I gave the door a push. He was alone, sitting on a chair, his riding breeches tucked up, and soaking his feet in a basin of hot water. He was adding boiling water from the kettle. That amazed me! "Matvei, what are you doing? Are you all right?" Never before had I seen anyone torturing himself with boiling water. I had seen people get killed, hacked up, shot. But people blanching their own feet, never.

"Obviously, the blood is bursting me open and making my head throb," he said. "Must get some leeches, but where from!" The druggist from Staroselskaya had turned out to be the enemy, so he was no longer. Obliterated. The orderly brought over a fresh kettle. I see that his feet are absolutely pink—boiled—yet he still goes on pouring. Superhuman willpower.

"How do you stand it?"

"This is nothing. It gets worse; it broils me, but I stand it."

I blurt out: I can't, I won't sign. I refuse. You can do what you like. Shoot me if you want.

"Your thinking is not proletarian," he said. "You can't see past your own navel. You'd do better to sit down here and read me the newspaper." His sight used to get bad in the evenings. Sometimes he would be holding a meeting, making a speech, and his eyelids would close of their own accord. The letters leap about on the page, my tongue can't get round the words because of the pounding in my head—this is the end! No way out. I cannot bear that boiling water. *Either he or I will have to go, before dawn!* Anyway, it was the end. She had told me, "You're done for." But nobody knew anything about that night. Not a single soul. I never even told Galya. I think that even I had forgotten— completely and utterly forgotten. Had I imagined it all? No. It happened. I take my revolver from my pocket, click the safety catch. And in that blind second I still do not know who is going to get it. That was exactly how it happened. I had absolutely no idea. But in the next second I would decide. He glanced at me, his cheek twitched, his little crimson mouth dropped open in astonishment. The kettle went one way, he went the other way and fell to the floor. He lay there, not breathing.

No, he did not die then. A month and a half later. Five others were executed along with him. The Steel Detachment was broken up; some were sent to prison, some to the fronts, to the North, near Tsaritsyn. They were tried by a special commission of the RMC of the Front, chaired by Comrade Maizel. Who later worked in Tsvetmet. But why didn't they touch Shigontsev? Inexplicable. Forgotten. Someone helped him out. I remember how his lungs rattled; he was emaciated, his face had turned black, he was spitting blood, but his expression was still fiery and satanic. "Why did that sterling fellow Motka Braslavsky die? Because the Cossacks revolted. And why did they revolt? Because he didn't burn them to ashes, he didn't finish them off. His own fault, the blind fool!" But the point was this: when the uprising began, Migulin was suddenly recalled from the southern front to Serpukhov, to the field headquarters of the Workers' and Peasants' Red Army. And from there he was chucked even farther west, to the Byelorussian-Lithuanian Army. Why the hell? At the very time that Denikin was advancing, when Migulin was more than ever needed on the Don.

Pavel Evgrafovich had tired himself out with the walking and the heat, and, as he no longer felt like lunch, he went to his room and lay down. He lay there for a long time. No one dropped by. About four hours passed. Occasionally he dozed. Coming out of his slumber, he heard voices from the veranda, and once Garik and someone else ran with a crunching noise across the crushed-brick path and Garik, gasping for breath from running, shouted out an odd phrase: "Did you pay her back with interest?" For some reason these words bothered Pavel Evgrafovich. He began thinking about them nervously, trying to fathom the meaning of that tiny spark of his grandson's soul which happened to fly past beneath his window down there, fluttering like a butterfly in its unspoiled nakedness, carrying with it something important, some essence, some secret thing, which vanished into the stillness of the hot day. He fell to thinking about how generations change; about women, revenge, gratitude; and about how love and understanding are in no way linked. Even understanding the fact that they are all pigs. Galya would have come by ten times and asked him, "Are you all right? What is it? Don't you want your lunch? Shall I give you some medicine?" His grandson was probably talking about Alyonka, Polina's granddaughter. Something was going on there. Suffering. God, is it any wonder? He was just the same age as Pavel Evgrafovich had been during his own schoolboy torments over Asya, sixty years ago in Piter. Garik's tormentress was to pay something back with interest. But the mystery was, was it repayment in vengeance? Or gratitude? The reason for Pavel Evgrafovich's agitation was that for some reason he thought he had to solve the mystery of that hastily shouted sentence because it had a connection with his own life, which was drawing to an end. If the real meaning was vengeance, then that was one thing; but if it was gratitude, then that was quite another thing. With chagrin, he was increasingly inclined to believe it was probably vengeance, childish and

trivial but vengeance nonetheless, it being, as it were, fashionable
nowadays: this "you give it to me, I give it to you," "you–me,
I–you" and all the possible variations.

At the timber station in Ust-Kamen a little gray-bearded old
man had suddenly asked him in a whisper whether Pavel Evgrafovich's surname was such and such. Upon hearing confirmation
that it was, he beamed toothlessly, bowed down to the ground
and pulled out of his pocket a fragment of yellowed lump sugar
wrapped up in a rag. "Accept my gratitude after twenty years!
From an unfrocked priest whom you saved from execution. You
remember Mikhailinskaya? Nineteen nineteen?" He then told
him an intriguing thing. One of the Church Fathers had written
that the feeling of gratitude was a manifestation of deity. That
was why it was rare. Ingratitude was much more common. "It's
not the fact that I can repay you with good that makes me rejoice:
I rejoice because this very minute I am talking with God."

That is what was evoked by his grandson's running and the
chance shout. At that point there was a knock at the door and
Vera entered.

"Papa, aren't you hungry? Aunt Polina has come to see you."

It was like this with Polina: For the first two years or so after
Galya's death he could not bear to see her or talk to her; everything
reminded him, made the wound bleed. Everything, everything:
Polina's long-nosed, wrinkled, black-eyed face, her soft southern
kh sounds, like the way Galya spoke—they were both from Elizavetgrad—her gutteral *r*'s, her way of joking. Although of course
Galya's jokes were more subtle, wittier; she had a marvelous sense
of humor. There was no comparison, in fact. Galya was a deep,
clever woman, and Polina was really not that bright. But then
he became reconciled to her, to the fact that she *continued to
exist* while Galya was no longer. Then after some time he began
to like her again; he was amazed at her tirelessness, pitied her
and tried to help her whenever he met her, an old woman, on
the highroad, weighed down with baggage, dragging a wheeled
handcart and looking like a slow, decrepit beetle. He hated her

daughter, son-in-law and granddaughter—with the passionate hatred reserved for enemies—for permitting such a disgrace. He had had some sharp clashes with her son-in-law. On a couple of occasions he made some justified comments—My dear friends, how can you? You have a car and there's Grandma hitched up to a wagon—which were answered by some rude remark. So he had sworn never to try to change anything in that family; but whenever he met Polina with her load he always took the cart and her bag. Although the doctors had told him never to lift more than three kilos. Well, he had long given up on doctors.

Polina was telling him something in an undertone, something mysterious. Her black eyes became round, her wrinkled mouth twisted to one side. How she had aged, poor thing! A real old woman! Now Galya never became an old woman.

"What are you whispering for?" he said, irritated. "Speak normally. You know I don't like secrets."

He was irritated not because of any dislike for secrets, but because he had not heard properly. He had to remind her every time. It was so disagreeable. Just like begging for alms: help an old man! Speak louder! Of course, Polina was a good woman; she sincerely loved Galya and Galya loved her, but in Galya's attitude there was no rhyme or reason. She did not bestow her friendship on just anyone, but although she was so inflexible with everyone else she was tolerant toward her own circle. She forgave her friend the fact that she was not bright. Shortly after Galya's death Polina had come to visit in a bizarre, bright-colored outfit, her face powdered and her lips painted with lipstick. What was she trying? What sort of game was that? Pavel Evgrafovich had felt such a surge of irritation that he had muttered through his teeth, "Please remember never to come and see me with painted lips!"

She continued to speak in a whisper, but a loud, intense whisper as in the theater, and her eyes grew even rounder. Something about a reference, a certificate, moving out, moving in somewhere. Oh, the same old subject—Agrafena Lukinichna's house. He had given strict instructions that he was not to be involved in it. On either side. He had long since let Ruslan have his share in the cooperative; he did not attend the meetings and had no voting rights—so sort it out among yourselves!

"Pasha, I'm not asking you for anything: just give me a reference."

"I'm not an office that issues references. I don't have a stamp."

"Pasha, don't make jokes. Please. This is a matter of... well, to put it more bluntly—" her bumpy, many-dimpled chin twitched and her mouth slid farther to one side in a clumsy grin—"not my whole life, but just the very end of it. The last little bit!" And she indicated with two fingers what a tiny scrap was left of her life. Her sense of humor. But not apt. If Galya had wanted to be witty on that subject she would have thought up something wonderful!

"What sort of reference do you need?"

"I'm trying to tell you: a reference saying that I was engaged in revolutionary work."

"What work did you do?"

"What do you mean? In 1919 I was held by Denikin's counterespionage unit. Have you forgotten? Galya told you about it hundreds of times. Galya did it, too."

"Gracious, woman; you were fourteen years old. Galya was thirteen." He began to laugh. It was nice talking about Galya. "For heaven's sake, what kind of revolutionary work can you mean?"

"Pasha, we were politically conscious young girls. We loved the Revolution very much." And she went on jabbering in her usual garrulous way, pretending to be half joking, affecting wit, but in fact talking nonsense. Suddenly she finished talking and said, right on target too, "If Galya was alive she would give me a reference before you could turn around! You don't have to do anything; you just have to write down that you know from your late wife that Denikin's counterespionage unit had been after Polina Karlovna for revolutionary activities."

"Forgive me, but what were those activities?"

"We were scattering leaflets around the market for the Independent Students' League. We were hauled off to the police station and held for six days. They could have done whatever they wanted with us—beat us, rape us, shoot us—we were completely in their power."

She positively oozed stupidity. What could a reference like that possibly do? The cooperative board consisted of cynical, indifferent people who would just make fun of the pair of them. And really, it was funny. Polina said that she needed the reference for something else. She wanted to get into a veterans' home. Some special place in Uspenskoye, near Moscow. Pavel Evgrafovich had heard of it.

He was so stunned by this news that he was struck dumb: a veterans' home was Pavel Evgrafovich's secret horror. In his crazy dreams, in his night thoughts, he had a picture, from what other people told him, of a last resting place where the principal torture was that one was surrounded by *other people's old age*. No one and nothing apart from *other people's old age*—most excruciating for the old. Can one really feel happy hearing under one's window a grandson's enigmatic shout, "Did you pay her back with interest?" The more he read in stories about the poorhouse—descriptions of the gardens, the rugs, the libraries, the televisions—the tighter the chill grip around Pavel Evgrafovich's heart. The luxury of those homes was reminiscent of a Moslem paradise. Parting from the children and grandchildren meant parting from the last remaining piece of Galya. But thank God, that was no threat to him. What stunned him was the calm with which Polina spoke about the home.

"What nonsense," he said irately. "I'll have a word with Zinka and your son-in-law this very day. Have they taken leave of their senses or something?"

"They don't know. I haven't said anything yet."

"What made you think of this?"

"What do you mean, Pasha?" Polina faltered as if unable to

decide whether to tell him or not. Her thin, sinewy hands, the hands of a laundress and a bag-lugger, turned their palms up and to the side in a gesture of perplexity. "They don't need me, Pasha."

"Don't talk rot! Nonsense! Get it out of your head!" he shouted.

"It's the honest truth, Pasha. They did need me when Alyona was little, but not really now. In a sense I'm even a burden to them now. They're planning to go to Mexico for three years, and they want to put Alyona in a boarding school. Anyway, do they ever really need us?"

Pavel Evgrafovich said nothing. All this was not to his liking. First, why this "us"? Why lump them together? They were completely different people, in different situations; you can't treat them the same way. Secondly, there was in fact a grain of truth in her nonsense, and that was the worst thing. In addition to which, Polina's decision had required courage which he had not suspected the poor woman of possessing, and he felt wounded and even humiliated. The only thing he could find to say was, "In that case why have they put in a claim on Agrafena's house?"

"I don't know. I don't interfere in their affairs. Pasha, please: just a few words."

He sat down at the table, put on his glasses, tore a sheet of lined paper from a notebook and wrote. Polina folded it in four, poked it under her belt and, after giving Pavel Evgrafovich a smacking big kiss on the cheek, left. But a minute later she returned and said to him in a whisper, her eyes again taking on that meaningful round shape—an old schoolgirl habit, inappropriate in an old woman, she should drop it—"Only, I beg you, Pashuta, don't tell anything to the family!"

Pavel Evgrafovich sat awhile at the table mulling over Polina's eccentricities—for some reason she had smacked him a kiss on the cheek and called him Pashuta, which she should not have done, because only Galya called him that: again tactlessness from lack of intelligence—but then, giving up and putting the whole thing out of his mind, he immersed himself in Grozdov's letter and his reply. The work was progressing badly. Several times

either Vera or Ruslan would look in, summon him to eat, distract
him with questions, and he would chase them away and get
angry. The heat did not let up and he was bothered by an unpleasant smell from the garden, like singeing chicken feathers or
burning garbage. Most likely it was their neighbor Skandakov
making a nuisance of himself again. He had taken to burning
all his rubbish in an iron tank, producing a loathsome stink which
wafted into the neighboring plots. It had proven impossible to
put a stop to this hooliganism; they had tried shaming him into
stopping and summoning him before the governing board, and
Pavel Evgrafovich had sent a letter to Skandakov's organization,
but all to no avail. He had had the gall to say, "I'm not answerable
for the direction of the wind!"

After about an hour's wrangling, and having written all of four
sentences—albeit very meaty ones—Pavel Evgrafovich went out
onto the veranda to eat. The heat had prostrated everyone and
laid them low. Myuda was lying on a folding cot with a damp
towel on her head. Ruslan was sitting barefoot in his shorts in a
corner of the veranda at a small table, bent over his blueprints,
correcting them. Valentina served Pavel Evgrafovich some beet
soup and a dish of kasha and a chicken cutlet, the food he had
brought from the sanatorium. He had no appetite.

His daughter-in-law was wandering about, likewise barefoot
and half naked, her red bathing suit showing through the cotton
robe she wore thrown over her shoulders, her belly and navel on
general display—go right ahead and admire!—and she loitered
on the veranda as if she was expecting something from Pavel
Evgrafovich. A compliment on the food? But it wasn't hers: it
was government food. Yet one could sense that she was hanging
around for a purpose. Everyone was expecting something, some
conversation. Now Vera had appeared. She had obviously been
sleeping and her face was red and puffy. Goodness me, she too
was in her bra and linen shorts—outrageous with her legs.

Ruslan asked why Polina Karlovna had come. That's what
they're waiting for. That's the reason for the excitement. Even

Myuda, dead with the heat, turned her head to hear better and pushed the towel off her face.

Pavel Evgrafovich replied, "Nothing in particular; we talked a bit, recalled the old days. After all, she did go to school with Mama." The only person who had known Mama longer than he. He had known her since 1922 and Polina since 1915. He thought the serious, heart-to-heart tone would distract attention from practical considerations; they did not often bring up Mama, each out of pity for the other, and if he mentioned her name they would be expected to show interest and ask what his old friend had reminisced about and what they, the abandoned old-timers, had talked of.

But Ruslan questioned him relentlessly. "Nothing about the house? Not a single word?"

"No, nothing. She's not interested in it. She said she doesn't interfere in their affairs—I mean the affairs of Zina and Kandaurov."

"So you did have a conversation about the house?"

"Yes, yes," interrupted Pavel Evgrafovich, getting irritated. "Only it was about something else."

He naturally did not go on to explain exactly what. Heavens, what an interrogation! They're out to trap me. Well it won't work, my dears; you won't find out. Suddenly he blurted out, "She also said nobody needs us."

But this phrase came out rather like a joke, and Ruslan laughed. "Oh, no-o! I'm sorry, but we do need you. Papa, you simply have to speak with Prikhodko."

Pavel Evgrafovich said nothing and walked away.

Once again he remembered about the letter from Galya and he felt an urge to read it. Good God, from Galya? Not from Galya, from Asya. He was startled by how strangely and yet how easily he had confused them. As a matter of fact, it had happened because a letter from either one of them was inconceivable. But if *one* had appeared... He suddenly imagined with a quaking heart that he *had* received a letter from Galya. In the usual dark-blue envelope, airmail. Naturally, airmail. How else? It had been put into the mailbox together with the newspapers. There was no return address. But there was something written on it. One word: "There." Nobody knows anything, and so "There." Apart from that, no address, no return address, not a single word; blank. No envelope, even. A page with no envelope, at the top of which there is an opening sentence: "Pasha darling, don't torment yourself over trifles; let them do what they want—you won't offend Polina or me...."

He stopped on the wooden staircase and looked out the round window; the sultry evening sun was melting on the tree trunks. He thought, If Polina doesn't mind, then Galya doesn't mind, either, and neither do I. He could have a word with Prikhodko. It did not matter now. The bad thing was that they refused to think about anything or remember anything. Have a word with Prikhodko. There was a kind of connecting thread between the two women, Galya and Asya, who had never seen each other or known about each other. He never told Galya about Asya. Galya was jealous. She did not need to be jealous of the other woman, because they were composed of different molecules, of different stuff: at the time of Asya, Galya had not existed anywhere in the world, then when Galya appeared Asya ceased to exist. And then Galya disappeared and now, out of different matter, Asya had reappeared. One had belonged to him with her whole flesh, her whole being, while the other was air, unreachable. Now they had changed places: Galya was unreachable, whereas Asya—a train ride to Serpukhov, then the bus to...

By evening the heat had still not abated. As in the steppes of the River Sal in 1921. Then too there was a wind which blew not coolness but heat. There was a medicinal smell on the veranda. The women were taking valerian drops. Ruslan, Nikolai Erastovich and two guests who usually came on Saturdays—Laletsky, a gray-haired, young-looking fat man, and Grafchik, a

gymnastics teacher—were sitting at the big table playing Pref-
erence. By now their tea-drinking and their sitting under the
lamplight was over. Verochka, Myuda and Viktor had taken
refuge in the kitchen, sitting around the tiny laminated table
drinking tea.

Verochka's eyes were red, either because of the hot weather
or from crying. "Papa, the matter's practically settled," she whispered. "Kandaurov will get the house. Laletsky said... Well, of
course he has massive connections; the ministry gave him a letter;
they phoned Prikhodko from somewhere or other. I like Aunt
Polina, but Kandaurov's a bastard."

Pavel Evgrafovich shrugged his shoulders. Nothing to be done
if the man's a bastard. He was reluctant to show his utter indifference at the sight of her tears, but was unable to control himself.
The whole thing was nonsense. Not worth a brass farthing.

"How many other claimants are there?"

"Three. But they all dropped out. Now there's only us and
Kandaurov—yes, and Mitya from the state farm, a very distant
relative of Agrafena Lukinichna. But he doesn't count; he's a
drunkard and a cadger. You've seen him: he's often lounging
around here, trying to sell iron or glass or tiles of some kind—
all stolen, of course. Laletsky said Kandaurov will get it. It's
definite."

"Verochka, dear," said Pavel Evgrafovich, "why such despair?
What's the matter? We've lived for thirty years without that house
and we'll go on living without it. You'll go on living; I won't be
needing it."

Verochka lowered at him. She took him with her hot hand
and led him from the kitchen into the next room and closed the
door. Like when she was a child—to have a secret powwow.

"Papa, you know how complicated everything is with Nikolai
Erastovich. He's a strange, sick man. He often needs to have a
rest during the day, and where can he, here? He says if only he
had his own corner or a little veranda..."

"So? What else?"

"He says he can't bear it anymore. This living on sufferance. If only there was a veranda even. Do you understand? He's at the end of his tether."

"What does he love most, you or a veranda?"

"Don't talk like that." Verochka's round face with its girlish bangs, the harried, unhealthy face of an older woman, pursed up and her lips began to quiver. She turned and left the room. Pavel Evgrafovich stood in indecision. He felt sorry for her, but he did not know what he could do for her. A veranda wouldn't help. He left the room, went up to Verochka, who was wiping the kitchen table with a cloth while looking out the window, and put his arms around her.

"You can't do this, you can't, you can't. Especially to your family who love you," his daughter whispered.

"Well, what can I do for you?" He kissed her on the top of the head.

"I don't know what you can do. Have a word with Prikhodko. What if... I don't know. Try."

Verochka had a rare quality: she took offense instantly, but just as instantly forgot the offense completely. She would have made a marvelous wife for someone; she so much wanted to have children, but it was too late now; she was past it, and that man had made her have abortions. She had had two while Galya was alive and no one knew how many since Galya's death. Dear God, so hard to make head or tail of their affairs. For example, if he were Verochka he would not be able to stand living with that Erastovich for three days—he would tell him to go to hell—yet she lived with him and put up with him.

Pavel Evgrafovich returned to the veranda and sat awhile by the wide-open window. There was no feeling of relief in the air, although it was about eight o'clock and quite dark. The card players were conversing in undertones. Pavel Evgrafovich did not understand anything about cards, nor did he want to. He had done without cards for his whole life, and had retained from his youth a scornful prejudice about them as being a small-minded, bourgeois activity.

Viktor quietly ascended the wooden steps leading from the garden—he always walked and talked quietly. He went up to Pavel Evgrafovich and sat down on the floor beside him.

"Grandfather, I meant to ask you," he said under his breath, "what did she say about Grandmother?"

"What did Polina say?" said Pavel Evgrafovich, delighted. "I'll tell you! Let me remember now. She said something very interesting. . . . Oh yes, I know. When they were both thirteen, your grandmother and Polina, they were engaged in revolutionary activities and they even landed up in Denikin's prison in Elizavetgrad. Very young girls they were. They were intimidated and tortured, yet they didn't betray anyone."

Apart from Viktor, nobody on the veranda was listening to what Pavel Evgrafovich was saying. The card players were discussing their own business. Suddenly Ruslan said, "Papa, I'm sorry, but you must see Valentin Osipovich. So brace yourself; I know it won't exactly be pleasant."

"I'll have a word," said Pavel Evgrafovich. "I'll try."

"But don't delay. The board is meeting next week, then the general meeting will be at the end of the month."

"It's not the end of the month, it's the first Sunday in September," said Laletsky. "Anyway, it's all useless. The house will go to Kandaurov, as surely as you haven't got a three in your hand."

Laletsky guffawed. Once again they began speaking unintelligibly and slapping the cards down. Then Ruslan said, "Listen, you are underestimating the power of public opinion. *You* will be voting *against Kandaurov,* won't you?"

"I suppose," said Laletsky.

"As for me," said Grafchik, "I shall obliterate him with a stroke of my pencil. Types like that have grave contraindications for me."

"What's so bad about him?" asked Pavel Evgrafovich.

"I find it difficult to explain, Pavel Evgrafovich. Now, you, for example: I have deep respect for you. Whenever I visit you and talk with you or your son I feel my heart and soul at peace; I go all sort of relaxed, do you understand?—"

"Eloquent words, damn him," interrupted Ruslan.

"—But when I see that fellow, my blood-sugar level rises."

"Another claimant has muscled in, however," said Laletsky. "A certain Izvarin. Used to live there before the war. Prikhodko is dragging him into it for some reason. Can't see why; the house will still go to Kandaurov."

"What's to see? It's very simple—"

"Play, maestro! Throw down a card!"

"—*very* simple, in fact: he wants to milk Kandaurov for all he can get. The more claimants there are, the more... well, you can see for yourselves."

"Izvarin? Sanka Izvarin?" exclaimed Ruslan. "Surely he's not still around?"

They could gab away and slap their cards down all evening and all night. Pavel Evgrafovich said he was going into the garden for a breath of air; he suddenly had the idea of going straight off to see Prikhodko without further ado in order to remove the weight of a highly disagreeable conversation from his mind. But he was loath to tell them about it. He took his stick and began walking down the porch steps. It was dark and close in the garden. The usual sweetish scent of phlox and of tobacco plants—on August evenings they smelled mightily—was all but absent now. Everything had withered, wasted away and decayed. Above the blackness of the trees, in the pallid night sky made silvery by the stars, hung the red moon.

Feeling his way along the path with his stick, Pavel Evgrafovich emerged from the thicket of bushes and sapling lindens onto the path that led into the heart of the colony. They have an inkling that the idea of a conversation with Prikhodko is disagreeable, but none of them knows why. There is no one left who could know.

Galya knew. She was not on speaking terms with Prikhodko. She never spoke to him or his wife, although naturally his wife had nothing to do with it; but Galya was unbending. She would say, "You can do as you wish, pass the time of day with him, drink tea, discuss the international situation—it's your business, but I can't stomach him. To me he was and always will be a white louse. Because anyone who hurt my husband once is an enemy for life." That was the way she was! Pavel Evgrafovich stopped and, leaning his stick against a stone, looked up at the sky, and his eyes filled with tears. She would not have allowed him to go to Prikhodko. "Are you going to ask something from that louse? Let him bully you and feel as if he's giving you a handout?" It's for the children's sake, Galya; they need something. They still live badly, in cramped uncomfortable conditions, and they're mentally unsettled; they're not living the way they want to, but are living the way it is. They're unhappy, Galya. Nothing has changed over these five years. "Do you think they'll be any happier with a spare room and a veranda?" No, of course not. Happiness comes from something else. Impossible to say what. Happiness is what we had. But what can you do? I haven't the strength, the intelligence, the opportunity: nothing. There's only that little house, two rooms and a veranda. Let them. If they feel that strongly about it.

When you live for a long time, strange encounters take place, ridiculous chance meetings. As if someone had thought it all out on purpose. A long life has its inconveniences. Whoever could have woven this queer, tentacular web of circumstances, of gossamer threads and knots, in such a way that in 1925 Pavel Evgrafovich had been working in the Purges Commission in the Baumansky district of Moscow and had voted for the expulsion of Prikhodko, an employee of Gorpromkhoz (the Municipal Industrial Authority) who had concealed his having attended the Cadets College, as well as certain actions in Kiev, and that now, practically half a century later, this former cadet would determine whether his children were to be happy or not? It was the most unmitigated, monstrous nonsense if you thought about it seriously! But if you didn't think about it, it was nothing in particular. Run-of-the-mill nonsense.

Pavel Evgrafovich in fact had forgotten all about the petty little liar who floundered about as best he could to keep his head above water in his harsh life. Such people were not uncommon; he had no time to pity them and it was impossible to remember them. And really, nothing terrible had happened to Prikhodko at the time. And then six years later when they met at a dacha cooperative shareholders' meeting Pavel Evgrafovich saw a portly fair-haired man, wearing a *tolstovka* of raw silk and expensive shoes, who was the manager of a factory. Pavel Evgrafovich did not recognize him. He did not recognize him for a long time. At the time Pavel Evgrafovich was working in the Urals and came to Moscow on short visits. He never would have recognized Prikhodko had not the man himself told him in a very friendly, half-joking manner, "Do you know, my dear neighbor, that you threw me out of the Party way back when?" "You don't mean it!" "Yes indeed." And that was the end. Big joke. Everything settled down, worked out, became blurred and stabilized. Of an evening they would greet each other and raise their linen peaked caps and straw hats. Then years went by, involuntary separation. Pavel Evgrafovich came back before the war: impossible to live in Moscow; his dacha became his only refuge. Galya trembled, fearing that the authorities would see and guess: he was shuttling back and forth from Murom—his residence permit was for there. Then, again a meeting, a meaningless conversation about this and that: the children, the war. The war was on in Europe and we were on the brink of joining it. Then Prikhodko suddenly came up with "You haven't forgotten that you drove me out of the Party in 1925, have you?" "Yes, I had," Pavel Evgrafovich admitted. "Well, I haven't. I'll always remember." And he walked off with a smile. A day later the inspectors struck and all hell broke loose. Galya was convinced it was Prikhodko's doing. Who knows! It might have been. No one knew exactly. Nothing came

of it; there was no time, because June crashed, Pavel Evgrafovich
volunteered and he spent the whole war as a soldier. He survived
two injuries. He stumbled upon Ruslan one night in Poland in
1944 in a demolished farm. Some tank-crew members were
spending the night there. What a meeting! Then again years
passed, once again everything settled down, changed, stabilized.
The little dachas became dilapidated, began to rot, the iron rusted
through, while on the other hand gas cylinders appeared beside
the houses, and the plants in their gardens grew luxuriantly.
Again meetings here and there, on paths, other people's verandas.
Exchanges of bows, muttering about trivialities. Or else Prikhodko's daughter, a slovenly fat woman, would drop out of the
blue and ask, "Do you have a spare bulb you could lend us?
We'll give it back on Monday." Galya never gave them anything.
But he did. To him the past had all vanished somewhere down
a pit, down a hole in the ice, and it was pointless to remember
it. However, things reached a ludicrous pass once when a whole
gang of Pioneers visited Prikhodko and he received them in his
garden and told them stories *about the Civil War*. My God! What,
pray tell, could a poor little leftover cadet possibly have to tell
them? Sometimes you just itch to grab him by the necktie and
say, "You sniveling creep, whom are you trying to kid?" Then
you think, to hell with him—it's all over and done with. He
cheated everyone, that chameleon, so to hell with him. Only
don't ask him for anything.

The path went up a hillock where there was a bench; on sultry
evenings someone would always be sitting there under the pine
trees. Now too, as he walked past, Pavel Evgrafovich noticed a
motionless figure sitting at one end of the bench. It looked like
a woman. A pale dress was visible. He shouted out, "Who's
there?" After some hesitation the woman answered, "It's me,
Pavel Evgrafovich."

He recognized Valentina's voice. He was glad to sit down
beside her, thus putting off the unpleasant visit. Valentina was
smoking. He could not abide tobacco smoke in the house and

insisted that smokers go out into the garden. But she had gone very far afield indeed. She was sniffling as if she had a cold. He thought to himself, Something's amiss.

"What's the matter? Feeling bad?"

"Yes..."

"What is it, then?" He heard a voice telling him, Don't: don't get into this. "What's happened to you?"

"Nothing's happened. Nothing. Pavel Evgrafovich..." she hesitated, gave a sigh. "Nothing.... Your son doesn't love me."

"Don't be silly! Perhaps you're making a mistake?" The same voice told him there was no mistake.

"So tell me why he's always inviting his first wife out to the dacha? And Viktor? Myuda's a good woman, and I like Vitya too, but he doesn't care for them at all. It's not as if he can't live without them. He only invites them because of me...to vex me...to make me remember...to keep me constantly humiliated."

She's not stupid, he thought with amazement. Valentina blew her nose. Now it was obvious that things were bad. He was incapable of talking to weeping women. Galya never cried. Of course, Galya was extraordinary. She did not cry in Zlatoust when they very nearly parted; when she decided to leave and told him so. When that dark-complexioned woman had appeared from the first-aid post. It was a confused, difficult time—three months of something like intoxication, nonsense. Then everything cleared up. She didn't even cry when they were forced to part. Well, what could he tell Valentina?

"You know, Valya," he began cautiously, "I think that what you're doing wrong is that you allow him to drink."

"What's that got to do with it?" She buried her face in her hands and sobbed loudly. She gasped for breath; she wanted to speak but could not.

"I really don't know what to allow him...to make him...I allowed him everything. Let him! What of it?"

"He shouldn't."

"I know he had an affair with that fat fool of a woman."

"With whom?" asked Pavel Evgrafovich, but he cut himself short. "I'm really not interested; I don't want to know. I have no right to meddle in your business. The only thing I will try to do is something about Agrafena Lukinichna's house. I'll have a word with Prikhodko."

"Who needs the house? What the hell for?" retorted Valentina through her tears with sudden anger. "So he can take his women there? And going to Prikhodko to ask him for favors! Marvelous!"

She hates Prikhodko, too, thought Pavel Evgrafovich.

After sitting awhile and saying something meaninglessly re-assuring, he proceeded on his way. Everything was in a muddle. Some of them wanted the house, but others did not. It was all very confusing. He felt sorry for Valentina, but not for long. Why pity her? She was young and healthy.

At Prikhodko's dacha a light was burning on the open-air veranda. Two old women were drinking tea—or perhaps playing cards or simply talking—seated in wicker chairs at a small table covered with a tablecloth reaching down to the floor. A puny little dog leaped out from under the table with a yelp, making the tablecloth flutter, and started barking at Pavel Evgrafovich and keeping him at bay. He did not intend to go in, and he greeted them over the wooden fence and strained to understand their replies. The dog's barking made it impossible to hear. One of the old women, Prikhodko's wife, her gray hair combed into a tall pile, smiled at him while saying something and making gestures with her pale, plump hand—not inviting-in gestures, but gestures seemingly pointing him down into the garden: over there, over there! This went on for a minute, the old woman shouting and waving her hand, the dog barking and he unable to understand and standing like a suppliant by the little wooden fence twined all over with wild vine. Prikhodko's dacha was fa-mous for its wild vine. Standing there was intolerable, but going in was also impossible. A ridiculous situation. Finally, during an instant when the dog stopped barking, he managed to distinguish a shout: "He'll be back in a week! He's in Leningrad!"

Pavel Evgrafovich nodded with relief.

Everyone was laid low by the heat, each asking the other, "How do you feel? How are you standing this Africa?" Oleg Vasilevich Kandaurov replied with restraint, "I am not bearing up badly. My general state is pretty good." In fact, his general state was excellent and his body continued to function without any discomfort or stoppages. Everything worked, flowed, moved, functioned, relaxed and tensed regularly as it should.

"Your pressure is like a cosmonaut's," said the doctor at the public-health clinic. An unfamiliar young woman, this doctor, Angelina Fyodorovna. In fact, Oleg Vasilevich knew none of the doctors, as he rarely visited the clinic except to obtain papers. "Magnificent for your age."

"What do you mean, for my age, my dear Angelina Fyodorovna? I'm forty-five! Surely that's not old!"

"Well, you're not a boy any longer."

"Yes I am! I am a boy, Angelina Fyodorovna." And Oleg Vasilevich did a handstand, leaning his outstretched stockinged legs up against the wall. One of the simple yoga exercises. He did it every morning.

Angelina Fyodorovna laughed. "A little boy! That's enough, Oleg Vasilevich! Get down!"

Standing on his hands and looking up at Angelina Fyodorovna from below, he could see her beautiful bare thighs and he thought that there was no time for anything anymore. "Come on, listen to my pulse now. After that physical exertion." He stretched out his hand.

She took his wrist in her fingers. She herself, the poor thing, had red eyes and was sucking validol. Naturally, his pulse was a fraction higher than normal, but it was on the whole even. "Well, perfectly all right for Mexico!"

He could not resist joking, "And what do you mean by Mexico, Angelina Fyodorovna, eh?"

She smiled, shook her head reproachfully and wrote something down on the card.

But it was only to doctors, and especially young woman doctors, that Oleg Vasilevich told the whole truth. When friends and acquaintances asked him how he felt and how he was standing Africa, he would answer, "Quite well" and "Not badly," although he should have answered, "I'm bearing up splendidly" and "I feel wonderful." But the rule was, Never tell people anything that might upset them even slightly if you do not have to. To answer "Splendidly" and "Wonderful" while everyone else was gasping and dying would be hurtful. He even used to reply, "I don't feel bad, but my head's a bit achy." Or "Not bad, but the engine's knocking a bit." But talking with his boss too Oleg Vasilevich would not permit himself to lie and would speak the whole truth— "Fighting fit." That was a hard-and-fast rule: if you're ill and your engine is knocking, sit at home and rest.

He went to the clinic on Friday but did not manage to get the tests finished, and on Monday and Tuesday he was busy from early morning. The only day he could visit the clinic was Wednesday and that day turned out to be the most horrendous of all— the thermometer read ninety-four in the shade. A woman waiting with him on line for the laboratory felt sick and they made her lie down on the divan and dosed her with medicaments. He thought, She would not be given a clean bill of health for Mexico. He looked at her with sympathy.

Angelina Fyodorovna was running down the corridor, her heels clattering, when she stopped for a moment and asked, "How are you? Everything okay?"

"Everything's wonderful, except I have a massive favor to ask you: as an exception couldn't you give me the certificate today? Eh? I have absolutely no time at all tomorrow! Angelina, don't be a bureaucrat; you're such a kind, sweet, understanding, sympathetic person." He grabbed her moist little fingers, squeezed them, and looked into her eyes, remembering that any request needs to be backed up with some push, some passion. You get nowhere with either a listless or an arrogant manner. You have to humble yourself, wallow about in the dust, stun them with your almost romantic drive and disarm them with humor. "Besides, to be quite honest..." and then he whispered, "I'm fighting fit!"

"You are fighting fit," she said with a smile, "but I don't have the right without the tests. Come tomorrow morning. Or the day after tomorrow, as you wish. I can't, do you understand? Much as I'd like to. I'd get into trouble. You're a boy, you're fast on your feet. And you have a car. I saw you yesterday getting into a super dark-blue Volga. And you'll have another lucky chance of being alone with the doctor in her office. See you!" She waved her fingers and ran off.

He shouted after her, "What shall I bring you back from Mexico?" She answered without turning back, "A cactus!"

He was nonetheless distressed by this microscopic failure—he had hoped to wangle his certificate today—and he began thinking about how to plan the next day. Not a damned thing was working out. Tomorrow he had to be at the dacha to try to fight for the house, to talk to people; today he had thousands of things to see to, and at five there was Svetlana. High time to tell her. She was about to leave for the Baltic and by the time she returned he might no longer be there. So it was time to say goodbye. Of course he had spoken to her about it in general terms; she knew about his intention, but as for the details...

The point was that the rubber band had been pulled out incredibly long. Now this way, now that way; now yes, now no. Now in six months, now within a year; then the whole thing is off, unpack your suitcases. Then all of a sudden, decisions, stamps and visas all at once and he had to get ready immediately. He'd had a hard time beating them out of a month to get everything settled. Nothing had been done! The bother over the house was only the beginning. He had to talk to everyone. Take no chances. It was a unique matter and demanded a jeweler's touch—it could all collapse because of a single idiot. Four claimants! And how many were there in that vegetable-garden kingdom known as the Stormy Petrel Dacha Cooperative? Why "Stormy Petrel"? What "Stormy Petrel"? What idiotic self-deception had been afoot there forty years ago? How many dopes and miserable lice hated him merely because he drove around in a Volga and occasionally lived abroad? How would those shrimps vote at the general meeting? What would they take it into their stupid, envious little heads to do? If he could give each shrimp a shearling coat as a present—or even a Pierre Cardin shirt... Yet the basic cut of the garment was brilliant; that was the most important part! Pyotr Kalinovich's talk with Prikhodko; the letter from N.A.; Maximenkov's call. The rest should be a matter of technique. *Should* be. In theory. But in fact everything got stuck on account of people.

Those uncontrollable dopes. How would Aglaya Nikonovna Tarannikova behave? How would Laletsky act? How would Grafchik vote? That character especially worried him. There was no knowing why he was ill-disposed toward Oleg Vasilevich, never spoke to him and only darted scornful looks at him from afar. Well, to hell with him; after all, what was he but a physical-education teacher! Pathetic louse! Nevertheless, in that kingdom the louse was a leading force: chairman of the Auditing Committee. He had used various sly dodges to convince them all that he was a big wheel. They all thought Grafchik was someone to be reckoned with. "Grafchik said..." "Grafchik promised..." Oleg Vasilevich used to meet him in the mornings down by the river where Grafchik did his running and a primitive form of high-school gymnastics while Oleg Vasilevich did his yoga, stood on his head, and also ran, but in a special way with special breathing. They sometimes met face to face on the path and, like a well-brought-up person, Oleg Vasilevich would always nod or give him a look of greeting as if to say, "A good morning to you, Anatoly Zakharovich!," but Grafchik would always run past him in his tattered sweat suit—which should long ago have been used for mopping the kitchen floor—and his ragged sneakers, not seeing and not noticing, or even tossing his face back arrogantly as if to say, "I am Grafchik, and who are you?" Oleg Vasilevich began answering in kind and ignored him. Without delving any further. He needed him like a hole in the head. But later when he needed everyone—and especially such an important cog as the chairman of the Auditing Committee—he swallowed his pride and once again started to say hello and to nod to him in the mornings. Grafchik thawed somewhat and, while his replies were not loud and clear, at least he made a swallowing motion with his throat which caused his head to sort of nod, and a hint of a grimace appeared on his lips, a sign at one and the same time of a certain squeamishness and a kind of "Good morning." Sometimes Oleg Vasilevich's Volga would overtake Grafchik while he was walking to the trolleybus terminal in the morning. On occasion Grafchik even used to pump away on his bicycle to school. His school was quite nearby, on Karbyshev Boulevard. Once when Grafchik was trudging along the road in the rain, wrapped up in his plastic raincoat with the hood up, Oleg Vasilevich braked and flung open the car door. "Step in, dear colleague!" But Grafchik said, "No, no, I beg you. No, thank you! I'll walk," and gave the car door a hasty slam. With people like that anything might happen. But Oleg Vasilevich knew one thing for sure and that was an old principle he had held from his youth: If you want to achieve something, you've got to make an all-out effort and use all means and opportunities, everything, everything, everything—right up to the hilt! That was how, when he arrived in Moscow as a small boy, he had once bludgeoned his way into the Institute. That was how he'd won Zinaida once upon a time. That was how, in the highly intricate and involved struggle over Mexico, he had beaten the resourceful Osipyan. That was how he would get Agrafena's house.

Right up to the hilt—that was the point. In big things and in small things, everywhere, always, every day, every minute.

Again the heels clattered: Angelina Fyodorovna was returning from the far end of the corridor. Oleg Vasilevich tensed up; the blood was throbbing in his temples.

He leaped out of his chair and grabbed her by the elbow as she was rushing past.

"Angelina Fyodorovna, you priceless darling, I beg you, be a real angel for me." he mumbled incoherently and ardently, walking in step with Angelina Fyodorovna and pressing her moist, hot elbow to his side. "Understand the full monstrousness of the situation. Tomorrow morning I'm meeting the delegation; the minister is summoning me in the afternoon; the day after tomorrow I have to have left Moscow. And Personnel is demanding the damned certificate by today! Now, look, what will it cost you? Let's come to an understanding about it. I'm a man of my word: what the Spanish called a *gentilhombre* in olden times. So you'll give me the certificate, won't you? If you have even the slightest qualm about it I swear on my honor I'll bring it back tomorrow. Here," he said, taking his card out of his wallet. "Call this number anytime—morning, evening, in the middle of the night. Okay? Is it a deal? Don't forget, you're saving my life!"

They stood in front of her office door. Angelina Fyodorovna looked at him, smiling, but not as blithely as before, but rather pensively, and shook her head. "I can see the monstrousness of the situation in one respect: you are monstrously brazen-faced, Oleg Vasilevich."

"Well, what am I supposed to do? I have no alternative. Anyway, I'm fighting fit, Angelina Fyodorovna, so—"

"Yes, yes. Fighting fit." She nodded, unlocking the door. "Come in, you awful man. Especially awful for women; you can talk them into things."

She went into her office. He followed her, and felt a tiny, split-second twinge of joy. Once again that golden principle, which had always come to the rescue—right up to the hilt!

By five o'clock he had arrived at the Lyre Café on Pushkinskaya Street. Svetlana was not there. It was unbearable sitting and waiting in the sweltering car, so he walked over to the shade of the building and sat down on a low narrow ledge by the wall. He looked as if he were squatting down. Like a vagrant somewhere in Saïda or Tetuán. At siesta time. He was wearing a tattered T-shirt with the word YES on it, fringed jeans, sandals which looked straight out of the garbage can on his filthy feet: a genuine Scandinavian *clochard* who for some unknown reason had wandered into that back-of-beyond Arabian town. Before sitting down he spread out some newspaper and tried not to lean up against the wall in his white T-shirt. Svetlana would not arrive before five-fifteen. An ineradicable school habit: boys have to be *put to the test*. There had long since been no boys, no one, to test—he wished she'd stir her stumps—but the habit remained. He was not angry with her, because she would be getting hurt today.

She had appeared exactly a year ago. It was also a hot summer, though not hellishly so, like now; she was a trainee Spanish teacher, bright and quick-witted; she did everything quickly: talking, running up and down stairs, typing—even on a Roman-alphabet keyboard—fulfilling all the tasks he, as head of the department, gave her. And all the rest too. Incredible speed. She once made dinner in eighteen minutes! She could tidy Igor's room—that shed, that fetid pigsty which went for months without being ventilated—literally in half an hour. But that, he thought, was not on the first visit, but on the second or third, in September. Even on the first visit her speed had amazed him—he had just gone into the hallway to flip the lock and when he returned she was already in bed, curled up under the sheets head and all. All her clothes fanned out on the carpet. For five seconds he imagined that everything would be not quite as it later turned out. He imagined that everything would remain as easy, quick, serene and airy as it had started. But the way it turned out was blind passion and torment. A difference of twenty-two years—she could be his daughter. Giddy heights which made you catch your breath and made your head spin, and also the bottomless pit. There was a moment in bitterest winter, in December, when everything suddenly cracked, bent, burst and any minute now would collapse like an old building from an underground tremor. Girders bent, the roof creaked, broken tiles tumbled down, but the house still remained standing. Then in the spring came the anguish. Tallinn; quarrels, doctors, tests carried out on mice, and all the nightmares which accompany love, and it seemed that it was over forever. There was much about her that never ceased to astound him. She was a girl. But an amazing one, far more experienced and capable than other, mature women. She loved him—still did love him—like no other woman before, yet he felt there was a barrier that was not easy to surmount. No, not youth, not caprices or irascibility, not the naïve despotism, but something that had to do with himself. His own mirror image which he saw in her and which, on occasion, gave him the frightening feeling that suddenly fate had actually confronted him with his daughter as in the famous novel by Frisch. In fact there could not be any daughter. The reality was something else: they were fashioned from the same clay. The first woman in whom he had seen himself. And that frightened him.

She flew round the corner and dashed toward him, overtaking passersby, but not because she felt guilty—she was twenty minutes late—and not because she was in that much of a hurry to see him, to cling to him: just by force of habit. The way she tore off to the office in the morning was just as precipitous. Her ancestors had probably been running footmen in the courts of the Russian boyars. Or the Tatar mirzas. Unmistakable Tatar blood—dark skin, black hair, slightly slanting dark eyes, and the narrow, rather severe fold of the lips that betrays the East. She was born in Moscow, a Muscovite born and bred, but her father was from somewhere in the South. She dashed up, breathing heavily, did not apologize or even say "Hello!" or "*Hola!*," but inspected him penetratingly, snuggling up to him, and asked him, "Had a haircut?"

"Yes." They had not seen each other for twelve days. He took her by the shoulders, pulled her toward him and kissed the spot he liked to kiss—above the collarbone. And immediately he was infused with the smell of her dear clammy body. "Where shall we go to eat? Here? The Astoria? Perhaps to the Theater Club?"

"Nowhere."

"Why?"

"No reason. I don't feel like it."

He looked at her suspiciously. That "no reason" was unnecessary. Simply "I don't feel like it" was understandable. Because of the heat. He himself had absolutely no appetite at all. But "no reason"? He asked whether everything was all right with her. Whether there had been any trouble at work, at home, with her parents or her sister. Her sister was seriously ill. Last month he had tried to get a drug from France for her. Yes, everything was all right. Her sister was feeling better. Her parents, thank God, were at the dacha. He thought for a while; she sensed something. Just as dogs sense an impending earthquake women sense a break. Before there are any signs.

"Shall we go?" he asked, taking her by the arm.

They got into the car and drove off. She sat beside him and rustled her fan the whole time, cooling herself. She sometimes brought the fan up to his cheek and fanned him a bit: useless but pleasant. Igor's apartment was in the middle of nowhere in one of the remote southwestern neighborhoods. They were used to the long distance and usually chattered all the way, telling each other the news and what had happened during their brief separation, but right now the conversation was not going well: she was silent and he could not think of a suitable topic, because all his vital concerns of the moment were taboo. Until she knew about his going away he could not impart all that was bubbling inside him about this and that—the bureaucracy, the idiocy, the difficulties, the petty details that make you choke with anger. Even just today's episode with the doctor's certificate! What it took to persuade her! Then what should he do with the car? And

the apartment? Making arrangements for his daughter for the
summer and winter vacations? Unless he managed to get the
house everything would grow into a problem. The new owners
would not want to let it out, that was for sure. He had to wrench
the house away with his teeth. All this, which had been torturing
and tormenting him over the past few days, he could not discuss
with Svetlana, and he mumbled something about the heat, the
climate, the wisdom of old people and the helplessness of aca-
demics. He had decided to tell her everything today, but just
before parting. From the practical standpoint too that made sense,
because if he were to tell her immediately, their rendezvous might
come to an abrupt conclusion. That would be silly. They reached
the hills of the southwest. On the deserted streets stood the hulks
of some uninhabited, bare houses, blinding in the sun. It was as
if the sidewalks had been scoured by the intense heat; there were
no people in sight.

"I'm completely soaked through," said Oleg Vasilevich. "As
soon as we arrive we'll take a shower."

She did not respond. Again he was put on his guard. On hot
days they usually started by taking a shower. Sometimes even on
not so hot days as well. They liked it very much. Igor had a regal
bathroom, complete with wonderful fixtures and all the latest
accessories, which he had brought from West Germany. There
was even a telephone in a special little niche set into the wall so
if you felt ill you just had to reach for the phone and dial 03.
He asked somewhat impatiently, "Are you going to take a shower?"

The question meant something else. He should not have asked
it. He was revealing his weakness. But then his nerves were not
made of steel.

"Where?" she asked. "In the car?" And she sputtered with
laughter like a little girl. It cleared the air a bit. But when they
arrived at Igor's incredibly stuffy apartment—last time they had
stupidly not drawn the blinds and both rooms were scorching;
the air was like a steambath, nearly eighty degrees—she refused
to slip into the shower, saying she felt unwell. It could be a ruse.

Something was the matter. The water from the cold tap was warm, meaning that the earth had baked through to the depth of the water pipes. What'll happen to the spring crops? They'll all be burned out! he wondered, echoing the thoughts of Polina Karlovna, who liked to discuss the prospects for the harvest. The thought of his mother-in-law triggered a wave of anxiety—Alyonka had been entrusted to her. Their daughter did not listen to *them*, so why should she listen to her grandma? A prickly, explosive age. "Really and truly," said Zina, "we don't have any right to go away just now. Mama is hopeless at bringing up children. She's too kind." Zina's customary, meaningless token protests: she knew full well that they would be leaving anyway, so there was no alternative. They could not, after all, put her into a boarding school. These were Oleg Vasilevich's cogitations as he soaped his sweatiest places, feeling no relief, as the water brought no coolness.

When he stepped barefoot into the room, walking over the mats—Igor had mats everywhere, albeit mats covered in dust—Svetlana was sitting in the same position. The sheets had not been put on the bed, but the room felt a bit cooler: two Japanese fans were humming away flat out. He asked why she was sitting looking so pensive like the Lorelei. What was the matter? *Qué pasa?* She said she simply could not move. Well, okay, let's just lie. Let's rest. Let's talk about life. It was a while before she reluctantly pulled the bed linen out of the chest and tossed the pillows to the head of the bed, causing the dust to rise in the process and Svetlana's face to grimace fastidiously for an instant, which suddenly made him mad. He was on the point of saying, "Instead of making faces you could take it outside and give it a beating!," but he held his peace. There was no time to teach her how to live. He had not taught her when there was time.

Then suddenly he became passionately, deadly sorry for the girl he was leaving forever. He stroked her soft skin, kissed her neck, her shoulder blade, the fragile line of her backbone, saying nothing; there were no words. She lay beside him not quite as he would have preferred. But now, with this upsurge of blinding pity, he needed nothing but to embrace, stroke and say goodbye. This went on for several minutes. Then he spoke. What about? Heavens, what about? Not the things he should have talked about. About the fact that he felt worn out, badgered, driven; about that whole nonsense, that stupid business. Prikhodko, the chairman of the cooperative, was an old fogey, a schemer and a rogue. But he had found a way to get at him and Prikhodko had promised. There was someone called Gorobtsov who was first on line, not for that house in particular, but for the first share to become available, and now Oleg Vasilevich was arguing that co-owner-ship with him would not be difficult because Gorobtsov had performed no services to the cooperative. Whereas Oleg had. He had hustled for the telephones. Lugged roofing materials for the office. A year ago he had managed to get the Moscow Council, through Maximenkov, to fence off part of the river for the Stormy Petrel, with a swimming place and a small boat basin. A fat lot those dopes would have gotten without him! A fat lot of nothing! The authorities would have long since demolished the whole rotten cooperative. They'd been planning to for ages. They were going to build a State hostel if he hadn't once again arranged things through Maximenkov. Gratitude alone should make them grant the house to him. And not just grant it, but come and offer it to him! So much had been invested in it over the seven years, so much effort put into it.

The most disagreeable individual and the most dangerous rival was a certain Ruslan Pavlovich Letunov. That whole Letunov nest. They had put their roots down there. They were the really tough opponents, because of the legend which exists in any com-pany or corporation: old man Letunov was the legend in this case. He was a veteran, a participant in the Revolution; he had seen Lenin, had suffered, and he'd been around. Just try not to respect him! Out would come the commendations; all his ser-vices, wounds and scars would be trotted out. But Grandpop was okay; you could reach an understanding with him. He was made of the same stuff as those half-extinct gagas who need nothing apart from their memories, their principles and respect. A lie, of course: they need everything else as well! They all do. He doesn't turn down his regular "special lunch" and ambles over to the sanatorium every day with his covered dishes. But they still play that game: *we don't need anything.* Then there's the biological aspect as well. What do old people really need? A bed, a blanket and a potty. Lying down and reminiscing. But there's his frightful son—that one would pull the food out of your gullet. Ruslan Pavlovich. A lout and an alcoholic. Goes around the dachas asking for a loan of three, five rubles to go for a dose of the hair of the dog. Has the man no shame? After all, he's an engineer; he has higher education. The bastard. And his sister is round the bend, a real ding-dong. They've produced a slew of kids. They're running such a caravanserai you can't figure out who's who. People like that should be forbidden to breed at all. What a brood! What if he and Sveta were to have one? That Ruslan fellow used to come over to see Zinaida and bring her scarce books or cassette recordings—he was a music buff on top of everything else—or else he would simply tap on the window in the morning and say, "Zinochka, do you have some dregs of something left?" And once, when Oleg Vasilevich appeared on the veranda instead of his wife and asked him curtly what sort of behavior was this waking people up at an ungodly hour, that lout had replied, all innocent, "But my dear neighbor, there's no kinder person than your wife! Where are people down on their luck to go?" He'd had to give him a bit of a—

At that point Oleg Vasilevich broke off, remembering just in time that it would not be a good idea to describe how he had tossed the half-drunken Ruslan down the porch steps: it might remind her of the incident last year with her fiancé when he went for them near the Peking Restaurant. On both occasions Oleg had used a karate blow which works infallibly. The boy had fallen like a ton of bricks; his briefcase went one way, his eyeglasses the other way, and his head slumped back. She cried, "You've killed him!" He told her it was nothing terrible: just an ordinary self-defense maneuver. She shouted and wept. Five minutes later the boy came to but could not stand up. She stayed with him, and Oleg Vasilevich left. The next day she dashed over to say it was all over with her fiancé because he had called her a foul name. That she couldn't forgive. Heavens, what they had been through together!

"Do you know what's so awful?" he asked, continuing to stroke her. He stroked her tenderly and ever more insistently, his feelings of pity gradually waning and giving way to something else. She resisted. Her resistance was expressed by remaining unruffled and aloof; she wanted nothing; she reacted to nothing and occasionally she brushed away his fingers with a firm hand, to show her impatience. "The awful thing is that man is envious... in his very nature. I think envy is part of the struggle, the survival instinct. It's in the genes. Those dopes are wildly envious of me! And they'd massacre me. Man is fifty percent envy... well, some more, some less. There's less in you. I would think you're not very envious. Are you, Svetochka? Do you envy anyone?"

She said to the wall, "I envy women that men don't lie to."

Like the karate blow: instantaneous pain and unconsciousness. Three or four seconds passed before he said, "There aren't any women like that."

"There are."

He embraced her with all his might, clasping her and pressing her to himself ever tighter.

"Do you know any?"

"Yes. Let go; you're hurting. You shouldn't tell lies. All that prattle today was lies. I'm ashamed for you."

"But, Svetlana, what can I do? After all, it's my life, my work." He unclasped his hands and she moved aside to the wall. "I'm rolling like a billiard ball hemmed in by green baize. My path is into the pocket. Nowhere else. Or over the cushion."

"Oh, no." She grinned. "You won't fly over the cushion. Do you remember what you used to say? That you wanted to change everything and start everything over again from the beginning? You had some madly daring plans."

"Svetochka, I'm a functionary. Goethe said somewhere, 'You think you are moving? But it's they who are moving you.'"

"Don't talk drivel."

There was a pause. He could sense that she was crying. He finished his cigarette.

Suddenly she asked in a calm voice, "Listen. Just give me an honest answer. There are some material things which you already enjoy or which you aim to enjoy in the future. Well, let's say a woman—me. You enjoy me, right? There's your family, which also provides enjoyment of a different kind. There's Agrafena's house, which you're longing for like the seat of pleasures. There's Mexico, which I know you were trying to get and have gotten— you did the impossible, you conquered it like an inaccessible woman—and there's another important seat here in Moscow which promises to yield even higher pleasures: another dream of yours. Tell me now; if you had to choose one thing out of all of these, which one would it be?"

"What a strange quiz. What's the point?"

"I just want to know. How to live. You see, you're my teacher about life, so tell me finally, what should one give up first? In what order? A woman, family, property, travel, power... What do you want most of all?"

She turned over and looked at him, her eyes still moist with tears, but with a genuine, pupil-like curiosity. He looked at her with longing. Then slowly he clasped her in a tight, steely grip, drew her closer, closer, closer. She moved up to him obediently, because she was waiting for his answer, and his lips breathed out into her lips:

"I want all of it."

And when the sun went down and the day darkened, he got what he wanted, because, as always, he insisted *right up to the hilt*; it was a desperate, long and very bitter sweetness which is only possible on the eve of the final separation. Then when it became as dark as night they went into the bathroom and stood under the shower, and he sponged down the beloved body which he was about to leave forever, and said, *"Pónte el pie aquí,"* took her leg by the knee and placed the sole of her foot on the rim of the bathtub. She obeyed him; he embraced her, kissed her wet face and did not taste her tears with his lips. The water flowed and they stood under the shower until utter exhaustion; it flowed and flowed; they stood, it flowed, they stood, it flowed and flowed and flowed with all its might.

At about eleven he drove her to Starokonyushenny. He turned into the courtyard. There the darkness was stifling, hazy, asphyxiating. There was no escape from the closeness. All the windows of the dark apartments were open; voices could be heard; people could not sleep. Someone was sitting on a bench, someone else lying on a blanket on the grass. They could not linger there long; they had to say goodbye once and for all. They had said goodbye already, many times. He asked whether she needed any help with anything. Should he have a word with someone? To do with work? He would still be there through the end of August. For a long time she said nothing, then, well, now that he mentioned it she did need someone to have a word with Sheludyakov. They needed someone for Morocco. She didn't care where she went—Morocco, Zambia, the North Pole, wherever. Perhaps Morocco would be best, with her Spanish. He said it would be easy for him to speak to Sheludyakov. He was an old friend.

And that was it. She dashed over the fence, over the bushes, and rushed away without looking back; she knocked on a door on the other side of the little square. . . .

He sped along the nighttime highway. His heart gave an occasional twinge—damned stuffy heat. He even felt a slight spasm: that darling of an Angelina was right, he was no longer a boy— and he thought with sadness of Svetlana, then that he should fly via Paris and spend three days or so there. He reached the dacha at midnight. It struck him at once that they were not asleep; the veranda light was on. Grandma, Zinaida and Alyonka were sitting around the table and no one came out onto the porch although they could hear that the car had driven up.

"What's up with you?"

"Nothing's up. Everything's just fine," said Polina with a smile and a somewhat sheepish, mischievous expression which left no doubt that something definitely *was* up. And that the old girl was to blame.

"Mama wants to leave us and go into an old people's home. That is to say, the poorhouse," said Zina.

"No, Zinochka, not the poorhouse, but the Home for Veterans of the Revolution!" said Polina Karlovna, raising her finger. "There's a considerable difference."

"Oh, Mama, what difference is there? It's just as terrible and just as hurtful for us all."

"How so, Zinochka? It's a respected place. You should be happy to have your mother so well set up. I hope to God it works out. I haven't heard anything yet. I'm still just getting the papers together."

The blow was so forceful that Oleg Vasilevich seemed to reel, and he had to lean on the doorpost to recover his balance. Of course the old girl was play-acting. What did she need it for? No reason at all, just to flaunt the fact that she was irreplaceable in their household. Perhaps they could talk her out of it and the whole thing would fade away like a nightmare. The main thing was to be tactful and imploring, like when talking to a policeman who is threatening to give you a ticket. But even so, what a bitch!

"My dear Polina Karlovna, we have scraped along through good and bad together for fifteen years—surely we don't deserve this? You've mortally wounded us. I am absolutely shattered. You make this announcement just as we are on the point of leaving; I mean, well, really..." His nerves gave out. He could not sustain his calculated tone of humility and finished in a burst of seething rage, "A stab in the back without a knife! You're acting as if you were our worst enemy!"

The old woman shrugged her shoulders. "I understand. I know.

I'm very well aware of everything, Oleg. In fact, that's what Zinochka and I have been discussing all evening, what to do. What can I do? What I cannot do is take on the responsibility for the house and Alyona. I don't have the strength; I'm too old."

This was spoken so calmly that Oleg Vasilevich realized that it was useless. He was familiar with the old woman's uncommon obstinacy in everything—whether to cut an onion this way or that way, for example—and he knew that you could never tell her anything, that other people's opinions flew by her ears without even reaching her eardrums; and so he said nothing now, but cogitated in silence. Suddenly he remembered that Zina had once hinted that her mother had someone, a certain friend of advanced years; some theatrical artist or other. Aha! So that was it! Off to the poorhouse to be with her boyfriend? Too old to stay with her granddaughter, but still fine for indecent senile hanky-panky. It was on the tip of his tongue to say it, to slap her in the face with it, but he restrained himself. No, no; not in the heat of the moment. We'll keep that trump card for last. First get a good night's sleep. You needed a clear head for this sort of thing.

Alyonka sat at the table looking gloomy and mulish. She was scribbling something in pencil on a piece of paper, her bespectacled head bent low. In the obstinacy stakes that creature held second place to her grandmother. Obviously they had quarreled and Alyonka was in the sulks. Oleg Vasilevich looked at the uncomely girl with irritation and pity which turned for an instant into pain. What would become of her? Boarding school? Well, other people do it. Many do. Tomorrow, tomorrow. With a clear head.

Zina asked, "Where have you been so late? I called home, I called Leonid Vasilevich..." Her eyes were alight with a keen, burning curiosity.

Suddenly he yelled out, "What difference does it make where I was?! Is that really what you should be worrying about? We're going through a catastrophe here, a nightmare—all our plans are shot to hell; our whole life has gone to hell! But the most

important thing to her is where was I and why so late." He gave
up in desperation, left those silly people and went into the garden,
where his bed stood under an apple tree.

Suddenly the telephone rang. "May I speak to Sanya
Izvarin? I apologize for calling you, Sanya. You're a grown-up
man, but to me you're Sanya, just like forty years ago when you
picked lady apples in my garden and I chased you away, set Jack
on you—remember Jack the bulldog?—and complained to your
father. . . ." The old man muttered something quickly in a voice
half smothered by hoarseness, yet extremely chummy. From this,
Sanya gathered that he needed something; there was some impossible situation. His surname, a certain Prikhodko, meant nothing to Sanya.

"I'm sorry. Do you have some business to discuss with me,
Comrade Prikhodko?"

"Yes, urgent business. I must see you."

"Urgent?"

"Yes, extremely. *Cito*, as doctors write on prescriptions. You
should know, Sanya, that our talk will doubtless be of interest to
you. I don't live far—I'm literally a quarter of an hour away."

Alexander Martynovich was on the point of leaving for the
hospital to visit his wife. So he told him not later than midday.
The little old man turned up ten minutes later. And as soon as
Alexander Martynovich saw the bare knobbly skull, the nose like
a ship's prow and the large, elongated mouth stretched into a
somewhat fawning and cunning smile, he at once remembered.
He didn't remember Prikhodko; he remembered the guy they
nicknamed Potbelly or Knife-switch who lived all the way down
by the vegetable gardens. He had two children, a lad called Slavka
and a girl called Zoya. Slavka was the same age as he. They
made friends one summer. Oh yes, and Slavka was famous for
something: he loved to twist ears. Most often he would twist his
own ears; pull at them, fold them into a little envelope, poke the

lobe into the earhole, while sitting and talking or playing cards, calm and contented with his ears twisted up. But then suddenly he would start to grow nervous and he just couldn't wait to twist ears—even an ear belonging to someone else: Zhorik, Ruska, Skorpion or himself, Sanka Izvarin, and he would start whining, "Give me your ear, please! Give it to me! Gimme, gimme, gimme!" Or else he might just order Zhorik, "Give us your ear, you Dutch creampuff!" Zhorik would obediently proffer his head and Slavka, purring, would set about twisting Zhorik's wafer-thin dark-skinned ear. Yes indeed: Slavka Prikhodko. There was a veranda twined around with wild grapevine. So, was Slavka's father that old man with the big smiling mouth? He had played a dirty trick on Mama. For some reason she had given orders not to speak with him or to go onto their veranda. She did, however, allow Sanya to play with Slavka in the yard. Everything had faded away, burned out, dried through, vanished. Why hadn't the old man died? Why had he turned up?

"You too, Sanya, have a fair chance—I don't say a big chance—of getting the lodge. You see, you lived there for about twelve years, didn't you? From about 1926. I remember your dad well. I'm surprised they never raised the matter. They seem to have faded away, in fact—out of the picture. But you have a moral right."

"Yes," agreed Alexander Martynovich. "Tell me, how is your son? Slava?"

"Slavik didn't come back from the war. He died in the northern Caucasus in '42. My wife and I and Zoechka were evacuated to Chuvashiya." The old man gabbed so quickly it was as if he wanted to rid himself of the words as quickly as he could. "Well, now, Sanya, write out your claim and I'll try to help you."

Alexander Martynovich remained silent, thinking and secretly worrying. His heart was pounding. The thing that had just hit him so bizarrely out of the blue was like the old dreams that had tormented the entire first half of his life; the dreams about the unfulfillable past. A couple of times after the war he had stumbled

by chance into Sokoliny Bor—since then twenty years had
passed—and he purposely turned off into the wood and walked
to Liniya 4 so as not to see the fence, the pine trees and the
roofs. It had all rotted away. Suddenly he imagined that he was
already gray-haired; sick; had seen everyone buried, seen his son
buried; and that a mysterious bald old man with a scary nose
appears, a wizard perhaps, or the devil, and offers to give him
back his childhood in exchange for something: to give him back
those times when everyone was alive, when he used to run barefoot along the stony path and when the sun used to burn the hot
resin of the pine trees. . . . But what was the point? What did he
want?

"You know, it's rather unexpected. . ." Alexander Martynovich
mumbled. "I'll have to think it over. . . . I'm going over to the
hospital. My wife's sick."

He then traveled a long while on the trolleybus and made an
effort not to remember. But the memories came of their own
accord. The fact of the matter was that it was a godforsaken hole.
That was why it was so terrifying to go back there.

It was a godforsaken hole, although to look at it it seemed
nothing extraordinary: pine trees, lilacs, fences, little old dachas,
a steep riverbank with benches—which were moved back out of
the way of the water every two years because the sandy bank was
collapsing—and the road, roughly surfaced with fine gravel and
tar. The road had been tarred only in the midthirties, and even
then not right to the end, but just up to the turn onto Liniya 4,
or, as they used to call it probably before the Revolution, the
Fourth Cut, for at one time there had been a real pine forest
there and they used to have to drive cuts into it. But forty years
have passed since then on both sides of the *liniya* or the Cut or
the Grosse Allee: the name for the forest road which plunged
between the hills, given it by the brown-lipped, wrinkled Mariya
Adolfovna, whose face reminded you of a crumpled old sock,
but an infinitely kind, gentle and incredibly homey sock. What
became of her later, after that summer when she tearfully left

Sanya's life forever? Stretching out on both sides of the Grosse
Allee were the colonies of colossal new dachas. And the pines,
enclosed by fences, were now creaking under the wind, exuding
their resinous fragrance into the hot air as their personal gesture,
like musicians invited to play for a wedding. Ah, never mind, it
still felt good! One could listen to the music standing out on the
street. The air by the pine trees, the fences and the Cut was
stunningly pure; the purity was so powerful that it could knock
over a person who carelessly stumbled out into that air straight
from a jam-packed bus from the city. That was what was happening to Sanya that summer: just like the grown-ups, he shuttled
from one institution or waiting room to the next and stood in
lines. He would turn up at Sokoliny Bor only toward evening
and he would gulp down the air and choke. He felt the sweetness
of the air and the bitterness of forebodings. Yes, yes; it was a
godforsaken place. Or rather, a cursed place. Despite all its charms.
Because for some strange reason people perished there: some
drowned in the river while swimming at night; others were cut
down by sudden illness; and certain individuals settled their scores
to the death in the lofts of their dachas.

Mariya Adolfovna whispered, "O, *jetzt muss ich mich auf den
Weg machen,*" and for the tenth time shifted something somewhere else, packed things up, sat down on the sofa and drank
her tincture of valerian. And again, "O, *jetzt muss ich...*" Her
books with their gold-tooled antique bindings smelled of sachet.
Mariya Adolfovna had an octagonal wooden frame on which she
wove two-color napkins; she taught Sanya to weave them, as well
as his cousin Zhenya and Zhenya's mother, Aunt Kira.

"O, *jetzt muss ich mich...*" Mariya Adolfovna whispered, and
stayed where she was. Sanya's mother looked at the old woman
with pity and wiped her eyes. But on the whole Mariya Adolfovna
was not to be pitied. She was going back to Moscow, to her little
room on Arbat Street opposite the Ars Cinema, to all the interesting ferment of city life. On the other hand, Mariya Adolfovna
was utterly alone, did not like the cinema and rarely went outside.

"Mariya Adolfovna, dear, there's no need to rush off any-where," said Sanya's mother. "You're perfectly welcome to spend the night."

"No, no! Why? I realize I'm an outsider here."

"You're not at all an outsider, Mariya Adolfovna, but you must understand that I shan't have any way of paying you now. That's all. There's no secret about it."

"*Ach, Gott.*" Mariya Adolfovna nodded and blew her nose; the hand holding her handkerchief was large, with gnarled fingers like a man's, and big veins. Mariya Adolfovna did not have the strength to leave. Sanya's mother was worried.

Then Mariya Adolfovna said they did not need to pay her anything; she would work for nothing. But his mother could not agree to that. No, that would not be suitable. That was not possible. She kissed the old woman, told her what a marvelous person she was, how over the past three years they had become friends so that they were like close family now, but how life had changed and could never be the same again. His mother said, "We'll probably have to part with the dacha as well."

Sanya stood in the corner of the room, listening pensively to the conversation and looking at the women. His mother's words about having to part with the dacha hurt him badly and he felt fear in the face of the inevitable. They weren't merely leaving it; they were parting with it. And Mother could talk so calmly about such terrible things.

Mariya Adolfovna suddenly embraced Sanya's mother and said reproachfully, "Why don't you let me help you a bit? *Ach, Gott.*" And then she whispered, "I'm cross with that Kira of yours."

"No, no; thank you," said his mother. "I have a son; he'll help. Thank you, dear Mariya Adolfovna. Don't be cross with Kira; it's just that Boris Alexandrovich had to make an urgent business trip and he took them with him."

Sanya knew that that was not quite true. His mother was dissembling, hiding the truth. The fact was that mother's sister, Aunt Kira, her husband Boris and their little daughter Zhenya used to go to the dacha often and stay there for long periods. His father had a joke about them: "Only with DDT!" The origin of the joke was this: Father was once given some unexpected leave time and he decided to go and stay at the dacha: but with Mother and Sanya, and no relatives. How could they get rid of Boris and Kira? They decided to pretend that the dacha needed to be fumigated because of the bugs and that everyone had to go back to Moscow. There were in fact quite a few bugs around. Boris and Kira left. And Father and Mother stayed. Granted, with the bugs, but at least on their own—and with Sanya, of course. Hence the catchphrase "Only with DDT." And now, two days ago, Boris had turned up unexpectedly and said that Aunt Kira and Zhenya must leave immediately, that same evening, because they were late. Aunt Kira was crying and explaining something to Sanya's mother. Sanya guessed that they were not late for anything, but that they did not want to live in Sokoliny Bor anymore; that Boris didn't want to: Aunt Kira perhaps would have stayed, but she was afraid of quarrelling with Boris. Yet Mother did not take offense and said, "They have no choice."

Now Mariya Adolfovna had left also. It became empty and quiet at the dacha. Mother was out working during the day and he wandered through the rooms alone, lounging about with a book, first on one bed, then on another, doing what he wanted, while everything around him was at his disposal, but bare and lifeless. Once at the end of summer Mariya Adolfovna turned up again, ostensibly to take a stroll to Sokoliny Bor. Excruciating moments. Mariya Adolfovna shed tears again, pressed a few sweets into his hand and then disappeared forever. A year later, Sanya's mother decided to visit her—there had been no word from the old woman and they were afraid she had died; but Mother found her alive and well on the boulevard with some children. Mariya Adolfovna was glad to see her and dried her eyes with her gnarled mannish fingers. Taking Sanya's mother to one side, she told her in a whisper, as if divulging a tremendous secret, "They told me *es ist besser, ich sehe Sie* never again!" His mother had for

some reason never connected this simple—and so very familiar—reason for dropping out of sight with Mariya Adolfovna.
She had considered her too old and lonely for such circumspection. But now the old woman wanted to take her charges along
Gogol Boulevard with an easy mind and in complete compliance
with the laws in force, and she shouted at the laggards and scolded
those who ran ahead with "Remember, Seryozha: *der Esel geht
immer voran!*" This "ass's wisdom" was practically the only thing
that stuck in Sanya's memory from the homilies of Mariya Adolfovna, may she rest on a bed of down. The circumspection and
the tears were unable to cajole the fates—there was thunder in
the heavens; gigantic forces collided, and the destinies of millions
of old women were merely flashes which sparked for an instant:
in the summer of '41 Mariya Adolfovna left Moscow and went
east. And of course soon died, for she was on the threshold of
the final disappearance. Who knew, though? Perhaps she did not
die soon. Perhaps to this day she was even alive, ninety-seven
years old, and in the evenings still weaving woolen napkins on
her octagonal frame.

With the departure of Aunt Kira and Boris and Mariya Adolfovna, people began breaking away. Mother had guessed it would
be like that and was herself the first to make haste, without
recriminations against anyone. She found excuses for them all.
This one was ill, that one was fainthearted, he had too large a
family, the other one's job was too responsible. And when the
neighbors came by with their nasty gossip, such as that frightful
bore Elza Petrovna or the loudmouthed hussy Agrafena, the wife
of Vasily Kuzmich the dacha caretaker (everyone called her
Granka; she would scold and swear over the slightest trifle, the
linen, the vegetable garden or the fact that Sanya had squashed
a flower bed with his bicycle, but in actual fact because she
wanted to sting people a bit, tickle their nerves and take pleasure
in it)—in those days, people didn't dare just come over and start
a fight—even for them Mother would find words of justification.

"You have to feel sorry for Elza," she used to say to Sanya.

"Since Yan Yanovich died, her character has gone downhill. Granya, the poor thing, is just very envious, especially of people who have children...."

But Mother was not always kind, and sometimes would come out with something venomous or extraordinarily witty. "Elza's face is like a stomach pickled in formaldehyde. It is, isn't it?"

Sanya guffawed. If his mother says it, it must be so! Yes, yes! Such a nice little stomach pickled in formaldehyde. With tiny little bristles. But more likely a cow's stomach than a human's. She can't talk about anything but her grass and the vegetable garden. Incidentally, he never had visited her garden. The visitations were the work of the hands—or rather the legs—of Ruska or Skorpion.

Granya and Vasily Kuzmich lived in the basement of the big house. Everyone tried to ingratiate himself a bit with Kuzmich, and all were even slightly afraid of him although he was a quiet man, uncommunicative, good-natured, mustached, not a drinker or a smoker; he just used to walk about the colony with his broom and rake, burning trash and forever repairing the well. This repair work consisted of his hiring laborers from the village of Tatarovo and of their squatting around the well and smoking. The reason people sucked up to Kuzmich was that he was the most stable and long-standing member of the community, in contrast to the others, whose tenancy was as precarious as the birds'. One day they were living there, next day they were not; now a whole horde of them would be making whoopee, now they were boarding up the windows and doors; now you see them, now you don't. Others appeared. Everything was constantly confused and ever-changing, but Granya and Kuzmich were always in residence in their basement home at any time of the year, through the depths of winter and the impassable autumn slush.

Once upon a time on the land where the five cooperative dachas now stood there had been a manor house, which was burned down in the Revolution—in the summer of 1917 actually, so that it was not the new regime which was guilty of this act of arson but some spirited fellows from across the river who decided to take the law into their own hands. The name of the lady of the manor lingered on in the memories of the dairymaids and woodcutters and the old women who came around the dachas hawking mushrooms and berries: it was Korzinkina. Korzinkina: not a trace was left of her apart from the beautiful white stone gateposts, like those of a cemetery, with pyramid tops, gateposts they did not manage to burn down, and the stony road paved in ancient cement—cracked and extremely dangerous for cyclists: Sanya often used to take a tumble there and scrape his knees. That legendary Korzinkina appeared quite distinctly in Sanya's imagination: corpulent, with a large face and thick, drooping lips, wearing a long black coat flared out at the bottom like a bell, who sometimes would be whisked off the ground by some supernatural power and would fly about in a blaze of sparks over the houses, over the pines like Gogol's witch.

Something else remained of the former estate besides its cemetery gates: the little wooden house near the entrance where the caretaker had lived. The only reason the little lodge escaped burning was probably because it belonged to a workingman— who nonetheless vanished together with the owners. The lodge was neatly constructed of heavy beams on a stone foundation, with high porch steps, a small veranda, two rooms and a kitchen. In 1926, when a group of educated Muscovites of proletarian extraction selected this burned-out waste ground for the Stormy Petrel Dacha Cooperative (another cooperative, the Falcon, had its origins at the same time; it subsequently grew into an enormous Moscow district with its own Metro station), that lodge was the only building on the land. Nobody had his eye on it and so Martyn Ivanovich Izvarin, an employee of the Workers' and Peasants' Inspectorate, the Rabkrin, moved in with his wife and son.

A year later the dachas were already springing up. The first was a cumbersome two-story affair, with four verandas and an attic, which housed several families. That was where Sanya's first

friend lived, Ruska Letunov—protector, offender, fighter of Ta-
tars and discoverer of the seamy secrets of life—along with his
little crybaby sister Vera. In the attic of the same house lived red-
haired Myuda, so named in honor of MYD, International Youth
Day. Then two slightly smaller dachas appeared, in one of which
lived a famous professor who strolled about the cooperative in a
silk dressing gown and a *tyubeteika*, and who was called for by
a black Rolls-Royce which had a little window in the roof for
ventilation; the professor's son Skorpion used to invite Sanya to
come for a ride to the bus terminal and back. In the other dacha
lived the Marchioness, who adored dogs and cats and detested
children. Then, finally, a two-story detached house went up
which for some reason was named "The Cottage"; in one of its
apartments lived Slavka Prikhodko and in the other lived and
bellowed the rambunctious family of Burmin, an old lecturer
and propagandist. Sanya's father knew Burmin from the eastern
front, but they did not have much to do with each other in
Sokoliny Bor, and whenever they met outdoors they would ban-
ter. Father thought Burmin was stupid (Sanya used to hear him
say, "That fool Semyon") and adopted a skeptical attitude to his
feats of military prowess and even to his decoration. On the other
hand, he did respect Letunov, Ruska's father, and called him a
sensible fellow. Alexander Martynovich could remember his
mother saying, "Pasha Letunov was the only one who did the
sensible thing: after the war he went and got a degree and became
an engineer, not like us duffers." Ruska's father visited Sokoliny
Bor only seldom, sometimes not for months—he was working
up north in the Urals; and Ruska's mother, Aunt Galya, a good
woman, used to go away on long visits to him while Ruska and
Vera would be left on their own—the rickety woman responsible
for looking after them, who was either a maid or a relation, did
not count. In any case, she would go off to Moscow for weeks
on end, leaving Ruska and Vera to their own devices.

In their apartment, games and entertainments were invented,
tournaments, card games, heaven knows what. Canvas curtains

would be hung on the veranda, the hullabaloo would start, and the floor above would be pounded with a stick. What Ruska called the Bolshoi Theater...darkness and shame, crushed out of memory and buried. He wanted to become a great artist, a great writer, but the first thing he ever did—at age eight—was a great piece of stupidity; parents bawled at each other, thrashed their children, forbade them to go outside. Yet, was it Ruska's fault? Everyone was to blame. First and foremost the foolish grown-ups who abandoned their children to silly women and dashed off to health resorts or meetings or—in the case of some, like the chin-tufted Burmin—set themselves up as the smashers of old norms of behavior and the creators of new ones.

Well, of course it all started with Burmin's eccentric ideas, which seemed so silly and such fun! Burmin, his wife, his wife's sisters and their husbands were devotees of "the naked body" and of the "down with modesty" society, and often used to walk around near their dacha in the garden—and sometimes even in the public vegetable plots where many people would assemble in the evenings—in an indecent state: that is, in their birthday suits. The other residents were outraged—the professor wanted to write to the Moscow Council—but Sanya's mother just laughed and said it was an illustration of the tale of the emperor's new clothes. She once quarreled with his father, who forbade Sanya to go to the vegetable plots while those "buffoons" were larking about. Father really had it in for Burmin because of that "down with modesty" business. Yet the others just laughed. Burmin was gaunt, tall and bespectacled and reminded one more of Don Quixote than of Apollo; the Burmin women were no raving beauties, either. True enough, they were marvelously sunburned. And all of them striking, straw-color blondes. The smallest of the straw-color blondes was Maiya, Sanya's coeval and friend. The face has vanished, the voice has been forgotten, but to the end of his days he will feel a kind of wafting breath of warmth from the name Maiya. Could it have been love at that grassy, butterfly age? For Sanya it was. He was in love with her hair. When he glimpsed her shining golden head bobbing among the verdure, he felt terrified and joyful and as if his strength was abandoning him; he wanted to fall down and lie there motionless like a beetle, pretending to be dead. Maiya was not like the other Burmins: she talked slowly, looked at things pensively and never walked around the garden without a stitch like the others.

He remembered his feeling of disgust and terror the first time he saw grown-up people naked. At the time, Burmin was teaching somewhere. Precisely what and precisely where no one knew; he used to write articles on questions of education, enlightenment and history about which Izvarin Senior commented disrespectfully, employing the word "poppycock." It was a mystery what lectures Burmin could be capable of giving. He had spent two years in a parish school, and the rest he had picked up in exile with the help of books and friends. He played an important part in the Civil War, but since then had been eclipsed and pushed to one side and had given his mind over to silly twaddle—the same tomfoolery Sanya's father referred to scornfully—such as pedagogics, raising children in communes, and sun worship. Nudism, but with a sort of *progressive* tinge. It all came to a head once in a full-scale row. But was it really stupidity as his father said? Was he truly stupid, that land surveyor's son with the goatee who was swept up onto the crest of a wave of monstrous force? Now, more than three decades later, what seemed axiomatic then, Burmin's stupidity, seemed doubtful. After all, he alone of those educated people who founded the Stormy Petrel bored right through those years of red-hot coals, ablaze with fire, and emerged *unscathed* from the flames into the cool of ripe old age and new times. They say he died recently. Apparently Ruska's father is still alive, though he had a plateful: he got scorched; and it was not stupidity that saved him, but fate.

Sanya had heard about old man Letunov from Ruslan, whom he met by chance on the street several years ago. His former friend had become incredibly self-important, respectable and paunchy, his head of gray hair fluffed up like a provincial actor's.

He was chief engineer of some factory or other. What about the other old people? Wiped out, carried off, drowned, rumbled away... Sanya was only guessing, for he had not been there for decades, was not keen to know anything, shunned people and got talking only because Ruslan had buttonholed him and bawled, "Sanka! Still alive, goddam you?"

Back then, in those rooms with the window blinds (surely he hadn't forgotten?) that gray-haired paunchy boy had made them— some with a whisper, others by force—take off their underwear and nonchalantly do as the grown-up Burmins did in their garden: without embarrassment walk around stark naked, jump, lie around or fight. This was his Bolshoi Theater. The land surveyor's son countered the raging dacha dwellers with "Children have to see and know everything! Don't be sanctimonious hypocrites!" Sanya saw the little golden body with a shudder as it flew from room to room, quivering involuntarily like a butterfly in flight. "Only petit bourgeois people are afraid of a beautiful naked body!" Burmin roared, his color heightening, his fist shaking. "The bourgeois hide their filthy souls beneath their hypocritical clothes!"

Then followed beatings, slaps, beltings and Sanya's mother's cry of "Martyn Ivanovich will tell the Rabkrin! Unless that obscenity stops!" And forever and ever that sunburned, shame-free, forbidden thing aglow in the golden beam which percolated through the chink. Then at the end of summer—even before the river became navigable and turbid from fuel oil, when on both sides yellow sandbanks were still visible and you could even wade across the river in some parts—Sanya heard a woman wailing. Terrible and low like the horn of a steamship. Maiya's mother ran along the riverbank and wailed; suddenly she fell and several people rushed over to her. A crowd was milling about by the water. Some boys dashed down the slope, taking enormous leaps in their haste, over to the crowd. Sanya too ran up to them and saw Maiya, the same as always, only with her eyes closed and her hair lying across her face like grass....

Far, far away—from everything: from childhood, from book

madness, from steamships, from the stream, from people breaking away... From Ruska's shout when he was hit by an iron pipe and fell. They were seeing who could throw a piece of water pipe the farthest. When it came to Sanya's turn, the thing shot out of his hand, flew to one side and hit Ruska on the shin. He lay in a cast for a month and a half. Ruska's mother, Aunt Galya, uttered not a word of reproach! But someone—it could almost have been that same old man with the big nose—said at the meeting, "The father sabotaged the job he was on and the son is doing the same thing in his own circle, crippling other children." Mother could not bear it. She burst out crying and started shouting at the meeting. Aunt Galya took her by the hand and led her home, took care of her like an invalid, and the next day Mother told him not to set foot on that old man's veranda and never to speak to him. "You've never seen a scoundrel, have you, Sanya? From now on you'll know: that bald man is a scoundrel." He asked, could he still play with Slavka? "You can play with Slavka," said his mother. "A son is not responsible for his father."

One day, Agrafena came by and asked if she could take a look at the cellar and the woodshed. Sanya's mother said, yes, of course she could, but then suddenly wondered, "But why do you want to look, Granya?" Agrafena had already opened the little door under the veranda which was held shut by a nail, and was about to dive into the darkness of the cellar, when she stopped halfway.

"What do you mean, 'why?,' Klavdiya Alexeevna? Your house is passing to us. You don't expect us to take it sight unseen."

"How is that possible, passing to you? Who said?"

"They said. How do I know?" Agrafena looked at Mother, offended and perplexed. "Why shouldn't it go to us? We've been working for you all this time, living for years on end in that basement. Do you know how damp it is there? Just you try living there."

"I am a full member of this cooperative!" shouted his mother in such a voice that Sanya was terrified. "You wouldn't dare! Not as long as I'm alive! Go away, Granya. Close the cellar door and don't come back here with that nonsense ever again!"

Agrafena left grumbling, "People are living in the basement and a fat lot they care about it."

But it was all over. Mother knew it and Sanya guessed. At the end of the summer Sanya's mother organized a birthday party for him. She wanted it to be the way it was before, in previous years. She did not realize that Sanya knew what had happened and that her endeavors were unnecessary. He could perfectly well have done without the party and not been in the least upset. Of course, he would not have wanted to forgo his new album and the little transparent envelopes with the stamps of the French colonies, but the pie, the flowers, the candy... Of his pals only Ruska and Vera and red-haired Myuda came. Later apparently, about ten years later, Myuda became Ruska's wife. Such a kind creature with her thick lips and her chubby cheeks. Whereas Vera was something of a burden because, he felt, she was attracted to him. And that was the last August with pie, phlox and evening strolls along the riverbank. Mama tried very hard to make everything the way it had always been. It was an incredibly cold evening, unusual for August, even for late August. It was like an October evening. Nobody went swimming. Someone lit a bonfire on the opposite bank, where the ground was low and given to flooding, and, barely visible in the twilight, the fire cast a long, glowing yellow reflection on the icy water, like a candle.

Mama died that winter. His former life crumbled and collapsed like a sandy bank: quietly and suddenly. Something different began: different school, different pals, different beds, different town, not like a town at all, with its wooden pavements and wooden houses. In the dead of winter they brought in the machinery, and a munitions factory was transplanted from Moscow. Why go back and unearth things that are buried in the sand? The bank has collapsed. Along with the pine trees, the benches, the paths strewn with fine gray sand and white dust, the pinecones, the cigarette butts, the pine needles, the shreds of bus tickets, the French letters, the hairpins, the kopek coins which fell out of the pockets of those who once embraced here on warm evenings. Everything was swept downstream in the swirl of the water.

Alexander Martynovich sat at his wife's bedside in the unbearably stuffy, sunbaked ward. He held her hand in his, talked to her about something and thought, I won't tell her. What's the point? Anyway, it's impossible. She might be able to, but I'm not. He was quite calm. The only thing that puzzled him was why the old man had turned up thirty-five years later. He put the question to him bluntly when he phoned him as agreed the evening of the following day.

"Errrr..." He heard a drawn-out bleating sound, then a cough, then a sigh and then that chummy, mumbling voice again. "It's fairly complicated to answer that one. Or perhaps it's too easy; but, you see, you won't believe me. It's a great pity you don't want it. But when I come to think of it, you're right; it isn't an easy business winning a house: there are many pros and cons. You're right, my dear Sanya, to stay away from trouble."

"Do you remember," asked Alexander Martynovich, "that my mother, God rest her soul, once called you a scoundrel?"

There was a pause. In those four or five seconds, Alexander Martynovich had time to think that life was a system in which everything, in some mysterious way and according to some higher plan, was interlaced. Nothing existed independently as bits and pieces; everything stretched on and on, one thing intertwining with another, nothing ever disappearing completely. And therefore, the fairy-tale house, that object of such longing and the cause of night tears, absolutely had to reappear. And here it was: like a lost, once-loved puppy turning up as a doleful, half-dead dog. The old man wheezed scarcely audibly, "You haven't learned a thing about life, Sanya." And hung up.

The next morning they all departed except Ruslan, who had been hanging around the dacha for about a week. Hard to tell whether he was on vacation, whether he had brought work home or whether he was working for such a bunch of amateurs that he could collect his pay without having to go in. Who knows? Useless trying to ask; they wouldn't give you a straight answer. And why were they always so sarcastic? Facetious about everything, whether appropriate or not. Oh, aren't we clever! The two of them had breakfast together. The sun was beating down. Ruslan was barefoot and naked apart from his shorts. Gloomy and unshaven; he drank very strong tea, smoked, and said nothing.

A smell of burning wafted in from the garden. The grim silence was tiring and, unable to restrain himself, Pavel Evgrafovich asked, "Might I inquire why you're not at work today?"

Ruslan put the empty cup on the table and, bunching his fingers together, wiped his mouth—just as Galya used to wipe her mouth. He sat there rocking on his chair as if he had not heard, then picked up the teapot and took a couple of gulps from the spout. Only then did he answer, "Why do you ask? Will it affect the World Revolution?"

Serves you right. Don't butt in, you old goat. Pavel Evgrafovich said peaceably, "You should have a word with him, Ruslan. He's burning his garbage in that tank again, the hooligan."

"Who?"

"Skandakov. Can't you smell that stink coming over?"

"Skandakov!" Ruslan humphed. "Skandakov died days ago. It's he who's gotten burned: cremated. Myocardiac infarction. Don't you know what the smell's from? The forests the other side of Moscow are on fire. The peat's burning. As in the ancient Chronicles: 'And there came to pass a great drought in that season...' Do you remember? That drought was a thousand years ago."

"Yes." Pavel Evgrafovich fell silent, then asked, "Tell me, why do you always use that idiotic, clownish tone of voice when you talk to your father?"

"What?" Ruslan cupped his palm to his ear. "What's that?"

"That's just what I mean. Oh God, I see." Pavel Evgrafovich was in haste to get up and leave him, but Ruslan unexpectedly took him by the arm, pulled him back and forcibly sat him down on the chair like a little boy. He often made use of his superior strength, the impudent puppy.

"By the way, I've been meaning to ask you something: In your opinion is collective reason always right? And is the individual always wrong?"

"Well, how... how can I put it?" Pavel Evgrafovich was glad that his son had asked him a serious question, and wanted to give him a thorough, intelligent reply. He braced himself, collecting his thoughts. "I don't think I can offer you a cut-and-dried answer. Each case has to be examined with all its implications and inconsistencies—in a dialectical manner. What aspect are you interested in?"

"My own. The personal aspect. You see, there's a farce going on: I have to change my job. They're hounding me out of the factory."

"What are you saying?" asked Pavel Evgrafovich, alarmed.

"Nothing terrible about it. I'll find work in no time. But the thing that eats me up is, what if they're right, the bastards? They say I'm a man who's impossible to work with. They say I'm arrogant, rude, this and that, selfish. I don't take other people's interests into account. I've set my colleagues against me. And this is coming from people I simply didn't expect would talk that way. You could have knocked me over with a feather. The fact is, it's a real persecution campaign; the situation is so bad I can't stay there. That's it, Papa. But that's not my point. I'm not desperate to stay in that hole. What gets me is something else: if *everyone* says I'm bad, perhaps I really *am* bad. Maybe I really am such a bastard."

"No, Rusik. No, no. Don't even give it a thought," said Pavel

Evgrafovich heatedly, feeling sudden pity for his son, almost like forty years ago. "You have your faults, of course; who doesn't? But it is possible to work with you. And live with you. I think they've got it wrong—you're not so very selfish; you're not so very concerned about yourself."

"Well, they think differently. I really don't know what to think about myself. It's not nice, you know, when people tell you you're a bad person. If they say, 'You're a bad employee, a bad engineer,' you can think, to hell with them, let them—but when they call you a bad person... it's not nice."

"You're not a bad person at all. But, of course..." Pavel Evgrafovich hesitated; he was about to say that Ruslan's faults included a certain slovenliness, a flippancy and a disrespectful way of talking which might not be to the liking of his co-workers. However, he thought it better not to spell it out. He stroked his son's graying hair and said, "Deep down, you're a good, kind person. You don't live exactly the way I'd like you to, but what can you do?"

They fell silent. Ruslan mumbled something incoherent as he rocked back and forth on his chair, looking into the garden.

"What's bad in my life?" he asked.

"Bad? Nothing. But there's no good either. You don't have a home. There's no warmth."

Ruslan let out an "Ah" as if to say, "So that's what you want." Then he sighed and agreed, "You're right, Father. Yes, yes. You're right. I have neither one nor the other, not a blessed thing. I don't have a blue Volga either, like that show-off over there," he said, and nodded in the direction of the path where, behind the trees, Kandaurov's Volga was slowly turning around. "And why is it I've ended up with nothing? When everyone else has it all? It's not Moscow he's zoomed off to; he's been someplace else: a state farm, maybe. So he must have had a reason. He's not about to waste gas on nothing. Good God, why do I make all this fuss? It's almost all been done, the picture's painted; the only thing left is a trifle, a few petty details. Well, to hell with

them. By the way, I'm off in a couple of days. Going to fight
fires. Somewhere near Egorevsk. They were calling for volunteers. 'Whosoever thou mayest be; gentle knight or simple soldier.'"

"You volunteered?" exclaimed Pavel Evgrafovich, seriously
alarmed. "Why? You're out of your mind! Let the young ones
go, but you're fifty years old. And your heart, you idiot. My
goodness..."

"Rubbish. My heart's okay. But sitting in the office and looking
at their ugly mugs—that makes me sick! I can't vouch for myself—I'll either say something or hurt somebody. I'll take a swing
at someone; then you'll be bringing me care packages. Better to
be on the fire line, saving our forests, our wealth."

Shattered and perplexed, Pavel Evgrafovich looked at his son.
Was he really fifty years old? There was something adolescent
about him, immature; a rowdy, a playboy, a wastrel. His hair
was graying, he dressed like an engineer, yet he spoke like a bum.
He pointed his finger at his father in a threatening, derisive,
patronizing way as if he were the father and Pavel Evgrafovich
the son.

"I know you, my fine friend! You'll take advantage of my
absence. You'll turn around and break your promise. Be sure to
talk to Prikhodko, okay?"

Oleg Vasilevich set off early in the morning for
the state farm to look for Mitya, nicknamed Zhalizo, and Krivoi—One-Eye—and also Zuchkovsky, from the little village of
Zhuchkovo where Mitya was born but where he never managed
to live: he either got dragged off to Moscow on construction jobs
or wound up on a state farm, or in a dacha colony as a caretaker,
or got recruited along with his cronies to go out to Kuban—good
jobs all. The name Zhalizo was because he was forever appearing
with some business proposition, always asking in a soft conspir-
atorial tone, "Need any jalousies for the window?" Oleg Vasi-

levich knew Mitya well, considered him to be an artful dodger
and a knave and did not believe a single word he said or any of
his promises, but reckoned that there was no point quarreling
with him, that he was a *necessary* artful dodger and a *useful*
knave—although he had quarreled with him and bawled him
out on more than one occasion, and had banished him in fits of
temper, swearing that he would not shell out a single ruble more.
But after a while he would roll up again with another one of his
wretched propositions or his enticing wares, such as watering
cans or cement paving stones, and Oleg Vasilevich, swallowing
his pride, once more would start up his disreputable relationship
with him, lending him money and drinking vodka with him on
the veranda. But those long-standing contacts were with the old
Mitya he had grown used to, the one he could coddle and be
benevolent to, and tell him at any time where to get off—the
wheeler-dealer Mitya, the dodger, the slogger, the sponger and
fellow boozer. But not at all the Mitya he had now become.
After all, now he was a rival! It was true he was not a major
threat, probably quite a doubtful one—he wasn't a member of
Agrafena's immediate family, but was a nephew—but anything
could happen. Good people and kind neighbors never failed to
spring something on you, some dirty trick. Mitya had made an
appearance in his new role only twice: at the funeral and the day
after, when he and two of his pals pulled up in a truck with the
intention of loading up all Agrafena's stuff right then and there,
dresser, bed, television, sewing machine, and making a quick
getaway. If Polina Karlovna had been home on her own, they
would have pulled it off smoothly. But Zina sent for one of the
board members and Taisiya the bookkeeper, who asked him what
grounds did he have? They told him he had to prove his inher-
itance rights. Mitya bawled at them, and his pals hurled curses
at him in his turn. The three of them were slightly tipsy, in that
wonderful frame of mind of anticipating a great spree any minute
now, but then it was taken away—if not forever, then at least
postponed indefinitely—which was unbearable. They flew into

a purple rage, and Taisiya ran for the police. Taisiya was a reliable sort. Quite a lot had been put into it, but it would not go to waste, for it was like money in a Swiss bank—it would never disappear, and would keep earning interest. Taisiya could roar and curse with the best of the men. But Mitya's wife—totally unsuited to him; a nice-looking woman, how did she live with that creature?—did not get down from the cab and only groaned plaintively, "Mitya, leave them be. Mitya, let's go."

The co-op party held their ground, with the help of Valera the policeman, who roared up in his boneshaker. After which, Mitya disappeared for a long time. He went off somewhere with a work crew. And then a week ago he turned up again. Polina Karlovna heard someone rattling along with a wheelbarrow. She stepped onto the porch and saw Mitya walking along the flagstone path with Agrafena's iron wheelbarrow, a very practical thing in which Agrafena used to tote earth, fertilizer, bricks and fallen leaves.

"Mitya," said Polina Karlovna, "how come you're taking it without permission? It doesn't belong to you, you know."

"Nor to you neither!" snapped Mitya. And he walked away with the wheelbarrow without looking back.

But this was nothing. Mitya did not scare Oleg Vasilevich. The main thing was not to let him get away with his insolence. He remembered their first summer here about eight years ago when they did not know anyone yet and were living on their own (Agrafena was in the hospital—she was always somewhere getting treatment, being examined or under observation, a highly tedious woman: all conversations with her were about illness and medicine). A lopsided fellow came along wearing a hand-me-down jacket, a cloth cap down over his nose, one eye screwed up— whence the nickname Krivoi—and asked whether they needed any glass. He was holding under his arm two large panes of glass wrapped up in cloth. Oleg Vasilevich told him they did not need any. The other insisted they take it, saying that the lady of the house, his aunt, had ordered it, and here it was. The fellow smelled of alcohol, and Oleg Vasilevich chased him away. In the middle of the night they were awakened by a crashing and a clinking. They tore out of their room and saw that the glassed-in side of the veranda facing the fence had been smashed and was lying in smithereens on the ground. Also lying on the ground was a massive cobblestone. Someone had thrown it from the road. And there was no doubt who. The next day the smart aleck showed up as if nothing had happened and again started whining that maybe they would take the glass. Maybe they needed it? "You told me to get it; I've paid money for it." Oleg Vasilevich complained to him that some rascals had thrown a stone over the fence and that now the glass would come in handy. There happened to be nails, a hammer and a glass cutter in Mitya's pocket, so he got down to work at once and within an hour had repaired the whole thing beautifully.

"Thank you, thank you," said Oleg Vasilevich, shaking Mitya by the hand. "Take care of yourself! Come and see us sometime, my dear fellow."

"What about the sixteen rubles?" said Mitya in surprise. "As we agreed?"

"Wha-a-at?" roared Oleg Vasilevich, and, grabbing the nape of Mitya's scrawny neck in his steely fingers, he squeezed him so tightly that Mitya winced and dropped down. "I'll teach you to throw stones around! I'll put you inside for three years, you lousy bastard! I'll smash your jaw for you, you bag of bitch's guts! Clear out before I kill you!"

And you can bet that Mitya did clear out, for Oleg Vasilevich had pounded him good and hard—he fell to his knees, then onto his side, rolled over, jumped up and ran away in shock. Since then, relations had normalized. Agrafena did not like her nephew and was afraid of him; often when Mitya paid a visit she would lock herself in her room and tell them to say she was not at home. He used to try to get money out of her; he was persistent and bad-tempered, and she did not have the willpower to refuse him.

Oleg Vasilevich found Mitya in the workshop at the copper-work bench, where he was hammering out a tinplate gutter on the mandrel with a wooden mallet. Judging by the zeal with which Mitya was working—the sweat was streaming down his shoulders and cheeks, his mouth was open and his eyes gazed at the visitor with a senseless look, not recognizing at once who it was—it was obvious that he was engaged on a rush job, and not for the State, that the client could not wait and that Mitya was in a hurry.

"Well? What's up?" He reluctantly tore himself away from his mandrel and mallet.

They went outside and sat down in the shade. Mitya's bare chest sported a tattoo of an eagle with an inscription below it: "Life is like a baby's nightdress...." The second line was lost in the crease of his stomach. But Oleg Vasilevich knew it well. Trying to sound as equable and good-humored as possible, although he had a feeling that he was in for a hard and bad time, and that Mitya had somehow changed, he asked, "What's it to be, then, artful dodger?"

"So when are you moving to Moscow? September, or earlier?" asked Mitya instead of answering.

Oleg Vasilevich grinned, took out a pack of Philip Morrises and flicked out a cigarette. He offered it to Mitya, who—surprise again!—scornfully shook his head and produced from his trousers pocket a crumpled, squalid-looking pack of Dukats. He placed half a broken Dukat in a cigarette holder and lit up with an important air.

"Got your hopes up?" asked Oleg Vasilevich. "Well, forget it! You don't have anything to hope for. You're not a direct heir; you're a nephew and according to the law nephews don't inherit. I'm giving it to you straight. You can believe me. So, Mitya, things don't look so good for you."

"Well!" said Mitya, and he bent his head down low, screwed up his eyes and gave Oleg Vasilevich a very crafty look. "Well, what the fucking hell have you come for?"

"I'm just about to tell you. But first you've got to understand that you don't have any rights. Absolutely no rights whatsoever. You're on what you might call a wild-goose chase."

"Well!" repeated Mitya in a more mocking tone of voice, bending his head lower and screwing up his eyes even more craftily. "What about a dependant? If someone's a dependant?"

"I take it you mean that you're a dependant? Agrafena's dependant? Oh, Mitya! Don't make me laugh! Ha, ha! They've been leading you on and you believe them, you ninny. Who told you that crap?"

"Smart people told me. There are smarter people than you, you know. Anatoly Zakharych told me: Grafchikov. He's a top-notch guy; he gave me the whole picture."

"You know where you can go kiss your Grafchikov, don't you?" said Oleg Vasilevich, heating up. "Why is he trying to confuse you, the creep? You're not a dependant at all. Granka never kept you. She couldn't bear the sight of you! You were like the plague to her. She would hide under the bed from you."

"But she gave me money all the way."

"Vodka money!"

"Who's to know?"

"Everyone knows! You're a famous boozer. Everyone'll bear me out."

"Well, you're an idiot to think that way," said Mitya calmly. "No one'll believe you, 'cause you know yourself... they don't exactly worship you, Vasilych. Anyway, Grafchikov—Anatoly Zakharych—he told me. 'I'll confirm,' he says, 'that Granya gave you money for your room and board. Don't you worry,' he says to me."

"That's a load of rubbish. How can you be her dependant when you've got a wife? She should be the one to keep you, not your aunt."

"What the fucking hell for? Klavka's not my wife; she's a sort of stray. We aren't registered."

"Okay, but you work, you have a trade: you're a tinsmith and a roofer. Hell, you can provide for yourself. Stronghearts like you, dependants! It's ludicrous!"

"It's not so ludicrous, my friend, when you don't have your health. I work a month, then I'm out sick for two. My heart is weak. My liver's bad. My liver's really calling it quits. I'm taking drops for it, you understand? So don't buck me, Vasilych. My message to you is, clear out. Get it?"

Oleg Vasilevich said nothing while he thought. Then he said, "Okay! This is all idle chatter, a waste of time. Now I'm going to tell you why I came. But not here. I don't like it here." Oleg Vasilevich surveyed the workshop yard with disgust. There really was little of beauty to be seen—rusty machine tools, axles, a wheelless trailer, boxes and garbage. "Let's go to the junction, sit there quietly and have a serious talk."

For a split second a desperate zigzag of inner struggle was visible on Mitya's face, then without a word he went inside the building, returned and made a quick victory sign with his hand, the kind soccer players make when they have scored a goal, which meant "Let's go!" Half an hour later they were sitting at a table beneath the white awning of the Rest Café. They ordered three bottles of sour Romanian wine, that being the only thing there was, a package of wafer cookies and a few candies—Oleg Vasilevich noticed that Mitya was pleased with the humble repast, although he did not eat a single cooky or candy—and they conducted their conversation in an undertone.

Oleg Vasilevich told him bluntly that it was a complex matter and perhaps Mitya would win, perhaps he wouldn't; he probably wouldn't, because the highest trumps were in Oleg Vasilevich's hand. This and that, and, into the bargain, the other thing. "So don't waste your effort, buddy, you'll sink to the bottom." They ordered another two bottles. The place they had to run to turned out to be nearby, so they just hopped over the fence. Mitya was getting sober, not drunk: the situation was becoming clear to him. "If you fight it, go to court and get into a legal wrangle, you'll get nothing; you'll just give yourself a bad time." On the

other hand there was compensation: ready cash. A hundred rubles. Either goose egg or a hundred—which was better? But of
course Mitya—no fool he—scoffed at that amount and made
his own suggestion: five hundred. They began haggling. It went
on for a long time; they sparred, got excited, worked themselves
up into a sweat, then finally agreed on a hundred and seventy.

"Just one thing, though, Vasilych, do you hear me?" said
Mitya, pointing a threatening finger at him. "The money now!
Or else it'll be what you always do—next week, on Tuesday or
Screwsday."

"Here's the money. A hundred rubles. You'll get the seventy
after the general meeting; the same day. Now sign here."

Mitya wrinkled up his brow as he scrutinized the sheet of paper
where Oleg Vasilevich, on his Triumph typewriter, had spelled
out Mitya's terse renunciation of any claim on Agrafena's house.
He gave a grunt and a sweat and looked at Oleg Vasilevich as if
a thought had suddenly occurred to him, which was on the tip
of his tongue and which would stalemate his opponent, but then
he did not say what it was and signed. It was four o'clock. The
whole day had gone on Mitya; he too had to be pressed *right up
to the hilt*. Nothing yields without a struggle; everything has to
be grabbed, squeezed out! Many pressing jobs he had planned
for today had fallen by the wayside.

Oleg Vasilevich felt weighed down and enervated from the
sour wine and the hellish heat; there was a racket in his head.
He felt like diving into the river and sitting in the water until
evening, but the two hours he still had in hand until the offices
closed sent him to Moscow. And he did manage to achieve a
certain amount. That evening, he sat after his shower in a wicker
chair on the balcony of his Moscow apartment, wearing knit
shorts and rubber beach sandals as if he were at the seaside, and,
as he relished the peace, the shade, the feeling of success and
the sensation of the rightness of his whole up-to-the-hilt life, he
took a pencil and checked off in his notebook the errands he had
accomplished. He crossed off the list: Mitya; Shipping Office;

Housing Office; next volumes; and Potapov. Potapov was his code name for Svetlana. He had said goodbye to Potapov. So that errand too, however bitter, however heartrending, had been completed and should be crossed off. Come to think of it, she was leaving tomorrow. What about today? The evening was free. He hesitated a bit, feeling sorry for her and rather disapproving of himself. But to forgo this evening would be to betray his principle, for this evening, the eve of her departure: that was *the hilt*. Quickly getting up from his chair, he went inside to the telephone. Svetlana's number did not answer. He tried twice and waited a long time.

Just when he had replaced the receiver his telephone rang.

A familiar, melodious voice said, "Oleg Vasilevich? Finally! I've been ringing you all day. You weren't there. It's Angelina Fyodorovna."

"Yes!" he said, not grasping immediately who it was. "Oh, Angelina Fyodorovna! What can I do for you?"

"It's nothing special, Oleg Vasilevich. I just wanted to ask you to come tomorrow and bring another urine sample. Could you do that?"

Before Oleg Vasilevich had time to think, a slight, instantaneous chill in the pit of his stomach came in response to her words. He asked stupidly, "Why?"

"We occasionally request a second sample in certain cases. When we're in doubt about something and we want to be sure."

"Angelina Fyodorovna, tomorrow is really impossible for me. I'm meeting a delegation at Sheremetyevo Airport," Oleg Vasilevich lied, unconsciously on the defensive.

"That's all right, you can come the day after tomorrow," agreed Angelina Fyodorovna. "Come the day after tomorrow in the morning."

A cast-iron weight; the forests were burning, Mos-
cow was dying of asphyxia, suffocating from the livid, ashy, brown,
reddish, black fog—different colors at different times—that filled
the streets and houses with a slow-moving cloud which spread
like mist or like poison gas. The smell of burning permeated
everywhere; there was no escaping it. The lakes turned to sandy
shallows, the river revealed its rocks, the water barely trickled
from the faucets, the birds did not sing; life on this planet had
come to an end, killed by the sun. In the evening they related
all sorts of horrors. Vera had seen a man fall down on the street.
It was like a slow-motion film: he marched in place for a few
paces, throwing his knees up high, then his head slumped back
and he collapsed. In the Metro a woman had fainted. *Evening
Moscow* was full of funeral announcements. Stray dogs were being
shot. One old man said the hot weather would last to the end of
October. Pavel Evgrafovich's sister-in-law kept on saying that it
was the nuclear tests which had spoiled the climate—nonsense,
of course. He was annoyed by his sister-in-law's goody-goodiness,
the way she paraded her virtues, and also by her stupidity.

No one denied her merits. Everyone remembered. Galya used
to say, "I'll never forget what Lyuba did for us. If it hadn't been
for Lyuba, the children would have had it." True enough: for
three years until 1940, while they were away—and he was away
even longer because he went to the war—Lyuba was with the
children; she carried them around with her, minded them, went
with them and Galya when they were evacuated to Lysva, and
from there accompanied Ruslan to the front. She saved the dacha
in Sokoliny Bor as well. Thank you for all that. So where was
the stupidity? No, not in the fact that she didn't listen to the
radio and wasn't interested in newspapers and talked stuff and
nonsense at the table, but in her secret belief that she could
somehow stand comparison with Galya. Come on, Lyubochka!
You may be five years younger than your sister, but you don't

compare with Galya either on points or in face or, of course, eyes, so don't even try. Not to speak of intelligence. But you are a good woman. Kind, decent. A thoroughly good woman, unquestionably; everyone knows. All the friends and relations say, "What a good woman Lyuba is!" And some add, "You might say she sacrificed her life for the sake of her sister." Well, not quite. Although it's partly true. In '37, when Lyuba was twenty-nine, a railwayman proposed to her, but she refused him because of the burden she had taken on her shoulders: her sister's children. We all know, remember, appreciate; nothing will make us forget—but to go around like that in an open sarafan as if you were twenty, with your bare back dappled with age spots, is unseemly, Lyubochka.

The doctors had given her some good news and she returned from Moscow cheered up, rejuvenated and bearing strawberries. They sat out on the veranda eating strawberries and drinking tea. They kept the glass casements and the garden door closed to keep out the burning smell. It did not help much. The terrible, bitter smell still got in. When anyone entered or left the veranda, everybody shouted, "The door! The door! Shut the door!" During Ruslan's absence—he had gone to Egorevsk as a fireman, another one of his crazy ideas (though it was clearly no joking matter: the peat bogs were on fire and it was extremely difficult to put them out; the fire had burned far down into the soil)—Nikolai Erastovich had taken upon himself the role of leading man and society entertainer, and was relating news about the fires. Actually not news but essays on the subject. About an old man in the Altai who two years ago had apparently predicted the present drought. And about predictions, forecasts and prophesies in general.

"They say the Ministry of Agriculture takes the old man's advice very seriously. And he gives extremely precise recommendations. He's never once made a mistake...."

The sister-in-law was oohing and ahing in amazement. Silly

goose, she'd believe any old nonsense. Vera, of course, was gazing in adoration at her better half, and the rest of them, sitting around the table—Myuda, Viktor and Valentina—were lapping up what the blatherskite was saying. And what utter rubbish it was! Apparently, science had proven its impotence in the field of prognostication: not a darn thing ever comes true; they always miss the mark. Can't even forecast such a simple thing as next week's weather, not to mention more important matters. They can't, they can't; it's beyond them. Even with the building blocks they have it doesn't follow that they can erect a building. You need something extra. What? you may ask. A fresh approach to everything.

Viktor asked timidly, Why could the Ministry of Agriculture not find out from the old fellow what forecasting methods he used?

Nikolai Erastovich smirked and threw up his hands. "What could he tell them? He himself doesn't understand his methods."

"He probably just doesn't want to," surmised Valentina. "Why should he reveal his secrets?"

"No, that's not the point. He can't."

"Why not?"

"Well, how can I put it?" Nikolai Erastovich hesitated, looked at Vera as if to ask "Should I tell them or not?," then said, "You see, the point is that it is *not the old man in the Altai himself who speaks.*"

"Ah!" said Viktor. "I understand."

"What's there to understand?" Pavel Evgrafovich said, unable to contain himself. "Don't fib, Vitka! There's no understanding that rubbish."

There was a pause. Nikolai Erastovich made no protest, as if he had not heard Pavel Evgrafovich; the others too seemed not to have heard, and in the silence the beating of the gray moths against the windows of the veranda became audible. But naturally his sister-in-law could not sit quietly and let the subject drop. In a sheepish whisper she asked, "Nikolai Erastovich, my dear, please forgive a silly old woman, but I didn't quite understand. What do you mean, it's not he himself who speaks?"

Once again he smirked and shrugged his shoulders. "I didn't mean anything in particular. If you don't understand, then you don't need to understand." He made a magnanimous gesture as if to say "you can go on living: I permit it." "Especially as it would take a long time to explain."

"A long time?" asked Lyuba, surprised. "How long?"

"Very long. A lifetime."

"You're just poking fun at me. Vitya, what do you understand by it? Please explain to your auntie."

Viktor frowned darkly as he gathered his thoughts and his words. He wanted to give an honest explanation, but he could not find the right words and thoughts. At that point, his mother, poor Myuda—Pavel Evgrafovich always pitied her somehow although there was no reason to—came to his assistance:

"You probably meant that the old man makes his predictions in a state of trance? Like in his sleep?"

"Don't gild the pill," said Pavel Evgrafovich. "Lyubov Davydovna, what they're trying to suggest is that the Lord is speaking through the mouth of the old man. That's the whole secret. Nikolai Erastovich is religious and you and I aren't. Therefore, we'll never understand him or he us."

"Really? I don't believe it!" His sister-in-law displayed even greater amazement, as if she had heard a piece of news, although they had spoken and argued about the subject on more than one occasion.

"Surely you, Nikolai Erastovich, an educated man, don't believe in God? Well, I never! I can't agree with that at all! You're talking nonsense!"

Nikolai Erastovich's lips twitched, his cheek grew crimson and he sat for a minute staring straight ahead at the bowl of strawberries. Then he silently stood up and went inside the house.

Verochka whispered in embarrassment, "Lyuba, why are you so tactless?"

"What did I say? I'm simply astounded."

"You're not astounded at all. You've known about it for a long time, don't pretend you haven't. It's not nice the way you both— you and my father—always make out that... You've got to respect other people, different views. There's no prying into another person's soul."

"There isn't any soul!" shouted Pavel Evgrafovich, and he hit his stick against the floor.

Verochka got up with as much alacrity as her bulky body was capable of and looked at her father in senseless stupefaction as if something had struck her dumb, and she followed her spouse off the veranda. Valentina collected the dirty dishes and also left. Viktor rushed into the garden and Pavel Evgrafovich remained alone on the veranda with his sister-in-law, to whom he had nothing to say.

"Vera needs to have thyroid treatments," she said.

Pavel Evgrafovich did not answer. She irritated him. They all did. He did not look in her direction and did not listen to her mumbling. In the black glass were reflected the lampshade, the tablecloth and the hunchbacked figure of an old man at the table with a single tuft of white hair down to his shoulders. Then his sister-in-law left and he had sat by himself for a while when the door opened and Nikolai Erastovich appeared with a lighted cigarette, meaning that he was on his way into the garden, as smoking was not permitted in the house. But Nikolai Erastovich was in no hurry to go outside, and he stood on the veranda puffing tobacco smoke around—an act of brazenness—and then said softly, "They showed their real gratitude to you for your loyal service."

Pavel Evgrafovich felt everything inside him starting to shake with hatred—what hatred exactly he did not know: whether it was his hatred of Nikolai Erastovich or Nikolai Erastovich's tangible hatred of him—and said in a barely audible, sinking voice, "I rendered *no service* to anyone and did not expect any *gratitude*."

Nikolai Erastovich, emitting puffs of smoke, went outside onto the steps. Shortly afterward, Verochka appeared from inside and, passing by without looking at her father, said, "Rusik asked me to remind you about Prikhodko."

"He isn't there," Pavel Evgrafovich called after her.

"He's back. I saw him this morning."

Pavel Evgrafovich went on sitting at the table by himself, looking at his reflection in the black glass. No, he couldn't go anywhere today; his legs were hurting. And his head felt heavy. His pressure had gone up. Go to his room? Seemed early yet. Read? His eyes were bad. Sleep? He wouldn't fall asleep, he would toss around in the dark until about three. Better, then, to stay on the veranda where there were people around. It was light there; the lamp under the big shade was on. He sat like that for a long time. People stopped there on their way from the garden to the house and from the house to the garden, complained about things, sighed, talked among themselves, disappeared behind the door—he paid no attention to them. He looked to the side, engrossed in thought. Though he had no thoughts in particular, as his head was tired. Then the deep night silence set in and there came the sound of light paws padding up the steps and scratching at the door. Arapka entered, embarrassed, apologetic because of the late hour, his head bowed to the ground and his tail swishing. Most delicate animal! Pavel Evgrafovich was happy to see him and went off, trying not to creak or shuffle—everyone had gone to bed by now, some in the house, some in the garden— to find something for the dog in the kitchen.

The same stifling August night: 1919. A village, its name forgotten. The smell of youth—wormwood. Never again were you so strongly permeated by that bitter stuff—wormwood. A courier galloped along with a telegraph message. No one was

asleep that night. How could they be? Mamontov's breakthrough
had numbed us like a hailstorm. At the meeting point of the
Eighth and Ninth Armies about a hundred versts to the west. It
was not in our direction he was straining, but to the north, and
he seemed to be far away, but the whole front was quivering like
a wound that had been barely stitched up. Tambov and Kozlov
had been taken. Then suddenly the night courier arrives with a
telegram: Migulin's corps has moved from Saransk to the front!
Violating all orders. Unauthorized action. Treachery? Turned
coats? Joining forces with Denikin? *Has what they warned about
happened?*

The clear nighttime horror in the steppe with the smell of the
burning grass and the wormwood. First thing: is she really with
him? Asya is tearing herself farther and farther away from me,
over ever more boundless barriers. By now she was over the edge,
reachable only by bayonet and death. Don't lie to yourself. Your
first thought was precisely that: by bayonet and death. There is
even a split second of joy, a moment of hope; for there is a way,
because you immediately *believed it*. Some people from the political department of SouthFront, a wounded commander who
had attempted to fight his way through to Kozlov, a rowdy and
a loudmouth, all of us—cut off by Mamontov's movement from
the headquarters of SouthFront, which used to be in Kozlov and
has vanished northward goodness knows where—all of us, apart
from Shura, instantly accepted the news on faith: By order of
SouthFront, Migulin was declared a traitor and outlawed.

Spending the night with us is a young priest. No, not a priest,
a seminarian. A villager took him in out of pity. The seminarian
is crazy, always laughing quietly and crying; mumbling something. No one notices him or hears his mumblings. He twitters
away in his corner like a bird. All of a sudden he comes up to
me, squats down beside me—he was lanky and gaunt—and,
speaking with significance and sorrow, and pointing a warning
finger at me, says, "'Understand that the name of the star is called
Wormwood: and the third part of the waters became wormwood;

and many men died of the waters, because they were made bitter.'"

I was struck by the words "star" and "wormwood." I did not know that it was a verse from the Bible. They told me afterward, and strangely enough it was someone from the political department who told me, a literate fellow; but at the time I thought it was gibberish, nonsense. The reason he was that way was that they had wiped out his whole family. Somewhere in the South. But we could not understand who had done it, the Whites or the Grigorevites or some Maruska Nikiforova or other. These Maruskas had multiplied like rabbits; each bandit detachment had its own, though I did see a real Maruska Nikiforova in May of '18 near Rostov. Wearing a white Circassian coat with cartridge slots. The priest mumbled incoherently, "'The locusts have devoured... Unclean toads...'"

So there we were sitting that night, discussing, droning on, smoking, when the telegram arrived. Sergei Kirillovich—outlawed. Migulin the hero, the old fighter of the Revolution, could be shot down by anyone. The wounded commander was ranting and raving worse than everyone else: "Traitor! Self-seeker! No wonder the rumors were flying about him! He gave in, the brute! I'd let him have it in a minute, without a second thought."

Everyone was shaken and they were all howling and yelling, blasting and cursing Migulin. Shura alone, as usual, cannot be drawn in.

"Wait until we get the details."

"What details? It's as plain as anything! He chose his time dead right: neither earlier nor later, but precisely now, when Mamontov has broken through the front."

"They had arranged it beforehand!"

"The creep! Colonel!"

"You know, I can't believe it."

"Can't believe the telegram?"

"No, I believe the telegram. And I believe that he has moved. But I don't know the reason."

"Do you believe that SouthFront has declared him an outlaw?"

"I believe that, because there are people who wanted it that way."

"I don't understand what proof you need. When he stands you up against a wall and gives the squad the order to fire, you'll still have doubts, I suppose."

The wounded commander waved his Mauser. "If I had my way, I'd finish that filthy counterrevolutionary bastard off. And no argument!" And he fired into the air from an excess of emotion.

They were angry with Migulin something horrible. Everyone was worked up and nervous; they wanted to do something immediately: move off somewhere, charge off to Borisoglebsk or to Saransk. And then an incident as quick as lightning was played out: basically insignificant, without influence on the course of the war or the destiny of peoples—apart from the destiny of one person, which was indeed irreversibly sealed that night—but an incident which cut into my memory like a knife. The accidental death of a vagrant in the tempest of war. Why did he hurl himself at the man with the Mauser and start shrieking and going berserk? An outburst of madness, an attack of illness. He shouted, "Beast! Begone! Out of my sight!" and grabbed the wounded man painfully by the arm, and the other—also in a moment of madness—discharged his Mauser at the seminarian. Shura ordered him arrested on the spot. I do not recall what they did with him. He was convoyed to Saransk, and then what? Don't recall, don't recall. Then there was a hunt for Migulin, who was moving away westward through the forests.

When people have been afraid of something for too long, that terrible thing happens. But what actually? I believed it in the first minute, then I had doubts, and after that my belief would sometimes grow stronger and sometimes new doubts would appear. After a long life and endless dissection, here I am now, an old man—an "old piece of garbage," as Vera once said when angry not with her father but with another old man who had done her a bad turn—on a hot night in Sokoliny Bor, when life is over. I require nothing; sleeping pills do not help—anyway, what's the point? The sleep which no one can escape is near. So answer this: Why did he do it? I do not need articles, the immortalizing of his memory, the street in Serafimovich: I do not need the monumental truth; I need the small truth, not declaimed publicly but spoken confidentially: *why?*

Here's the file, its cardboard worn shiny, with the yellow rectangle of tracing paper stuck onto the top corner bearing the inscription "Everything on S. K. Migulin." Leaflets, notebooks, letters, copies of documents—everything collected over the years. One more time. Why not now? Why not now, after one o'clock at night? After all, I'm not sleepy. Silly to spare my eyes when I soon won't be needing them.

B ack, back! Back a few months. In order to understand what happened. My heart was broken. But such a dull, tormenting pain.

We parted in March. He was transferred to Serpukhov, then to Smolensk, into the Byelorussian-Lithuanian Army, an absurd banishment, since that army was not conducting operations at the time. Assistant commander of an inactive army. And this at a time when things were really blazing and crackling away on the Don. Denikin was advancing, the Cossack uprising was in full swing, and they wrested him from the battlefield and dumped him out to grass in peace and quiet! Khvesin's corps, which was created to fight the insurgents, botched the job, panicked and retreated. In June they remembered Migulin again. Here is the telegram from Sokolsky, member of the Revolutionary Military Council of the Southern Front, to the Chairman of the RMC of the Republic:

KOZLOV, JUNE 10. DENIKIN DETACHMENT CONSISTING APPARENTLY THREE CAVALRY REGIMENTS BROKEN THROUGH KAZAN-SKAYA. DANGER OF UPRISING SPREADING TO KHOPERSKY AND

UST-MEDVEDITSKY DISTRICTS SIGNIFICANTLY INCREASED. NOW THAT SOUTH FRONT OPEN, TASK OF EXPEDITIONARY CORPS IS OCCUPY LEFT BANK OF DON FROM BOGUCHAR TO UST-MED-VEDITSA, PREVENT UPRISING NORTHERN DISTRICTS. KHVESIN DISCOVERED HELPLESS CONDITION. URGE IMMEDIATE APPOINT-MENT COMMANDING OFFICER OF CORPS MIGULIN, FORMER COMMANDER TWENTY-THIRD DIVISION. MIGULIN'S NAME WILL GUARANTEE NEUTRALITY AND SUPPORT OF NORTHERN DIS-TRICTS, IF NOT TOO LATE. REQUEST IMMEDIATE REPLY KOZLOV. COMMANDER SOUTHFRONT IN COMPLETE AGREEMENT.

SOKOLSKY

The next day, the Chairman of the RMC had this message transmitted by direct telephone:

MOSCOW TO SKLYANSKY. SOKOLSKY INSISTS THAT MIGULIN BE APPOINTED COMMANDER OF EXPEDITIONARY CORPS. NO OBJEC-TION. COMMUNICATE WITH SERPUKHOV. IF REPLY IS AFFIRMA-TIVE, SUMMON MIGULIN IMMEDIATELY.

JUNE 11, 1919
RMC CHAIRMAN TROTSKY

The same people who had *kicked him out and dumped him out to pasture!* Commander-in-Chief Vatsetis agreed to the appointment. Migulin received his orders and the very same day— what am I saying? the very same *hour*—rushed to the Don. Shura was appointed corps commissar, and I of course went with him. Another extract from the file:

INSTRUCTION FROM RMC OF SOUTHFRONT. CHANGE NAME EX-PEDITIONARY CORPS TO SPECIAL CORPS. DIRECTLY SUBORDI-NATE TO SOUTHFRONT. COMMANDER EXP-CORPS COMRADE KHVESIN RELEASED FROM COMMAND WITH PERMISSION ON SURRENDER OF POST TO TAKE PERSONAL SICK LEAVE WHILE REMAINING ON RESERVE COMMAND STAFF OF SOUTHFRONT. COMRADE MIGULIN APPOINTED COMMANDER OF SPECIAL CORPS WITH AUTHORITY OF ARMY COMMANDER. COMRADE MIGULIN IMMEDIATELY ASSUME COMMAND OF CORPS UPON TAKING OVER FROM COMRADE KHVESIN. REPORT ON REACTIONS AND HAND-ING OVER.

End of June, cool summer, rain, warm. We were traveling by armored train to Buturlinovka, where the Corps headquarters was. I met Asya in the train. We had been apart for only four months, and what a transformation! As soon as I saw her I had an impulse to rush forward, embrace her and smother her with kisses, darling person, no one more darling—only Shura—but her cool smile and a nod of her head restrained me. I shook her hand.

"Aska, I'm so pleased to see you! Why are you so thin? Your cheekbones are standing out! Are you lugging guns for him?"

She grinned drily. "I'd be happy to lug them, but you don't give us any guns."

Everything about her was different; she did not get jokes and her look was guarded and wary. Why? It seemed not to show any of the old friendship. No embraces, no horsing around? The whole of the first day after our arrival, and even after that, she tried not to spend much time with me. Migulin too had become thin and shriveled, with his black tuft of a beard, his burning expression, his hasty movements, his sharp voice; he shouted when he spoke, with violent emotion. At the drop of a hat he would call a meeting, assemble a bunch of Cossacks and thunder out a speech—a man possessed. Right now he had one passion: to create his Corps, to create an army and to command it—to save the Revolution! Yet even while thinking of nothing else and taking notice of nothing around him, he still managed to keep a sharp eye on Asya, seeing if she was around and with whom. Those glances of his, naïve, searching, split-second looks of anxiety, at the height of an argument or a speech when he was haranguing mobilized Cossacks—the mobilization in the northern districts had been sluggish and unsuccessful, but when Migulin appeared things started moving, they knew him and trusted him, he was a Cossack celebrity, the pride of the Cossacks—those candid looks of an almost old man staggered me. He was in love! He couldn't live without her! And she, she... Somewhat taken aback by the transformation in her—what was there to be surprised about, fool that I was?—I seized a moment to ask her, "Why do you treat me like a stranger? What's happened?"

"Nothing." She smiled in the old way, softly; but immediately the dourness returned. "I don't know what your attitude is to Sergei Kirillovich."

"Oh, so that's it, is it?"

"Yes."

"Do you divide people up according to that principle?"

"Yes, I do."

"I see, but please forgive me . . ." I was dumbstruck, speechless. I mumbled, "It's sort of strange; it's unlike you. I can't recognize you."

"That's understandable. The old me is long gone. That little girl has died," said Asya implacably. But was it really Asya? I looked at her coolly. "You were probably present at my death. I never met anyone like Sergei Kirillovich, and life is so different for me. He is extraordinary, don't you see? Not like everyone else; not like you and me! That's why I've changed—from being with him. And naturally he has enemies, ill-wishers, the envious, and simply scoundrels who would like to see him dead."

"I hope you don't put me in that category."

"Not in that one. But, Pavlik, I honestly don't feel that you truly . . . I have a nose like a dog and I can scent . . ."

She then started talking a bit, telling me about their ordeals in Serpukhov and Kozlov, their journey to Moscow, whence he was summoned to the staff of the Workers' and Peasants' Red Army, where the high command had promised him work— mustering a cavalry division of Cossacks from the liberated districts. Sergei Kirillovich agreed, but for some reason everything died down and he ended up being sent to Smolensk. What anguish, what humiliation! He fretted and fumed. He had no desire to live. She was terribly anxious for him, for he was on the brink of suicide. Just imagine it: a mettlesome, courageous man bursting with fierce strength, doomed to peace and quiet. While on the Don the battle was raging! How could he endure it? He was going out of his mind. Peace and quiet were worse than prison. What was it all about? Who was the obstacle? Who was his enemy?

She questioned him intensely, scrutinizing him passionately, wanting to understand, to find out—for him. That whole confession was for him. I cannot help you. I haven't got a clue myself. There's chronic distrust of him, but why? It was dangerous discussing it with her because I could see that everything was inflamed and painful.

"Aska, I don't think he has direct enemies. There was a kind of prejudice, like a blind fear."

"Who?"

"Really and truly I don't know. Perhaps there are people in the Don Bureau, perhaps in the Revolutionary Military Council of the Southern Front..."

I knew of certain direct enemies—Kuptsov, Khutoryansky, Simkin. She probably knew about them, too, and certainly *he* did. There was no point in naming names. Probably in the RMC of the Republic as well there were, if not direct, physical enemies, then theoretical—that is, ideological—enemies: not excluding the Chairman. They would never see eye to eye on some issues. Cossack self-government, for example. After all, he was a People's Socialist, and the theoreticians would always remember that. As Naum Orlik said, "Fifty percent spontaneous rebelliousness, thirty percent something else and five percent Marxism."

Asya continued to interrogate me avidly. "You're talking about the RMC of the Southern Front. What about Sokolsky? He's on our side! He insisted that Sergei Kirillovich should be given the Corps."

How to explain that in these circumstances, battle to the death, people act not under the influence of feelings, whether sympathies or antipathies, but under the effect of mighty and higher forces which you can call the forces of history or the forces of fate. What does it mean, "on our side"? (My God, why "*our*"? So quickly? So finally?) "Our" is beside the point; the point is that the Don is collapsing and it has to be saved. Things were desperate. The risk was great, but there was a chance. Sokolsky's brains were a bit more alert, but Kuptsov's and Khutoryansky's minds had become calloused: that was the difference. But to labor under the delusion that he was *on our side* was pointless. None of that should be spoken of. I nodded: yes, yes, naturally, Sokolsky insisted and sent telegrams. (What was I to do?) My true understanding of the situation was that it was a gigantic muddle! I have become confused. One understanding has merged with another; they have piled up in layers, heaped themselves one on top of the other, and have become fused together over the years. Now, a lifetime later, it's not clear: did I think like that then? Is that how I understood things? All my understandings have gotten mixed up. No, in the summer of '19 there was something different. That was why I was wary talking to Asya, holding back the fact that there was a particle of evil in me too, which later lacerated him: distrust. Well, perhaps it was an in-significant, barely visible particle. Not many were spared that confusion.

Ah, but this is all as I see it today, today—a lifetime later! But then it seemed one way and was another. Then... spring 1919. Denikin was advancing, the uprising was blazing away. Migulin was recalled to Moscow, then to Smolensk. At that time an act of distrust was, you might say, confirmation of that distrust, and there was no need for any evidence. *If they kicked him out, then there was a reason for it.* Leave Migulin on the Don during the Cossack mutiny? Put a wolf in charge of the sheep? Not realizing that he would have done everything in his power, would have laid down his life, to stop and quell it. Because he had devoted everything to that; he had no other life. His trouble was that he bawled everything out point-blank. And he would justify his views, foaming at the mouth and with drawn sword. Even about things he did not know much about. He would bawl about people's representation. He would bawl about maximalism. He would bawl about Anarcho-Communists. He would bawl at meetings and say that not all commissars were courageous and noble, that some were cowards. He would bawl about not all poor peasants being good people, that some were villains and cutthroats. He also bawled about wanting to establish a strong people's authority on the Don, a genuine Soviet regime, as ordered by Comrade Lenin and Comrade Kalinin, without generals or landowners, with Bolsheviks at the head but with no commissars.

And some were dumbfounded by all that bawling. Others scratched the backs of their heads. And certain people said, "Well, all right, let him bawl, but we will still give him an army." And then again some said: militaristic bluster. In the spring of 1919 the celebrated military leaders were on the boil in Russia—ours, the Whites, the Greens, the Blacks... The regimental commander, former NCO Maslyuk, could not hear Migulin's name without emotion. His lips tightened, the muscles over his wide cheekbones twitched, and the scar across his forehead—the mark of an Austrian cutlass—turned livid. Maslyuk did not say anything against Migulin because Maslyuk's tongue was incapable of forming any words about Migulin, good or bad. And the reason was not, as people thought, that Migulin was a Don Cossack and Maslyuk a Voronezh peasant, or that one was an NCO and the other a lieutenant colonel: it was that someone else's fame can seize up the throat like the touch of a knife blade.

But I did not speak about Maslyuk to Asya—though he really was a foe—because I did not have the sense to do so. I did not realize it immediately. Our conversation ended with her joyful whisper, with a happy radiance in her eyes: "He's unrecognizable now! A completely different man. Heavens, how glad I am that they gave us the Corps!" Then again, all of a sudden, the worried "But what does your Shura think of Sergei Kirillovich?"

I answer that he respects him.

But what began so well, the first few days... Ah yes! Well, briskly, fleetly, energetically! Mobilization, training, shooting, meetings, speeches, the nightly drafting of loudmouthed, inflammatory leaflets, dictated to Asya for typing on the Underwood, which he would sign "Citizen of Mikhailinskaya *stanitsa*, Cossack of the Don Army, S. K. Migulin." Here is a page, on the one side marked out in little purple squares for candy wrappers for the Buturlinovka candy factory, and on the other side an appeal: "To the Refugees of the Don Region." His style:

CITIZEN COSSACKS AND PEASANTS!
    Last year many of you were compelled by the Krasnov counterrevolutionary wave to abandon your native steppes and suffer greatly.... If General Denikin triumphs there will be no salvation for anyone. Try as you may to escape, to get away, somewhere or other a wall will be waiting for you where the cadet gangs will finish you off. But if *we* triumph! Therefore, Citizen Exiles, come to me, all of you! Fear lest the dead should hear and rise up and you should be asleep! Fear lest the chains of slavery be already over your heads!

Plus, of course, the splendid finale:

Long live the Social Revolution! Long live the pure truth!

Asya told me in confidence—and asked me not to pass it on, as Migulin did not want people to know—that the Denikinists had cruelly punished his family when they captured Mikhailinskaya. They tortured his mother and shot his father and brother. Migulin's wife—he had left her before the war—escaped with her daughters and was saved. But his eldest son died on the German front. Refugees related that they burned Migulin's homestead and on the ashes erected a pole with the inscription "Here was spawned the degenerate snake, the Judas of the Don, Migulin." Pride did not permit them to express their sympathy and sorrow. But that massacre served for a guarantee that he would not turn traitor and defect.
    "Why did he ask you not to tell anyone?"
    "Pavlik, he's strange. He's so odd, so guileless."
    I remember that the word astounded me: guileless. What she

probably meant was, unable or reluctant to derive any benefit for himself from anything. He did not tell her for a long time. And then when he did he warned her, "Everything was burned to the ground: I want no one to mention it." He truly was a strange man. Once Asya and I were standing beside the command car, talking. Asya was pressed up close against the car, afraid to move thirty paces away. She had been told to stay close at hand because (was it the real reason?) she might be needed at any moment to bash out an order or an appeal. I was arguing with her and said, "Asya, listen..." Whereupon Migulin appeared and gave me a queer, dark look.

"Young man, it behooves you to address my wife as Anna Konstantinovna." He followed this with a coarse bark, "None of your Asyas, get it?"

To give him his due, it happened at a time when he was all exercised and agitated and incapable of speaking calmly. SouthFront was giving no assistance. Once again the same thing had happened: Migulin's Corps was being treated like an outsider! Again the stepchild among the beloved children. In fact, the very name—Corps. In late June, Migulin and Shura sent a telegram to SouthFront headquarters:

HAVING TAKEN COMMAND OF SPECIAL CORPS AND HAVING AC-QUAINTED SELF WITH SITUATION, COMBAT EFFECTIVES AND STATE OF MORALE, WISH TO REPORT FIGHTING BEING CON-DUCTED IN EXCEPTIONALLY DIFFICULT CIRCUMSTANCES IN VIEW OF VASTNESS OF FRONT AND WEAK SUPPLIES OF MATÉRIEL. SOME REGIMENTS NO MORE THAN EIGHTY BAYONETS. MANY UNITS NOTABLY UNSTABLE OWING TO INSUFFICIENT TRAINING AND LACK OF COHESIVENESS. (FIRST COMMUNIST REGIMENT SCAT-TERED DURING NIGHT OF NINETEENTH TO TWENTIETH.) WHEN COSSACK SQUADRONS PASS THEIR STANITSA THEY GO OVER TO ENEMY (FEDOSEEVSKAYA AND USTBUZULUKSKAYA SQUADRONS. BECAUSE UNITS EXHAUSTED FROM LONG PERIOD OF FIGHTING, HAVE SUSTAINED HEAVY CASUALTIES AND HAVE LOST LARGE NUMBER OFFICERS AND COMMISSARS DURING UNREMITTING AND FIERCE FIGHTING. MORAL RESILIENCE EXTREMELY LOW

AND THEY CAN BE USED ONLY AS LIGHT SCREEN BEHIND WHICH
FORMATION AND TRAINING OF FRESH UNITS AN URGENT NE-
CESSITY. DISCHARGE OF ANY ACTIVE ASSIGNMENTS WITH THESE
TROOPS WITHOUT APPROPRIATE RESPITE IMPOSSIBLE. ACCORD-
ING TO MOST RECENT REPORT FROM COMMANDER DIVISION
TWO, NO MORE THAN 150 BAYONETS LEFT PER BRIGADE.
                    COMMANDER SPECIAL CORPS MIGULIN,
                    MEMBER OF RMC DANILOV

The telegram bears the marks of Shura's hand. "Moral resilience" is Shura's. But here are some pages I copied from a
document at a difficult time, six years ago. Galya was dying and
I almost died myself from the torture of sorrow. My only salvation
was in my archive. A mammoth telegram from Migulin to Moscow and to the RMC of the Front. How overjoyed I was to have
found it in the midst of my torment! A little old man gave me
the lead, told me the archive and inventory numbers. Nice old
chap, and open too, even though he was doing some ferreting
at the same time. The old fellow is dead now. Galya too.

                    JUNE 24, 1900 HOURS, STATION ANNA
ON APPOINTING ME CORPS COMMANDER OF THE SPECIAL
CORPS, THE RMC OF THE SOUTHERN FRONT STATED THAT THIS
FORMER EXPEDITIONARY CORPS WAS STRONG, THAT IT HAD UP
TO FIFTEEN THOUSAND BAYONETS AND UP TO FIVE THOUSAND
TRAINEES AND THAT IT WAS ONE OF THE FRONT'S FIGHTING
UNITS. IF SUCH INFORMATION WAS SUPPLIED TO YOU, I DEEM
IT MY REVOLUTIONARY DUTY TO INFORM YOU OF THE TOTAL
DISCREPANCY BETWEEN THAT INFORMATION AND THE TRUE
STATE OF AFFAIRS. I FIND THIS INADMISSIBLE, FOR, OWING TO
THE FACT THAT WE TOOK THE DATA AS FAVORABLE, WE HAVE
BEEN CLOSING OUR EYES TO THE REAL DANGER AND, LULLED,
HAVE NOT TAKEN TIMELY MEASURES; WERE WE NOW TO TAKE
THEM IT WOULD BE TOO LATE. I CONTINUE AS BEFORE TO AD-
VOCATE NOT SECRET BUILDING OF SOCIAL LIFE ACCORDING TO
A NARROW PARTY PROGRAM, BUT PUBLIC BUILDING, BUILDING
IN WHICH THE PEOPLE WOULD ACTIVELY PARTICIPATE. I DO NOT
MEAN THE BOURGEOISIE OR KULAK ELEMENTS. THAT KIND OF

BUILDING ALONE WILL AROUSE THE SYMPATHIES OF THE BULK
OF THE PEASANTS AND PART OF THE TRUE INTELLIGENTSIA. I
WISH TO REPORT THAT THE SPECIAL CORPS HAS ABOUT THREE
THOUSAND BAYONETS FOR A 145-VERST AREA ALONG THE FRONT
LINE. THE TROOPS ARE WORN OUT AND DRAINED. APART FROM
THREE TRAINEE GROUPS, THEY ARE BENEATH CRITICISM, AND
OUT OF THE IMPRESSIVE-SOUNDING THOUSANDS THERE RE-
MAIN A FEW PATHETIC HUNDREDS AND DOZENS. THE COM-
MUNIST REGIMENT HAS SCATTERED; IT CONTAINED PEOPLE WHO
WERE UNABLE TO LOAD A RIFLE. THE SPECIAL CORPS CAN PLAY
THE ROLE OF A SCREEN. THE SPECIAL CORPS'S POSITION IS NOW
HELD ONLY BECAUSE MOBILIZED COSSACKS FROM THE KHO-
PERSKY DISTRICT HAVE BEEN BROUGHT OUT. GENERAL DENI-
KIN'S PLAN FOR THAT DISTRICT HAS BEEN PROVEN COMPLETELY
WRONG. AS SOON AS THE WHITE GUARDS REDRESS THAT DE-
FICIENCY THE SPECIAL CORPS WILL BE RENT THROUGH LIKE A
SCREEN. NOT ONLY ON THE DON HAVE THE ACTIVITIES OF CER-
TAIN REVKOMS, SPECIAL SECTIONS, TRIBUNALS AND SOME COM-
MISSARS PROVOKED A GENERAL UPRISING, BUT THIS UPRISING
THREATENS TO SPREAD IN A BROAD WAVE TO PEASANT VILLAGES
OVER THE ENTIRE FACE OF THE REPUBLIC. IF I SAY THAT AT THE
PEOPLE'S MEETINGS IN THE VILLAGES OF NOVAYA CHIGLA, VER-
KHO-TISHANKA AND OTHERS THERE WERE OPEN CRIES OF "BRING
BACK THE TSAR," YOU WILL COMPREHEND THE MOOD OF THE
PEASANT MASS, WHICH HAS PRODUCED SUCH A HIGH PERCENT-
AGE OF DESERTERS WHO HAVE FORMED GREEN DETACHMENTS.
ALTHOUGH THE UPRISING IN ILOVATKA ON THE RIVER TERSA
IS STILL MUFFLED, THE STRONG FERMENT IN THE MAJORITY
OF DISTRICTS OF SARATOV PROVINCE IS THREATENING COM-
PLETELY TO WRECK THE CAUSE OF THE SOCIAL REVOLUTION. I
AM A NON-PARTY MAN, BUT I HAVE GIVEN TOO MUCH OF MY
STRENGTH AND HEALTH TO THE STRUGGLE FOR THE SOCIAL
REVOLUTION TO LOOK ON INDIFFERENTLY WHILE GENERAL DE-
NIKIN TRAMPLES THE RED BANNER OF LABOR UNDERFOOT.
CASTING MY MIND'S EYE FORWARD AND SEEING THE RUIN OF
THE SOCIAL REVOLUTION—FOR THERE IS NOTHING TO INCLINE
ONE TO OPTIMISM AND AS A PESSIMIST I AM RARELY MISTAKEN—
I CONSIDER IT NECESSARY TO RECOMMEND THE FOLLOWING
URGENT MEASURES: FIRST, REINFORCE THE SPECIAL CORPS WITH
A FRESH DIVISION; SECONDLY, TRANSFER TO IT, AS THE BASIS
OF THE SPECIAL CORPS'S BATTLE ORDER, THE TWENTY-THIRD

DIVISION . . . OR ELSE APPOINT ME COMMANDER OF THE NINTH.
. . . A CONVOCATION OF THE PEOPLE'S REPRESENTATIVES . . . I
HAVE COMMUNICATED MANY STATEMENTS FROM STANICHNIKI
TO THE RMC OF THE FRONT . . . AND WHEN A PEASANT COM-
PLAINED THEY KILLED HIM. YOU WILL SEE FOR YOURSELF WHO
IS A TRUE COMMUNIST AND WHO IS OUT FOR HIS OWN SKIN. . . .

A confused, vicious, desperate tract, difficult to sort out at
three in the morning. My head felt weary, but when I arrived
home with that text, terribly thrilled, and sat down at once by
Galya's bedside and began reading it aloud, Galya suddenly interrupted me and asked, "Pasha, do you think anyone's interested
in that right now?" Extremely unlike Galya. She is always interested. And if she is not interested now, then that must mean
her life is ending.

Let me explain: The truth which was created in those days,
in which we all believed so ardently, has perforce lived on to this
day in a reflected, refracted form, has become the light and air
which people do not notice and do not even guess at. The children
do not understand. But we know. Don't we? We can clearly see
the reflection, the refraction. That is why it is so important now,
half a century later, to understand the reason for Migulin's downfall. People fall not from a bullet, an illness or an accident, but
because they are confronted by supremely powerful forces and
they are grazed by blazing death.

She gives me a long, an unprecedentedly long, dark and deep-
down look—a look of farewell. I shall always remember her face,
weakened, bloodless, with her cheek on the pillow, hoarfrosty
from the imminent parting—only her expression was infinitely
passionate and penetrating—when she asked me, "Why is it I
am dying?" Her soft whisper and that hint of a smile indicate
that no answer is required. A rhetorical question. To herself, or
to nobody.

I tell her angrily, "You're not dying! Please don't talk nonsense!" The usual lies as I think to myself, They'll never understand later how we endured it all . . . the forces that tore us up.

Migulin was destroyed because at a fatal instant two streams, hot and cold, collided in the heavens, two clouds the size of continents, and they produced a discharge of colossal might—two streams of belief and unbelief, which hurtled and swept him away in a hurricane of comingled hot and cold, belief and unbelief. Displacement always brings on a storm, and the downpour drenches the earth. This merciless heat will end in a downpour like that. And I shall enjoy the coolness if I survive. Galya and I are standing in the garden pavilion where we have rushed to take shelter from the rain—the heavy cloudburst is lashing down onto the felt-covered roof. The mist in the garden is swirling about in white, watery billows. "I *must* speak with you! Two o'clock in the garden."

The downpour, the pavilion, the soaked dress, Galya's terrified face—a high-school look of yesteryear. This is where we arranged to meet. The names carved with a penknife...

"What's happened?"

"Pavlik, I'm afraid for him again! He's had a terrible row with Logachev and Kharin. He threatened to kill someone."

God. My blood runs cold with horror. My Galya is terrified for someone—not for me! She is crying because of someone else. I ask her, my lips growing numb, "Do you love him that much?" Odd, it's as if I know who "he" is, yet at the same time I cannot understand. I make a fantastic effort, trying to guess who the man is, so familiar.

"Surely you can see? I can't live without him."

Suddenly. Not Galya, but Asya. Asya in the pavilion! In the garden of a provincial military chief's house. A note from her had summoned me. This was after Migulin's return from the second Moscow trip, in July, after his talk with the Central Committee Cossack Section, when he came back heartened and full of strength. The Special Corps, which had been created to combat the rebels, had now lost its significance; the front had moved northward, Denikin had captured the Don, Tsaritsyn and Kharkov. Now it was a matter of waging war on Denikin, not on the insurgents! Migulin is raising a new corps, the Don Cossack Corps. We are stationed in Saransk. The Corps is taking a staggeringly long time to form. But Shura has a new appointment— to the RMC of the Ninth Army. That is what Asya is frightened about.

"You see, he's the only person Sergei Kirillovich can talk to! Even though he argues with him. But he can't stomach the others. The others are enemies."

"Enemies? Really?"

"Yes, enemies!" In Asya's eyes I saw relentlessness and wrath, the wrath of Migulin. She whispers, "They're sending them to us deliberately... from the northern districts... we know they got up to mischief there. He can't bear the sight of them! Hates them worse than Denikin!"

"Where are they sending them to?"

"All our political commissars come from there... from the Khopyor area."

Preparations on the eve of departure. A conversation with Shura in the owner's room with its smell of thyme, its chests and icons. The owner asks sympathetically, "Where have you retreated to? Where is the front? Why are the workers of the world dozing and not rousing themselves?" He acts concerned, but his smirking clean-shaven mug shows he's happy. Suddenly he announces in a whisper, "I can tell you quite frankly, Citizen Communists, why your war lacks derring-do: you don't have any generals. Booksellers and clerks on the staffs and at headquarters. That Lyovka* with the spectacles. Do you think he can outwit a general?"

Shura is loath to leave Migulin's ill-starred Corps, but cannot bear to remain any longer. True, true, the smack in the face does smart: there are no generals. And if anyone does turn up we put them into pickle like wild mushrooms. Unbelievable stupidity. Shura's pet expression, "unbelievable stupidity." Be-

---

* Presumably a reference to Trotsky.—EDITOR.

cause all Shura's efforts to make some headway, all his telegrams, all his bad language with the SouthFront representatives, face to face or on the telephone, get no results. As the saying goes, one minute they blow hot, the next minute they blow cold. In June they're desperate, in July they aren't so keen. First one thing, then another. That is why Shura is so mad. Because he cannot din into anyone, "You must trust him to the last!" He is angry at Migulin too, because of his ranting and raving, which does harm to himself—he almost came to blows with the special representative from SouthFront when he sent him packing after he had come to check up on the work of the political department.

Enter Logachev and Kharin, both political commissars. Quite young; Logachev is about twenty-three, Kharin a little older. Logachev is a student from Novocherkassk and Kharin a worker from Rostov, a boilermaker. They had both been on commandeering assignment in the northern districts in February and March and had won renown for being staunch and intrepid *carriers out*—they call them the "Khopyor Communists"—and naturally Migulin is at odds with them.

"So you're abandoning us, Alexander Pimenovich?" asks the palely smiling, sharp-nosed little Logachev. As always, his look is arrogant, his head thrown back. "Does not your departure resemble the flight of certain well-known creatures from a ship?"

"I'm a soldier. Orders," explains Shura glumly, without taking umbrage.

"But what do you really think? What do you feel deep down?"

They are young. One minute they are transported by passionate enthusiasm, the next minute they are overcome with terror. In an access of rage, Migulin threatens to shoot them. In turn, they threaten to arrest and shoot him. How can they work together? None of the work is progressing at all. The Corps is rotting away in inactivity. Meanwhile, Denikin is preparing to break through to the front, and in a few days Mamontov's cavalry will wedge itself right between the armies.

"Deep down, I feel sorry for you fellows. I don't want to leave you to the mercy of the Corps Commander. He'll make a meal of you."

"Or vice versa, maybe? The enemy carrion!" says the big-fisted boilermaker, screwing up his eyes.

"He isn't enemy carrion. He's a revolutionary, but a peasant revolutionary—that is, a petit-bourgeois revolutionary. He's valuable to us because he's the enemy of our enemies. Get it? Unless you get that fact straight you're going to find the going rough and dangerous."

Shura understands it all so well, yet he lacks the strength and patience to work with an outstanding revolutionary. Trotsky wrote on one of Migulin's first telegrams, "Don Cossack Establishmentarianism and Left Socialist Revolutionaryism." And that stuck like a permanent red wax seal. Naum Orlik! He too loved to define staff members and stick labels on them. That pharmacist's approach to humanity—or, more exactly, to individuals—survived for decades, for there is nothing more convenient than cut-and-dried formulas, but now everything has grown turbid. The vials have been broken and all the solutions and acids have run into one pool. There is a lot I do not understand nowadays. At times, not a darn thing. Young people and the middle-aged crowd seem particularly mysterious to me. I have an inkling about old people. Old people are closer. I could equal Orlik in going around sticking labels on old people, but the young ones stonewall me. Such a muddle; such murky waters! Even Naum would get bogged down. Even he would ask to be forgiven.

Oh, of how much, how much we are guilty in all this! The Don was abandoned, left to take care of itself and then to choke in its own blood. . . .

What's this I'm reading? Goodness me, it's the letter to the Central Executive Committee. What Migulin said to Vladimir Ilych Lenin during their meeting in July.

. . . In March and April the outlying districts of the Don fell victim to a plague of agents. Huge numbers of them had infiltrated the ranks of the then Red Guards. Someday impartial history will shed light on the terrible plight of the frontline Cossacks. There were innocent people among the hundreds of Cossacks who were exiled or executed. The Revolution has made such deep inroads that the poor mind of the *stanichnik* is powerless to analyze the events that are unfolding. The requisitioning of cattle and grain now taking place in the Don, a result of the famine in the land, is incomprehensible to him. I am profoundly convinced that the Cossacks are not as counterrevolutionary as people assume. . . . Whatever lies or slander people have spread about me, I solemnly state before the proletariat that I never have betrayed its cause and never shall. I ask for one thing: understand me as a member of no party, but as one who has been a custodian of the Revolution since 1906. . . .

I well recall what happened next. Vladimir Ilych apparently said—according to a member of the Cossack Section—"We need people like that. They must be used skillfully." According to the same person, Kalenin's attitude was also sympathetic; he merely expressed the apprehension that Migulin would go from criticizing certain unworthy Communists to opposing the Party.

My God, it is so unthinkable to explain him in a single word! Yet they try it every time. They tried it while Migulin was still alive, shrieking out words like "traitor" and "betrayer"; and they're still trying it today, with cries of "Leninist" and "revolutionary." If he could simply be explained in a single word I would not be sitting here in the middle of the night rummaging through papers. Although it is thanks to those papers that I'm managing to kill the nighttime hours. Past two. No sign of sleep. And my head seems clear. I am thinking again, and pondering over everything. Here I am reading about Migulin in an agony of conjecture, yet at the back of my mind is the thought, How is Ruska doing out there in the burning forests? Has he fallen ill? He's a muddle-

headed boy, silly—in his own affairs: silly *toward himself*—he's
bound to do something wrong.

Another letter, a late one; long, ebullient, breathtaking:

> I will not accept this madness, which only now has risen
> up before my eyes, and with all the strength that is still within
> me I shall fight against the policy of the dispossession of the
> Cossacks. I advocate that, while not interfering with the peas-
> ants' daily life and religious traditions or violating their cus-
> toms, we lead them to a brighter and better life through personal
> example, by demonstration, and not through the grand, high-
> falutin slogans of homespun Communists who are still wet
> behind the ears, the majority of whom can't tell the difference
> between wheat and barley, although at their meetings they try
> to teach the peasants with great self-assurance about agricul-
> tural management. . . .

(Was that intended for me? Each time I read that part I think
it's for me. I too used to hold forth at meetings about "let's smash
Denikin and we'll be in time for the harvest.")

> I wish to remain a genuine worker for the people, a genuine
> defender of its aspirations for land and freedom, and, once
> and for all, I disassociate myself from all the slander put about
> by the pseudo-Communists. . . . That devilish plan which has
> been revealed to dispossess the Cossacks compels me to repeat
> points I have made at meetings:
> 1. I am not a Party member.
> 2. I shall go along with the Bolshevik Party, as I have always
> done, right to the end.
> 3. I deem inadmissible any interference by pseudo-Com-
> munists in the military and educational work of the staff
> officers.
> 4. In the name of the Revolution, and on behalf of the
> sorely tried Cossacks, I demand an end to . . . And all the
> scoundrels who artificially stirred up the population as a
> pretext to exterminate them should be arrested and prose-
> cuted forthwith. . . .

I am combatting the evil perpetrated by certain agents of the authorities. That is to say I am in favor of what was stated recently by the representative of the All-Russian Central Executive Committee, and I quote him verbatim: "We shall most decisively remove from office commissars who are bringing ruin and disruption to the country, and we shall request the peasants to elect those they consider to be needed and useful. . . ." I know that I am exposing an evil which is totally unacceptable to the Party. . . . Yet why is it that people who try to point out the evil and to combat it openly are persecuted, even shot? Perhaps after this letter the same fate will await me too. . . ."

Those it was addressed to did not read it in time. Everything could have been different. But other people read it. The main evil turned out to be sincerity. And how! Running himself down like that! At this point the Corps Commander started rushing around. They were not giving him the people. He asked them to send captured deserters to the Corps. They refused. He proposed a mobilization of the peasants. No. Early in August he applied for Party membership. The political department, headed by Logachev and Kharin, did not accept their Corps Commander into the Party. The trouble was, there were no real commissars around. People like Furmanov and Chapaev. People like the ones cited at the Eighth Congress who, "hand in hand with the best of the officer elements, in a short time created an efficient army." Lenin did not know all the details, but he understood the crux of the problem.

The letter to Gusev! September of '19!

It is the best, *most energetic* commissars who should be sent to the South, not the sleepyheads. . . .

Lenin, Volume 51. There should be a bookmark somewhere. . . . Here it is. There! Letter to RMC member Gusev— Sergei Ivanovich.

. . . in actual fact, things are at a standstill—almost a total breakdown. . . . The standstill is due to Mamontov. There seems to have been one delay after another. The troops coming to Voronezh from the north were late. They were late in transferring the Twenty-first Division to the south. They were late with the machine guns. They were late setting up communications. We are also late forming up. If we miss autumn, then Denikin will organize his forces, get hold of tanks, etc., etc. That must be stopped. This sleepy pace of work must give way to a lively one.

Precisely what Migulin had been yelling about in the summer! It was *his* Corps which was being formed at that terrifyingly sleepy pace!

By that time, neither Shura nor I was in Saransk. We were in Kozlov. We found out all about it later from biased, unreliable sources.

This is from a report by Kazymbetov, a courier from the Cossack Section in Moscow. Kazymbetov spent several days visiting the corps:

As an individual, Comrade Migulin enjoys tremendous popularity on the southern front at the present time, among both Red and White. . . . his name is surrounded by an aura of honesty and profound devotion to the cause of the Social Revolution and the interests of working people. . . . Migulin is the only person to whom the Cossacks look with trust and hope as their deliverer from the oppression of generals, landowners and counterrevolution. He should be skillfully used for the Revolution despite his open, and at times sharp, words about "pseudo-Communists." . . .

And then, after that; let's see.

And so the fundamental cause of this distrust is his very popularity. . . .

Reading on. "The mood of the Corps. . ." Here we are!

The Corps has not been formed and is only barely being formed. The Red Army men are dead set against the political workers and the political workers are dead set against Comrade Migulin. Migulin is indignant not only at the fact that they do not trust him—a true fighter for the Social Revolution who sacrificed his health on the front—but also at the fact that they are even trying to dig his grave by sending in what he sees as unfounded denunciations against him. As a result of this, Migulin gives the impression of a desperate man at bay. Of late, Comrade Migulin, fearing arrest or an attempt on his life, has been keeping a bodyguard close by him. The political workers are afraid of Migulin. The Red Army men are in a state of excitement and are ready at any minute to defend Migulin by force of arms from attack. In my opinion, Migulin is nothing like Grigorev and is far from being an adventurist. However, grounds are being contrived for the charge of "Grigorevism." Migulin may be forced to make a desperate move. . . .

The dark backwoods of Rostov, small, mean houses, fences, a frosty night, the flickering of candles through the warm windows, people celebrating Christmas, no one guessing our presence. We crash into a sort of lane and knock down a wicket gate. How should they know that we have dashed eighty versts in one day? Rushing down from Nakhichevan. As if to Belshazzar's feast. Near one house, with a light shining in the window, and from which voices can be heard, stands an officer wearing a hood and a long greatcoat; he is embracing a woman and has swept her back passionately, bending her so far down that he might drop her into the snow at any moment, although she is wearing only a dress and is bareheaded. The door of the house is wide open; obviously they have just jumped from the warm inside out into the freezing cold. I look at them from the porch and see that it is Migulin and Asya. "Don't you dare!" I shout. He went for his holster and started back from Asya, and, from above as if from a horse, I dealt him a short, fearsome blow with my saber; there was a *chock* like the sound of a watermelon being split open. All he managed to say was, "Ah . . ." .

Pavel Evgrafovich woke up out of his nightmarish vision and for a long time was unable to calm his heart. His hands were shaking, everything inside was pounding, his mouth was dry. My God, what came over me to dream such a horrible and ridiculous—above all ridiculous—thing? What the hell? Where did it come from? The thing that had bored its way into my dream was the liberation of Rostov: the way we attacked them like a bolt from the blue. Christmastime, on the brink of 1920. And there was a house, a courtyard, music from the window, shooting along the street and an officer and a girl kissing. The soldier finished him off in a second, right then and there; the officer had taken it into his head to kick up a racket—if he had kept quiet he would have lived. We rushed into the house, where everything was in readiness—the table laid, bottles of wine, *zakuski*, women shouting, the gramophone playing. . . .

Finally in the middle of August Asya's reply arrived in a thick envelope which turned out to contain a school notebook folded in half and filled with small handwriting. Pavel Evgrafovich read:

DEAR PAVEL,
   I was ever so pleased to get your letter telling me that you are alive and well, and living with your children and grandchildren, and that on the whole your life has turned out well apart from the loss of a person near and dear to you—but then very few people of our age have escaped such bereavements, and I have lived through that sorrow three times. So I understand you and am full of sympathy, dear Pavel. I delayed answering you because I wanted to remember as much as possible and write down as many details as I could, just as you asked. This is what my memory has retained.
   You ask what happened after you and your uncle A. P. Danilov left the Corps. Of course you could not have known all the ins and outs. And all kinds of terrible rumors were going around. I think that Sergei Kirillovich's enemies were

deliberately spreading them. Naturally, in a fit of temper he was capable of calling a panicking subordinate a bad name, about which I always felt ashamed and used to tell him off. But you know he was rabid! In the heat of the moment he was capable of swearing even at Communists, although he hated the enemies of Communism with a passion and waged war upon them throughout his life. I think the fatal blow was dealt in August when he applied for Party membership and was turned down. His own political department refused him. I don't recall the names of those people anymore, apart from one—Logachev. Sergei Kirillovich used to repeat it often, always with enmity and scorn, sometimes with a threat: "One day that milksop will go too far; and then BANG!" There was someone else; tall, swarthy, shaggy-haired. And another one too—middle-aged, lean: a Latvian, I think; spoke bad Russian. But Sergei Kirillovich especially hated a few of his fellow countrymen from the Ust-Medveditsky district. They used to be in the Revkoms and pursued an incorrect line, one that Sergei Kirillovich disagreed with, and so he quarreled with them. He always used to quarrel about the Cossacks. At the time there was a lot of talk about the Cossacks, sometimes for, sometimes against. Right now I don't rightly recall the point of contention; I just remember that S. K. was fretful and called some people boobs and scoundrels and said that the Revolution would be destroyed by scoundrels. He believed they were purposely sending him people who were disagreeable and hostile to him, and whose job it was to watch him and check up on him. He used to call them—among his own people, of course—stool pigeons and overseers. He didn't mince his words. In general, the atmosphere in the Corps was uneasy. Particularly when your uncle Danilov left. I've remembered his name now: Danilov. They had a falling out. I don't remember why. I think it was over some commission they sent from Front headquarters. Sergei Kirillovich used to say, "They send snoopers, but they can't send me reinforcements, however much I ask."

He was very pained at their unfair treatment of him. Of course I am not a historian or a political expert and I can't make definitive evaluations, but as someone who observed him closely during those weeks I would like to say that he was devoted to the Revolution and the Soviet regime, but that certain people were making him into an enemy. Granted, he did criticize the shortcomings and behavior of his men. That cannot be denied. I remember he would come to the command car in the evening, send his orderly Ivan off somewhere and pace like a tiger, silent except for almost painful groans. "Seryozha," I would ask, "what's happened?" "Oh, I don't feel like talking about it." Then he would suddenly start shouting, "Denikin is advancing! But here I am, held in captivity. I can't wait to get to the front! I'll force them to give the order." When Danilov left, he came home extremely depressed and said, "If a former prisoner has reached the end of his tether, then what am I supposed to do? Put a bullet through my head?"

It was both of you leaving that killed him. Well, what happened next? Endless, all-night meetings with the staff officers and commanders. The atmosphere was highly charged. Some of them consulted among themselves and did not let the others in. I remember that Sergei Kirillovich was working intensely, writing up some program or other, which I typed up—but now I don't recall at all what it was. Later at the trial I believe it was used as evidence against him, to try to prove that his betrayal had been premeditated. But that is not true. He was writing in the abstract, discoursing on a historical topic. He was very fond of philosophizing, discussing and debating, and although he had no real education he used to stump a lot of clever people. He sent some telegrams to SouthFront and to the RMC of the Republic which were all replied to unfavorably, and finally I feel he arrived at a decision. You see, Denikin's offensive was very successful. The news was disquieting. He could not stand it. Someone with a different character—more reasonable—might have controlled himself, but Sergei Kirillovich exploded. I'm not defending him, Pavel. I just cry, weep, when I remember how he came running to me, cursing someone, and asked, "Well, what am I to do? Tell me; advise me!" Of course, he knew that I could not advise him at all. It was just his desperation. What could I do? I myself was almost delirious. Then I just loved him and felt awfully sorry for him.

Suddenly he told me, "You must leave at once!" Why? "You must." No explanation. I guessed. "You're setting off for the front? Then I'm going with you!" We argued the whole night through. He didn't want to take me with him for anything, but I had nowhere else to go. Mama, Papa and my sister Varya were in the South, in Rostov or Ekaterinodar, I didn't exactly know—in any event beyond the front line. We had another relative, Aunt Agniya, Papa's sister, who lived in Smolensk, but I flatly refused to go to her. She was a stranger to me, married to a Pole, and a convert to Catholicism—but that was beside the point. The fact was, I could not leave Sergei Kirillovich. Then he began trying to persuade me to visit his sister in Voronezh province, but no one knew whose territory that was, ours or the Whites'. So fortunately there was nowhere to go to and I stayed with him.

Everything started moving swiftly. I remember he wrote an appeal. His assistant, Korovin, said it was too sharply worded and asked him to tone it down. Once again they argued and cursed each other for some time. The people from the political department demanded that Sergei Kirillovich fire some of his commanding officers and prosecute them, but he refused. I remember also that his friend Misha Bogdanov shot himself. That hit him very hard. All of a sudden, Sergei Kirillovich lost heart and seemed to give up the idea of taking unauthorized action. But then he had a telephone conversation with one of the SouthFront leaders; perhaps it was Yanson—I don't rightly recall. I remember the conversation very well because I was in the room; also, Sergei Kirillovich related it to me in detail afterward. That conversation affected him too. It was like the first stone hurtling down a mountain: a whole avalanche crashed down after it.

Of course Sergei Kirillovich's decision may have been foolhardy, maybe not. I do not intend to pass judgment on my husband. I only know he was an honest man and he said there was no way out. Although it was all discussed behind closed doors among his closest and most trusted circle, it naturally became known at Front headquarters. Because there were people who turned out to be informers. Sergei Kirillovich was too guileless: he trusted many people mistakenly. For instance, he regarded Yurganov the regimental commander as a loyal friend, yet he behaved worse than anyone, and at the trial he even tried to make excuses for his failure to have shot Sergei Kirillovich—the bastard. He even lied that he had tried to shoot him somewhere but had missed; he was trying to wheedle himself a pardon—to no avail, however. But I've digressed.

Yanson asked if it was true that Sergei Kirillovich was intending to proceed to the front without Command's knowledge. Sergei Kirillovich explained the situation in a forthright voice. I remember phrases such as "I am surrounded by an atmosphere which is suffocating me," "I would agree to take a squadron of men who are loyal to me and join up with my own division." He had in mind the Twenty-third Division, of whose command he had been relieved in March. His friend Malikov had been made its divisional commander. On the whole he spoke calmly and reasonably at first, untypically so for him. Yanson said he was ordering him, in the name of the RMC, not to dispatch a single detachment without authorization.

Sergei Kirillovich said, "Then I shall go alone. I cannot remain here any longer; I am being vilely insulted!" Yanson demanded that Sergei Kirillovich come to Penza. The headquarters of the Front was in Penza at that time. Incidentally, I remember him saying, "Come. We'll think it over together. Comrade Danilov is commander of the front here now." But Sergei Kirillovich answered him frankly that he feared for his safety and would not travel without a convoy. Yanson tried to convince him that there was nothing to be afraid of but eventually agreed to the convoy. Sergei Kirillovich demanded a hundred and fifty men. All right, take a hundred and fifty men and come at once. I also remember Sergei Kirillovich's final words when his composure failed him. He stood there, pale, the sweat pouring down his face—it also happened to be a very hot day—and he shouted down the receiver as I stood in front of him. He was looking at me the whole time but did not see me, and he shouted, "Kindly inform the Twenty-third Division that I have been summoned to Penza. I want them to know in case anything happens. I place myself in your hands, Comrade Yanson, as someone I trust!"

That seemed naïve to me. But I was in any case horror-struck. I felt that something terrible was drawing near. He replaced the receiver and said, "That's it, then!" Then he asked me how I thought he had spoken. I told him very well and forthrightly. He was satisfied. What he really wanted to know was had he acted properly. Then his torments began, the

vacillations which went on for days on end. First he would
decide to start out, then he would change his mind. Incidentally, what affected him was the fact that Yanson had said
Danilov was in Penza. Although he had had words with your
uncle too (with whom hadn't he?) he still respected him. I can
remember sensing that because he was secretly upset when
Danilov was transferred. He felt that things would be worse
without him, and they were. He said that Danilov would be
odd man out in the political department, that he would have
been accepted as a Party member but that the young fiends
had taken it into their heads to destroy him. For some reason
he called your uncle "odd man out." I don't remember him
looking odd at all. All I remember is something stocky and
solid, with a shaven head. He reasoned, "If Danilov's in Penza,
why didn't he come to the phone and say a few words to me?"
He thought that this was no mere chance. He thought Danilov
would not take upon himself the responsibility of summoning
him to Penza because he was not sure about the others. I don't
know the real reason Danilov did not want to speak to him.
After all, Yanson called twice—the following day also, when
Sergei Kirillovich had already given the order to march. This
time the tone of the conversation was coarse and vicious.
Yanson threatened to outlaw Sergei Kirillovich, and S. K.
cursed him roundly. The day before, however, after their first
telephone conversation, something had happened. Someone
surreptitiously left a note in an envelope in the command car,
which I found on the floor and read. Just a single line in large
block capitals: DO NOT GO TO PENZA. THEY WILL ARREST YOU
AND KILL YOU. I began to wonder feverishly what to do. Tell
him? For some reason I thought of one person from headquarters whom I disliked. He was always trying to incite Sergei
Kirillovich against the political department people and was in
favor of S. K.'s venture; he was in general wicked-tongued.
He once grabbed me in the dark, pretending to mistake me
for another woman—although he could see perfectly well it
was me. When I tore myself away and said, "Aren't you afraid
of the Corps Commander? If he finds out he'll kill you on the
spot," he gave a nasty smile and said, "But how do you know
who'll get to the other first?" I didn't like that one bit. I thought
that that man might harm Sergei Kirillovich. Pavel, forgive

me. I'm going into too much detail and can't stop myself;
everything's coming back to me, all these new memories—
one thing clings to the next and draws it out. You must understand that I've tried for a long time to forget about it. Since
the time Sergei Kirillovich was declared an enemy, I haven't
said a thing to anyone, still less written anything. I'm amazed
myself at how much stuff my memory has still retained. After
all, more than fifty years have gone by. You know, the human
memory is truly a miracle of nature.

Anyway, there I was, standing with the note in my hands,
wondering what to do. To be honest, I was not in favor of this
unauthorized march to the front, not because of any higher
considerations such as the Revolution or discipline, which
were alien to me—politics is not my strong subject—but
simply because I was afraid for him: I felt he was straining at
the leash to enter the fray, to die, to be slain, anything rather
than vegetate. Death was not in the least frightening to him,
while to me death, his death, was very frightening indeed. I
am like that; I always worry about my nearest and dearest. I
wanted for him to go to Penza, for the whole situation to settle
down somehow and become calm. I did not believe that they
could arrest Migulin or—even more ridiculous—kill him!
His name was too renowned. Suddenly he stepped into the
command car. Not stepped in, but burst in: just flew in with
a single bound like a young lad—he was on the whole very
fleet and nimble for his age. He saw the note, asked, "What's
that?" and tore it out of my hands. He was very jealous. I was
right when I told that man that if Migulin had seen him trying
to squeeze me in the dark like a stableboy groping for a tart,
he would have killed him on the spot. He read the note, smiled
and tore it up. By that time he had made up his mind not to
go to Penza, but that note caused a complete about-face: he
suddenly felt embarrassed in front of me; his pride was wounded.
He thought I might think that he had refused to go to Penza
for the talks because he had taken fright at the contents of the
note. At once he gave orders to go to the station and make
arrangements for the train. Many railway cars were needed for
people and horses—an entire train. Shortly afterward, one of
his close associates, the machine gunners' commander, galloped up and said that the stationmaster at Saransk had said

that there were no cars. He did not know when there would
be any. He could supply a locomotive and one car, and that
was all. Migulin took that to be a ploy; that in fact they wanted
him to set off without a convoy. Then he became enraged and
started shouting, "You can't arrange anything with those people! They don't keep their promises!" Once more everything
had turned around a hundred and eighty degrees.

He gave orders to assemble the Cossacks for a meeting. All
the roads into and out of the town were closed off. He ordered
that certain officers be arrested and held as hostages. At the
meeting he read out a statement in which, I well remember,
he called on them to go to the front and beat Denikin, to save
the Revolution and also to beat what he termed the "pseudo-
Communists." It was a sort of general debate; he consulted
the troops about what action to take. The tension was terrific;
there was shouting, and shots were even fired into the air. I
was standing behind the rostrum, unable to calm myself. I
was shaking the whole time, afraid that someone would take
a shot at him from the crowd. He could talk in such a tremendously inspiring way. I had never heard an orator like that
before. Incidentally, some who spoke tried to dissuade the Red
Army men from following Sergei Kirillovich and openly threatened and cursed Sergei Kirillovich, calling him an outlaw. I
was amazed at their nerve, because the main mass of the people
were against them. But Sergei Kirillovich allowed everyone to
speak, although he himself was fidgety and would interrupt
and yell out protests. And suddenly he chased that swarthy,
shaggy-haired fellow from the rostrum, shouting, "I won't allow you to agitate my men!" After that, some soldiers from
the commandant's squadron arrested that dark member of the
political department. He shouted out, "You can have me shot,
Migulin, but still I call you a traitor!" Sergei Kirillovich said
he was not going to shoot anyone, because he was against the
death sentence. I remember another argument about some
money which had been taken from the treasury. A commander
by the name of Zabei-Boroda accused Korovin of taking it.
Sergei Kirillovich later explained to me that in fact the money
had been taken to pay the men's wages, and that they had
paid for a horse from some of the other funds. In general,
Sergei Kirillovich was indifferent to money and did not keep

track of it. I remember him at the meeting, asking the men, "Look, are you prepared to set out?" They answered, "Yes!" "There's a bird," he said, "known as the swan. Well, I'm like that bird: I'm singing my swan song. Do you get me?" "Yes!" they cried. "Are you ready?" "We're ready!"

Well, the following day we set off. Only a few thousand people followed us—perhaps four or five thousand—but a few days later, when Yanson's declaring Sergei Kirillovich a rebel became known, and the order was given to deliver him to headquarters dead or alive, many people took fright and our detachment was whittled down by half. There were some small engagements and skirmishes. Morale was falling all the time. There was a general feeling of anxiety and doom. Sergei Kirillovich was longing to get to the front line as soon as possible and engage Denikin in battle and rout the Mamontovists—but of course it was just a dream.

Again he tried to leave me. He put me in a britska, detailed three men and ordered them to head north, but I said I would shoot myself if he sent me away. I had a revolver. So again he had not succeeded in getting rid of me, about which I must say he was glad. I do not remember all the details of the campaign, which lasted about three weeks, during which we marched through forests, along out-of-the-way paths, and spent the nights in the woods as our detachment melted away. When Brigade Commander Skvortsov stopped us and ordered us to lay down our arms, there were about five hundred men left, no more. We could have fought—and died, as Skvortsov was in a determined frame of mind—but Sergei Kirillovich gave the order to give no resistance and to surrender arms.

I shall remember that terrible day until I die. It was terrible, but not because we were captives of our own people: as we were not enemies, I could not comprehend that fully. I just felt in my heart that it was terrible for him: his hopes had been dashed, and he had been unable to prove a thing. He had never been afraid of death; he was dejected by the fact that he could not prove anything. There was a certain regimental commander too, Maslyuk, who behaved spitefully and humiliatingly. He came up on his horse smirking in an uncommonly arrogant and conceited manner like a ham actor, and asked, "Where are the people from the political department?

Alive?" Sergei Kirillovich said, yes, they were, and he indicated behind him. They had taken two political department people as hostages. Sergei Kirillovich was sitting in the britska. Maslyuk turned purple in the face and barked, "Stand up when you're talking to me, you pig!" And he raised his hand, threatening to strike him. Sergei Kirillovich gave a start. I was horrified, but Sergei Kirillovich restrained himself and said calmly, "Vanka, don't whistle. Play a nice dance tune instead." Why he said to play a nice dance tune I don't rightly know. But I remember that very clearly.

Sergei Kirillovich had such contempt for him! I don't know what became of Maslyuk later. I won't forget his haughty face; the way he looked down on Sergei Kirillovich and took delight in calling him a pig. He demanded that Sergei Kirillovich and several commanding officers be executed; he had the right to order executions on the spot and he wanted to exercise it, so he put pressure on Brigade Commander Skvortsov to allow him to do so. Sergei Kirillovich behaved calmly. I could not hold back the tears while he tried to reassure me and to tell me what I should do after his death and how I should deal with his legacy. Legacy! God! He had nothing. The man had almost reached the age of fifty, and had no house, money or valuables—nothing apart from a pair of boots, a pair of baggy Cossack trousers with a stripe down the legs, a horse and a gun. He did not even have so much as the poorest, most indigent Cossack: a strip of land. However, he did have some papers and notes which he cherished, and he asked me to give them to someone in Moscow, I forget whom. I think they were his thoughts on Cossack self-government and about the organization of the Don region in general. They were all lost later; I'll never forgive myself. When I was traveling from Balashov to Moscow, my suitcase was stolen with those papers inside.

They did not execute anyone at that stage; attached to Skvortsov's unit was a certain important military official, one of the top people, I don't remember precisely who; I saw him for only two seconds when he was getting into a car: short, in a service tunic, black beard, pince-nez; a civilian look about him. At the time, of course, I knew who it was, although I've forgotten now. He gave orders that they be sent to Balashov and tried there by court-martial. This was done not out of magnanimity, but because they decided at once that a widely publicized trial would carry more weight than a hasty execution in the forest.

At that point they separated me from him, and I did not see him again until three weeks later, after sentence had been passed and they granted us a meeting. You know how the trial went. You wrote in your article that after the sentence had been pronounced, those who had been convicted sang revolutionary songs all through the night. Perhaps that's true; I don't know. But I did hear something because I spent the night standing at the foot of the prison wall, and snatches of song did reach me. I heard the Cossack songs, "Dearest Father, Glorious, Quiet Don" and "Can the Falcon Be Kept in Bondage." This latter song was Sergei Kirillovich's favorite; he used to sing it often. True, his voice was nothing special, nor was his ear.

Pavel, you ask why I expressed surprise in my letter that it was you who wrote the piece on Sergei Kirillovich. That's inaccurate. It is true I was slightly surprised, but that was not the overriding feeling I felt when I read the piece. What I mainly felt was tremendously happy and tremendously grateful to you for having remembered a name I cherish. My slight surprise stemmed merely from the fact that you had been a member of the court secretariat in Balashov in 1919. I remember that you were unable to help me to get a meeting with the defense attorney on the first day of the session because you said it was too late. On the whole, Pavel, I think that you did somehow believe that Sergei Kirillovich was guilty. I'm not blaming you—at the time that's what most people believed. People were in the throes of war and they saw things quite differently from now, when they can evaluate everything calmly.

Pavel, I'm weary of this letter, and I'm afraid the whole time that I haven't managed to say anything. I have a sort of terror that I've forgotten to make the most important, the most precious point about Sergei Kirillovich. Yesterday I called the doctor and spent the whole day in bed, all churned up. So I'm going to close. Otherwise I could go on reminiscing forever. By chance I still have Sergei Kirillovich's last letters and a few of his documents, but I'm not going to send them to you yet. Perhaps we'll meet here in Klyukvino or I'll go to Moscow. My daughter-in-law has a car; she sometimes goes to Moscow on business or to shop. But I should prefer to see you here, dear Pavel. I've become sickly: a real old woman. I embrace you. Answer me quickly.

Your ASYA

Incidentally, my daughter-in-law, quite a plain-spoken woman, read my memoir and concluded, "You know, Mumsy (she calls me Mumsy; thinks it sounds funny), you've lived your life all wrong: you should have written novels. When I read your stuff I can't put it down. It's like a detective story." Such compliments in my old age! Tell me how you're standing up to the heat. Here, everything has been blasted; there won't be any potatoes and we haven't seen any berries at all.

Pavel Evgrafovich read through the letter twice, then read certain passages once more, and felt delight as well as a kind of vague anxiety which gave him palpitations and made his hands go cold. He took some medicine and calmed down somewhat. The delight was because the dead past throbbed and lived in the pages of that school notebook, and the anxiety was—goodness knows. Certainly not because of that nonsense Asya had written about his having believed in Migulin's guilt. Even though he might have believed in it, *it was not to the same extent as the others*. It was impossible not to have believed in it at all. She should not have said that, blaming him half a century later. She simply did not remember the way things really were. Things were very rough and straightforward—Migulin was a traitor and that was that! What was she asking him to do? Why these accusations? He felt like answering her immediately and sending her a few documents so that she could get the point about how difficult it had been trying to push his article through into the magazine! Even nowadays. She took a narrow view of things—there was much she did not see, did not remember and did not want to hear. Should he not perhaps send her this appeal, which Migulin issued immediately after the campaign?

SORELY TRIED PEOPLE OF RUSSIA:
At the sight of your sufferings and torments, of the outrages committed against you and your consciences, no honest and truth-loving citizen should be able to bear and endure the violence any longer. Take into your hands all power, all land, factories and plants.

We, the genuine defenders of your interests, are going to the front to fight against your evil enemy General Denikin in the profound belief that you would not wish for a return of the landowner and the capitalist and that you yourselves will try . . .

Yes, yes. Then we have:

On the red banners of the Don Cossack Revolutionary Corps it is written: All land to the peasants. All factories and plants to the workers. All power to the working people in the form of the true Soviets of Workers', Peasants' and Cossacks' Deputies. All so-called deserters shall join forces with me and will constitute an awesome force, before which Denikin will quake and the Communists bow down.

COMMANDER OF THE DON COSSACK
REVOLUTIONARY CORPS
CITIZEN MIGULIN

What a mess followed; everything was in a holy mess. He hoped the Corps would grow, and yet it petered out. Then, take his relations with the Cossack Section. True, at first relations were not bad. When he went to Moscow he met with people from the Section who promised him help, and he spoke kindly of them. Then some emissaries from the Section visited the Corps and wrote sympathetic reports about it. But for some reason, Asya, you don't mention the fact that at that meeting which you describe in such detail, he called the Cossack Section the "Mongrel Section" and the "dead end of the bowels." His very words!

And as for who believed it and who did not—well, if we're going to be honest about it, everyone believed it! To a man. How could one not believe it when addresses such as this one were being read:

COMRADES!
We took all measures to bring about a peaceful settlement of the conflict between Migulin and the Soviet Republic. Now the time for talking is over and, in order that you might know where you are being led and what you are being thrust into, we are transmitting to you the decision of the Revolutionary Council of the Republic:

"Migulin has been declared a rebel, and powerful battalions have been moved against him. He is to be dealt with as an outlaw. Inform the troops of this and warn them that anyone daring to take up arms against the Soviet regime will be wiped off the face of the earth. In order to avoid bloodshed, I am offering Migulin one last chance to return to the fulfillment of his military duty. Otherwise he will be considered a traitor to the Revolution. If he obeys of his own free will I guarantee his safety. Otherwise his perdition is inevitable. . . ."

The following is taken from the indictment:

The appeals which he issued along his line of march contain indications that he wants to overthrow the Communist Party. One appeal states: "I have raised a rebellion against the Soviet regime, a regime which is not to your liking, men of the Red Army. . . ." He invites into his ranks deserters, who are the greatest bane of Soviet Russia, for they undermined our position on the southern front. . . . Along Migulin's line of march several battles took place with our Red Army units; according to the testimony of some, these numbered four, and according to others five. Hence, at the time when it was learned that the Soviet regime could not permit any partisan campaigns, Migulin was pressing his way through to the front by force of arms. . . . Late in the evening of August 24, Migulin knew that if he set out for the front he would be outlawed. . . . As a result

of skirmishes among our very troops, many people were killed
and wounded; there were losses on Migulin's side as well. In
the midst of our operational difficulties, Migulin gave orders
to destroy the telephone and telegraph lines. There is information showing that on the way, Migulin arrested some Communists and several peasants—true, he later released them—
because they had refused to give him their carts; he even
threatened to shoot them On the way, one factory was robbed
and a certain sum of money was seized from the manager.

(You see, Asenka, these facts somehow slipped your memory.
Yes, the human memory is even more of a miracle: it has the
amazing ability to discard some things and retain others!)

   As Migulin drew nearer to the front, as his situation became
quite dangerous and as he began to feel that the game was up,
he started to hesitate, but still, instead of surrendering peacefully, he attempted to press on further. . . . Migulin arrested
two Communists, Logachev and Kharin, on suspicion of their
having made an attempt on his life. But there is no evidence
establishing that such an attempt took place. Migulin declared
those Communists to be hostages and threatened to kill them
at the first shot from the Soviet side. The arrested Communists
marched for several days with the Red Army men, with the
threat of being shot at any time hanging over them, and it was
only the panic caused by shots from our side that gave them
a chance to flee. . . .

Yet the way she describes it, the arrested men were in the
ranks of the Corps and when Maslyuk asked where they were
Migulin waved his hand behind him as if to say "There they
are." My goodness, memory is an unreliable thing. One needs
these old bits of paper, these documents wearing away at the
folds, the faded ink, the pale Underwood typeface. *But I cannot
send all that to her.*
   Pavel Evgrafovich sat down immediately to answer her.

DEAR ASYA,
    Thank you for your engrossing reminiscences. I learned very many interesting things from them, which disclose . . .

Here he spent a long time wondering what expression to use: "the whole story" or "the entire course of events" or simply "the events." However, upon further reflection he decided on "certain details." Then he continued: ". . . about the march of the Don Cossack Corps to the front," whereupon he heard a shot somewhere nearby. He paid no attention to it, because there was always a shot or two being fired in the Corps. Discipline there was not of the best. He had just begun the next sentence when two shots rang out one after the other, which he thought did not sound as if they had come from a .375 rifle. It sounded as if they had come from a sporting gun, which seemed strange—where would they get a sporting gun? Some thin voices, either women's or children's, were shouting. Pavel Evgrafovich set down his pen and, just as he was, in his mesh undershirt and striped pajama trousers, left his room and went out the back door, across the large common porch and down into the courtyard.
    At the bend in the road leading from the gate into the heart of the cooperative he saw a truck. Several people were crowded around the truck, women and young kids, shouting, howling and even crying. Polina's granddaughter, the overgrown Alyona, rushed toward Pavel Evgrafovich, sobbing.
    "Help! They're killing them!"
    "Whom?!" asked Pavel Evgrafovich in amazement.
    "They've already killed Guslik! Now they're looking for Arapka. They want to kill him! They're wild animals! My God, they're animals! Animals!"
    A man with a sporting gun on his shoulder was moving away toward the sheds. Pavel Evgrafovich caught a fleeting glimpse of another man walking by his side, who he thought was Prikhodko, wearing a straw hat and with some white garment flapping about

him. A crowd of children was running after them. Pavel Evgrafovich heard a heated shout.

"Tolya! Come on! Let's shoot Arapka!"

He recognized with horror the voice of his grandson. Standing
alongside the back of the truck was a familiar lad—State Farm
Mitya, a scoundrel and drunkard who looked as if he was under
the influence right now: his face was red and he could scarcely
get his tongue around his words. He was having a terrible time
trying to tell the women something while they shrieked at him
and waved their arms about. The dogs that had been shot were
lying in the back of the truck. Some small boys were jumping
up and down trying to peep over the side. Pavel Evgrafovich
rushed over, panting, to the sheds, where a man with a gun was
darting from one shed to another in search of Arapka. One boy
was crying. Another was shouting gleefully, "Over there! Over
there! There he is!"

The murderer was throwing aside a heap of planks.

"What can you do?" said Prikhodko. "Orders from the dacha
trust. It's got nothing to do with us, folks."

"Stop it!" shouted Pavel Evgrafovich with all his might. For
some reason nobody heard. He sank down onto something re-
sembling a crate, something wooden. His legs would not support
him. He felt a pain in his chest. He suddenly imagined he was
sitting on a long wooden object, like a coffin. All of a sudden,
out jumped Arapka from under the planks, whimpering, and ran
over to Pavel Evgrafovich. He jumped up onto Pavel Evgrafovich's knees and thrust his nose into the pit of his arm. Pavel
Evgrafovich put his arms around the dog and could feel him
shivering. Pavel Evgrafovich was gasping for breath, and there
was a pain in his chest.

"This is my dog. . . . He's not a stray . . . ," he said in a weak
voice.

People were shouting something. A woman was cursing at
Prikhodko. He understood that the reason Prikhodko wanted Ar-

apka dead was because Arapka pestered his own little dog. Shoot him just because he was a mongrel! He was the best of the lot. They were the mad ones, those drunks—they were the ones that should be shot. He felt like shouting all this out to the man with the gun and to Prikhodko and telling Prikhodko that he was contemptible. That he was a former cadet. That he was a traitor. That he was the one who ought to be shot. But he was too weak even to speak, let alone shout; there was a pain in his chest, so he hugged the dog and trembled along with him. He felt nausea welling up. No one would take the dog away from him no matter how much they yelled or breathed their stinking vodka breath into his face.

Prikhodko cast an evil look at him. "You're in violation of the paragraph! Orders from the Moscow Council!"

Pavel Evgrafovich formed a glob of saliva in his mouth to spit. A boy ran up to him, sat down by his side and put his arms around Arapka. Now there were two of them hugging the dog. Then a small girl approached from the other side and put her hand on the back of Arapka's head, which was sticking out from under Pavel Evgrafovich's arm. Suddenly he felt the dog stop shivering.

Someone wheezed into his ear, "Go get some dough. I'll give it to the creep, otherwise he won't leave you alone." It was State Farm Mitka.

The boy who had sat down beside Pavel Evgrafovich carried Arapka in his arms, then grew tired and let him go. Arapka ran alongside, sticking close to his legs. Pavel Evgrafovich stopped whenever the pain was too crushing. He looked for some money at home, rummaged about all over, went through pockets and drawers, and asked Valentina, but found only three rubles plus about forty kopeks in change.

Mitka was not pleased, but, after grumbling, eventually agreed.

"Okay, give it here!" And he ran off, jumping over the plant beds, cracking through the bushes, in his hurry to get to the truck, to move on to new dogs and new three-ruble bills.

Pavel Evgrafovich went inside the house and closed the door behind him. He did not feel like talking with anyone. His chest was still aching, but that was not why he did not want to talk. No, that was not why. Everything taken together produced a feeling of loathing. He had saved Arapka. But how could he save the rest? For instance, that boy who had shouted, "Over there! Over there!"? And his own grandson? How could he talk to Prikhodko now? It occurred to him that when Galya was alive all this would have been impossible. There could not have been such dog butchers, such curious little boys, such heat. The heat was inhuman, unearthly; heat from the other world. Everything was different when Galya was there.

He was sitting in his rocking chair when he suddenly heard voices, Verochka talking to Erastych. Somewhere below his window. Down there, quite nearby. They were not talking loudly in fact, but, wouldn't you know it, he could hear every word. He was amazed at how clearly and distinctly.

Verochka was complaining, "I'm terribly worried. It pains me to look at him. He's become so old; so pathetic and odd. He can hardly walk."

Erastych: "Don't let it get to you." (What a stupid expression, "Don't let it get to you"; the man works in an institution of learning and uses such God-awful expressions.) "You can't force your brother to give up drinking, can you? You can't bring the old man's health back, can you? So don't let it get to you."

He listened calmly. It was nothing new. The only thing that bothered him was that he was eavesdropping, but it was not an easy matter to get up out of his rocking chair. It required an effort, and he hesitated for some time, wondering whether to embark on the complex operation of hoisting himself out of the chair, hoping all the while that the tedious conversation down below would stop. He gave a loud cough and banged his stick on the floor to let them know he was sitting nearby. But no, they did not hear, and continued their conversation.

Verochka said even more plaintively, "But, you know, I feel sorry for him, I really do. Well, why does he sit up all night, not sleeping, sorting through his papers?"

"Thank God he has an occupation."

"It's not an occupation, Kolya. It's something..."

"All old people are a bit bats. Old age is a type of schizophrenia." And they went off.

He pondered that strange expression, "All old people are a bit bats." What did that unpleasant fellow mean? The sentence made him uneasy. The schizophrenia part he could understand. They thought he was a schizophrenic. But why bats? My God, they are the ones who are sick; sick with a lack of understanding, sick with insensitivity. It was as though they had achieved the ideal of that man with the bare, crumpled skull—what was his name? He used to say that one should get rid of one's emotions. Had they gotten rid of theirs already? He clean forgot the man's name. His skull was like a kulich—an Easter cake. He was killed in the spring of 1920.

No. I won't go and talk to him. All this talk is devoid of interest. And if there's no interest, there's no sense either, so why worry about it? It was all over long ago and was absolutely pointless. Mercy me, how terribly intriguing won't it be to know who gets the little house of the old woman who left no heirs! No, no. It holds no interest for me. The only interesting thing is, *what drove Migulin out of Saransk in pursuit of Denikin?* That was the real sore point, the real problem, the question of questions!

In order to answer her charge that "you did somehow believe that he was guilty."

Ask the ants scurrying along in single file across the windowsill right here, one after the other, whether they believe that in the place they are running to there will be food, salvation, truth.... As always, one person snorted skeptically.

We arrived in Balashov at dawn. Hazy, dark October. Living in the apartment that had been rented for us was Lev, a correspondent for the Revolutionary Military Council's paper *On the March*. He did not resemble the lion for which he was named: he was thin and pale, and his military jacket had a secondhand look about it. He had with him the latest issue of *On the March*, with the article entitled "Colonel Migulin." Written by Trotsky. The trial was to begin within two days.

"Look here, he really can't write this," says Shura, trying to grasp the import of the article, and I see that his face has coarsened and become covered in white blotches. I know that those white blotches are a sign of irritation. "Look what he writes:

"The career of former Colonel Migulin is coming to a shameful and sorry end. He considered himself to be—as did many others—a great 'revolutionary.' But what was the reason for Migulin associating himself with the Revolution for a time? It is now perfectly clear: personal ambition, careerism, the desire to mount onto the backs of the toiling masses...."

Then he comes straight out with: 'treachery.'"

"Well? Why don't you like it?" asked Lev.

"Because before a trial you can't write, 'It is now perfectly clear...'"

"I don't understand."

"If it's 'perfectly clear,' then there's no point in having a trial. All courts throughout the world are meant to establish the facts."

"We're not concerned about all courts throughout the world," said Lev. "A revolutionary court is unlike anything else. Never in history has there been anything like it."

Or was Lev his surname? His first name was something complicated; by force of habit everyone called him Lev. Lev. We had known each other for a long time—about three weeks. He would appear intermittently in Kozlov and, from time to time, at the Ninth Army headquarters.

Shura told him that if he had known that to be the case he would not have consented to take part in the trial.

Lev replied coldly, "Alexander Pimenovich, I do not think that the matter depends on your consent."

Starting with the dark dawn, the "Colonel Migulin" article and that unpleasant conversation with correspondent Lev, everything went off course. At once Shura began, as was his wont, to object to everything down the line. He was seething with exasperation and fury. He seemed to curse himself for not having gotten out of the way in time, and now he made it a point to fight with people, to be obstructive and to stalk out. Yet he was needed: his authority and his fame as a former prisoner lent weight to the court proceedings. Two other members of the tribunal were Kuban Cossacks. An old Party member called Syrenko was appointed president of the court. The chief prosecutor was Yanson, an old acquaintance of Shura's; they called each other *ty*. Yanson was the main one: all the quarreling, swearing and disputes were with him.

"Just get it into your head, you stubborn devil, that the point of this trial is not juridical, but political. Its point is propaganda! We have to shatter the Migulin legend. We have to deal a blow, number one, to the counterrevolutionary Cossacks; number two, to Bonapartism; and, number three, to guerrilla warfare."

And again to Shura: "Alexander, why do you always want everything your own way? Why are you always—and I remember you very well from the old days—so subservient to discipline and collective opinion?"

Shura said that he had come in order to take part in a court examination, not a theatrical performance. If it was going to be a show that had been fully rehearsed in advance, then he begged to take his leave. That wasn't quite true. The author of the "Colonel Migulin" article had wanted a show. But things turned out differently. Quite differently, although Shura did not guess what would happen.

An irritated Yanson assured him, "Don't worry. It will be a real trial with a prosecutor, defense counsel, judges, the public and the press"—although he, Yanson, had a clear-cut prior opinion: Migulin should be convicted of treason. "You don't agree?"

"I don't know. That's why I've come: to find out."

Their arguments became sharper and Shura took the bit between his teeth. It ended up in catastrophe: Shura left for Penza in the evening, flinging down the angry explanation that he was divesting himself of the duties of a member of the court owing to the fact that he disagreed with this, that and the other thing. I do not remember with what precisely. The president of the Military Revolutionary Tribunal of the Tenth Army was urgently summoned to replace him. Shura was acting dangerously. I was terrified for him. There was a moment, immediately after his sudden departure, when Syrenko and Yanson, in their rage, talked about arresting him and putting him on trial. But it was all nonsense, of course! They agreed afterward that it was perhaps for the best: that, with the mood he was in, goodness knows what he might have gotten up to at the trial.

But I stayed on in Balashov. Because I had already been appointed assistant court secretary. A lot of red tape, a lot of papers, names. Apart from Migulin there were twelve commanding officers and Cossack associates of his on trial, and about fifteen people to be called as witnesses. Besides, all four hundred and thirty of the men taken by Skvortsov were considered as defendants and were waiting for their fate to be decided.

Gloomy, emaciated, suddenly an old man—the streaks of gray were more pronounced than ever before in his black hair— Migulin was sitting on the first bench by the side of the judges' desk, and over and over again he would scan the room, his body jerkily bending forward, his shoulders strained to their limits. He was looking for Asya, but she was not there. The public was not admitted on the first day. I met Asya that evening.

And here is the rarity of rarities, a one-hundred-sixty-page gem in a dark-blue file: the shorthand report of the trial. If ever fire breaks out in this house and I have to grab my most valuable possession, I will go for this file. Why, though? It has all been read and reread.

THE PRESIDENT: Prisoner at the bar Migulin, have you heard the accusation against you?

MIGULIN: Yes.

THE PRESIDENT: Do you plead guilty?

MIGULIN: I plead guilty to all charges with the exception of a few details, but I request that my confession be heard during the trial. . . .

It has all been read and reread, rethought and readjusted by memory. But every time there is something new. Galya read it, too. She used to say that Migulin was an upright, honest man, but with a narrow outlook. This she deduced from the shorthand report. She had real understanding. She knew nothing about Asya. Galya was truly excellent at figuring people out, especially men. She was not very interested in women. Indeed, she had no women friends, only Polina. She used to say, "They bore me. There's so much nonsense in them."

MIGULIN: I was not opposed to Communist ideology, but to certain individuals who were sapping the authority of the Soviet regime. I drew a detailed picture of all those individuals at the meetings. So I should like to call attention to the impossible political atmosphere which surrounded me in Saransk. Then the rumor spread that Tambov had fallen and it seemed to me that in those circumstances the cadets might move on Bogo-yavlensk. It seemed likely to me that Denikin's forces would drive a wedge into our position, going in the direction of Ryazhsk, especially as rumors had been circulating about the evacuation of Kozlov. I decided to go forward with the forces I had, convinced that by so doing I would halt the movement of the front at all points. . . .

THE PRESIDENT: Did you threaten to arrest any Communists?

MIGULIN: That was only a tactical move, as I wanted no one to obstruct my path. At first I stated that Kharin and Logachev would be executed, but then I gave orders not to do so as I am opposed in principle to the death penalty. I did not execute a single Communist who was arrested.

THE PRESIDENT: When did you write your declaration "Long Live the Russian Proletarian Working Peasantry"?

MIGULIN: Early in August when at a meeting someone handed me a note asking the question "What is the Social Revolution and how should humanity live?"

THE PRESIDENT: Did you not regret the fact that you had no guns because if you had had them you would have blown Penza off the face of the earth?

MIGULIN: No. I never said that.

THE PRESIDENT: What, if any, fighting was conducted under your command during the campaign?

MIGULIN: We tried to avoid all fighting; before we got to the River Sura we consulted with Yurganov as to the best way to proceed in order to avoid a confrontation. . . . Quite frankly, my initial destination was Penza because I wanted Comrade Yanson finally to understand me. . . .

YANSON: Tell me, when you set out with your detachment, ostensibly to defend the front, was it logical of you to establish a new front at the rear of the Soviet-held ground? As an officer did you give that any thought?

MIGULIN: Of course I acted illogically, but try to understand my state of mind; try to understand that atmosphere. . . .

YANSON: Have you felt normal over these past days or has your mind been confused?

MIGULIN: You have already heard me say that I was not aware of what was going on. When I had those talks with you I was rushing about; I went to the telephone exchange several times, and more than once picked up the telephone receiver; in the end, worn out by that struggle, I . . .

How did she know I was at the theater? Lev and I had gone in the evening to the theater, or rather to the club at which the Saratov company was performing. They were doing *The Lady from Torzhok*. All I remember about it is the name. And the fact that Lev was incredibly scornful in his assessment—he was a theater buff, an expert, a city slicker who was friendly with actors from the Moscow Art Theater. He would be returning to Moscow immediately after the trial. "If this is the sort of rubbish that is going to flourish on the stage, we'll have to have another revolution!"

The actors piled into a cart and were taken to the station. A sack of flour was placed in the cart with them. And then out of the blue appeared Asya. I did not recognize her immediately: she was wrapped up to the eyes in a scarf and was wearing a long black coat. She grabbed me by the arm and dragged me from the doorway off into the darkness.

"Pavlik, I must see you for a minute."

She asked me to arrange a meeting with Migulin. I was stunned. She was speaking an overwhelming flow of gibberish; she was beside herself, sick, crazy. She was feverish, her lips were burning; she kissed me, squeezed me, begged me, and tried to persuade me. "I know I've done you wrong. You love me, you're my darling, you'll do it... you'll help. If I don't see him tomorrow I'll die. It was so terrible what he said today. He slandered himself! He said his mind was confused...."

It turned out that she had been present at the trial; she had prevailed upon someone, forced her way in, and had sat there hidden away. He did not see her for a long time, although he was constantly on the lookout for her, but then she did something to *make* him see!

I told her it was impossible. I was small fry there. Because of Shura, my relations with Yanson and Syrenko were bad: they were angry with him and would do nothing for me.

"But they're going to shoot him! There's no other way!"

I said nothing, because it was the truth. What could I tell her? I felt terribly sorry for her, and at the same time my amazement at her love was suffocating me. And when in her madness she seized my fingers and, looking into my eyes yet not seeing me, babbled that if I helped her she would be prepared to do anything, that she would stay with me, I asked her, "Forever? Or only for today?" Terrible, mean question, but it wasn't me! It wasn't me! I could never have asked it if I had been myself! But I too got carried away. I was like a lunatic.

She looked at me and suddenly burst out sobbing, and whispered, squeezing my hand, "Forever, forever! Forever—if only I can have one minute with him."

That is something she does not mention in the letter. That is something she has forgotten about. As if there had been no meeting on the street, no sobs or madness; as if we had never gone afterward to the apartment where Lev snored in the next room—the apartment *where she stayed* until morning, and where nothing happened apart from conversation, hour after hour of explanations, love for another, pangs, fantastical plans. Yet nothing could come of it all. Nothing, nothing. That is why she forgot. She remembers only that I could not arrange a meeting with the lawyer. She refuses to try to understand and does not want to know anything about it.

I said to her, "Try to imagine the situation. Denikin is advancing, Kursk is taken, a plot has been exposed, a bomb has exploded in Leontevsky Lane, our comrades have been killed. In this hour of mortal danger, how do you suppose a man accused of treason should be judged?"

"I'll swear any oath you like: he's not a traitor!"

"But even Yurganov, one of his close associates, says he wanted to kill him for treason."

"That's a lie! There was nothing more disgusting than Yurganov's answers. I've seen through him now. He's like putrid waste whipped up from the bottom by the storm. . . ."

Where are Yurganov's answers? Unforgettable, the way Migulin looked at him.

YURGANOV: I was expelled from the sixth class of high school on suspicion of murder, then about two years later became a local teacher. But as a result of constant clashes with the priests—with whom I found it impossible to reach any understanding—I gave it up, roamed around, roughed it. Then I was called up for the war. Under Kerensky I was admitted to military school and attained the rank of ensign. After the October Revolution I joined the Red Army, in which I serve to this day. . . .

THE PRESIDENT: What posts have you held?

YURGANOV: First I was in the ranks, then was elected commander. I commanded a brigade, and in Migulin's Corps I was a division commander. . . . I could see that Migulin was deranged and wrong. He was mistaken in his wholesale attacks on the political people. . . . I explained Migulin's error by his morbid nervousness and suspicion. . . . I tried to reconcile the hostile sides in the quarrels.

THE PRESIDENT: Did you write a letter to Brigade Commander Skvortsov calling Migulin a leader of the World Revolution?

YURGANOV: Yes, I did. But at the meeting on August 21, when Migulin appealed to everyone to go to the front, and when the masses, roused up by his appeal, shouted out, "Onward to the front!," Migulin asked me, "Are you going to defend your comrades?" What could I answer? I told him I was. He later arrested a commissar at the meeting and, when I went up to him and pointed out that he had acted improperly, he said to me, "I got worked up." I was outraged by Migulin's action and told him that if he took a step to the right I would kill him.

(Migulin shouted something out with a laugh. The President reprimanded him.)

In the end, when I realized that under no circumstances should Migulin be allowed to go to the front, I decided to do what I had considered doing a long time before: kill him. An opportunity had not arisen earlier because he had surrounded himself by loyal associates, his "janissaries."

THE PRESIDENT: Why did you advise the Brigade Commander of Migulin's march in the letter?

YURGANOV: I wrote that he might do something outstanding.

THE PRESIDENT: And you wanted the Brigade Commander to support your adventure.

YURGANOV: I repeat again that the letter was written under pressure from Migulin.

THE PRESIDENT: I shall read out the most significant sentences: "Migulin is not only a great strategist, but a great prophet too." Did you write that sentence?

YURGANOV: Yes, that is my sentence.

THE PRESIDENT: "If he revolts it will be to defend truth and freedom."

YURGANOV: Those are my words.

THE PRESIDENT: "The peasants are prepared to throw themselves into Denikin's bondage if only to escape those torments..."

YURGANOV: Those are Migulin's words.

THE PRESIDENT: Why do you write at the end of the letter, "I embrace you heartily, perhaps for the last time"?

YURGANOV: That's really just a closing formula to which I don't attach any particular importance—especially as, at the time, I was vacillating about whether to kill Migulin and then commit suicide....

The questioning of Dronov. He was asked what he did before the October Revolution and what he did during the war.

DRONOV: I was a sub-*esaul*, then I became a regimental aide-de-camp. After the October Revolution I lived in Kiev and joined the Red Army. On August 15, I got into Migulin's

Corps and was given the post of aide-de-camp of the Second Regiment. . . .

THE PRESIDENT: Were you in the army under Skoropadsky?

DRONOV: I had to serve in staff posts under six governments. . . .

THE PRESIDENT: Why did you follow Migulin?

DRONOV: Partly for personal reasons: because I had received no salary for a month and a half.

THE PRESIDENT: Did you understand the meaning of his having been declared an outlaw?

DRONOV: I did not attach much importance to it."

It somehow seems to me that it was this Dronov—I suddenly have an image of a dandified, lanky man respectfully extending forward a neck with a prominent Adam's apple and even cocking an ear toward the President in order to hear him better—that Asya was talking about in the letter. The one who bothered her and squeezed her in the dark. Was it he? I have an inkling it was, so it makes me angry to read:

THE PRESIDENT: Before he was disarmed, Migulin addressed the troops, did he not?

DRONOV: It was like this: Migulin ordered the regiment to form up and said in his own words, "I am sacrificing my life to avoid bloodshed. We're going to join forces with the Cossacks. Forward, singers!" And the regiment set off in song. That was in Krutenkiye, just before you get to Mokrenkiye. . . .

THE PRESIDENT: Tell me, did you ever hear Migulin express an opinion about Trotsky?

DRONOV: Yes, I did. During the campaign, meetings were called in some villages, at which the following words were spoken: "Recently, I read in a paper that Russia will need a strong dictatorship for some years. Is Lev Trotsky not already thinking to become dictator of Russia?"

THE PRESIDENT: When did you find out that Migulin had been outlawed?

DRONOV: About five or ten minutes before setting out. . . .

THE PRESIDENT: Migulin, did you know that in the morning of the twenty-second, and on the twenty-third of August, some Cossacks committed excesses and arrested Communists?

MIGULIN: I was not aware of that.

A two-hour recess was called. That evening Yanson made his statement for the prosecution. He was twenty-eight at the time. But in that tow-haired, short-legged little man on the rostrum I did not see—no one saw—either his youth or his university past or his Baltic origins: it was the icy voice of the Revolution speaking; it was *the course of events*. And one's spirit froze and one's hands became rigid. I remember, I remember...

I remember: the cold brilliance of the sky through the window. The unexpected sunny day. I remember: Asya in one of the front rows, noticing and hearing nothing, staring at the Cossack with the gray whiskers. I remember my increasing amazement: how could I have doubted his guilt? It was all so terribly clear.

I accuse former Cossack Colonel Migulin and his accomplices, all of whom held responsible posts in our Red Army during the war between the Soviet regime and Denikin, of having fomented armed rebellion against the Soviet regime. We have before us a tremendous body of evidence which portrays a sufficiently clear picture of the uprising. On the night before August 23, I learned that something was amiss in Saransk, that the Corps was in a state of unrest and that Migulin was making mutinous speeches. I took all steps to bring about a peaceful settlement of the conflict. I informed Migulin by command telephone of the situation on the southern front and of Mamontov's raid. I told him that his unauthorized campaign could do great harm to the cause of defending the Soviet Republic. This was met with a confused, incoherent answer— he said he "could not take any more" and that he "felt stifled.".... Drawing his Corps away with him, he advanced from Saransk to the front, intending to join up with the Twenty-third Division and form a combined force for certain purposes known only to himself, Migulin....

Here in court, Migulin has been overhumble. He was contrite. He said that he was unbalanced; that he had been so to speak pushed into it and that he had not realized that he was committing such a crime. But there was a time when Migulin felt that he had a certain amount of support behind him and behaved differently. He had hoped to become a people's hero, something like a Russian Garibaldi. In those days he could even use threats. For example, in the appeal or manifesto in which he declared war on me, he writes, "I'll destroy you, sweep you away, if you dare oppose me...." After analyzing all the evidence relating to Migulin's case, I have reached the conclusion that this man is no eagle, but merely a drake— since the methods he used to inveigle his men into following him were not those of a leader.... I maintain that no one since the time of our Revolution has created a more muddled and nebulous ideology. One cannot help comparing Migulin to Kerensky of blessed memory, who said, choking with rage, "If you don't believe me I'll shoot myself."...

Migulin's prime accomplice, Yurganov, behaved in court like a coward, saying that he had opposed Migulin and that he had even tried to kill him. He described himself as a sympathizer with the Communist Party. This means that Yurganov is a criminal twice over: as a traitor to his Party, and to the Soviet regime. In revolutionary times the attitude to be taken toward such pathetic ditherers is rarely ever sympathetic. He should have overcome his faintheartedness and cowardice and told the men clearly and precisely, "Migulin is a traitor; you must remain in Saransk." A statement like that might have spared us the need to put over four hundred people on trial, among whom known traitors are undoubtedly in the minority. Of the commanding officers who followed Migulin, I am interested in the figure of Dronov, who, according to his own statement, served under six governments in the Ukraine. Evidently, these included the Soviet regime, then Petlyura, then Hetman Skoropadsky, then the Soviet regime again, et cetera. And yet under all these governments he retained his staff posts.

I think that this act of treachery will have been his last.... People like Migulin—unbalanced, but quite good speakers—are incapable, once they have aroused the benighted masses, of keeping them under control. So they are replaced by the Denikinists. Dronov, along with Mamontov, would really have established a front against the Soviet regime. That man did not follow Migulin for nothing: in his own words he claims to have followed him in order to be paid his back salary for one and a half months. That sounds ludicrous coming from a former regimental aide-de-camp: he followed Migulin because he caught a whiff of adventure and the chance of easy political gain. Here he behaves all meek and mild, like a simpleton, obligingly answering all the questions. Such a meekling and a cringer could never have held staff posts under six governments....

You all know that for almost two years now the very meaning and essence of our Revolution has been distilled into a struggle between extremes: the working class, the Communist Party and the Soviet regime on the one hand and the bourgeois counterrevolution—Denikin, Kolchak, Yudenich—on the other. All attempts by compromise groups—by the establishmentarianists, by the champions of various *radas* and so on— to find some kind of middle line have thus far proven to be in vain. We know, and anyone can verify it from a thousand facts, that any struggle raised against the Soviet regime and against the relentless iron logic of things has led to Denikin and to counterrevolution. The Czechoslovaks, the Left Socialist Revolutionaries, the democratic groups of Mensheviks and others have risen in revolt against us. All these groups have ultimately found themselves within the embrace of Denikin, who has dashed them all out of his way. He alone is a resolute and strong adversary, and only one of the two, either the Soviet regime or Denikin, will emerge victorious from this terrible, colossal struggle....

Edvard Yanovich was no fool; no fool at all in matters of reasoning! He could talk too, and had a lucid mind. But the times were catastrophic—October 1919. What were people thinking about then in godforsaken Balashov? What were they hoping for? My God, Denikin had taken Voronezh and was on his way to Orel and Bryansk. In the east, Tobolsk had fallen. Yudenich was in Krasnoye Selo; the Germans were in Riga. Everything hanging by a thread. *And not an instant's doubt about ultimate victory!* The next day, after the trial, we went hunting: we rose at dawn. First we went to the lake and shot some duck, then went off to a field to shoot partridges.

... Here he expounds a semi-Tolstoyan, semisentimental melodrama. He says that he favors a system which is to be introduced without any violence whatsoever. But who can believe that you, an old Cossack officer, who in the old war was awarded practically every military distinction, even the Saint George's Cross, have sincerely adopted such a point of view? Let us even take his theory of the state. He wants immediate freedom for all citizens. He does not understand that the path to socialism lies through the dictatorship of the oppressed over their oppressors. He does not understand that to demand freedom for all in a period of civil war is to demand freedom for counterrevolutionaries....

You expatiate at length on your love for the people and freedom, and moreover you write that ordinary people live badly in Russia, and for that you blame the Communist Party. That is a lie: it has nothing to do with the Communist Party! You know well that we have been ravaged by four years of war and you know that our plants and factories have been brought to a standstill because the counterrevolution has seized areas rich in oil, coal and grain.... You say that people should not be coerced, that they should do everything of their own free will and that the entire apparatus of the state should be weakened. Fine, but what would have happened by now if we did not have compulsory conscription into the Red Army and if we had no monopoly on grain? Not only would the Communists have been exterminated, but you too, Citizen Migulin, would not be flourishing in particular lushness under the dictatorship of a general. You complain that the peasant has a hard life. That is true, his lot is not an easy one, as the country lies in ruins! But in your criticism of our food policy, you forget to mention that the towns have become impoverished, that they have nothing to exchange for grain. The worker must surely die of hunger if the Soviet regime does not give him grain. That is a shameful state of affairs in a country which has a grain surplus. . . .

Now, about the outrages on the Don. The evidence makes it clear that outrages did take place. However, it also makes it clear that the main culprits in those horrors have already been executed. It should not be forgotten that all these deeds were perpetrated while the Civil War was going on, when passions had reached fever pitch. Look to the French Revolution and the struggle between the Vendée and the Convention. You will see that the forces of the Convention committed atrocious acts—atrocious from the point of view of the individual. The actions of the Convention forces are to be understood only in the light of a class analysis. They are justified by history because they were committed by a new progressive class which had swept from its path the vestiges of feudalism and popular ignorance. The same thing is happening now. You must understand.

We are experiencing the most enormous difficulties; the Revolution is surrounded by an iron circle; our army is straining itself to the breaking point to hang on to the achievements of October. Our army is beginning to eliminate the unruliness which used to thrive in Red Army units when each commander acted arbitrarily, amateurishly. Migulinism, in whatever self-satisfied, unrealistic verbiage it may be cloaked, is an expression of that unruliness of the amateur period.

We have before us a criminal who drivels on about the happiness of mankind but who in actual fact is opening up a path for Mamontov to march on Moscow. We should feel no pity for people like this. The detritus of petit-bourgeois ideology should be swept from the path of the Revolution and the Red Army. I consider that the severest punishment should be meted out to Migulin and his accomplices. . . .

I demand that Migulin, all his officers and all the commissars and Communists who followed him be executed.

Then spoke Stremoukhov, counsel for the defense, who looked probably like no one else on earth; a prewar, antediluvian figure with a pince-nez. He was stout and, what also struck one, he sounded short of breath when he spoke.

Comrades! The revolutionary tribunal has seen fit to entrust to me the onerous duty of defending the accused. Not the system of Migulinism — not the historical phenomenon known by the name of Migulinism — but the accused himself. . . . The prosecutor has presented to us a whole lecture on Migulinism and has stated the views of the ruling Communist Party; this is all nothing new, and if the prosecutor, in explaining that phenomenon in accordance with the Party line, addressed the public face to face, but addressed the court sideways —

(The President interrupted the counsel for the defense and pointed out that such expressions were inappropriate.)

— then I, as a defender of human beings, am going to address your hearts. . . . I have given a great deal of thought to this case and I ask you now: What are these people charged with? Desertion. . . . But up to now we have dealt with and indicted people who were *fleeing the front*, whereas now we are prosecuting a group of people who marched *to the front!*

Whom exactly are we charging here? Not a drake as the prosecutor said. We have before us a lion of the Revolution. From the very dawn of Soviet Russia he fought in the ranks of the defenders of the Revolution, fought honestly for two years — and how he fought! I repeat, that drake has fought from the very beginning of the proletarian Revolution. True, he did not quite succeed in conceiving a political program, nor could he comprehend all the niceties of politics, as can the prosecutor — who is evidently an old Party worker, and to whom we listened with pleasure. Nevertheless, this lion of the Revolution understood all these matters in his heart, and in his heart he felt that the Party was giving the hapless working class what it needed. . . . Wherever there was trouble, wherever the White Guard gangs broke our Red front, that is where this drake would head for. He was trusted at such crucial times, hopes were pinned on him, and he lived up to them. Allow me to remind you that last year — my knowledge of the events of our recent military history is rather poor — our Red Army units in the Khopyor sector were unable to break through the wire entanglements, and so it was this very drake who struck

the enemy's rear, overran him and drove the foe back southward. Surely, this is no drake who advanced forward right up
to Novocherkassk!

So what was the offense of this man who now stands before
us in the dock? It was this: that a Red Army soldier was a bad
politician, that he did not have a clear grasp of the political
atmosphere surrounding him and that, soldierlike, he was
forthright in his actions. A man of integrity—as in his heart,
so in his deeds—he did not hide his thoughts. . . . In a conversation with me in Cell Nineteen he expressed regret that
all his correspondence has landed here. It included letters of
a personal nature. He requested that they not be quoted—it
is in any case not necessary. However, I venture to go against
his wishes as regards one sentence only: I read a remarkable
phrase which sums him up completely. He writes to the woman
he loves: "Be mine entirely or leave me." That short sentence
expresses the whole of Migulin's nature. . . .

As hard as I try I cannot recall that sentence, although I listened
attentively to the defense counsel's statement. Even more than
attentively—greedily, enthusiastically! It thrilled and upset me
just as Yanson's speech had earlier thrilled and upset me. But if
it's there in the shorthand report, then he must have said it.
When? In February? When Volodya was still alive? When she
was dividing her love between the two of them?

. . . Things were bad for the internal administration on the
Don. Migulin cried out, "There is trouble! As a result, our
successes will be reduced to nothing!" But his voice was barely
heeded. He was told that Moscow had not forgotten about the
Don and that orders were being issued. But surely the point
is not to issue orders stating that we shall combat all the outrages; the point is that those outrages nevertheless continue. . . . True to himself and to Soviet Russia, Migulin cried
out from the depths of his soul: "We cannot go on living like
this! Help! Do something to alleviate the present situation!"

And who knows but that Moscow's well-known appeal to
the Cossacks was triggered by that cry? We know that recently
the policy of the Soviet regime has changed with regard to the

Cossacks. The newspaper *The Red Plowman* stated on September 11 that the policy toward the Cossacks would be changed and would take account of the social conditions on the Don. . . . Migulin cried out, and his cry acted as a goad to cure one of the plagues of Soviet Russia. That was his achievement and because of that achievement he should be pardoned. And, as a defender of human beings, I crave your great indulgence and beg you with all my heart to weigh the circumstances of this trial, consider them and only then to pronounce your judgment.

And here is Migulin's statement:

Citizen Judges, when I found myself in Cell Nineteen, I noted down my impressions during the first moments of incarceration on a scrap of paper which will remain after me. My first minute in that dungeon was so queer: when the door slams shut, your immediate feeling is that you don't understand what has happened. My entire life has been devoted to the Revolution, yet it has sent me to this jail; my whole life long I have fought for freedom and as a result I have been robbed of that freedom. In that dungeon I was able to meditate in peace, perhaps for the first time. There was no one to intrude and I pondered on who I was.

Yanson said I am not familiar with Marx. True, I do not know him, but there in my cell I read for the first time a small book about the social movement in France and I unexpectedly happened upon a definition which sums up people like myself. In France there were Socialists who were concerned with the idea of justice and who sought after it everywhere. They were exceedingly sincere, yet were devoid of scientific knowledge and method. . . . I am just such a person, and this has been my downfall. . . . And I beg the revolutionary tribunal to lend an ear to that. I shall say something about the revolutionary actions I have had occasion to perform in the course of my life.

In 1895, when I was still in the ranks, one of the commanders deducted six rubles from my nine-ruble salary. I rebelled against that and said I would shoot the bastard. The resulting situation was so difficult that I was unable to bear it for long, and so transferred to the post of magistrate. By 1904 I had been made an officer and was chosen for the honorary post of *stanitsa* ataman. At that time I had to equip nine men at public expense, and this hit the Cossacks hard: it forced them into debt; and, as a fervent defender of Cossack interests, I took all steps to ease their burden. So, during the formal acceptance of the horses, I managed to get all nine animals past the commission. But when the ataman arrived he rejected all the horses and ordered me to submit others by twelve o'clock. However hard I tried to discover why the horses had been rejected I could get no answer, and so I decided to submit the same horses to the ataman. At twelve o'clock they produced the horses for him, the same ones, and the ataman selected six of them and rejected the rest, ordering me to produce the remaining horses by three o'clock. Again I decided to show him the same horses. In the end I succeeded in getting the original horses through, and eighteen Ust-Medveditsky *stanitsas* witnessed the event. . . . Then, when the Japanese declared war, I was mobilized and sent into combat. There I saw officers committing wanton enormities, and when the commander of the Fourth Cossack Division, General Teleshov, was put under military arrest for the enormities, excesses and crimes which he committed, I said in public to the commanding officer of the regiment that that was just how a commander should be treated, as outrages could not be tolerated in our army. For that I was sent to a military hospital for those suffering from nervous disorders. They wanted to declare me insane for having spoken the truth. I then had some difficult, cheerless times to endure, and I remember how gladdened I was by the October 17 manifesto. I remember how everyone welcomed it as they would celebrate a joyous holiday. . . . Nineteen six was a very difficult year for me. I shall not go into my run-in with General Shirokov, as a result of which I found myself in the Danilovskaya district. When the Union of Russian People was formed I explained its meaning to everyone, and when a secret letter from the Union of Russian People was intercepted I read it out to the Cossacks and explained its true import to them. When I was sent to the First Cossack Division under the leadership of Generals Samsonov and Vershinin, I endured some terribly difficult times. No one understood me, and after one of my clashes with the commanding officer I told him that he was not a man but a beast. So, wherever I was, no matter where, I always performed revolutionary acts in order to discredit authority. Everything I have said here is to show..."

Suddenly at supper, a terrible discovery: Ruska was ill, in the hospital, and they had been hiding it from him. Hiding it— hiding it from him! It had happened six days ago! The entire household knew, while he, his father, was kept in the dark. The despicable conspiracy was broken by Prikhodko's daughter, fat Zoya, who rushed over with wide-open eyes and asked, "How's Rusik getting on? I heard he's feeling better." Pavel Evgrafovich was stunned; his voice disappeared. A second of numbness while he waited to hear what the people around the table would answer. Without a moment's embarrassment, Vera replied that, yes, he was better; they had called up the hospital yesterday and his condition was satisfactory, but they wanted to keep him there for at least two weeks. He sent his regards to everyone.

"Who called up? And where to?" gasped Pavel Evgrafovich.

"I did," said Valentina. "I called Egorevsk."

"What's the matter with Ruska? Why don't I know anything about it?"

"Papa, what kind of nonsense is this? Aren't you ashamed of yourself?" said an apparently indignant Vera, and she waved her hand at Pavel Evgrafovich. "Do stop, please."

"*What is the matter with Ruska?!*" shouted Pavel Evgrafovich.

"Papa, don't get mad. Just drop the funny stuff."

Vera threatened him with her finger, and Erastovich looked at him crossly. Of course it was all a game they were playing, not wanting to appear as liars in front of a stranger. And, keeping up their game, they did not want to say anything about it! On the verge of tears and at the same time choking with rage, he demanded that they explain immediately! *He really had known nothing about it!* They looked at him as if he were a fool. No, as if he were a goner.

Putting on a soft, patient tone, Vera tried to point out to him, "Papa, how can you say that? On Tuesday you were sitting right here and we came in and talked. Then you went to your room."

"Pavel Evgrafovich, you're overworked. With those memoirs of yours," said Erastovich. "You should take a break."

Pavel Evgrafovich buried his face in his hands. "God Almighty, will somebody tell me?"

His sister-in-law piped up, "You know, one night I heard a bump and got scared, so I went into his room and found him on his bed, dressed—I mean in his pajamas—and asleep. The light was on, his file was on the floor and all his papers were strewn about."

Finally he learned that Ruska had suffered some burns—not too dangerous, thank God. As a former tank crew member, he had been working on a tractor out there. The tractor had overturned somewhere. Into the burning peat. No one knew any details, and for some reason no one made a move to go and see him immediately, which is what they should have done.

Fat Zoya suggested, as if in all innocence, "Folks, let me go, eh? To Egorevsk? I'm free right now; I'm on leave. It's absolutely no trouble at all; I'd gladly..."

And this in front of his present wife, his first wife, his sister and his sons. Such utter nonsense. Vera muttered unintelligibly, "Thank you, Zoyechka, but there doesn't seem to be any particular need right now."

Valentina, compressing her full lips, which made her face square and angry-looking—an expression which used to appear when she and Ruska quarreled (they had not quarreled for quite a while now; everything had died down)—clattered the dishes without saying a word and left the room. Whatever was brewing between those women was not his concern, but for goodness' sake, when a disaster has taken place... He felt deeply resentful of Valentina. Getting even at a time like this!

"I'm going. Give me the address. Quickly!" said Pavel Evgrafovich in a fuss, and he got up from the table.

Everyone started shouting. They all went for him. Shook their hands at him hypocritically. He almost did not hear them; he was thinking of Galya: it was a blessing that she had not lived to see this. The old man would go to the hospital because the woman who had been pulling the wool over his son's eyes for thirty years *could not share him.* Oh God, it's his own fault! His own fault, silly, unprincipled man that he is. His whole life he has done exactly as he pleased and this is his punishment—no one to give him so much as a drink of water. Well, croak, then, like a dog, among strangers. . . . And at the same time an incredibly powerful pity for his son was squeezing Pavel Evgrafovich to the point of tears. How can they just sit quietly around the table drinking tea? Valentina brings in the jam. Verochka selects some without pits and puts it into her jam dish. Does that mean, then, that it is not a matter of complete indifference to her now whether her jam has pits in it or not? The way they hissed and waved their hands at him, as if he were a hen which had flown onto the veranda from the yard!

Gasping for breath and forcing his way through their hands, shouts and alarm, he muttered, "Why are you eating. . . jam?"

"Vitya!" shouted Vera. "His drops! On his table!"

She helped him into bed. Everyone left. It was quiet again. She held his hand while she took his pulse, looking at him with panic in her eyes. She whispered to him, "Don't worry, Papochka, he's better now. You mustn't get worked up about it. Valya has spoken with him."

"But how could you? So many people. . ."

"Well, what could we do about it if he demanded—" and lowering her voice even more—"that no one should visit him? Do you understand? No one. Of course Valentina is offended, Myuda is afraid to go and I didn't want to, either."

Then, happy guess, "He's not alone, then?"

"I don't know. . . . I think. . . My brother's a very secretive person."

"Worthless man!" He made a movement with his fingers signifying that it was the end of everything. But he let his fingers drop.

Late that evening there was a soft knock at his door—it was Grafchik. He tiptoed in for some reason, the way people do when visiting a sick person, and spoke in a whisper. He brought the latest issue of *Abroad* with him.

"I've come to see you, Pavel Evgrafovich—and to send something to Ruslan: a positive thought."

"What's that?"

"How's his condition, first of all?"

So he had known all about it, too! Once again reminded of their villainous conspiracy, Pavel Evgrafovich became gloomy and answered curtly that it was satisfactory. Pavel Evgrafovich's feelings for Grafchik were benevolent; he thought of him as a smart, well-read person. Besides, this physical-education teacher paid attention to him, brought him magazines and books (he could get nothing out of the children), readily engaged him in conversation, listened to him with interest and asked quite intelligent questions. Yet now Pavel Evgrafovich knit his brows: the suspicion that Grafchik was part of the conspiracy had crept into his mind. Why hadn't he brought *Abroad* before?

Grafchik had plunked himself down on a small child's stool, which made him look as if he were squatting on his haunches— Pavel Evgrafovich used the stool to tie his shoelaces on—and was relating a funny story to him. About a friend of his.

"And you know, this kind of thing: 'Care for a positive thought? For five rubles?' Or else he'll call you up and say, 'I can give you a positive thought—for a ruble.' Ha ha!"

"What was it, a joke?"

"It was a joke. But at the same time, he would never turn down a ruble."

"Nice friends you have."

"He's not a bad lad. But he likes playing games, you see? His whole life he's made everything into a game...." He began telling him about his gambler friend, but it was not interesting.

Pavel Evgrafovich interrupted him. "My dear Anatoly Zakh-arovich, what was it you wished to impart to me? As a positive thought?"

"Oh yes. Well, tell Ruslan that it seems his main rival in the battle for the house has dropped out. Kandaurov."

"What do you mean, dropped out?"

"Dropped out," repeated Grafchik in a whisper, and he made a significant face, rounding his eyes and shooting out his lips into a tube. "That's how it looks to me. He's got other worries. He's seriously ill."

"Really?" asked Pavel Evgrafovich. He could not believe that young people could be seriously ill. Grafchik nodded. His expression was full of meaning. And this was not in keeping with his sitting on a child's stool, as if on his haunches. "What's the matter with him?"

"Something bad. I don't wish him any harm. I hope he gets over it. But in my opinion, things look bad."

Pavel Evgrafovich was sitting in silence on his bed, thinking. "What about you, Anatoly Zakharovich? Are you by any chance a gambler?"

"I? Come, come!" Grafchik gave a laugh and started up from the stool. "What are you saying? I have a family; I have no time for that. While I think of it, you can take it that I've told you nothing about this. Really—how silly!"

And he darted out in a trice. Just like that, Pavel Evgrafovich pushed off to Polina's. It was pitch dark and the twinkling stars were scarcely visible through the haze. Every day that smoky haze appeared intermittently. Why to Polina's? What could he say if things looked bad? Polina's husband Kolka had died many years ago; she was still young, about fifty. She could have begun a new life, but did not want to. Galya had advised her to make a fresh start. Indeed, to do so at once: there was no time to be lost. She had selected a pediatrician friend of hers for Polina. Polina refused. The fact was that people like Migulin were one-track lovers. They could love only one single thing: one woman, one idea, one revolution. When there was a choice, when they were pulled in different directions, when the ground underneath them was swaying and it was necessary to be flexible, such people would snap. How could Migulin not fall for her? When they announced the sentence—death, all commanding officers to be executed—they all listened calmly, apart from one man, I think: the commander of the Commandant's squadron, who fainted and fell to the floor. But Migulin did not budge during all the chaos; he looked on scornfully as they raised up the fallen man. Suddenly Asya cried out from in the room, "Seryozha! I'm with you!" Her cry was so poignant, piercing, powerful and impassioned that in that one instant the old, gray, hardened Migulin was transformed into a happy man: he smiled, his eyes twinkled, he whispered something and nodded his head. . . . When I came back from my hunting expedition the next day—it was like a gulp of water: I would have died of nervous exhaustion otherwise!—Asya met me by the gate of the house. She told me she had spent the whole night near the prison. She looked at me horrified. "You went hunting?!" Yes, yes, I went hunting; nothing could be changed, so I went hunting, because I couldn't see or talk to anyone. . . . There were thirty-two hours left before the sentence was to be carried out. She shouted, "You don't know any of it! A telegram has been sent to Moscow appealing for a pardon!" I knew nothing about that. I only knew that on the last day of the trial a telegram had arrived from the Revolutionary Military Council of the Republic with a request to take into consideration Migulin's behavior in court and to hand down a lenient sentence. Then Migulin closed his final statement by saying, "You see, my life has been a cross, and if I have to bear it to Golgotha I shall. And, whether you believe me or not, I shall shout out, 'Long live the Social Revolution! Long live the Commune and the Communists!'" But the RMC's telegram arrived late: the sentence had already been passed. That same evening, however, Yanson sent a telegram to the All-Russian Central Executive Committee requesting amnesty for Migulin and his followers. *That* I didn't know about. Nor, of course, did I know that late that night an answer had arrived from the All-Russian Central Executive Committee.

For some reason Pavel Evgrafovich picked up from the table his file with the shorthand report. He walked through the bushes in the darkness to Polina's little house, and on the way he suddenly noticed: he was carrying the file! Why? Why was he lugging it along to Polina's? He was going quite balmy in his old age. Couldn't remember what he was doing.

"I set off to come and see you," said Pavel Evgrafovich, "and for some reason I brought my file with me." And he slammed the file down on the table in a fit of temper.

There were three people sitting around an empty table on the veranda. Polina, her daughter Zina and little Alyonushka. They were talking about something and, when Pavel Evgrafovich appeared, they fell silent at once. Zina went inside the house. Polina said, "Pasha, darling! Will you have some tea with us?" She pulled the file toward her, undid the tapes and leafed through the papers. "Your work is very interesting. Do you want me to read it?"

"I don't want anything! Give it to me. I just took it with me accidentally. I happened to bring it with me out of the house, do you understand?"

"I understand, Pasha. I'm always glad to see you. Would you like some tea?"

He acquiesced. No one spoke. He was trying to recall—why had he come? At this late hour? It was after ten. He had come about something important. He could *not* remember what it was. At all. Try as he might he could not for the life of him remember. This simply would not do, dropping in on people late at night without rhyme or reason! But no, he could not remember. What he got was a baffling void and nothing, nothing, absolutely nothing to fill it with. He suddenly felt weak from his intense efforts to remember and became somewhat alarmed, because tension could cause a stroke. And so he decided to stop thinking. The only thing that came to him was that it was something to do with Migulin and Asya. With the way Migulin took the execution. That he'd taken it calmly—it was the pardon he could not endure. Yanson talks about that. In the book he wrote in 1926. There he says that they had to act quickly, as the time for carrying out the sentence was drawing near. A little more than twenty-four hours remained. Even if Moscow's reply was half an hour late for whatever reason, technical or meteorological, it was the end! I remember the oppressive waiting. I was not allowed in. Five of them consulted together—only the members of the court and Syrenko. Before requesting the pardon from the All-Russian Central Executive Committee they decided to demand that the condemned men give their word of honor. How naïve! But that was exactly how it was. Everything was decided in the heat of a seething revolutionary fever. In his memoirs, Yanson writes that his meeting with Migulin took place in the office of Balashov Prison, and with the others, in the cell. Migulin had aged considerably overnight. When Yanson told him that he would plead for mercy for him, the old man could not stand it and broke down crying. Yanson speaks of Migulin as an old man. At the time, Migulin was forty-seven and Yanson twenty-eight.

"If you only knew, my dears," said Pavel Evgrafovich, "what a relief it was! I was exultant—everyone was. And Yanson gives a very vivid description of it here. I'll just find it now—it's not together with the shorthand report; I copied it out separately from his book. Here it is! I've got it. Do you want to hear it? Are you interested? But are you really interested or are you just saying so out of politeness?"

Alyonka nodded her head and Polina seemed completely sincere when she whispered, "I'm very, very interested, Pasha. Really, very."

And he began to read.

"It was easier for the old soldier to take his leave of life than for him to return to it. As we approached the cell where the others were they stopped their singing of a revolutionary song. We entered, and one of the prisoners cried out, 'To your feet! Attention!' One after another they jumped up from the floor. When we informed them of the purpose of our visit, their joyful excitement was great. Cries of 'Let's get Denikin!' and 'Long live the Soviet regime!' filled the cell. They were glad of the chance to live and fight—"

He broke off for a minute because Zina came in and whispered something to Alyona, who left the room at once. Zina sat down in her place.

"Zinochka, this should interest you. You like psychological experiences. Do you want to learn about the feelings of a person who is sentenced to death? I'll read it out from Migulin's notes. It's in another section. He wrote this down in Moscow, from memory. Shall I read it to you, or is it too late maybe?"

"Read it, Pavel Evgrafovich," said Zina, and she lowered her head into her hands.

He had a feeling that perhaps it was not a good idea to read it. The mood was not quite right. And anyway, the hour was late. But he very much wanted to. Suddenly there was a knock at the porch door. His sister-in-law. They were looking for him. Polina immediately exclaimed, "Lyubochka, Lyubochka! Come here!"

The old women started whispering together. He no longer felt like reading, because his sister-in-law, he knew, was indifferent to Migulin's story. He turned to Zina.

"Zina, if you want me to read it, I will, but if not, then I can do it another time. I don't have to read it at all. It was purely by accident that I brought the file with me anyway."

"Pavel Evgrafovich, don't pay any attention to me. I'm dead beat, in a scarcely human state. The whole day in the heat, back and forth between the hospital and the Institute," said Zina, continuing to sit there with her head in her hands. "Please read it."

He hesitated a bit. "Well, all right. If you ask it, I'll read a little. Well, then. These are notes that Migulin made in the Alhambra Hotel in Moscow, where he was taken from Balashov.

"After we had heard our sentence, they did not refuse our request to assemble in one cell so as to be able to spend our last hours together. In that cell, knowing that in a few hours you would be shot, that in a few hours you would cease to be, it was extremely instructive to observe people like yourself on death row and to compare their condition with your own. Here the real man comes through, completely independent of his will. Any attempt to conceal the true state of the soul is useless. Death, snubnosed death, is staring you straight in the face, chilling the soul and the heart, paralyzing the will and the mind. It has already embraced you with its bony hands, but does not choke you at once; it slowly squeezes you in its chill embrace. Even in this situation some people are able to look it proudly in the eyes; some have to summon up their last drop of spiritual strength to try to put on a show of looking death in the face—but no one wants to appear faint-hearted. For instance, one of our cellmates suddenly leaps up and starts dancing a *chechotka*, rhythmically tapping his heels on the cement floor, in an effort to take us, and himself, in. Yet his face is immobile and his eyes are lackluster, and it is terrifying to see in them a living human being. But he soon starts flagging. One of the candidates for a bullet is lying on the floor. He is completely in the grip of horror. He does not have the strength to fight, nor do I have the strength to look at him without a profound, despairing feeling of pity. . . .

He writes marvelously, dammit! Don't you think? He writes well, doesn't he? His style is very beautiful—literary. He could even have become a writer."

"Pavel Evgrafovich. . ." Zina looked at him strangely, scarily, her eyes red. "I want to tell you something, by the way: that in our life, where there are no wars or revolutions. . . it also happens. . ."

"What. . . what?" asked Pavel Evgrafovich.

"I, for example, sometimes feel like. . . dancing the *chechotka.*"

She got up from her chair, placed her arms akimbo like a Gypsy, and her face started to quiver. Polina dashed over to her, put an arm around her shoulders and led her away.

His sister-in-law whispered, "Let's go, let's go, Pasha. We must go. Come on."

"Stop! I came..." He suddenly remembered: to help Polina. People do not survive to old age: they get sick and die and nobody can help them. Yet you must try to help. All of a sudden it all collapses. But still, you have to try. A red moon was rising above the pine trees. And the smell of burning was asphyxiating. Now they would suffer for a long time, struggle for a long time, hope to the last; and that unpleasant young fellow whom Polina did not respect and who treated her like a domestic servant would start sinking into his own perdition as if into a swamp, ever deeper, ever more inextricably, until the crown of his head disappeared into the leaden bog.

Pavel Evgrafovich sat there clasping his file to his chest, patiently waiting for the women to return to the veranda.

And one day at the end of August it was as if a string had snapped—the heat stopped. But not everyone survived intact to that marvelous time. Some had become terribly emaciated, the health of others was severely damaged by heart attacks. Still others did not live to see the cooler weather at all. But the ones who did survive felt wonderfully invigorated and, as it were, took new pleasure in life: their attitude to the city was changed now, their attitude to water was changed, as was their attitude to the sun, the trees, the rain. However, this period of pleasure did not last long: about two days. By the third day everyone had forgotten about their recent ordeal—helped by a fine rain which fell from early morning and which induced an autumnal tedium—and they began busying themselves with their own affairs.

Valentina and Garik moved back into town; there was school to get ready for, a uniform to be shopped for, schoolbooks, this and that. Myuda and Viktor disappeared, too. Viktor was sent off to a collective farm to pick potatoes. Verochka undertook to repaper the apartment in town, and Erastovich went away to Kislovodsk. The dachas emptied, the voices of the children died away. When Pavel Evgrafovich walked to the sanatorium with his covered dishes he met no one on the bank. The beaches were deserted, and the boats, now completely superfluous, jostled one another in the basin. Dogs whose owners had disappeared ran around the highway, having turned half wild. Pavel Evgrafovich finished his letter to Grozdov from Maikop.

Ruslan walked about the area with a cane. He had a medical certificate until the middle of September. Ruslan loved that silence when everyone had gone—late August, early September—but there was so little sweetness in his life! He had known it once in his youth, then once sometime in the midfifties when he had left the plant and had not yet found another job, and again now. He strolled around the dacha colony, where everything was so quietly becoming wild, where things were drying up and waiting for autumn, and he thought, It is possible to start over. It wasn't such a terrible thing. Take his old man: he had started over many times. That was all he did, in fact: start everything over from the beginning.

Ruslan was the first to catch sight of the black Volga that rolled into the courtyard, pulled up at the turning in the gravel path and let out three men. Having emerged, they started to smoke and look around them in a leisurely manner. One was holding a red file. Not in any particular hurry, Ruslan went up to them and asked them whom they were looking for. They replied that they were not looking for anyone. Talking among themselves, they walked away into the depths of the grounds. The man carrying the red file walked in the middle, holding the file behind him with his two hands and tapping his back with it from time to time. Ruslan did not like the way he kept tapping his back with the file. There was something rather insolent about it. They walked slowly at a strolling pace, not showing any interest in their surroundings, talking amongst themselves. As if they knew it all.

Ruslan went up to the black Volga, in which there sat a chauffeur wearing a suede jacket, and asked where the car was from.

"You really don't know?" asked the chauffeur.

"No."

"Come off it!"

"I don't know."

"The car is from the government. They're going to be building a residence here. For junior staff."

"What about the houses?" asked Ruslan in amazement. It was a silly question. He asked it only because he felt at a low ebb after the heat, his illness and the hospital.

"The houses!" The chauffeur grinned, shaking his head. Taking a look out the window, he saw the humble wooden abode with its darkened logs in which Ruslan had spent all his life, and again smiled, this time in a somewhat forced way, as if at a bad joke. "The houses..."

People do not understand that there's no time left. No time at all. If anyone were to ask me what old age is, I would say that it's a time of no time. Because, fools that we are, we don't live right; we squander time: we waste it on trifles, on this and that, not realizing what an incredibly precious gift it is, not given to us for no reason, but so that we can *fulfill* something, *achieve* something, and not just croak our lives away like frogs in a pond. For example, to fulfill the things one has dreamed about, to achieve what one has wanted to achieve. But there is always one little thing lacking: time! Because it has been frittered away and squandered over the years. My God... They say to me, Where do you think you're going at your age? The weather's foul; it's rainy and cold, you'll catch a chill and get pneumonia. At your age pneumonia is the end. Wait until spring; your Asya won't run away, Migulin is not about to take off. Urgent business my foot! Of state importance! Yet they don't ask themselves whether *I* won't take off before spring. There's no time for waiting, no time at all—not a single day.

They have started trying to coax me out of the dacha so as to be able to keep me under surveillance. Verochka begged me to leave, Ruslan ran over in a taxi, and my sister-in-law dragged herself along to say, "Pavlusha, I don't understand how a living being can stay here." She sat there in her overcoat, her teeth chattering from the cold. But I keep the temperature cool deliberately, not more than fifty-five degrees, because it does you good to live in a cold atmosphere, just as sleeping on a hard bed is healthy. "Pavlusha, please forgive me, but there's a strong smell in your room. Do you think that's healthy, too?" I shouted, "What about teaching an old man how to live: is that healthy? When his life is at its end?" No need to shout. It's not their fault. They don't understand. My sister-in-law burst into tears. Now they have left me in peace, alone in the dacha; not a soul around, some snow has fallen, the river is black—not yet frozen over. Its banks are white. The benches are damp. When Arapka and I go to get lunch from the sanatorium—and now it's a slow walk, about forty minutes each way—we rest standing up, not wishing to sit down on a damp spot. And breathing is difficult; the air is damp. As we walk along the riverbank we keep glancing at the highway to see whether Dusya the mail carrier is coming along on her bicycle. I'm waiting for a word from Asya. Telling me when. She wrote me that she was going into the hospital for a month in October to have her legs treated and that she would let me know as soon as she was out and I could set off to see her at once. There is no other time. So what if the weather is foul and it's cold—I have no choice now. Ah, lost, lost! So many years. . . . And yet perhaps the only reason my days have been prolonged at all, the only reason I have been spared, is to piece something together from the shards, a vase, say, and fill it with wine, the sweetest wine. It is called Truth. It is all the truth, of course: all the years that dragged by, that flew by, that weighed heavily on me, that tested me; all my losses, my labors; all the turbines, the trenches, the trees in the garden, the holes dug and the people around them—it is all the truth, yet there are clouds that shower your garden and there are storms that thunder over the country and envelop half the world. Once, I was set spinning by a whirlwind, hurled into the heavens; never again did I soar to such heights. The highest truth is *there!* Only a few of us have sojourned *there.* And then what? Always too busy, always too blind, always too slow. Youth, greediness, incomprehension, the enjoyment of the moment. One time work dragged me off— family, calamities—another time they tossed me to the back of beyond, albeit not for long, only two years, without rhyme or reason; I was considered lucky. Then there was war, the front lines, hospitals; then again, with my last particle of strength— quite usual, just like everyone else—I came back alive, and am still alive today. *But, my God, there was never any time!* The snow fell early, before the events of November, the year Migulin was sent from Balashov to Moscow, condemned, pardoned, demoted, but allowed to live. So back to the old tricks. The pot has overturned, so start the cooking from scratch. As I did at one point. In 1940 I left Svobodny and arrived in Moscow bedraggled and sick. How was I to live? My God, live, live! I was a clerk in some tinpot factory which riveted some rubbish or other. In August of the following year it was off to the war with the militia. While in November 1919 he became a civilian—head of the land department of the Don Executive Committee. Rostov had not yet been taken: they were waiting in Saratov. But two months later they gave him another regiment. . . .

Two people have arrived with Ruslan, a man and a woman. They want to rent accommodations for the winter. The man is recovering from a heart attack and needs air and quiet, and she's going to look after him. Both are quite young, around forty. Roman Vladimirovich and Maiya. Some tea? Fruit compote from the sanatorium? No, no, thank you; we're not staying long; we just want to discuss the details. It's cold on the veranda, so they sit inside. I get their number immediately; I know they'll immediately start fibbing. If they're going to start fibbing, then there's no need to have them as tenants at all. Ruslan is a poor judge of people; they can fool him.

I ask them sternly, point-blank, "Are you husband and wife?"

They glance at each other. The woman smiles. "Not quite, Pavel Evgrafovich. We're friends. Colleagues."

Her smile is open, alluring and *knowing*. A beautiful smile. Beautiful lips. A tasty morsel of a woman; chubby, a rosy complexion, though not in her first youth. Roman Vladimirovich is to be congratulated. However, I do not wish to rent the dacha to them. The woman asks permission to smoke and I give an affirmative, albeit curt nod which she understands—a woman of subtlety, sensitive!—and she immediately says, "Oh, it seems no one smokes around here. I'm sorry; I can wait."

I make no objection. Let her wait. There's something about them I don't like.

"May I ask what sort of work you do?"

"We're research assistants," answers Roman Vladimirovich. "Biologists. I am a Candidate of Sciences."

Then they start assailing me with questions: How do you fuel the stoves? Am I not frozen to death? Does the gas come in cylinders? Is there no hot water? And what about the plumbing? Does the toilet work? Do I shave every day? Don't I find the solitude oppressive? Am I not bothered by what is known as "the great country tedium"? Are there any neighbors? Dogs? Crows? And the old lady nicknamed the Marchioness? Does she live in this house or in the one next door? Do you ever visit her? But she never visits you? Why is that? Nothing to talk about? What do you do in the evenings? You don't have a television? Your eyes don't get tired? Do you take a sleeping pill? Then suddenly everything falls into place and I realize that this is not at all what I had thought! This is something quite different. Absolutely different. I see now. Silly children. As usual, I begin to feel sorry for them. Ruslan sits there crestfallen, not himself. As if he were in the power of these people. As if they had brought him here and not the other way around. But what if he really is in their power?

Roman Vladimirovich is piercing me all the while through thick spectacles with his smiling eyes, as he continually picks at his swarthy, Arabic-looking face with his forefinger—either digging down into his ear for something which he balled up in his fingers and threw onto the floor or else creeping up into a nostril or rubbing at his lip.

"Pavel Evgrafovich, since chance has brought us together, could you tell us—" he shoves his finger into his mouth and scrapes something off a tooth with his nail—"something at least about Migulin. I've heard that you're collecting material about him. A most interesting figure! If you have an odd moment free..."

"Why do you want to know?"

"I've heard of him and read something about him. It would be splendid if you could just tell us something."

Liar. He's never heard of him or read about him: only what Ruska told him.

"I could go on at length about Migulin. But today my son is not conducive to that kind of conversation. What's the matter with you, Ruslan Pavlovich? Are you off your rocker? Or have you murdered someone?"

"Tell them!" He nods gloomily. "You've been asked."

No, I cannot bring myself to tell them; I don't feel like it; there's no point in their knowing. They came for something else. I make an effort and mutter something out of politeness. They seem to be listening attentively; Roman Vladimirovich nods and keeps on saying, "I see, I see," while the woman has walked over to the wall and is scrutinizing Galya's portrait. The summer after the war, by the river. She looks at it for some time, but without asking any questions. Then, interrupting my narration, I ask her,

"Do you wish to ask me anything about my late wife? Please feel free. After all, you *have to* ask me about her."

I purposely stress the words "have to." But they pretend not to notice. Suddenly Roman Vladimirovich asks, "Your late wife was also somehow concerned with Migulin, wasn't she?"

At that point I see right through him. I have no further doubts at all.

"No," I say, "you are mistaken, my dear sir."

"What about *you*, Pavel Evgrafovich? Don't you feel—" and with his forefinger he pushes his glasses up the bridge of his nose, which make his eyes look as if they have leaped forward—"don't you feel, you know, a sort of intangible, insignificant... maybe a guilt about the memory of Migulin?"

"Guilt," I echo. And I sense he has me floored. He has thrust a cold dagger right into my heart. Why did he ask me that, the scoundrel? All my strength has abandoned me and I say nothing.

He apologizes, jumps up, clasps his hands to his chest, runs to the other room, brings in the teapot for some unknown reason—the old one whose solder is wearing out.

"No, my dear Doctor. I feel guilty not about *him*, but about all the rest, including you—yes, guilty."

"What are you guilty of, Pavel Evgrafovich?"

I explain as best I can that I am guilty of not having shared the truth. That I stashed it away for myself. And as I see it, the truth, my dear Candidate of Medical Sciences, is precious only when it is for everyone. If you keep it all to yourself, under your pillow like Shylock's gold, then *pfui*, it's not worth a spit. That is why I am so tormented in my old age: because there is no time left. I do not know whether he has grasped any of this. Most likely not, although he keeps on saying, "I see, yes," while his constantly smiling gaze, through his glasses, shows the same coldness as ever. Most likely he has decided that his fears have been confirmed: the old man is talking a load of rubbish. A manic-depressive psychosis engendered by a vague feeling of guilt.

Complicated by a widower's pangs. Poor children! I feel for them; I can appreciate their alarm, their fright, the fact that they rushed off to these smart alecks who are posing as dacha tenants. But they still can't understand.

"You can't understand," I whisper to Ruslan, having called him into the next room and closed the door, "because we're different beings. Forty years ago, when you were eleven and I was thirty-three, we were closer to each other than we are now. Because there was plenty of time left. But now you've got the time, while I have none left."

"Father!" He seizes my hands and presses them forcefully in his. "We're worried. We don't want you to live alone or to make that journey. You're such a marvelous man. People like you are..."

He clasps me to him as if I were a little boy in his hands; he strokes my head with his big palm, and my scrawny neck and my feeble back. How I love him!

"I forgive you," I say, "all this nonsense with the doctors."

"I'm sorry, Father! We wanted... They're friends..."

"It makes no matter. You still can't understand."

"We can't, Father! We can't, we can't. You're right."

"Of course I am. You see, *there is no time.*"

"Do whatever you like, then. Do whatever you will." And I see that there are tears in his eyes.

A few days later he sees me off at the station and puts me into a car of the train in a seat by the window. I have not traveled by rail for a long time. It is interesting looking at the rows upon rows of suburban high-rises which amaze and frighten you at the same time (where do they find the people for so many buildings?), at the wet asphalt roads, the lines of cars at the grade-crossing gates, the metallic gleam of headlights shining in broad daylight, the colored umbrellas, the children running in the rain with their book bags on their heads, the dacha verandas, the fences, the somber trees, the misty meadows, the little white dog sitting atop a sand heap; and again buildings, buildings, buildings: white, gray cinderblock hulks, nameless, fantastic, menacing, stretching as far as the eye can see. The ice-cream girl comes down the aisle and I buy an ice in a soggy wafer. Not that I have that much of a yen for ices, but everyone around me is buying them and munching away at them just as, at the dacha in Siverskaya, we used to munch away at the carrots we would steal from the Finn's vegetable garden. Mama gave me a good beating for it once. I am going back to Siverskaya. The dark, damp fences, the twilight sky—is it a November day or a white night in July? I am returning there by the suburban train. In Piter everything is troubled and uneasy; there is shooting every night. Mama has forbidden me to take the evening train on my own: recently a whole car was robbed. "If you're delayed in town, it's better to spend the night at home and travel the next morning." But I'm too impatient to wait! Even though it is nighttime I long to run through the summer darkness past the dacha where Asya's window on the second floor is always half open and swinging to and fro like a living thing. The white sky shines in the windowpane. Asya is asleep and does not know that I am running along the sandy path past her house. I shall see her tomorrow morning, however. That is why I cannot stay in Piter. The ice is inedible. The taste reminds me of the icicles I used to love in those times beyond memory, before Siverskaya.

At midday the bus delivers me to a strange town. Some people lead me along a sidewalk paved with concrete flagstones. The spaces in between the slabs are black with pine needles. They lead me by the arm as if I were a helpless old man and in danger of falling, even on level ground. The flagstones are wet; in some places there is unmelted snow and a crust of ice which makes them slippery, but I walk cautiously. I don't need to be held. I'm still all right; some old people are much worse than I.

"Over there!" says a woman, pointing at a tall building in among the pines. A twelve-story tower. The woman disappears into a store, from which people are emerging bearing glass beer mugs. Some are carrying three or four each. One man has made his mugs into a garland and hung it around his neck.

The amazing thing is that I feel no excitement whatsoever! I just want to see her as soon as possible, just as soon as I possibly can, in order to *find out*. Man lives by his passions; at one time I wanted love, success, a tremendous cause, the well-being of my kith and kin, but now I crave nothing except one thing only: to *find out*. My last passion. My God, what can I *find out* from Asya? What shall I ask her about?

The elevator smells like a hardware store. I stand on the twelfth-floor landing and look down. Pine trees, roofs, snow in skewbald patches, the bend in the river gleaming like mica, and beyond that the evergreen vista and the blue distance. There are pictures painted with ancient paints which, when found in underground tombs or crypts, have only to be touched for them to disintegrate. But what makes my heart pound is not the worry or the fear that they will disintegrate at my touch, but a premonition of what I am to *find out*.

By some mistake they take me for the doctor. A moment of foolery—Please do go in; here's a towel; my briefcase snatched out of my hands, my precious possession, and they are about to carry it off somewhere, but I do not let them. I say, "Some water, please. I have to take my medicine." And at the height of the confusion, a little old lady with tousled gray hair pokes round the door, all stooped forward as if bending over to meet me, wizened like a hobgoblin. I see the greenish crown of the head, the crumpled skin, and in her eyes—pale blue, familiar, Asya's— a gleam of terror. Around me is happy twittering, the lapping of voices, and light, branchlike arms embracing me. Then imme- diately we launch into everything, all the times, all the fifty-five years. Including the main subject I badly need to find out about. This: Why did he lead that march to the front? In August 1919. She must know. No one in the whole world knows. There is nobody left apart from her.

The mummylike old woman looks at me with her gleaming eyes and blinks strangely, batting her lids. "Is it important to you?"

"Oh yes, very. Very!"

"I see. Yes, yes. . . ." She nods sympathetically, condolingly. And goes on moving her eyelids while her lips stretch into an enigmatic half-smile. "Pavel, I remember you so well, my dear."

"I have to know the truth!"

"I understand. Yes, yes." She nods. "I understand, Pavel. Aren't you tired? You don't want to lie down awhile? I wrote down everything I could. I don't know anything more."

A young woman comes in and puts three glass beer mugs down onto the table. Then she lifts one mug up onto the sideboard, pours water into it and stands a spruce branch in the water. She inspects her work with admiration. All the time the woman is busy with the mug and the branch, the old woman is signaling me with her eyes. Gradually the old woman turns into Asya. I no longer notice the disheveled gray hair, the wrinkled cheeks; I see only the long familiar pale-blue eyes, secretly and slyly winking at me. Like the way she used to confide things she kept secret from the grown-ups, in Liniya-15 days. Shuffling in her slippers, the woman goes out, and Asya whispers to me with surprising agitation, "She must not know! I'll explain later. She guesses, but we won't hand her the trump cards so easily."

In Asya's room, a small, light corner room which I like—I am happy for Asya—there is a typewriter on the table, and paper and carbons are scattered about everywhere, even on the bed. Asya has worked as a typist all her life. Ever since 1919, when she learned to pound the Underwood in Migulin's headquarters. Of course she's on her pension now, has been for fourteen years. But she doesn't sit around idle. Pounds away at home. How can one not work? What sort of life would that be? In the first place, she doesn't want to be an idler; nor does she want to be anyone's dependant. What, have to depend on her dear grandchildren or her daughter-in-law? God forbid! Oh no, she'll always have a kopek or two of her own, so as to be independent and to slip a bit to them. They're a slovenly lot, always without money. . . . No, her daughter-in-law is a case apart: she does as she pleases— doesn't even want to eat her meals with Lyudmila and seems to have plans to settle down. Let her! One can't judge her; she's not old yet.

"Well, she's starting to go over the hill just a bit—on one side anyway." Asya snickers like a young girl, and her wrinkles scatter over her face. "Like a windfall apple. And interested candidates will appear and pick her up. She's a woman of high position. In the administration of the Institute. And they say she'll go even farther. Borka could do nothing." Then, in a whisper, "That's why she's so wary, you see? That's the reason she refuses to know or hear anything about Sergei Kirillovich. She's afraid it'll harm her. She's such a calculating woman. . . ."

Silence! Silence! Asya presses a finger to her lips and again plays that game with her eyes, as she did when she was a child. Now I see the drawback of the room: for some reason it has no door. It has a curtain instead. Everything is audible. In the next room you can hear her daughter-in-law shuffling around and talking to her son. When the shuffling comes close to the curtain, Asya either lowers her voice to the merest whisper—inaudible to my ears, so I ask her to repeat, with the usual irritation—or else she suddenly starts speaking with exaggerated loudness: "I used to have a fearsome stroke: I could bash through five carbons at a time. But now even the third copy is scarcely visible: I haven't got the strength. I used to be an incredible pounder. My late husband would say, 'You should be a blacksmith, not a typist.'"

Can it really be this funny hobgoblin I am holding in my arms, almost dropping from desperation? Her young, heavy body, her pale stomach, her pale legs, the smell of sweat and blood as pungent as turpentine, the smell of 1919; and he wrenches her from my arms as if she were his possession. Later in Balashov, in the room, with the lights out, when I felt stifled by longing and by her love for another, I had the same bewilderment: "Why did he march off to the front? What was behind it all?" And then later still, her shaven typhoid head, her thin little neck, the suffering in her eyes, her mother's anger. At the time it seemed—after Shigontsev's murder—that this was the end, that it was Migulin, not Shigontsev, who had been killed, murdered in the gully one night. Shigontsev on a tan horse and a stranger on a dark one had been seen leaving the headquarters courtyard and galloping off toward the village. Shigontsev was carrying the marching orders as well as the seals and the cipher. His orderly was wounded, so they gave him someone from the staff; Migulin could not abide that sick, savage devil Shigontsev because of old scores, because of the Steel Detachment. Sending him as a commissar was stupid, but someone had done it on purpose—their distrust of him rankled; they were trying to throttle him, to curb him, even though he had been fully acquitted and was working in the land department of the Don Executive Committee. Then there was the regiment, the brigade, feats of derring-do in the South; again he was gaining strength; then that spot of trouble on the River Manych. He got held up; paced back and forth in Novocherkassk; then the ice started drifting down: it was treacherous trying to make it across. And then they sent Shigontsev on purpose, that iron fool who was adamant about subjugating Migulin to the revolutionary will—which he fancied he himself personified with his blinkered, crazed look; he had it coming to him and he got what he deserved: they did away with him that night, shot him through the head, that strange head like a badly baked loaf. His horse trudged back riderless the next morning. Their names would never be discovered; they had vanished, sunk to the bottom. No, you mustn't think that everything always has to be made as clear as the noonday sky; some things do disappear. They didn't start looking for the murderers; an investigation was never conducted. Yet they did not manage to kill Migulin—the Commission of the Revolutionary Tribunal of the front could find no evidence—so once again he was up on his horse, with Frunze's troops, routing Vrangel along with Blyukher and Budyonny. Per-

ekop, Voinka Station, Dzhankoi, the Saint George's Cross and
the Order of the Red Banner; then suddenly, one winter's day
in my cold room, by the light of the oil lamp, I read three lines
in the paper saying that the former Corps Commander has been
arrested for participation in a counterrevolutionary conspiracy.
February of '21, Rostov starving, I am in the middle of medical
treatment and hobble about distraught: I've lost everybody one
by one. Then work on the Requisition Commission. My God,
well do I remember that winter: papers, complaints, shooting,
Kifarov the Turk, the profiteers, old women weeping—and we
small-time pushcart hucksters have the audacity to say that we
are not speculators or hoarders, and that whatever we've bought
is on the table, but meanwhile the agent came and put down
some of our stout rope to be requisitioned. However, since I have
just gotten back from the front and am now serving as commissar
in the liaison office, I ask him to issue an order only for the bed,
with the right to requisition it based on its having belonged to a
theatrical performer who had run off with a White gang. Well,
I abandon the petitioners, the deponents, the disabled, the pathetic, the hapless orphans, the honest toilers and well-wishers
of the Soviet regime, to dash off to the Mikhailinskaya *stanitsa*,
where the Corps Commander has been arrested, and the next
day to take Asya away with me. Now or never. Then that dark
fellow in the sheepskin coat, with a Mauser in a yellow box
holster, meets me on the front steps, sizes me up with his eyes
of ice, holds out a hand for identification, then says, "She was
taken with him, on a joint charge. And who are you to her?" I
do not remember what I answered. Perhaps "A friend," perhaps
"Her brother" or perhaps "No one." And that was that; the end,
forever, for life. The front steps covered with ice, the Red Army
man in the sheepskin coat; and I sit down in the snow. The rest
is not interesting. Can that dried-up, bent little old woman really
be she?

He spent two days in his native *stanitsa*. Only two days. On his way to Moscow. He hesitated about whether to stop by or not. His friends tried to talk him out of it, and she was not terribly keen, either. No, not because his first wife's family was there—she was not afraid of that—but she had a presentiment. Such an ominous feeling, a kind of sudden depression which made her cry all through the night without a stop. He got scared. "What on earth's the matter with you?" Of course, she could not understand. She blamed herself. "What are you eating your heart out for, silly girl? What can happen to me, a war hero? I've just been given a decoration." But then there happened the same thing as always used to happen: he could not bear not getting into a fight, not leaping to someone's defense. He had an over-powering need to defend one side and to give the other side a punch in the face. At the time—February 1921—there was un-rest among the Cossacks over the forced grain requisitioning. Once again an uprising was brewing. A certain Vakulin was rabble-rousing in the district and some of his followers were intimidating people. And this Vakulin, a former Cossack in Mig-ulin's division, started the rumor that Migulin had returned to the Don to join with the uprising. While in fact Migulin was calmly and peaceably—although with a heavy heart—making his way to Moscow to receive the honorary post of principal inspector of cavalry of the Red Army. The last thing he needed, that post! It was the same thing again: getting him as far away as possible from the Don. Perhaps it wasn't Vakulin but someone else who started the rumor going. The first day there were shout-ing matches with the Cossacks, complaints, women crying, stories about the people on food-requisitioning detachment. Migulin felt he had their support, and, fearing no one, he cursed the local authorities and threatened them: "I'm headed for Moscow, and the first thing I'll do is go right to Lenin and tell him about your villainous crimes." The authorities got the wind up, and palmed one of their agents off onto him, a certain Skobinenko. In fact, he had been shadowing Sergei Kirillovich for some time. I can see that scoundrel's ugly mug now—that thick-lipped bastard: chubby cheeks, curly hair. Whatever Migulin shouted out in his anger—and he was capable of quite a mouthful, nothing could hold him back!—Skobinenko remembered and noted down. Well, what sort of things in particular? Something that was soon afterward acknowledged and realized by everyone: that the forced food requisitioning should be replaced by a tax in kind. Well, at dawn on the third day they made up their minds. They surrounded the house and pounded their gun butts against the door....

"Asya, one thing isn't clear to me—I want to ask you one question: Where was he heading for in August 1919? And what did he want?" The old woman says nothing; nods her head pensively, trying to remember. Her old woman's eyelids flutter like the withered wings of a butterfly, hiding her faded pale blue. After a pause she says, having remembered all there is to remember, "I'll answer that I never loved anyone as much as him in the whole of my long, wearisome life."

A year later, after the old man's death, a graduate student from the university appeared, Igor Vyacheslavovich. He was writing a dissertation about Migulin. When Pavel Evgrafovich was alive the student corresponded with him, even telephoning from Rostov, and now he was eager to get hold of his memoirs and all the documents the old man had collected. Ruslan gave them to him. Ruslan liked Igor Vyacheslavovich. They sat until four in the morning, drinking vodka, talking about the Revolution, Russia, the Bolsheviks, the volunteers, the Chekaists, General Kornilov, the Marquis de Custine, the Cossacks, Peter the Great, Tsar Ivan; about the fact that there is such a thing as the truth; about love for people; the fact that Migulin did not escape his fate; that there was no conspiracy—he died in vain. They also talked of oil, linen and the harvest prospects. And when they left the house the next day—Ivan Vyacheslavovich was in a hurry to get to the station—they were caught in a sudden icy downpour of hail. They fled the taxi stand and took shelter under the archway of a building, and Ruslan, morose and hung over, thought, The truth is that Valentina has gone to her mother's, the second woman isn't around, there's no news of the third, and this rain has turned my jacket into a rag.

Igor Vyacheslavovich, a bony young man in a tight provincial jacket, wearing glasses spattered with rain, was thinking, The truth is that when the investigator asked that sweet man Pavel Evgrafovich in 1921 whether he could admit the possibility of Migulin's having participated in the counterrevolutionary uprising, he answered in all sincerity, "Yes." But of course he forgot about that. Nothing surprising about it: everyone—or nearly everyone—thought so at the time, and there are times when truth and belief become so tightly, inextricably fused together that it's difficult to sort out what's what. But we'll sort it out.

He said aloud, "I think I've missed my train."

The rain was sheeting down. There was a smell of ozone. Two little girls, covered with a transparent sheet of plastic, ran barefoot over the asphalt.

GLOSSARY

ataman—Cossack chieftain.

Blyukher, General V. (Blucher)—Leading Red Army general against Kolchak. Had been commander-in-chief of armed forces of the Far Eastern Republic.

britska—Open carriage with folding top and space for passengers to recline.

Budyonny, Semyon Mikhailovich (Budenny)—Born 1883 near Rostov. Marshal of Soviet Union. Cossack cavalry officer who played an important part in the victory of the Revolutionary forces in the civil war. Twice served as inspector of cavalry. Served in World War II. Member of Central Committee and of Presidium.

Cheka—Political police established in 1917 by Lenin. Full name Extraordinary Commissions to Combat Counter-revolution, Sabotage and Speculation. Replaced 1922 by Unified State Political Administration (OGPU).

Chernyshevsky, Nikolai Gavrilovich, 1828–1889. Radical journalist and author. Opposed nationalism and considered as forerunner of Lenin.

Denikin, Anton Ivanovich, 1872–1947. White leader. Son of a serf who distinguished himself in Russo-Japanese war. Greatly disturbed by the breakdown in discipline in the army, for which he blamed the provisional government. In 1917 dismissed as chief of staff to commander-in-chief Alexeev and appointed commander of western front. Supported Kornilov's bid for power. Died in USA.

dessiatine—Measure of area equal to about 2½ acres.

druzhinnik—Member of militia detachment.

263

Dukhonin, N.—Commander-in-chief in the field. Refused to carry out government orders to negotiate an armistice in November 1917.

dukhobors—Peasant sect dating from eighteenth century. Belief based on direct individual revelation supported by an oral scripture of canticles and proverbs. The majority now live in Canada.

duma—Lower house in imperial Russian legislature during the constitutional era of 1906 to 1917.

Dutov, A.—*Ataman* of Orenberg Cossacks; he led an uprising which severed communications between Europe and Central Asia for a period of almost two years.

Eisner, Kurt, 1867–1919. Socialist writer and statesman who became a pacifist and a Bavarian citizen. Imprisoned as strike leader in 1918 but released after protests from socialist Reichstag members. Proclaimed a Bavarian republic in 1918; murdered the following year.

esaul—Cossack captain.

Frunze, Mikhail Vasilievich, 1885–1925. Army officer and military theorist; joined with Bolsheviks at the very outset. One of outstanding commanders in civil war. Replaced Trotsky as people's commissar for war in 1925.

haydamak—Ukrainian Cossack, and also, specifically, a member of anti-Bolshevik Ukrainian cavalry detachment ca. 1918.

inogorodny—Non-Cossack peasant living in a Cossack community.

Kaledin, Alexei Maximovich, 1861–1918. First Cossack leader to organize effective resistance to Reds in 1917–18. Opposed provisional government's military reforms and was dismissed from his command in 1917. Supported regional autonomy for Cossacks. Elected Don *ataman* in 1917 but could not consolidate his authority in time to resist Red troops at the beginning of 1918.

Kalinin, M.—Former peasant and Petrograd worker. On *Pravda* editorial board in 1917. In 1919 president of All-Russian Central Executive Committee and effectively head of state.

Kalmyks—Buddhist Mongol people of western USSR.

Kerensky, Alexander Fyodorovich—Born 1881. Trudovik (q.v.) deputy to *duma*. Accepted post in provisional government in 1917; later minister of war. His own reforms slackened military discipline. As prime minister he dismissed Kornilov and he ended up being distrusted by all. Emigrated to Europe, then to USA.

Kolchak, Alexander Vasilevich, 1874–1920. A naval officer who came to be regarded by the Whites as absolute ruler of Russia as a result of a coup at which he connived in Omsk in 1918.

Kornilov, Lavr Georgievich, 1870–1918. Army officer given charge of Petrograd military district in March 1917, but he soon resigned and returned to the front. Appointed commander-in-chief by Kerensky, but hoped to achieve "firm authority"—i.e., a personal dictatorship. After conflict with Kerensky, he sent troops to suppress the Petrograd soviet and he was detained but escaped to form, with Alexeev and Kaledin, the anti-Bolshevik volunteer army.

Kshesinskaya's Palace—A Petersburg palace belonging to a ballerina who had been a favorite of the Tsar; taken over for Bolshevik Party headquarters.

Kuban—Northern Caucasus river. Cossacks established there in the late eighteenth century.

kulak—Well-to-do peasant.

kulich—Sweet Russian Easter bread shaped like a tall cylinder.

Left Socialist Revolutionaries—Group within radical peasant Socialist Revolutionary party; sided with Bolsheviks.

Lunacharsky, Anatoly Vasilevich, 1875–1933. People's commissar for education, in which post he was able, along with Gorky, to save many works of art and historic buildings from destruction. He wrote plays and was interested in the question of the place of religion in the new order.

Milyukov, Pavel Nikolaevich, 1859–1943. A historian who advocated westernization and a freely and democratically elected national assembly. Headed Constitutional Democratic party; sought in 1917 to preserve monarchy. Political adviser to Denikin. Died in France.

muzhik—Peasant.

Narkomvoen—People's Commissar for Military Affairs.

oblast—Province: administrative division of USSR.

okhranka—Tsarist secret police: the "defensive police" founded in 1881 to combat terrorism.

okrug—District: administrative division of USSR.

Order Number One—Provided for reorganization of army: officers were to be elected, committees were established for weapons control, etc.

papakha—Caucasian fur cap.

Petlyura, Semyon, 1879–1926. Soldier and Ukrainian nationalist. Minister of defense in Ukrainian government in July 1917. After the German occupation appointed *ataman* of Ukrainian army in 1918. Concluded alliance with Poland which came to naught after Russo-Polish war. He led his government from Paris afterwards. He was killed there.

Pioneers—Soviet Communist Party youth organization for children aged 10 to 15.

pirog—A large savory pie, often with a yeast crust.

Piter—Affectionate nickname for Petrograd.

pood—Equals 36 pounds.

rada—In the Ukraine and Byelorussia, a soviet or council.

Revkom—Contraction of revolutionary committee.

sarafan—Sleeveless peasant dress buttoning in front.

sotnik—Cossack lieutenant.

Sovdep—Soviet of Workers', Peasants' and Red Army Deputies.

stanitsa—Large Cossack village.

stanichnik—Inhabitant of *stanitsa*.

Svobodny—Town in Siberia.

tolstovka—Long, belted blouse.

Trudovik—Labor Party 1906–1920. Small but influential non-Marxist socialist party; left of center. Kerensky among members.

ty and *vy*—Respectively, the familiar and formal second person singular pronouns.

tyubeteika—Central Asian embroidered skullcap.

uyezd—The lowest of the administrative divisions (but see *volost*).

verst—Equals approximately two thirds of a mile.

vesiga—Spinal marrow of a sturgeon.

volost—A further subdivision of an *uyezd*.

voyenspets—Professional officer in Tsarist army who agreed to serve in Red Army under varying degrees of coercion. Always had a political commissar attached to him to assure loyalty and to check on the political correctness of his statements.

Vrangel, Peter Nikolaevich (Wrangel), 1878–1928. Officer and commander in Cossack units and horse guards. Joined Kaledin against the Bolsheviks and was commander-in-chief of the volunteer army. After 1920 defeat, lived in exile.

Yudenich, Nikolai Nikolaevich, 1862–1933. Tsarist general who led anti-Bolshevik forces against Petrograd in 1919.

zakuski—Roughly equivalent to hors d'oeuvre, but more substantial and more of a national institution.

Yuri Trifonov was born in 1925 into the privileged world of high-ranking Soviet society. His father, however, one of the Old Bolsheviks who had joined the Party before the Revolution, disappeared in the Stalinist purges, and his name was expunged from Party history. Yuri, after having won a Stalin Prize for an early novel, devoted ten years of his life to rehabilitating his father's name. It was not until he was forty-four that Trifonov found his true voice as a writer. There followed throughout the 1970s his series of short novels, culminating with *Another Life* and *The House on the Embankment*, that established him as one of the foremost novelists of his generation. He died suddenly on March 28, 1981. *The Old Man* was his last novel.